A Light in the Arcane

IN THE

Serendipity Series | 1

Amal Kimal

Cover design by @mgsdesiigns (IG)
Part break, interlude interior, and end design by Amal Kimal
Scene break, chapter headings, and title page interior design by @mgsdesiigns (IG)
Character art by @lyyzis_art and @lvcrvart
Copy editing and proofreading by Kayleigh Allery

ISBNs:
979-8-9928016-0-6 (e-book)
979-8-9928016-1-3 (paperback)
979-8-9928016-2-0 (hardcover)

For those who brave their demons, and dance *with* them.

Table of Contents

Author's Note

Thank you for deciding to read *A Light in the Arcane*—it means the world to me that my words have wound their way to you, and I hope you enjoy reading! Please note that this is the first book in a series, and while Layla and Jaxon's story ends on a HEA, certain elements are incomplete and pick up in the next book.

Additionally, while this is a contemporary romance, the plot does contain darker elements that may be triggering. If you feel that this list is missing anything, please contact the author. This is a new adult romance book meant for readers 18+ and includes the following:

- Mentions of depression, anxiety, suicidal thoughts, and PTSD.
- Mentions of drug usage by the main character and a near overdose and hospitalization. If you or anyone you know needs substance use support, visit crisistextline.org
- Mentions of organized crime, including selling drugs, implied human trafficking, and gun violence.
- Mentions of racism and xenophobia (toward the MCs, not by the MCs, and it isn't "promoted").
- Chronic illness (side character).
- Arranged engagement to a character other than the MMC, mention of physical abuse to another character, a scene of physical abuse toward the FMC (not by the MMC), and molestation.
- Witnessing the loss of loved ones and unhealthy coping mechanisms in the aftermath.
- Sexually mature content (chapters 23, 26, 27).

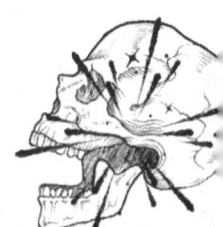

Author's Note

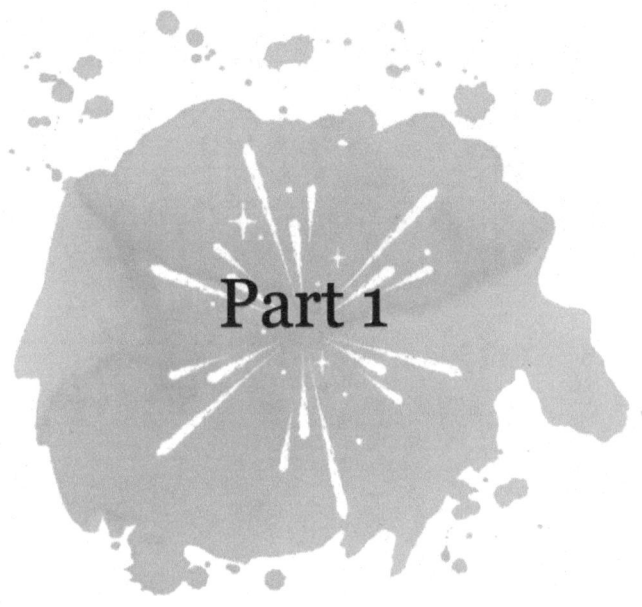

Part 1

Amal Kimal

Chapter 1

Now

There are claw marks on the walls. They're long, jagged, and deep—endless even. Like if I stare hard enough, they won't be claw marks anymore, but just brutal gaps, black holes that might one day finally swallow me whole.

I would know, I put them there after all.

They're less a mark of destruction, and more of a plea, a way to mark it down, to give my thoughts an *out*, until they are tangible. They're a way to show the panic and the monstrosity that has grown in me every day for the past one thousand eight hundred and ninety-five days.

It's a sick, festering feeling. A feeling that never fails to make my heart clench and bile rise in my throat as panic, rage, and helplessness claw at me. *Claw*. The irony isn't beyond me.

Except the marks on my wall are not real. No creature slashed the wall with wickedly long and sharp claws.

But I *did* put those claw marks there. With a steady hand, I have done each and every one. Painstakingly exact and vivid, that if anyone were to ever come into my room and see them, they would scream.

And I'd laugh.

5

I would laugh because I have been hearing that sound in my head for *years*. I haven't spoken a word, and sometimes, it's noticed, questioned, but never realized it's because I am too loud in my head. I am screaming in my head, clawing at a way to escape my mind, and it's always so *loud*. So to hear an actual scream again, because of *me*, would be *hilarious*.

In truth, no beast lurks in my room, and the marks on the wall are all painted. They are fake, a fraud, and a lie.

Just.

Like.

Me.

Swaths of light flicker over the walls from the moonlight streaming in through the shutters, but I already know what's on the walls. There are one, two, three, four, five, six, seven, eight surfaces in my room, and every single one is covered in paint, from the armoire to the ceiling.

They're all similarly haunting, eerie, and depressing paintings until it's almost pathetic.

I run my gaze over the splashes of vibrant colors and deep hues, over and over again, even though I already have them committed to memory. But I want to be able to remember them. Not because of what they all symbolize, but because painting has been the one thing that's kept me sane. Well, sane to a degree.

After today, I have no plan to ever see them or any part of this room and house again. That is, if I don't get caught. I'm sure that if I do, things will become infinitely worse. I can imagine deals made years ago finalizing, imagine having to exchange the bars of this house for another, forced into a role I never want.

The imagination is enough for the panic to seize me again, until my breathing quickens and pure fear tears its way up my throat. What if it doesn't work? Will I never leave this place then? Darkness swarms over my vision, crawls into my throat to wrap around my heart and *squeeze*, so visceral I'm sure there's a weight over my chest.

I heave in a breath, trying to force the thoughts away and cease the panic attack. But black spots still dance in my vision, the covers over me are suffocating, and I half expect to look down and see that they are snakes, scaly and slithering, their red tongues flicking, as they tighten and *tighten* around my ribcage.

Vaguely, I register that the sun has risen and that my clock reads eight. Soon enough, I will have to start moving, but before that, I must feign sleep.

Even though it's quiet, the silence suffocating, it's still blaring. Blood rushes in my ears, my pulse pounding and rapid breathing too loud, and I'm so sure I'll be heard. That this will all be over before it starts.

Breathe.

Calm down.

I close my eyes, and I try to remember. A smile, promises, stolen kisses, dark hair, and deep amber eyes, almost black out of the sunlight.

The panic eases, even if the memories don't matter. I know I won't meet him again, that the odds are too great and it's been too long. But remembering is like basking in the sunlight on a spring day, spread over freshly cut grass, watching the clouds roll above. It's like taking a pause in life despite the many problems pressing around me like a noose.

It doesn't help much, but it's enough for now. Enough for me to untangle the covers, pull them to my chin, and school my features into a semblance of sleep—brow unfurrowed, lips slightly parted, shoulders relaxed, and body loose. I strain my hearing, trying to pick up the routine noise of shuffling, keys clinging, and then the door shutting. But today, he's late.

I've planned this day for *years*. There are a plethora of backup plans and lies ready in case, but most importantly, I have to be sure I will never be found.

The shuffling sound starts, muffled and beyond a few walls, in another room. Heart pounding, I wait for the routine to start. A few moments later, and he doesn't disappoint.

It's funny how people, no matter how much they say they like change or mess, always have something in their lives that stays permanent. Some are detailed and exact, relentless in having their lives "perfect" and planned, while others are chaos in human form.

But everyone, regardless of interests and lifestyles, has something in their lives that is the same, every day, every time.

A door opens, knob scraping, the sound louder and closer before footsteps pad across the carpeted floor on the hall outside. He makes it to my bedroom, standing outside like he does every morning, the silhouette of his shadow visible. He always takes a deep breath, as if he's about to face the world, before he opens the door. Every time he sees that I am still in bed, in one piece, "asleep" soundly, he lets out a sigh of relief that always has me scoffing inwardly.

If he's always so relieved to see I'm alive and still here, then why does he pretend he isn't when I'm awake? Why did he curse me to the pits of hell and always glare at me after *the accident* happened, years ago?

For someone I used to trust, no one has ever confused me more than my father.

He takes a breath, and I know he's about to say something. Maybe a confession or a truth, or something that would explain *why*. For the past six years, he has been the only face I consistently see, the only other person to live in this house. But despite all that time, I can count all of our one-sided conversations on one hand.

"Happy birthday," every year.

"Say something."

"Eat something."

On the days I would stay in bed for hours at a time, drained in a way I could not explain, just knowing that there was this deep pit of pure black in me, gnawing at my mind, he would grow frustrated, and say, "I don't know what to do with you anymore."

And sometimes, when he's in an apologetic mood, "It's for the better, you'll see. He has to live."

Like every time, I don't say anything. He got what he wanted, so it shouldn't matter to him whether I respond. And I'm tired of his riddles.

He stays for a moment, his body silhouetted by the light filtering from the window in the hallways, casting a shadow in my room, over my closed eyes. I can tell he's probably running his gaze over the room, over the painted walls and painted *everything*.

I try to keep my breathing even as fear climbs into my head, wondering if, of all the days to start searching my room, he's going to pick today. I am so sure he'll find the packed suitcase, the returned college applications. But he doesn't, and soon, I hear the door groan and creak as it closes, and then the sound of footfalls over the staircase.

The loud coffee machine starts, buzzing and whirring, and a few moments later—finally—the front door opens, keys jangling, and it shuts.

And now it begins.

I don't waste a moment. Springing into motion, I push the covers back and swing my legs off the bed. I scramble around the room, stripping it of anything valuable, throwing them onto the bed before I pull the mostly filled suitcase out of the closet.

Blindly, I stuff it with the few possessions I gathered before slamming the top closed. My heart hammers the whole time, sure he will come back. Trying to zip it shut, I wrestle with the old thing. The black, tough cloth is worn and scratched, with one of the wheels slightly out of place, but it has to hold on for a little longer.

Pulling it to the floor and upright, I take one last look at my room, and for a moment my heart tugs at the thought of leaving it. Before it became my prison, it had been my sanctuary. But even then, it never chased away the loneliness.

The realization that I'm finally leaving, that I have packed my entire life into one suitcase, still hasn't settled in. I wonder, when my father comes home, how long will it be before he's even realized I've left? My room looks nearly exactly the same, after all.

Shaking my head, I look around, trying to see if I forgot anything. Turning in a circle, I take it all in, the painted walls, the bed with its dark covers, duvets, and throw pillows, the desk still crowded with paints and papers. I check under the loose tile on the floorboard. It's empty too.

Taking a deep breath, I stop examining the room and close the mirrored closet, the wheels of the closet door sliding over metal, smooth and silent, before it closes all the way and I see myself in its reflection. I take a step back, looking at myself, ignoring the gnawing sense that I'm delaying.

I'm wearing sweatpants, the elastic hanging low on my hips, not as fashion, but because they won't hold any higher than that. I remember a time when I used to hate my body type, the once-wide hips and corded thighs. What I wouldn't give to hold that girl and tell her nothing was wrong with her body.

I know I'm delaying the inevitable, not ready for change nor to leave the comforting routine of my prison, but I still don't move, hesitancy seeping into my blood, even though this day is all I've wanted for years.

Instead, I look higher to my face, a familiar face, though not because it's mine. I look like my mother, mostly. Same high cheekbones that are more prominent and hollow beneath them than they should be, same dark brown, wavy hair, and the same lips, a cupid's bow with the lower one fuller. I also have her nose, straight and snub at the end. The only thing I have from my father are my eyes, dark moss green framed with thick lashes behind my round glasses.

I hate the way exhaustion cuts across my every feature, the way defeat slumps my shoulders. I hate that I let the demons win over the years, eating away at me.

Maybe some would've told me to try harder, to find a sense of normalcy despite the walls that always closed around me in my head. That all I should have done was hold out. The truth is, I *did* hold out. Some days, it would feel like I was always holding up the universe. Two people died because of me, and I held out.

Angry, I slam my hands against the mirror until the sound reverberates in the room, and snarl at my reflection, "You don't even deserve to leave."

And maybe I believe that, but I still drag the suitcase behind me, leaving the room. When I get to the stairs, I don't bother picking it up—I don't want to find out just *how* out of shape I am—and drag it behind me.

I walk through the halls of my house like a stranger, as though there aren't memories wrapped around every corner of this house. I stare at a hidden alcove, and viscerally, remember hiding there as a child, barely able to contain my giggles as I would hear my brother searching for me.

The memory steals my breath until I have to tighten my hand into a fist, as though I will fall apart if I don't. Tilting my head back, I close my eyes and take a deep breath, until the angry pit of despair lessens, its maw closing for now.

The thing with this house, though, is that the memories are both bittersweet and nightmarish, and I hate the ways in which my father tainted the memories of my childhood home.

I tear out of the hallway, angry, like a woman possessed, until I reach the front door. My hand settles over the handle, breath catching, looking over my shoulder as though I will see my father or one of his men behind me.

But no one is there.

It's been years since I've passed this door, and I've been thinking about this day for so long, and *merda santa*, I'm actually going to do it.

My hands grow clammy with sweat at the idea, even as a smile tugs at my lips. No one is here, all the cameras are disabled, and by the time he gets home, I'll be long gone to the other side of the country. The smile stretches further across my face, as I turn the knob. It's cold against my skin, making goosebumps spread across my flesh, and when I push the door open, the outside world greets me.

It's not very sunny outside, but the light sears me anyway, a shock to my system as I gape and blink, immediately squeezing my eyes shut, hands shooting up to clamp over them. It hurts in a way I didn't expect, until I am half sure I've been blinded. Even as the initial shock passes, pulses of light glitter behind my eyelids every time I blink.

The view is familiar from years ago, but still disorienting, and I wonder what parts have always been here and what is different. Stepping over the threshold, I close the door behind me. It's a simple step, but I know my life will be irrevocably changed.

The air is brisk and fresh, smelling of mildew and something that jars my senses, all the colors somehow different here than they have been inside, through the window. Overhead, the sky is picturesque, a deep blue with rolling clouds. I want to stop walking and just stare at everything around me, fingers twitching for a brush.

The urge to paint is one I almost forgot, until it surprises me.

The house was big enough that I never felt claustrophobic, but now I wonder how I managed to survive for so long inside.

I drag in deep breaths of the air, savoring it. It's surreal being outside, and I am sure I will be dragged out of it, that I will find out this has all been a dream.

But I know it isn't, and with that, I start walking away until the house disappears behind me. It takes longer than I expected, the minutes stretching and the suitcase growing heavy until my arm hurts, and I'm always, always looking behind me. While most of his prestige and wealth are gone, enough that the guards were laid off a while ago, I can't help but fear that he knows anyway. Every passerby is a threat, every squeal of a tire is someone chasing after me.

Despite that, I make it, breath sawing in and out of my lungs, legs shaking until I want to collapse. There are no longer as many trees, and instead, skyscrapers reach up to the sky, rivaling each other in height, their metal and glass panes reflecting the sunlight, bright and blinding.

The cars blare their horns on the congested road, and there are others on the sidewalk, waving for taxis just like I am. From being hidden away and used to the blanketing silence, the sound of cars honking and wheels screeching, along with the loud murmur of voices, sets me on edge until I feel on the brink of experiencing a sensory overload.

But I expected this and pull out my headphones from my backpack and place them over my ears, the sound muffled. I don't know how long it takes for a taxi to pull up, and the trunk pops open before someone climbs out. Whoever he is, he appears to be in his twenties, maybe a few months older than me, and wears a faded black t-shirt over a pair of jeans. In one swift movement, he picks up my suitcase and places it in the trunk along with my backpack.

"I don't have all day," he barks when I don't move.

I almost grin, because I missed that, too. The city, with its confusing people. Some who are rude on the outside, but if you pull back the layers, they bloom like a flower, sweet inside.

I pull open the door and slide inside, my shoulders drawn tight, as I try not to look at everything. The leather seat is soft against my back as I lean into it, strapping myself in. It's surreal being in here, too. Of course, I haven't forgotten what the inside of a car looks like, but being in one again feels alien.

Worrying at my hands, I wonder if the panic will set in, old memories resurfacing of the accident, but there is nothing beyond the wary trepidation and hesitant excitement.

It smells of body spray, butter, and above that, the strong scent of perfume as if trying to purge the other scents. I wrinkle my nose, looking around as the car pulls away from the curb, and murmur, "The airport, and fast, please."

My voice is husky and thick from the lack of use, but he doesn't take anything by it.

"If I get a ticket, you're paying for it."

I look at the crumpled pieces of paper in the cup holder and grab one. As expected, it's a ticket, and I raise one brow.

In response, the car lurches forward, going faster, until I press roughly back into my seat. He messes with the radio in the car, and soon, music blasts out of the speakers. I still have the headphones over my ears, but the sound is comforting, too, in its loudness.

Like I'm seizing back my life and all the chaos it has to offer.

Pulling down the window, the wind whips my hair as he pulls onto I-90. It's exhilarating, the way the car speeds down the freeway, the wind a wild sound in my ears, pulling my hair and making my eyes sting. Not caring, I let out a cheer. It's loud, and free, and I don't care who hears or who finds it strange.

I'm buoyant, and I never want this feeling to end.

I let out another whoop and belt the lyrics to the song, not caring about propriety. The singer croons to his lover about leaving somewhere far away, about going wherever they want to, and leaving their world behind.

The driver joins me, his voice off-key, but he sings with such enthusiasm I laugh. I've never met him before, and don't think I will again, but a stranger is exactly what I needed.

The lyrics repeat in my head, and our voices are dissonant, mine too gruff and his not matching the tune, but I've never felt more free.

Like I'm flying and nothing can stop me.

Chapter 2

Then

Almost six years ago....

It's a horrible feeling knowing that someone *hates* you. Not the mild kind of hate, bordering on displeasure, but pure, unadulterated hate.

I.

Mean.

Hate.

It's a horrible feeling to know that whatever I've done has painted me even worse than a macabre villain to someone. That there's no going back, and there's no changing it. It's like spiraling down and down, with no way of getting away, with acid crawling down my throat.

And yet, he doesn't know that I deserve it, and I wonder how much worse things would be if he knew that it was all my fault. But he must suspect, doesn't he? If not, then how can he hate me just because I survived and they didn't?

How could he look at me and say, "Why did it have to be *you* who made it out?"

The words play over and over in my head as I get dressed for the first day of this school year. I should have my father telling me not to trust any of the boys, should have my mother giving me a warm hug and telling me to enjoy my first day, and I should have my little brother brimming with excitement for the day it's finally his turn to start high school. But I don't have any of that, and I never will.

And whose fault is that? I think, already knowing the answer.

Unbidden, my throat tightens and eyes well, but I furiously blink the tears away. Instead, I think of the words, "Why did it have to be *you* who made it out?"

The words are a visceral, unwanted mantra, one that never fails to crash me down. I push them back, locking away the memories behind a barricaded door and throwing away the key. Imagining it, even though it doesn't work, helps for now as I finish getting ready. I already pay the price for being the only one to have made it out. I pay the price every night when I cannot sleep, and I pay it more through the lengths I go to try.

I look around my room before stepping out. The walls are a plain beige, and I want to paint them, but I don't know how he'll react, and I don't want him to make me clean it up. But then again, if I paint everything, he *has* to say something then, right?

As I leave, the house is quiet, like it always is, not because it's still early but because it's *always* quiet. What can I expect when it's so large but only houses two people? It's too vast, mammoth-like, and hollow, and the space and silence make it desolate and lonely. It gives us an excuse to pretend we don't exist to each other.

Everywhere over the house, there are imprints of her and my younger brother, from the framed pictures to the carefully picked out pieces of furniture. It only brings back memories and makes it worse. *Your fault, your fault, your fault,* the voice in my head says.

Opening the front door, I make sure the house keys are in my pocket before I shut it behind me, and pull the wool cap lower on my head. This early in the morning, it's cold, and the world is still quiet. It's peaceful but desolate. The sky is a dark, dark blue, almost navy, but it's that time of the day when there isn't any sunlight, but no moon in the sky either.

From where I live, the school is at least a forty-five-minute walk, which is why I had to wake up at an ungodly hour. Ever since the accident, I've been banned from taking the bus or being in any car other than his. He's an extremist in that way, and I can add public transport to the ever-growing list of things that are too dangerous for me.

But then I remember the pure terror that settled over me like a thorny blanket the first time I sat in a car after an accident, the knee-jerk reaction to flinch whenever the light would turn red. Maybe it's a good thing I don't take the bus to school.

I steer my thoughts away from the accident, and to make the walk seem quicker, I pull out my music player, pressing the first thing that comes up without paying attention to it. The beat starts, soft, sad, and slightly haunting, before the melody begins.

I hum along to the lyrics, even though it makes it easy to spiral into the pit of my mind. I haven't even started the school year yet, but already I feel as though my skin is too tight, the routine of life too dreary. I have an ever-persistent itch to leave this place, to close my eyes and wake up years later. Better yet, to leave behind the memories and give up.

I wait for the panic attack to come.

There are throngs of people entering the school. *Stampedes* of students. I stand back, watching them cross the streets, with some loitering in the parking lot and others marching straight inside. I can already make out the cliques of people, the different age groups.

Inside, it's loud, with voices rising over others and boisterous laughter filling the halls. Bodies press against me in the hallway, the heavy scent of body spray and perfume bombarding my senses. I press past those heading to the lockers, deciding I'll get my schedule first.

The secretary, with what seems to be pajamas and a pencil shoved through her hair, is not what I expected her to be. I decide I like her. She's helpful, and when she notices the smudge marks on my fingers, she passes me a slip with information for art classes and competitions.

I pocket the paper and look for my locker, wrinkling my nose at the smell that wafts from it. Shoes squeak across the floor, and the sound becomes more faint as I load my things in.

It takes me five minutes to get the damn thing to close, and I step back with a sigh, but groan when it pops out again.

"*Chiudere,*" I mutter under my breath.

With no warning, a hand comes down beside me, slamming against the locker, the flesh smacking hard against the metal. The sound resounds in my ears, and I let out a shriek. I try to catch my breath and calm my hammering heart as I look at the hand on my locker.

With the size of it and the fine dusting of hair at the sleeve, I can tell it belongs to a male. His fingers are long, with smudges of paint on them, and I calm down a little at the sight. A fellow painter, then. The nails are trimmed neatly, and a scar runs over one of his knuckles. Immediately, the calm evanesces.

My gaze travels up from his hand to a black sleeve, then higher, to his bicep, noting the strongly outlined muscles. Someone on a sports team then? I look higher to his face. Dark eyes regard me, the shape of them hooded as he looks down, chin tilted up, and I can tell from here that his lashes are long, the edges of them curling. His eyes are dark enough that I can't tell where his iris ends and pupil begins, and their darkness makes his gaze seem harder, even though he seems slightly spaced out.

Hair as dark as his eyes falls in waves around his ears and over his forehead. High cheekbones make his face seem sharper, more defined, until he looks older than he probably is. With his lips tipped up at a corner, I can see that his incisors are crooked. I don't know why the thought satisfies me, as though I've finally found a fault.

Except it's not a fault, not really.

I draw my gaze back to his eyes, and his brows are arched, as if he's laughing at me. I've never been good at painting people, but I'm

17

filled with the inexplicable urge to try putting his likeness on a canvas.

"You should take a picture, it'll last longer."

A flush spreads up my neck at his words, and I blurt the first thing I can think of, "I think I'm good. You ruined it with what came out of your mouth."

Seriously, he scares the *merda* out of me, and then doesn't apologize?

At my glare, he takes a step back, hands raised in surrender. "Relax, I was joking. And I'm sorry, I didn't mean to scare you, I just wanted to help." He gestures toward the lockers. "All the lockers on this aisle are a pain to close because of a prank. You have to slam it *really* hard."

"I figured."

There's no hiding the snark in my tone, and he looks at me in appraisal, but also something else. I recognize that look—I have it every time I challenge myself to go beyond my comfort zone in painting, or read a six-hundred-page book in one night. He looks like he's found a challenge and will take it against his better judgment.

He doesn't say anything, and I pull my backpack higher over my shoulder. "Well, then. Thank you. But next time, go give some other girl a heart attack."

I turn on my heels, looking at the folded schedule and layout of the school in my hands, trying to find out where to go. I hear him laugh behind me, before he catches up, long legs making it easy. He towers above me, and from the way his shirt fits snug over his body, accentuating his shoulders and toned arms, I know that he's at least a grade or two above me.

But it's not as though he seems much older. Not age-wise, at least, or in the way he speaks. He's still like most teenagers in that way, on the cusp of adulthood, teetering between being a boy and being a man. No, he seems older in the way he *holds* himself. Relaxed, shoulders set back, head high, with a sort of confidence I don't often find.

But I know that confidence is faked, that there is somewhere dark his mind goes when he zones out.

"Nice to meet you, too," he says. "My name is Jaxon, a nice, charming name, worth swooning over, I know. What's yours?"

I pause, turning to face him, and he does too. I have to tilt my chin up to hold his gaze properly, and I can tell he likes it. *Okay, we can't all be trees.*

"Why don't you cut the act? The cocky one. We both know that's not who you are."

That smirk falls from his lips, and he regards me like he's just noticing me, slightly dumbfounded. That look I'd seen in his eyes earlier is back, and then I know exactly who he's like. He's someone who experienced life a little too early, and someone who still hasn't learned to cover it well. I turn around, leaving him there, a small frown pulling at his brows and a faraway look in his eyes.

"Are you this perceptive with everyone, or am I just lucky?"

I shrug, still not looking back. "I guess you'll never know." He doesn't follow me, and over my shoulder, I throw, "And the name's Layla."

I can't stop the grin that spreads over my face as I enter my classroom, the teacher taking attendance. First period hasn't even passed, and I already managed to render someone speechless.

In my eyes, that's an achievement.

The cafeteria smells like I imagined it would—of spices, bread, and slowly rotting food. Beneath it all, there's the smell of too many bodies packed together. From the size of the room and the amount of people crammed inside, I want to bet the school has been taking on more students than it's allowed to.

I'd planned to sneak off to the library anyway, but maybe now I'll have to, since every bench looks to be crowded. Or maybe... I could stay, and find a spot, and make some friends. Maybe the next time a catastrophe happens, I won't ghost them, and I won't hide in a house made of only haunted memories.

Immediately, I shake my head at the thought, my gaze going to the linoleum tiles beneath me. Ever since the accident and what I've learned, my world has tilted on its axis, putting me in a bubble. Everyone else is now *other*, who doesn't know about the monsters lurking in this city, wearing a false skin of humanity. *You don't deserve friends, anyway. What if they also die because of you?*

Lately, I've been agreeing with those thoughts more and more, but what I wouldn't give for normalcy, for forgetting what I know.

I'm rudely yanked from my thoughts when someone collides into me with an *oomph*, and hands come over my shoulders, steadying me.

"Would you *watch* where—oh, it's you."

Jaxon quirks a brow, his hands still over my shoulders, and somehow, he seems even taller like this. I can't deny his hands are warm, though, and I wonder when was the last time someone touched me. Was it really my mother? Before the accident?

"That wasn't very nice, *you* bumped into *me*."

"No," I insist. "You did."

He narrows his eyes, serious, as though I've offended him. "Are you calling me a liar?"

Grabbing his wrists, the material of his sleeves soft beneath my skin, I pull his hands away but don't let go. It's likely I was the one to bump into him, but I still say, "If the shoe fits."

He opens his mouth to say something, but I drop his hands and head toward the food. Grabbing a juice box and something pre-packed, I quickly make my escape.

Eventually, I find the library, and quickly learn that it's probably another under-funded part of the school. It looks to be the size of a classroom, maybe a little bigger, with thin metal shelves propped across the room, some barely holding their weight. In all the previous schools I'd been to, everything was new, polished, and larger than needed. At the time, I thought it was the norm, but now I wonder how much of it was a privilege funded by my father's... unsavory ventures.

But a library is still a library, so I look for a book and a quiet corner to sit in. Not five minutes later, and I hear someone else walking through the shelves, footfalls soft over carpet, before whoever it is comes my way. And they stop, expectant.

I keep my eyes on the book in front of me, even if I'm not really paying attention. Surely they'll go away.

They don't.

"Do you need this chair?"

Looking up, I can't hide the scowl on my face when I recognize who it is, even if a little guilt surfaces from earlier. I can admit it was rude of me to bump into him, insinuate—insist, really—that it was his fault, call him a liar, and then run.

"Oh, it's you." My eyes narrow. "Did you follow me?"

"I realize it can be very easy to believe the world revolves around you, but other people *do* like to come to the library during lunch."

The urge to snap back rises, but I sigh instead. "No. I don't need that chair." Pausing, I clear my throat. "I'm sorry for implying you were a liar earlier."

He scrutinizes me with his dark eyes, until I fidget. I'm sure he's going to throw my apology in my face, but what he does next surprises me. Instead, he smiles, and I think it's the most beautiful thing I've ever seen. *Seriously, Layla?*

His eyes crinkle at the corners, pure mirth written on his features. When was the last time someone was that *happy* over something I said? And also, it can't be *this* easy to make someone happy, can it?

"It's refreshing to see someone who states their mind but apologizes when they go too far."

I pause. "Thank you…?"

"On that note, I'm sorry for saying you believe the world revolves around you."

"Um, it's okay."

Nodding awkwardly, I wonder why he's still here, admitting that as pretty as his smile is, his temperament—quick to smile, quick to forgive—is a bit odd. But then again, maybe it's just because it's different.

"So, since that's out of the way, how about this? Instead of taking this chair to another lonely corner, I sit here, and then this lonely corner of one can become a lonely corner of two."

"You're weird," I quip, but don't stop him from sitting.

It's also exhilarating to have his attention on me, wholly focused. From the way others have glanced at him in the halls and in the cafeteria, I know that others probably want his attention.

"I could say you're a little weird too."

"But I'm not."

He gives me a look as though to say, *sure*, and unbidden, my mouth tugs up a little at the corner. I anticipated hating today, but for some reason, I don't.

Even more odd, I find myself actually looking forward to tomorrow.

Chapter 3

Now

This side of the coast is everything I expected, but at the same time, not. The airport is crowded, and I try to block out the drone of voices, but can't stop myself from looking at everyone, not much different from a person seeing color for the first time. Some smile when they catch me looking, others frown and turn away. Some of the men wink, and I have to bite my lip from laughing when one blows an over-the-top kiss.

But as much as I can't stop staring, a nervous giddiness thrumming within me, I keep glancing over my shoulder as I exit, heading for the parking lot.

I still can't believe I've made it this far; that no one stopped the taxi driver back home—not home anymore, I remind myself—or at the airport. I knew, and counted on my father's diminishing power and how he got lulled into a sense of comfort, but it's still shocking that it's actually *working*.

It's such a surprise, I don't believe it. In the parking garage, every shadow is a nightmare, every sound is someone behind me, until it's hard to focus on finding her car.

I repeat the license plate and general description in my head as I stand on the tips of my toes and survey the parking lot, some of it cast in shadows while the rest is encased in a yellow glow from the overhead lights. It smells of exhaust and fumes, pungent enough that I cover my nose.

And then I find it. Stark, bright red, and with a customized license plate, I can't believe I didn't spot it quicker. I mouth her name, testing the syllables on my tongue. Harlow.

She's a spitfire, with a creative mind and even more creative insults, but a teddy bear on the inside. We coordinated everything, from the timing to the apartment I'd share with her and the interviews I have to take tomorrow. Even though I've never had a face-to-face conversation with her, I love her, as though she's the sister I always wished for, and the person I will always be indebted to.

Bending down, I knock on the glass, hoping my voice isn't as scratchy as it was before. With a low whir, the glass lowers, and I finally get to see her. She is everything I expected, and at the same time, not. As though, while my eyes do not recognize her, my soul does.

Simultaneously, I try to study her and pay attention to what she's saying. Her straight black hair is cut to her chin, with neat bangs over her brows. She has a small, pert nose, with a light smattering of freckles over it, and sharp, dramatic eyeliner adorns her dark eyes, stark against her pale skin.

"Layla, right?" she asks, tone conversational until I wonder if picking up near strangers from the airport is a regular occurrence for her.

I nod my head slowly and refrain from reaching over and pulling her into a hug. Even though I've known her for years, that was all over the texts. And sporadic texts at that, since I often felt it wasn't safe for either of us, despite the numerous precautions I took.

Like this, it's easy to wonder if I actually really know her at all. Not when she doesn't know so much about me, by design.

"Great. Just so I know it's you. Code?"

"Big fishy."

She smiles. "Favorite artist?"

24

My earlier fear easily loosens. She's the same person I've known for the past two and a half years. "You mean one? Joking, it's obviously you."

She grins slowly, and there's a budding excitement taking root in my marrow. I've always known she's someone I effortlessly click with, but to experience it in person is nearly rhapsodic. "Favorite book couple?"

"Again, not *one*, but Cerise and Mikael are close to the top."

She squeals, and the laugh that bursts out of me isn't forced. It's odd, the way a laugh feels in my throat, the soft echoes of it in my chest, and I wonder at what point I forgot how it felt. When did I laugh before that? Was it all those years ago, with him?

"Get in. I've waited to have an in-person conversation with you for years, and we have some catching up to do. Prepare yourself. We're binge-watching that show I keep talking about."

She reaches down, presses a button, and the trunk lid pops open. As I throw in my backpack and suitcase, I can't help but let out a sigh. It seems strange to have such a... carefree, mundane conversation.

When I slide into the passenger seat, she turns her gaze to me, scrutinizing. "You good?"

I nod, and wordlessly, she reaches over and turns on the radio, the melody and beat soon filling in the silence.

"Come on, Layla!" she cheers, her head moving back and forth to the beat, every limb carefree.

I roll down my own window, until the wind pulls at my braid. There's enough for me to worry over, enough for my anxiety to feast on, like the interviews, the classes coming up, whether I'm being followed or not, and that list extends, but for now, I don't think of them.

There'll always be problems in my life, but it's how I push through them that matters. And right now, even for only a few hours, I'm letting them go.

The first interview sucked. I stammered through the entire thing even though it was for a relatively easy position at a small company, and I wondered if they could tell my last name was fake. That all the documents were fake and I don't behave my age, socially stunted, years past the normal pattern of life with only a high school diploma. While I know an education level is not an indication of worth, I carry the knowledge like it's an acidic shortcoming, another thing about myself to hate.

The second interview, right after that, wasn't much better, but I managed to *not* stammer the entire time. Just maybe half.

It was hard enough to find these job postings, and it's as though I'm sludging through murky water, my head still stuck on the other side of the country. I'm still in that house, waiting for the next set of parties with the next set of sharks, with men vying for the hand of the daughter to a dead empire as my father decides just how much I'm worth.

But I'm not there, I remind myself, and life's new responsibilities aren't waiting for me. There's money needed for school, for the credit card loans it took me to get here, and as much as Harlow insists she's got it, there's also money needed for the apartment. I refuse to live off her more than I already am.

I try not to really panic about it, because I would take these problems over the situation I was in a week ago any time. But sometimes, when I'm alone, the ache resettles over my bones, worming its way into my veins. I'm not there anymore, but I still just want to lie down and not wake up.

Dark, like my past, these thoughts leave a weight in my gut and possibilities in my mind that I cannot turn off. I hate the direction my thoughts go in when I see balconies and flat roofs, or speeding cars as I walk close to the edge of a sidewalk. One, maybe two steps is all it'd take, and then everything would be quiet.

"How'd it go?" I hear Harlow holler from the kitchen, and wearily, I trudge over to where she is, shrugging out of my jacket.

"Horrible. I stuttered." I run the word over in my head. "That's an onomatopoeia. Whoever invented it needs to be strangled."

Collapsing on the couch, I stare at the ceiling as Harlow moves around in the kitchen. It's been a week since I got here, which means that next week, classes start. Even though it excites me, enough that I grin at the thought, dread churns in my stomach all the same.

Everything is moving so suddenly, and even though I wouldn't want to change it, I can't help but be terrified. Do I really want to get a degree anyway? I'll be years older than my peers but socially inept, veering between the lost teenager and the stumbling adult.

It's exhausting to remind myself of the reasons I applied in the first place, and that it's alright to start college well after finishing high school. I tell myself they accepted me, one of the most prestigious schools this side of the country, and that alone is something I should be happy about.

The fact that the nightmares don't want to leave only makes things worse. Harlow says I should get help, maybe take some medication, but the idea of it fills me with a cold panic that flushes my skin until I cannot breathe. I shut my eyes against the onslaught of memories and get up to help her. She's trying to make some fancy dish that has the kitchen smelling like a restaurant and my stomach growling.

A stack of plates are thrust into my hands, and while looking at the pot in front of her, she says, "Set the table up, please, and call over Mrs. Darcy."

I do as she asks, because I've quickly learned that in this friendship, she wears the pants, and as I make my way to the door, she hollers, "And tell her to bring her daughter! I miss her."

Harlow always cooks enough to feed a village, and then either packs some food away to give to the neighbors or takes it to the local homeless shelters. I help her when I can, but there's always a frenzy to her, as though something bad will happen if she misses taking the food, and I wonder why.

Normally, nothing ever made me hesitate with her before, but that was over text. I know her, better than I know almost anyone, and yet the dynamic of living with her tilts our relationship. I know it's the same for her when I only hear her medical vest turned on late at night, when she thinks I'm asleep, and how she doesn't meet my gaze when she says she's stepping out for a doctor's appointment.

I open the front door, with scratches on the back from what I hope was the previous owner's pet. We live in a decent part of the city, but it's not a state-of-the-art place. The carpet that furnishes the hallway is in need of at least one deep cleaning, the paint peels in the hallway, and there are stickers on the wall, no doubt from one of the children. They always remind me of my dead brother, and I bury the pang of pain and guilt that smarts at the reminder. Everything gets buried these days, but then again, when have they not?

When did I start letting the demons win? Will there ever be a day I once again hide them so successfully no one can ever see them? Will they ever go back into their cage?

I knew it would be huge, that there would be thousands of students, but I wasn't expecting *this*. How the hell am I not going to get lost?

The New Student Orientation isn't starting until next week, but the next three days are going to be spent seeing the university president, familiarizing ourselves with some of the buildings, meeting our advisors, and registering for classes. Today, we get to meet with the advisors. Harlow is just as clueless and nervous as I am, so she wasn't much help in the morning.

I turn to face her now, and she puts her hands on my shoulders, shaking me once. She's not wearing her signature eyeliner today, and it makes her face somehow seem vulnerable, the angle of her eyes slender.

"I'm not supposed to go to this building; I'm meeting my advisor somewhere else." She looks down at her phone, checking her email. "I think. But don't worry too much. Do those breathing exercises to stay calm, and it's okay to stress sometimes. You wanted this, and you got it, but don't push yourself too hard and doubt yourself."

She gives me that "inspirational speech" for a while longer before turning around and hurrying away. I watch her retreating figure for a while, grateful for the umpteenth time that I have her even if it's been slow getting used to, before pushing my glasses higher up my nose and walking inside. Students buzz around me, some looking nervous like me, freshmen I assume, while others are more relaxed, chatting away as they walk.

But none of the noise and people can take away from the architecture of the building. The campus was built over a century ago, from what I remember, with a few of the buildings either remodeled or extended, but this one evidently hasn't been tampered with much.

It's on an incline surrounded by shrubs and bushes, and certain sections of it have thin, turret-like towers. Arches, done in black stone, cover the front, through which I can see the doors. With the clouds dark today, it seems less of a university building and more like an abandoned monastery.

Climbing up the stairs and passing under the arches, I push open the glass doors. They open up to a wide, circular space, with the glass ceiling high enough that all sound dulls out and I can see the sky, hinting to rain. On either side of the entrance are hallways that seem to branch into darkness, and at the far end are a set of stairs that lead up into a tower. I'm struck with the urge to go there first, but the hallway entrances are marked, and one reads "faculty offices."

I recall the email; *At eight, come straight to the offices. Mine has my name over it.*

There's still time, but the paranoia that has been nagging at me all morning surges. I am sure that I will mess up somehow, that it'd be better to find her office a little early rather than chance being late. Sometimes, I am so certain that my admission was a mistake and they need only a minor slip-up to expel me.

I head down that hall, passing by each office until I see her name, and the riot in my chest settles a little. But I have at least ten more minutes, and so I keep walking. A little ahead and there's a lounge area, and like the rest of the building, it's both archaic and cozy. Instead of plastic chairs, there are upholstered couches pushed against the walls with the center having a display full of posters.

As I sit and wait, other students enter the building, passing where I'm seated, and enter respective offices. Leaning back, I take out my best form of distraction—a sketchbook. Flipping to a blank page, I smooth it out, skin rasping over rough paper. I lean down, my hair forming a curtain around me, blocking most of the world, and everything fades away.

Without even realizing it, I sketch out a familiar alleyway, capturing a design I shouldn't remember as well as I do. Before me, familiar painted walls and designs slowly unravel across the page with every stroke of my pencil. The day plays over in my head as I sketch it, hand moving over the paper, but my mind is elsewhere.

Words repeat in my head. *"Maybe I just want you."*

"For someone so straightforward and unashamed, you often doubt what others feel for you."

More and more filter from the past, moments and words and kisses. They are images running through my mind, words playing in my head, feelings surfacing from the past. The memories should've disappeared long ago, but much like with everything else, I'm stuck in that time, always wondering over *what could have been.* How different would things be now, I wonder, if I never entered the office that day? How different would things be if I hadn't had to go to the hospital?

I need to move on, I know I do, and I'm angry at myself that I can't. I'm not that teenage girl anymore, but sometimes, it feels like it. Viciously, I snap the sketchbook closed and stuff it back in my bag. Looking at the clock, I catch sight of the time and mutter something incoherent. Only three minutes have passed.

To keep myself busy from remembering anything else, I turn to the glass doors and start guessing the stories behind the students that enter and leave. Most of the theories are probably nothing close, but it's amusing nonetheless.

A redhead enters, and for some reason, my gaze snags on him. Maybe because something about him is different from the rest of the students I've seen so far, or maybe it's just his hair, red like fire, red like blood, and his sharp features, eyes wide-set and upturned.

That red hair straddles the line between being curly and wavy, with light curls curving slightly around his brow and ears. His nose is slightly straight and snubbed at the end. There's a smattering of freckles over his nose, light brown from what I can tell, accentuating his sharp cheekbones.

I decide that he has the kind of face worth sketching, and I would, if taking a picture of him unabashedly wouldn't be strange.

Instead, I look down, fidget with the ring on my finger, and look back up, resolving to study him some more.

Until he looks straight at me.

I quickly slide my gaze away, hoping that he thinks nothing of the pink on my cheeks. Pretending to study the hem of my shirt, my fingers play with the cloth, until I see someone sit down beside me from the corner of my eye even though at least two other couches are empty.

Please leave, please leave, please leave, I repeat in my head. *I don't do conversations.*

I already know who it is as I look up, refraining from chewing my lips at how nervous I am. The thought is hilarious. I come from a life where nothing is supposed to make me nervous, not when I lived in the underbelly of a city that pretended there were no monsters hiding in mansions. Instead, the thought of even talking to someone fills me with a cold dread.

It's the redhead, and with him this close, looking at me, I can see that his eyes are brown. Almost like honey but darker. But not as dark as someone else's.

"Layla, right?" he asks, his voice light like he walks up and sits next to random people every day.

But then his words register, and I stare at him in alarm, stuck between wanting to punch him and getting up and bolting. How the hell does he know my name? All I can think is that he's here on behalf of someone else, that I've been found and I shouldn't have gotten comfortable with this new life. I shouldn't have settled in a place, and I should've just kept running.

I'm convinced he's going to pull out a gun and discreetly press it against my leg and tell me to stand up and walk outside. The familiar dredges of panic creep around my neck, tightening into a noose, and I know I won't be able to breathe soon.

Except he doesn't do any of that. "I'm Aaron, a friend of Harlow's. She told me to come see you."

He takes out his phone and pulls up a contact with her picture to show me proof, and from the texts, I know it's her. The sight calms me down, and I try to refrain from snapping or punching his arm. He couldn't have led with that?

But then I realize that if he's a friend of Harlow's, then she sent him here to either make sure I'm not having a panic attack, or worse, try to get me to go on a date with the guy.

Eventually, I settle with, "Great to know." It sounds forced and dry and horribly awkward, so I hope he gets the message.

His eyes brighten with laughter, even though there seems to be something sorrowful behind them. I wonder if that really is him, or if I'm just seeing sadness in everybody, as if looking at a reflection.

"I think she's trying to set us up," he says honestly, leaning back in his chair and regarding me with a look I know well.

He used to always look at me like that. My throat thickens at the memories, and I shove them away. I've been annoyed with Harlow's one-track mind to setting me up with someone, but maybe the idea has some merit.

"I think it's a good idea," he says, straightforward. It's an admirable quality, I'll admit, for him to be honest about what he thinks and wants, but I narrow my eyes at him. "Not to be too blunt, but the whole point of going out is to know someone better, and I want to know you better."

"Why?"

"Because," he starts, ticking up a finger for every reason he gives. "Harlow has told me a lot of you, I'm curious about you, it wouldn't hurt, and I can say for sure I'd at least get to be your friend." His response is quick and unashamed, before he adds, "And because life's too short to waste it behind the fear of rejection."

And there it is. Seems that my intuition was correct. For a moment, I don't know what to say in reply, because while meeting him certainly wouldn't hurt, for a split second, a part of me thinks, *but you're not* him.

I shake the thought. I haven't seen him for years, and it's been more than enough time for him to move on. I never expected him to wait for me, and I still don't. That's not fair of me, and it's not fair *for* me to wait for him either. And I know I'm being unreasonable, that the little flutter of hope in my stomach every time I see a familiar head of dark hair, is unreasonable.

Besides, going out with Aaron could be good for me. If anything, maybe I can get another friend, and the whole reason I came here anyway was to try. To try having a semblance of normalcy.

"Okay then. I'm going to throttle Harlow when I see her, but sure, I don't see why not." *You're certainly not bad on the eyes*, I think.

"Thank you."

He laughs, a light sound, and my cheeks flame.

I cover my face, groaning. "Did I say that *out loud?*"

"Yep."

I narrow my eyes at him, because he could've at least pretended not to hear me, instead of letting me stew in embarrassment.

His grin is easy. "I think we're going to have loads of fun."

I wish I could say the same.

Chapter 4

Then

I shouldn't be doing this, and I know that this decision is going to come and bite me where it hurts tomorrow. I *especially* shouldn't be trying it now, with tomorrow being a school day. Quite frankly, I shouldn't do the other option either—they're both bad. But this one, in the long run, could be beneficial.

It's a lose-lose situation, and I don't know how anyone in their right mind can actually enjoy these things.

It's past midnight—five more hours of this to go—and my mind is too tired to read or paint, but not too tired that I can't down another cup of coffee, trying my hardest to not fall asleep. Waking up screaming would be the perfect excuse for him to put me in a psychiatric ward. Not that I really think he would, but I never imagined he wouldn't speak to me either.

Which is a shame, because while I always loved my mother, I aspired to be my father—before. I used to steal his sunglasses and wear them on my face, over my own glasses. When I was five, I took one of the disposable razors from his sink and "shaved" the nonexistent hair over my lip to the point I bled. Over the years, though, the need to mimic him became less. Not only because I grew older, but because I inherited his stubborn will, until we both butted heads over everything.

But the final rift wedged between us was when I found out what he'd lied about for years. Sometimes, it's surprising how quickly his image tarnished in my eyes, until the man who was my father might as well have not existed at all. My mother's death was the final nail in the coffin.

For all the power his "line of business" gave him, he never could save her.

Drinking all the coffee in the house to stay awake is definitely a good decision. Based on how easy it is for my thoughts to veer south, the nightmares would've started soon after falling asleep.

Immediately, in my mind, a shrill scream sounds, followed by a sharp crash. I viciously start the machine again, glad the heater is on, the sound drowning out the whirring of the coffee machine as the warm, almost-black liquid pours. Inhaling deeply, the smell alone is enough to shake off some of the drowsiness, startling my senses. Without pouring milk, I down the glass, coughing as it sears down my throat.

And all I can think about is, *I'm going to fail my test tomorrow.*

Well, things could always get worse.

As expected, I look like *merda*. It's not a surprise, and I know that tonight I'm going to cave and take some of those stronger sleeping pills. The guy called them depressants or whatever, but they're sleeping pills. They have to be.

I'll figure it out, I tell myself, though I'm already planning on waking up earlier someday this week so I can get some more before school.

Somewhere, metal slams and shoes squeak, shaking me from my stupor, shocking me for a moment until the migraine pounding behind my eyes briefly retreats. My limbs don't want to coordinate with me, and the world spins as I glare at my locker's door before slamming it hard.

Like he promised, it latches.

I wait at the lockers a bit longer, already used to him showing up before classes start. When he doesn't come, I tell myself disappointment doesn't churn in my chest. I haven't grown used to him or anything.

Stumbling to first period, I pull at the collar of my shirt, familiar with the flushed, fervid feeling that overtakes me. I've tried this before, so the drowsiness, irritation, and rising fever is nothing new. When I'm not in the middle of it, it's almost interesting to think about how badly the body needs sleep. Only a few days without and soon it begins to shut down. For beings so weak and needing many things to survive, it's comedic how far the human race has come.

But for me, it's only been two nights of little to no sleep, so it won't be too bad.

I slide into my seat, rubbing a hand over my eyes as the weariness gnaws at my limbs. When I drop my hand, I see a cup on my table, one I am sure I did not put there. A frown tugs at my brows. Am I really hallucinating?

Looking up, I see one of my classmates, her name on the tip of my tongue, with nervousness written across her features. I regard her, and if I wasn't so tired, maybe I'd ask what she uses to have her bronze skin practically gleaming. Her features are soft, and from here, I can tell that her lashes are thick and long, framing her large, almond-colored eyes.

"Hi," she starts nervously. "I'm Aaradhya. I just thought you could use this."

I blink, slow, and the nervousness spreads across her limbs, her fingers fidgeting as she slides into the seat beside me. Finally, I remember what I'm missing.

"Thank you," I rasp, immediately pulling the cup closer and taking a sip.

It isn't coffee, but rather something citrusy and sharp. It's strong nonetheless, and I sit a little straighter in my seat. It's probably bad practice to drink things random people give me, but she seems nice.

"It's good, right? It's a family recipe my mom uses, since she hates coffee, and has insomnia." Her eyes widen. "Not that I think you look bad or anything, when I said I thought you needed it."

"You're good. And it's amazing, though I would never swear off coffee."

She laughs and tilts her head to the side, studying me, eyes tracing around my head, and this time, I fidget. Noticing, she blurts out, "Your color, it's blue, and you have no taste, thankfully."

I stare at her, maybe a little stupidly, because I'm sure the sleep deprivation is getting to me and I didn't hear her right. "I'm blue? And have no taste? Should I be offended?"

"I have the... bad habit"—she punctuates it with a groan—"of saying these things off the bat. But no, don't be offended. I can see colors when I look at a person... like they have a halo of color around them in a way, and when I look at someone, usually, I will 'taste' something in my mouth—like they have a taste. My senses basically don't work right."

I try to understand what she's saying. What does she mean by her senses "don't work right"? Like a condition? I wonder if that's how she sees it, or if it's what everyone else has told her. That rather than having something different, she has something wrong. I settle with saying, "I'm curious. Very curious. And seems cool."

Visibly relaxing, she smiles, hands moving vivaciously as she rambles, "I have synesthesia. My gustatory sense and olfactory sense aren't, well, 'normal.' So when I look at a person, I get a taste in my mouth, although you don't have a taste. As for the color, I see it around a person, sometimes on their skin, and sometimes it's like they have dragon's breath in that color."

She tries to avoid eye contact with the person who just started staring at her, and I wonder if she's ashamed of it, or if someone's made fun of her for it before. I have a million questions I want to ask her. Does it affect her? Make her feel unstable at times? Or is it like a normal, everyday thing for her that she can't imagine living without? Are the "colors" and "tastes" she can see and experience related to the person's personality in any way, or is it related to how she perceives the person?

Instead of bombarding her with questions, not wanting to make her feel like an anomaly when I can just search it up later, I say, "It's like you have a superpower."

She grins, twin dimples showing. Someone nudges her shoulder, murmuring something I don't catch before carrying on, and the grin immediately falls from her face.

Turning over, I glare at the girl that just walked by, even though it makes my incessant migraine worse, the tension behind my eyes flaring.

"Was she bothering you?"

Aaradhya shakes her head. "It's fine—I know her from another class and accidentally said she tastes like lemon. I explained it to her and apologized, but I think she just thinks it's weird."

My glare narrows further, even though the girl can't see me. "If she bothers you, let me know." I realize how that sounds, and add, "Not that you can't stand up for yourself or anything."

"You know, sometimes people like you remind me that the world can be a very beautiful place sometimes. But I know that I need to speak up for myself. I would, but..." She trails off, fear tightening her expression. "Never mind."

"Okay. But let me know. I'll happily put some people in their place in exchange for more of"—I pick up the drink—"this."

She grins. "You have a deal. Friends?"

There's no hiding the nervousness in my voice when I say, "Sure."

And despite the incessant voice of reason in my head, the one of caution, I grin back at her.

The silence is suffocating, as usual, hammering in that it's all we know now. Sometimes, when I turn my head, I'm sure I can catch a whiff of the perfume she would love to wear, and I wonder if my father is just spritzing it in his car to pretend she's still here.

The car slows down, the engine a low rumble as he stops in front of a nondescript building. Only once it's stopped does my knee stop bouncing, do my hands stop nervously grabbing onto the seat, as though my body is braced for an impact.

I close my eyes, and the world tilts, like I'm spinning, over and over—

With a start, I open them, and practically bolt out of the vehicle. The triggers are always worse in that car, always worse around him. And still, I turn to face him. Still, I say, "See you, *papà*."

And like always, he doesn't say anything. Like always, a vise tightens around my throat, and I want to slam the door hard enough it reverberates.

The air is brisk and cold as I walk to the building, one that resembles an office complex with its darkly tinted glass and neatly trimmed bushes lining the walls. From four to six, every other Wednesday, without fail, he drops me here, since the distance is too far to walk. At first, I thought it was because he cared, that this was his way of showing it.

Then I realized it was to keep me out of the house during this time. It didn't take two and two to piece it together when he was late one day and I decided to walk home, out of cash to cave and take a bus. Despite arriving nearly two hours later, he was still busy, unknown cars in the driveway, and I snuck in through the back door.

It's still hard to forget the image of the men seated in our living room, the sight of the guns strapped to their waists, as they all spoke in low voices. Worse, it's hard to erase the image of my father seated in the front of the room, in an impeccable suit, hair slicked back, and his own weapon within reach. He didn't look like my father then, but a man with ruthlessness as his closest ally. I'd ducked out of view, but from the way he'd glared at me the next day, the words *"don't interrupt business"* unsaid but clear, he knew I saw.

This new version of my father burns in my mind as I'm unable to reconcile his present and past selves. Looking back, I'm shocked he hid this part of him for so long and so successfully, and undoubtedly hid us from his world as well.

After all, I don't remember guards in my childhood, I don't remember incidents with rivals, but then again, how much do I really know? My father rules a ruthless empire, something I haven't known my entire life, and now that I do, the pieces are a mess, ones I try to puzzle together with the internet and fiction, but still not really understanding how his world works.

I step inside, and I know I'm angry, the rage a live wire nestled in my gut, snaking around my throat, that he doesn't really care to hide it from me as successfully. That my worth to him as a daughter only existed alongside my mother and brother.

I'm dragged to the present when a familiar voice says, "You can come with me, Layla."

My therapist is what some might describe as a motherly figure. She smiles a lot and is quick to say things like, "dear," "sweetie," and "darling," even when I frustrate her to no end. Sometimes, when I say something sarcastic in a deadpan tone, and she takes me seriously for a bit before realizing I'm being sardonic, I can tell she wants to glare at me, frustrated that weeks have gone by and I haven't given her anything.

I wonder if she would have a field day or send me to a psychiatric ward if I finally told her everything. What would she do if I finally let her see the signs I painstakingly hide every time I come here—the slight occasional tremors in my fingers, the bags under my eyes, the ways I sometimes twitch or fade, mind lost? Will the signs eventually grow worse?

What would she do, I wonder, if I told her about my father? Or about what caused the accident? Then again, it's luck to hope anyone on his payroll isn't already sworn into secrecy.

She smiles, a bit hopeful, like today, I'll let her give me the tools to fix myself. I smile back, knowing it's all teeth, all a facade to hide the demons behind my eyes, the demons in my thoughts.

"Well, Layla," she starts, a notepad in her hands and a pen poised in her fingers. "Let's begin."

Despite all my clipped words, Ms. Rose is always patient with me. Even when she's trying to crack me open with her words like an anvil with a clam, or when I sometimes stay in the lobby for hours after our session is over.

My house is too far away from here for me to walk and reach home before sunset, and while I would still try to make it, I don't want to walk in the dark again, not when I know what the city is like now. Not when I know the things men like my father sell.

Besides, I like staying here. The lobby is cozy and peaceful at this time of the day. Footfalls are muted from the gray carpets, the sunlight outside dims, and most are calm as the day unwinds to nightfall. Right now, it's the perfect environment for reading with no interruptions.

At least, until someone says my name.

It's soft, like a whisper, my name a caress as though the speaker doesn't want to disturb me. I look up, thinking that it's the receptionist trying to tell me that my father is here.

Instead, it's the person I least expect—Jaxon. Although, with my theories, maybe it makes sense he would be here. He smiles softly, wincing a little, as if in apology. The book I'm reading really is amazing, but I don't mind the distraction. At least not yet.

"So, what are you in here for?" I blurt, saying the first thing that came to my mind.

I also want to ask why I haven't seen him here before, but then maybe today is his first day or he usually comes on different days. It's still an interesting coincidence seeing him here, though. I can't say I mind it.

Once I register my words, immediately, I want to smack my hand over my forehead. It's like I went straight for the jugular despite knowing from experience that *you don't ask why a person is getting therapy.* That I made it seem as if we're in a prison only makes it worse. Although, in a sense, we are. We're prisoners of our own mind. But I don't think he'll see it like that.

Instead of being offended, he laughs. It's reserved almost, and more of a chuckle. Reserved like everything else about him so far. I wonder what he looks like relaxed, what a full laugh looks like, and tell myself I shouldn't care.

All too soon, it's over, but he's still smiling at me, eyes shining. It's odd seeing someone so happy to see me, not since my mother and brother passed away.

"I'm not here for the services. My… aunt is a therapist here, and I come here some days so she can teach me psychology."

"You want to be a psychologist?"

"I plan on studying it in college, but not too sure what I'd want to specialize in. Anyway, do you know what your name means?"

I blink. And blink again. Even though it's not new, it still comes as a surprise how quickly he changes the subject; how random he can be at times. Heck, everything about him comes off as a surprise.

"It's an Arabic word, coming from the word 'lail' or 'night'" he continues. "It means darkness, or beautiful night. Also 'dark beauty.'"

My mother named me, and a pang surfaces in her memory, sharper than the usual pain. She'd always loved language, and when I was born at midnight sharp, she felt that the name would be perfect.

"It fits you."

Nervous excitement pulses in my stomach, one I don't understand, but I want to ask him why he thinks it suits me.

"You study Arabic?" I ask instead.

He nods, a dark look momentarily crossing over his expression, eyes drifting away as though in a memory. I want to ask him what he's remembered, even though I know I shouldn't. Nothing good will come from learning more about him, nothing good will come from blending the line of polite formality into friendship.

And yet, there is the incessant belief that getting to know him would be all worth it.

Chapter 5

Now

The scream rips out of me violently as I throw myself up, my hands braced on the soft duvets. My heart palpitates wildly, sweat rolling down my spine as I pant. Scrambling over, I turn on the bedside lamp, and the familiar view of my room greets me. My new room, far, far away from there. I lie back down, my hair sticking to the back of my neck and my forehead, and everything is blurry without my glasses, but I don't care.

Instead, I smile. *I'm not there*, I repeat. There's a lot, normally, to be anxious about, but lately, I've been trying to reframe the way I look at things. Could I do without the nightmares and night terrors? Sure. Would I rather have the nightmares here, on the other side of the country, than be there? One hundred percent.

While this new practice is not fail-proof, it still helps, and I repeat the words, *I'm not there, I'm not there*, until my breathing evens out.

So even when Harlow barges in the room, her short, black hair in a disarray, I'm grinning in untempered glee. The men of my father's world thought they could have me, thought they could use me as the heir to a dying legacy, and now they will never find me.

Harlow stops at the sight of me smiling like the Cheshire Cat. "Are you crazier than I thought?" she mumbles, yawning.

Instantly, the grin melts, because I know it's not wise to mess with Harlow's beauty sleep. "Nope. Same amount of crazy. Don't worry, you can go back to sleep."

"You were *screaming*, like pure terror and oh-my-god-I'm-going-to-die screaming."

I shrug. "Don't remember any of it. It was a night terror, not a nightmare. So while night terrors can have a more visceral reaction, like screaming and sweating, you don't usually remember them."

She rolls her eyes and collapses beside me on the bed, immediately burying her head into a pillow. One of her pajama pant legs is hiked up to her knee, while the other one is past her ankles.

"Yeah, yeah," she mutters, her voice muffled from the pillows. "Don't tell me—you researched all about the differences and now you're going to give me a psychology lesson."

"No," I start, clearing my throat. "Jaxon told me. He was—maybe still is—into psychology."

She turns her head to look at me, and I'm not sure I like what I see written on her face. "He really was the love of your life, wasn't he? I'm expecting an angel in the human flesh, but I'm sure he's probably not that great. You know, since he's a guy."

"Harlow. That's not nice."

"Fair enough." She sighs, like I'm being unreasonable. "They have their moments. But you're telling me you've never been interested in any other guy?"

I don't tell her that for years, my options consisted of men who either viewed me as property, or men only interested in me for my father—most probably, they were all both. "Almost every guy who's talked to me or asked to go on a date so far has said they'd like to know what my accent sounds like in bed. Ew, no thank you."

"You do have a hot accent."

I narrow my eyes at her, but also don't tell her that with everyone else, it was not only disinterest that made me refuse their numbers, but also… fear. How would they react, I wonder, if they woke up one night to me screaming? What lies would I need to say to appear "normal"? At what point would those lies catch up to me?

"Besides," I continue. "Those guys don't matter and will not get my number, because I'm talking to Aaron, remember?"

Not only have we been talking, but we'll be going on a date soon. I wonder if I'm broken when excitement doesn't surge at the thought, when I regard the idea with mild interest, wondering how long it will take. But we share enough similar interests, and conversations are easy with him like they are with Harlow.

I turn to look at her when she doesn't respond, only to see that she's asleep, burrowed into the bed as she hugs one of my pillows. Sometimes, her ease to lie anywhere and simply fall asleep reminds me of a cat.

Rolling my eyes, I swing my legs off the bed, knowing sleep has long since evaded me, and when I glance at the clock, I decide I might as well go for a run. Every time, I hate it, as though I'm purposefully torturing myself when my lungs burn and legs ache. But with each run, my body hurts a little less, and my breathing grows more sturdy. Every time, I'm able to go a little farther before I want to keel over and die. But best of all, I'm usually so focused on putting one foot in front of the other that my mind empties of everything.

And right now, that's exactly what I need.

I've quickly come to realize that there's a bias surrounding art and humanity classes—a bias that they are easy. Sure, I don't need to memorize human anatomy or hybridization, but that doesn't mean my classes are *easy*. There's hours that go into every assignment and project. There's always the hammered-in mentality that once we get the degree, it only gets harder, the world of art full of sharks with only a few making it to actual success. After all, most are quick to say, "Artists either do big, or starve," for a reason.

It freaked me out enough that when I was picking my classes and possible specializations, I chose archaeology too. The idea of working in a museum during the day and painting at night seemed too good to not work toward.

Right now, I'm too absorbed in the white space of paper in front of me to notice that some of my classmates are leaving the lecture hall, until the professor tells me I shouldn't take too much time since the next class will be coming soon.

For the few weeks I've been here so far, I can safely say that this professor will be one of my favorites. Since the first day of classes, she's made sure that every student draws, paints, or sketches something at the end of lecture and hangs it on the bulletin boards. By the end of the semester, we should have our respective boards full, and compare our progress over the weeks.

As I put up my latest piece, I can already see the ways in which my art has changed as I track the various projects I've done. Some are of flowers, others are of scenery and cities, and another is the back profile of someone covered in shadows until he is discernible. I tell myself the drawing doesn't represent anyone.

I pause at the sight of another piece, a watercolor one of flowers, branching off one of my other pieces. Head tilted to the side, I study it, sure that I did not paint it. But then, why does the style look familiar? And this isn't the first one, either. There have been other drawings pinned on my board, ones I'm sure I haven't done, but can't figure out the culprit—I know they're not from my class, not when I'm almost always the first and last in the lecture hall.

Art styles are familiar, I try to reason, as I pin my new project. Still, I take a post-it note, write *Why are you putting pieces over my board?* and stick it to the latest mystery project.

It's probably nothing, and if it's someone else, does it really matter? But the style is familiar in a way that gnaws at me, hurt and stupid hope searing across my chest, and I need the paintings to stop.

I already know I want to leave when I step inside, anxiety riddling its way up my throat. I want to go home, wash the makeup from my face, put on my pajamas, and burrow underneath the blankets. Which is a shame, because I know this is the kind of place I would love to come to any other time. But the expectations that come with being here now, with who I'm going to be with, make me want to call it a night and leave.

Is it because of a lack of interest, or am I worried that I will botch this first date? Worse, am I worried that any hope this could be more will snuff out by the end of today? *You* want *it to be more*, I tell myself. But sometimes, when I think about it, I wonder if I really want him or if I've just idolized him for giving me attention after I've craved it for so long.

Before I can change my mind, a familiar arm wraps around my shoulders, my body coming to recognize the way he feels next to me.

"Sorry I'm late, Layla. The professor kept us waiting for a last-minute project."

His body is warm against mine as I'm slightly pressed to his side. It's not a romantic gesture, because he does this with everyone. With Harlow, his friends, and sometimes even his classmates, when they look like they need it. With his boyish charm, it's impossible for one to not relax around him.

I can't help but be glad that it's not a romantic gesture.

"That's alright," I reply. "This is a cute place."

And it is. With the miniature displays outside, lights strung over the storefront, and the various pieces pressed against the glass, the craft store is cute and different. It doesn't have the industrial look of a craft chain store, and is more inviting, almost personal, instead. I wonder if the pieces are from local artists, and when we go inside, there are tables with more art. In front of each piece are the supplies the artist used, from the paint brand, colors, brushes, or other medium tools, and then the aisle number for where to find each item.

It's unique, and regardless of how this goes, I know I'll be coming here again, even if it's a little far away from where I live, farther north into the bay.

"You like it," Aaron murmurs beside me, the pride in his voice unmistakable. "I knew you would."

"I do. How did you even find this place?"

"Harlow recommended it."

The annoyance that Harlow is meddling in my dates is brief, because maybe he asked for help to begin with. Honestly, I'm surprised she managed to not say anything for the whole day. Knowing her, Aaron had to bribe her for her silence, and probably by promising to update her with every detail. *"Impicciona,"* I mutter.

"What language is that?"

For a moment, I freeze, hating the way I've subconsciously come to associate the language with something else, with something dark, after years of hearing it used to say things best left unsaid, to make the kind of deals no person should.

"Italian," I answer.

"Oh, that's cool. You should teach me some words one day."

He takes me to the painting aisle, with its rows of paints, brushes, easels, and everything in between. In places like these, I regret having the budget of a college student, but I'd rather be here with a budget than there with money funded through blood and people in exchange for wilting behind metaphorical bars.

"You look like you want to clear the shelves," Aaron muses, dragging me from my thoughts.

"Hey, I'd be supporting a local business and giving these lovely supplies a home."

"Everyone needs a home," he agrees.

"That's the spirit."

Minutes or hours later, we walk out of the shop, and I look up at him as we walk to the parking lot, taking in his features—the freckles, brown eyes, sharp cheekbones, and small smile. I can't deny that it's a comforting feeling knowing I'm wanted. Over the last few weeks, I've gotten to know him better, since Harlow is always inviting him over and we message each other. But when I'm alone, I don't think about him, not unless it's in doubt over whether it's worth it to explore more with him at all.

A feathery sensation on my neck pulls me out of my thoughts, and it happens again, until I giggle. Blinking, I see that he's swiping a strand of my hair over my neck.

"You have a cute laugh."

Unbidden, a memory surges, an echo to what he just said. *"Because it's a pretty laugh. I like hearing it, and I'd like to see it."*

I want this, I tell myself. *I know I do.*

I want to be happy, and the only one keeping me back is, well, me. So what if my breath doesn't catch in excitement when he touches me? The body is easy enough to trick, and soon, the mind follows.

"Thanks. You have a nice laugh too."

I couldn't sound more awkward, but he grins, his endearing smile coming to view. When we reach his car, I blurt, "So, are you going to kiss me? Now that we've had our first date?"

He pauses, brows shooting up as he regards me. "I think it goes first kiss at your front door after I drop you off, since Harlow isn't picking you up. But do you want me to?"

I nod, and placing his hands on my arms, he walks me backward one, two steps until my back hits the car. His hands move to my face, cupping them. They're warm and chase away the lingering cold from the coming winter, and it'd be easy to melt into them. Just a softening of a few muscles and leaning my cheek just so, but my body does not comply.

He leans down, kissing my cheek, his lips soft against my skin. I focus on the soft strands of his hair that brush against the side of my head, the way his hands move to rest on my waist, warm, and his proximity. If I focus hard enough, maybe my breath will hitch, maybe I'll be filled with the urge to hold him and not let go.

Or maybe I'm just dead inside. Maybe it has nothing to do with compatibility and everything to do with spending years full of the fear that the next day would be it. That the deals made long ago would be finalized, that I'd finally have to trade one prison for another far worse, with not only my mind in pain, but my body too, and that fear has made me detached from my body.

Aaron nips my ear, teeth blunt and hard. I punch him lightly on the arm. "Are you trying to eat me? My ear's not edible."

Leaning away, he frowns and fakes a pout. "You've ruined the mood, Layla. Ruined. I was thinking naughty things, and then you have to go say 'eat me' like that. Like I'm a cannibal who's going to rip your lobe off."

I laugh, the sound light and free because he makes it easy. Placing my hands on his shoulders, I push myself up to my toes, balancing on my toes. Bending forward, I place an open-mouthed kiss on his throat, where his cologne is strongest, and pray that I did it right. From the way his breath hitches, I assume I did.

"There," I murmur. "Mood better? I'm pretty sure you were planning on kissing me."

"You think correctly."

I can hear the smile in his voice, but before I can say anything, he seals my mouth with his. His lips are warm, soft, and slightly moist against mine.

I close my eyes because I'm supposed to, and lean into him. He tilts his head to the side, tongue probing at my lips, and I open them. He tastes like mint, like a pack of gum. Slowly, my body responds, and I should be relieved. Relieved that the body can be brought to attention easily enough, even if the mind is an entirely different matter.

The hands on my waist hold me tighter as he pulls me closer and kisses me harder, tongue against mine, tasting me.

I wind my arms around his neck, because I think he likes that.

It's comfortable. *You like it*, I tell myself. I don't need fireworks in my veins and addiction in my mind for a person. I don't need *obsession*.

I remind myself of all of this as I kiss him deeper.

In class the next day, as I pin my latest project, there's a note beneath the one I left, done in a handwriting that is slightly unrecognizable. *Handwriting can change, Layla*, a part of me says, but I ignore it.

And then I notice the words.

You remind me of someone. She has a talent for art just like you do.

I should leave it at that and push the note to the back of my mind. Even if I'm imagining similarities when there are none, nothing good can come from this.

I write down *Who?* beneath the note anyway.

Chapter 6

Then

There's another reason I don't try to use coffee to stay awake—I usually fail, and then end up late for school. Worse, to get there quicker, I have to often take other, more unsavory, routes.

Like I'm doing right now.

This is a metropolis city, and being the third largest in the country, with a population of nearly three million, it gives "huge" a new meaning. Like any big city, it has parts one knows to stay far away from. It has routes people make sure to avoid if they're walking somewhere early in the morning or at night. Sure, the streets are safer now than at night, but with everyone at school or work, no one is around to hear a scream.

With that morbid thought, I hurry my pace, trying not to grimace at the grimy sidewalk and dark alleyways littered with trash. It even smells bad here, like rust, mildew, smog, and beneath all that, vomit. The roads are narrow, littered with potholes and trash, until every step is careful.

The buildings and apartments are in a similar state, paint peeling, windows dirtied or broken, with some boarded up. It's clear that this side of the city doesn't see a penny of the tax money put aside for renovations. Here, the decision is starkly noticed, impossible to miss, but in the city hall, it probably only took a simple signature.

Somewhere, I hear glass shatter and try not to scream or break out into a run, my body immediately jolting, the urge to flee irresistible.

Maybe someone simply dropped a glass cup in their home as an accident, but it could also be something else. Breaking out into a jog, my backpack thumps against my back every time I move, and my heart beats a wild crescendo in my chest, not from exertion, but from the increasing urgency and fear.

You'll be fine, I tell myself. I have a phone, and my stamina isn't so bad that I can't run a couple of blocks. *And if there's two people? Three? Grown, hulking men at that? What then?*

With every little noise, I nearly scream, jumping in fright, and my heart damn near wants to beat out of my chest. I know that my fear is unfounded. My father is able to track my phone, probably to make sure I've reached school every morning and am alive.

It tells me that he does still care about me. Or that he's just making sure the last *thing* he has left of my mother is alive. Something in the back of my mind tells me to look into what he does further, because maybe there's something else, some other reason why he doesn't care anymore. He's pretended for so long to be a normal man and have a normal life for my mother, but now that she's gone I can see the pieces fraying, see the way his eyes are darker, like morality has no meaning to him.

I pull my hood over my face, shielding my face until it gives me a semblance of comfort, and repeat my mantra in my head. *Eyes up, ears sharp, and calm down.*

There's another noise, and this time, I can *hear* my heart. *Thump, thump, thump.*

There's a scream, and then glass shatters again, the sound familiar to a night years ago, and now I can't tell whether my mind is playing tricks on me, repeating memories, or if I heard something real.

The memories converge over me, one after the other, until I'm not here but somewhere else. Until I'm not living in the *now*, but in the *then*.

"Don't worry, we'll be okay."

"Mamma, you're going too fast."

Another voice. A boy's, soft and fearful. *"Where are we going, Mamma?"*

Bright lights flash, and a horn blares. There's a scream as the car careens out of control, and then the deafening sound of glass shattering, my world thrown off its axis as it flips over and over. There's panic, fear, regret, and I don't want to die yet. Not yet, please. *And then calm acceptance, bittersweet acceptance, as the world goes black.*

Except it doesn't stay that way.

Right now, I want to place my hands over my ears, squeeze my eyes shut, and keel over. I want to forget how they looked, broken and bloody and *dead.*

Vaguely, muted in the haze of my thoughts, I register the sound of tires rolling over pebbles and an engine purring. Roughly, I'm shoved back into the present, to another dread. The car's moving too slow, right behind me.

My breath comes out in small pants as fear tightens its hold on me, a familiar rope winding around my midriff, making it hard to breathe. *I should run,* I think. Bolt like a deer and try not to scream or look behind me.

But like my will is not my own, I start to turn my head, looking behind me as I walk faster, hoisting my backpack further up my shoulders. It's a car, black as night. The windowpanes are too tinted for me to tell who is driving, and even though it looks slightly familiar, I whip my head back around, pull my beanie further down my head, and increase my pace.

I'm about to run, bolt, dash, do whatever, so long as it gets me *away*, when I hear a shout. "Layla!"

Frowning, I turn around, my grip on the straps of my backpack still tight, until someone I recognize leans out of the window. A frown still pulls my brows as I walk toward the now-idle vehicle and open the door.

"Jaxon? What the hell are you doing here?"

Now I know why the car seemed familiar. But why didn't I recognize it immediately? It's certainly not something I would forget, not when it's something about him.

He regards me, eyes narrowing a bit, and his words are aloof. "Looking for you, obviously. Get in, it's cold outside."

With as much grace as I can muster, I climb inside and pull the seatbelt across my chest. I wonder if this car is entirely his, or something he shares with a parent, and what it'd feel like to have a mode of freedom so readily available. To be able to just go somewhere miles away until everything fades away. The familiar itch grows over my skin, until I want to just close my eyes and wake up when I'm older and have the means to go somewhere far away from here.

Shaking my head, I go back to examining the car. It's clean, too; there are no wrappers in the cup holders, crumbs on the carpet, or stains anywhere. The space between our seats is smaller than I'm used to, until he is almost too close.

I shift over the leather seat, looking at him. "How did you know I'm here?"

How does he even know I walk to school?

He's still glowering, scowling even, until his features are sharper and black eyes even darker. "You told me that you walk to school and some of the places you pass on your way. There are a few routes from those places to the school, and it wasn't hard to figure it out. I... got worried when you didn't show, and just had a bad feeling."

I swallow, really wondering why he's so sour and furious, and I'm unsure of what to say. But why can't I remember telling him that? Or recognize immediately that this car is his? Now that I think about it, there are many things that are hazy. Things that have been becoming increasingly hazy over the weeks.

"I-I can't remember. Thank you though." Trying to lighten the mood, I add, "But try not to give me a heart attack frequently."

I woefully fail, and if anything, he seems even angrier. That's how I know he's mad at me, and I try to think back to a few days ago. Did I say or do something? If I did, I can't remember, though that's nothing new.

His knuckles are white as he grips the steering wheel, and his gaze moves to the road in front of us, giving me a side profile of his stern features; the clenched jaw, slightly flared nostrils, harshly pulled down brows, and thinned lips. But none of it can hide the shimmer of fear in his eyes, and I wonder what I did to put it there.

"How long have you been doing drugs, Layla?"

The blood drains from my face—I can almost feel it as my skin chills, a sharp revulsion stealing my breath—and I tear my gaze away from him, eyes wide. Immediately, my hands shake, and I wonder how far this goes. God, I won't even call it what it is—an addiction. The words are vicious in my head, and I want them to go away. That's not *me*. Worse, I don't know if the worry is because I don't want him to think differently about me or because I think he's going to take it away.

"What?" I whisper, pushing myself farther into my seat as if it'll swallow me whole. My blood hammers in my veins, echoing in my ears. *This wasn't supposed to happen.*

"I said, *how long have you been doing drugs, Layla?*"

Each word is delivered harshly, until shame swallows me, bile rising in my throat as my lower lip quivers. I bite it harshly. With all his normal ease and smiles, I forget the sadness that lingers in his eyes, the quick darkening that indicates a propensity to harshness. But it'd never been used *on* me before, only ever *for* me.

"I'm not"—I swallow, starting the lie because all I can think is that I don't want him to treat me differently. I want the other Jaxon, not this one who brings ugly things into the light—"doing drugs."

He turns, facing me fully, but I don't meet his gaze, and know that he will catch onto my lie quick enough. Faster than I can blink, he grabs my wrist and pulls my arm up, as if showing it to me, and I'm forced to look at him.

The despair behind his eyes is so fierce I want to scream at him. Disgust with myself crawls up my throat, and I want to hate him for making me feel this way. I hate it because this is another part of my life I've now ruined. He was someone I looked forward to seeing nearly every day, and now I won't have that anymore, and it makes vicious tears stain my eyesight.

"Your hands are shaking, your memory is getting bad, you always seem tired, and you're experiencing weight loss," he explains, the grip on my wrist urgent, tremors coursing through his hand. "And I can see a bag of it peeking from your backpack. You want to try that lie again?"

I look to my bag, to the slightly unzipped pocket, and realize that he's right. When did I even put it in my bag? "I–I..."

My throat closes, no words coming out, but I don't know what to say anyway. I just know that something is broken inside of me, that it's been for a while, and I'm forced to look at the jagged pieces now.

He goes on, each word delivered with venom until I curl in on myself, shoulders rolling inward. "And the symptoms will get worse, much worse. You could *die*. Do you not care about what this would do to your family? You can't leave this world, not yet. You *can't* leave me too. Not like that."

My eyes dart to his, and in the haze of my disgust, worry peeks through. Who did he lose? But he doesn't stop. "How did you even *get* it? Your body's tolerance will increase, and you will constantly need more and more and more. Did you think of your parents? Those around you? How it would feel for *them*?"

And quickly, hate surfaces. I hate his words, hate his judging, hate how I know he's disgusted, and I hate that I care. I viciously rip my wrist from his grip, turning on him to glare.

"You don't know *anything* about me, and you have no right to scream at me and berate me as if I'm harming *you*. I don't need you to act like *my* problems are a personal offense to *you*." My next words are a broken whisper, and for an aspiring psychologist, he's really crappy at confronting someone he thinks is doing drugs. "I don't need you to give me more reasons to hate myself."

I bite my lip harshly, until it stings, and I know it'll start bleeding soon. *I will not cry, I will not cry, I will not cry, I will not cry.*

"You think I don't know that?" I continue, voice hoarse. "That I'm getting worse, and that if my mother were to see me she would be beyond disappointed? You don't *know* me. You know nothing about my situation, you know nothing about why, and you've already deemed that I'm worth your disgust and hate. You can't call me *selfish* for what I've done."

I will not cry.

The mantra doesn't work, and I hate that, too. The tears are hot and burning, just like my shame, as they trail across my face, and my vision blurs. I try, and fail, to keep my face from scrunching up.

"Although I can't get mad at you for that, I suppose," I add, utterly *angry* at how my voice quivers.

Reaching over, I grab the handle, and am about to pull it when he grabs my wrist. I wish I could despise the way the warmth of his hands seeps into me, chasing away some of the perpetual chill. I wish I could resist when he pulls me closer.

But I don't.

I slide over the leather seats until I'm as close to him as I can be, and I refuse to look at him, instead staring outside and trying to keep the tears from running any harder.

The earlier rage has fled, and all that's left is a bone-aching tiredness, not just at him but because I know what he says is true. Will that be how I die? Constantly needing to escape my mind that I just start taking stronger and stronger things? When I started with the prescribed sleeping pills I never thought it'd grow bigger, but it was easy to convince myself when things just kept getting worse. What if the nightmares bleed out of my sleep and into my waking life?

"Layla, look at me." His voice is soft and imploring, so different compared to earlier, and I briefly entertain the idea that this is a trick as I adamantly refuse to meet his gaze.

His hands move to my face, palms large against my cheeks as he cradles my head, and my breath hitches. "Layla, look at me," he repeats. "Please look at me."

I never knew a voice could sound so pleading, and I cave, meeting his gaze, until his eyes are the only thing I can see, so full of worry and regret, I am sure they will spill over. With his thumbs, he gently brushes my tears away, and I want to cry harder, because I can't remember the last time someone touched me like this. I can't remember the last time someone held me like I'm something worth fighting for.

"I don't hate you. I could never hate you. And I'm sorry for being harsh, and telling you without knowing anything. *I'm so sorry.*" His forehead falls over mine, skin warm, nose brushing mine, and I never knew two faces could be this close to each other. "It wasn't fair of me, it was a jerk move, and I promise I'll do everything to make it up. I care about you, and I expressed that worry in the worst way imaginable. It doesn't change, though, that I'm worried about you, and while my intention was to help you, I hurt you.

"I was mad at myself for not seeing it earlier and hurt that you didn't talk to me about it, but this isn't about me. It's about you, and it's too big for one person to handle. Let me carry some of your pain. Let me help you."

He pulls me closer, until I'm half on him, and hugs me, his arms warm and solid around me, my head on his chest. My hands are around his waist and he's real beneath me, not going anywhere. Pathetically, I cry harder, sobs wracking my body. With the way he's hugging me, it's as though he's thawing something inside of me. As if in all those months, my heart hardened and the quiet inside is all I've known. Like I'm used to holding myself up, and him holding me breaks my resolve. With his arms encasing me, his sweatshirt soft against my face, and the warmth that radiates off of him, I don't want to hold myself up anymore. I want to stay here forever.

Even though I'm getting his shirt wet, I squeeze him back and keep crying until it becomes cathartic. When he starts brushing my hair with his fingers, I think I sigh. I want to bottle this feeling and play it again when the days get too hard and my head is too loud. Eventually, my tears stop, and eventually, the hiccuping stops as well as I—*merda, friends* don't do this—snuggle into him. My body rises and falls with each breath he takes, and it's comforting in a way I know I will always crave.

His hands rub circles over my back as he speaks up again. "You're right, I don't know about you, beyond what you've told me and what I've seen. I'd like to change that, though. You can talk to me, Layla. Open up to me, let me help. You can trust me. I promise to do better. And don't ever let me, or anyone else, talk to you like I did earlier, okay? It was shitty, and you deserve better than that."

I nod against his chest. "Okay."

And I realize that he *can* help me. He can make it easier, and maybe talking to someone, someone I trust, is all I need to get better. Though a part of me, a very large part, doubts and reminds me of the sleepless nights and the *fear* of going to sleep.

I push it away to the back of my mind.

"Tell me why."

I know what he's asking, for me to tell him everything. And maybe foolishly, I do. I tell him about my mother's and brother's deaths, about the nightmares, and how I need help going and staying asleep. The words spill out of me, as though my mouth is not my own, but with every whispered confession something loosens within me, a relief I never knew I needed slipping in.

But I don't tell him about what my father is. And don't think I ever want to.

When I'm done, I regrettably pull back to look at him and gauge his expression. There isn't pity in his gaze, and for that I'm glad, but there is worry and other emotions I can't place.

"How do you feel, now that you've told someone?"

I almost scoff, because now he sounds like a therapist so well it's no wonder he wants to study psychology. "Well, Mr. Therapist, I suppose I feel lighter."

He flicks my nose and I wrinkle it. Smiling at my joke, he shifts in his seat slightly, and I remember how I'm practically on top of him. Sheepishly, I move back to my seat, already craving his warmth. But I don't miss how his hand reaches out as if to pull me back before he drops it and clears his throat.

I worry I've made it awkward until he says, "Don't ever feel like you can't reach out to someone. People do care about you, and you *are* worth it."

Clearing my throat, I look at the dashboard, and my eyes go wide at the time. "We're late. Very late."

The car rumbles to life as he turns the key, and he's the epitome of ease as he moves the joystick to drive. With one hand on the steering wheel, and the other on the stick, he pulls the car to the road.

"We're skipping today," he announces, like it's a simple thing, and I stare at him, thoroughly befuddled. Him? The nerd who's nearly always poring over a textbook, skipping class?

Instead of calling him out on it, I ask, "Where are we going?"

He grins, eyes on the road, but I know that if he were facing me, I would fully see that it's a beautiful smile, the hint of a dimple coming out to play. A grin breaks over my own face, feeling foreign on my face considering that it's streaked with tears.

"Where do you think we're going?"

"I don't know. A lake? Some hidden jewel?"

"I should've known you'd like lakes. But you'll see."

We spend the drive in a comfortable silence, enjoying it but not awkwardly. It feels *right* being around him, somehow. At one point it starts raining, the sound of the water droplets hitting the roof of the car filling in the silence. The rain makes me want to burrow under a blanket and go to sleep.

Yawning, I cover my mouth with the back of my hand and pull my hood lower over my face. Refusing to go to sleep, I tell him, "You *really* like psychology. At first, I thought you were going to pursue swimming."

He's part of the school swim team, something I figured out quick enough, which explains his fit but trim body, and the fluid-like grace with which he moves. Though he does have the signature *swagger*— the one most teenage males have. With a pang, I wonder if my brother would've grown up to have it too.

He clenches his jaw, body tightening. "I'm supposed to pursue swimming, and I like it, but as a hobby. I would much rather do psychology."

"Why don't you?"

"It's not as easy as it seems," is all he says, and I know he's not talking about the subject in itself being hard.

I wait for him to elaborate, he owes me that much at least, and after a while, he sighs. "My guardians want my career to be professional swimming. You know, getting into the state championships and then the Olympics."

"Guardians?"

"I'm adopted."

I stare at him, a little shocked, but don't want him to feel weird. "And will you do what they want?"

I want him to tell me no, because it's so evident how much he loves psychology. Not only today, but always. Sometimes, he'll bring a notebook to lunch and pore over it as he eats, and when I peer over his shoulder, he'll patiently and eagerly explain whatever concept he's reading about to me, hands moving vivaciously, an eager light behind his eyes.

He sighs again. "I don't know."

I change the subject, curious. "What about your childhood? Were you adopted as a baby or did you have to go through the foster system?"

We stop at a red light, and he drums his fingers over the steering wheel as he bounces his knee. "I didn't spend long in the foster system. I was lucky to have mostly great caseworkers and be protected, but there are… depressing things you see and hear too early on."

I open my mouth to ask again, but he turns to look at me, clearly asking me to change the subject. "We all have our own demons, Layla, and more than facing them, we have to accept that they're there. I'm accepting mine, so you don't have anything to… worry about."

Resisting the urge to ask him more questions, or reach over and grab his hand just to touch him, I look back outside, listening to the sound of the rain and watching the water droplets drip down the window.

"We're here," he says, not even five minutes later.

The water beats harder, and completely unfazed, he opens the door and steps outside, languidly stretching in the rain, before coming around to the other side of the car. He opens the door for me, the perfect gentleman—he did let me bawl my eyes out all over him, after all.

Immediately, the water pours over me, drenching my beanie and jacket within seconds. Water drips on my glasses, blurring my world, forcing me to place a hand over my eyes.

He's more drenched than me, and dressed in less clothes that are quickly sticking to him, outlining his body. I note how water runs down his face in rivulets, sticking to his lashes and making his dark hair longer as it sticks to his forehead. With a small frown, he reaches over, rights my hood, pulls the zip higher to my throat, and then rolls my sleeves down until they cover my fingers.

"Cold?"

I shake my head even though I'm shivering. He catches on and wraps an arm around my shoulders, tucking me to his side as he steers me away from the car. Gravel crunches beneath our shoes as we walk, his body warm against mine, and I struggle to not lean into his touch. But I'm also confused.

And overthinking.

Does he like me, too? As in, more than a friend? Does his body hum every time I touch him just as his touch does to me? Does he feel like he can be himself around me like I do around him?

The rain falls around us like a heavy curtain, but I can see that we're in what seems to be a recreational park, or a trail. The trees' leaves shake in the wind, whispering as we walk. Between them, I catch glimpses of a lake, the water choppy in the rain and wind, dark beneath the covered sky.

We keep on walking until we come to the lake, and as we look at the wide expanse of water, I know the view is worth the rain and cold. Immediately, my hands itch for a brush.

"I want to paint this," I say.

He grins. "We can come back another time when it's not raining. Or we can go someplace else I know that's perfect for painting."

Immediately, I'm interested, not missing how he said we can do this again. So bringing me here right now isn't a one-time thing or done out of pity and a sense of responsibility. Or maybe it is out of pity, and the offer is a pity offer.

"It's fine," I say. "I don't want to be a bother."

He looks at me as though I'm crazy, expression incredulous. "It would never be a 'bother,' Layla."

"Okay," I murmur, trying to keep a grin off my face, and failing.

He smiles before turning around and steering me away to someplace else. It's not back to the parking lot, and I can't help but be relieved. I don't want this to end yet.

"What, you thought *that's* all I had to show you?" He shakes his head. "That wouldn't be exactly special, would it?"

We keep on walking to the tree line around the lake, and regardless of what he said, this place *is* a gem. At least here, in a city known for its size, skyscrapers, and congested streets, not for places like this.

"You know," he starts. "I cheated."

"What? On a quiz?"

He laughs. "No, I mean I cheated in bringing you here. I didn't come up with the idea to come to this place."

"Well then, Sherlock, how'd we get here?"

He pinches my nose and I glare at him. What is up with him and my nose? First he flicks it, now he's pinching it. Next thing I know, he's going to bite it.

Seeing my glare, he blinks innocently. "What? You have a cute nose. Anyway, I got you to pick the place without outwardly asking you where you want to go. Quite smart, if you ask me."

I frown, thinking back, and remember when he asked me to guess where we were going. That is smart, even if it's not foolproof.

"I wonder what else you're going to trick out of me."

His gaze turns serious, flicking down to me. Like this, chin tilted up, water sliding down every feature, he almost seems ethereal, until it's painful to see but not touch. "We'll see. Maybe I won't even have to trick you."

I don't even notice that we've been walking on the secluded trail in the forest for a long time, I just pay attention to him, and trust that if I stumble over a rock, I'll right myself up soon enough. And then I repeat his words in my head. Is he flirting?

Did he just flirt *with me?*

And I do one of the most embarrassing things I could ever do. I let out a little squeal like I'm a child. Immediately, my cheeks heat up, a feat considering how cold it is from the rain, and I want the ground to swallow me up or to have my existence erased from everyone's minds.

He bursts out laughing, and this one's a true laugh, because his lips pull back wide, dimple coming in full view. Why must every smile of his be so utterly beautiful? "Glad to know you like it."

I frown. It? *No, dimwit, I like* you.

That's when I notice that we've stopped, and I look around me. To my left, I can see the lake a distance away from behind the trees, and above us, the rainfall lessens. The weather isn't better, but the leaves are a canopy above us. We're a little higher, enough that I can see past the lake, toward the city.

Closing my eyes, I lean my head back and smile as the rain drips onto my face, and take a deep breath.

"Thank you," I say. "For bringing me here."

"Nature-lover," he teases. "I'll keep it in mind. When you see a plant, do you pet it, give it a name, and talk to it?"

Opening my eyes, I attempt to glare at him but can't when he's grinning like that. Truth is, I *did* do that, years ago. One was a fern, the other was the apricot tree in our backyard, and the last one was a fig tree. I think I named them Little Greenie, Bob, and Gremlin.

"Shut up," I grumble.

He places a hand over his heart as if I've wounded him, but concedes and stays quiet. Involuntarily, I shiver from the cold, and he reaches over, putting an arm around me.

"Thank you," I say again, needing him to take it seriously this time.

"Of course. What are friends for?"

I ignore the pang of disappointment, unable to help the sad sigh I let out.

Friends.

That's all we can ever be.

Chapter 7

Now

"No, Harlow, I'm not getting that."

She pouts but doesn't put it away. "Seriously. Your wardrobe is either sweatpants and t-shirts, or tights and sweatshirts. And while those are comfortable, they're very... well, repetitive and bland. And everything is black."

"I like black. It's my comfort color."

She waves the red dress in front of my face again. "Well then, you need to get out of your comfort zone."

She thrusts the dress into my hands, and I shoot Aaron a pleading look, but he doesn't notice. He leans against the wall, looking down at his shoes because Harlow confiscated his phone. There's something tomorrow night, and Harlow's been dragging us through the mall, shop after shop, in preparation.

It took two shops before Aaron was already looking for a furniture store so he could fall asleep on one of the couches. I didn't mind as much in the beginning, but after the fourth or fifth store, I wanted to collapse, too.

This routine has been going on for a while. Harlow will show me a dress, I will tell her no, we'll argue, and she'll put it away. Repeat. Her zeal to visit every shop, I've come to learn, is much the way she is with everything—like she's almost frantic to see everything life has to offer. I glance at the bags beneath her eyes with worry, not entirely believing she's just been staying up late to study for exams. But I take the dress she gives me.

With my arms exaggeratingly stretched in front of me, I inspect the dress. Compared to the other outfits she's shown me so far, it's not too revealing, but I still look at it warily. It's fitted around the waist, before there are added layers of what appears to be tulle and gauzy silk over the skirt. A skirt that probably ends at the knees, maybe even higher.

"No."

She throws tights into the basket—a basket I'm carrying—and glares at me before yanking the dress out of my hands and putting it into the basket as well. "You can wear the tights then. Or ruin the look and wear jeans or sweatpants with it!" She points a finger at me. "But you. Are. Getting. It."

I swallow audibly and follow her to the cash register. What Harlow wants, Harlow gets. I learned that the hard way and don't plan on making the mistake again. When I get home, I'll just hide it and won't wear it. She side-eyes me as if she can hear my thoughts, and a part of me wants to laugh at how… adorable she looks, all four-foot-eleven-inches of her glaring at me. Of course, I don't do that. I value my life.

As we leave, I don't people-watch as much, nor am I as riveted with my surroundings as I was a few months ago—has it really been months? Have I really been that lucky?

"So, what do you say, Layla? Are you driving us home?" Harlow asks.

"And get us all killed?" I joke. "I still need more time to learn, and I don't have my license yet."

In truth, I want nothing more than to accept the keys Aaron waves at me, start the car, and drive until it runs out of gas. I imagine that with the window down, the wind whipping my hair, my foot on the accelerator, and an endless road ahead of me with the ever-unreachable horizon, I'd feel free.

Aaron and Harlow have been teaching me from time to time, showing me what to do, and the other day, I did go around the parking lot of our apartment. Albeit at a snail's pace, and only because the parking lot was mostly empty.

"You know, there isn't actually any more for you to learn. Driving isn't *that* hard. You just need to look out for motorcycles and drunk drivers. Now you need to practice and get comfortable. Think of this as practice," Aaron says, taking the bags from Harlow and putting them in the trunk before giving her a look that reads, *I'm never letting you drag me along again.*

Despite my wariness, and the fear that still surfaces from time to time with being in a car, I grab his keys. Harlow lets out a cheer, punching me in the arm like it's a good thing. Except it *hurts*. I rub the spot and grumble something under my breath. Fine then, I'll just dye one of her outfits a bright neon color and hope it blinds her.

Turning the key, the ignition starts, and the car rumbles to life beneath me. I move the stick to reverse, hyper-aware of my surroundings as I back out, shoulders nearly raised to my ears.

"Can you put in the directions? And no highways."

As much as I'm willing to do this, I don't have a death wish. The automated voice starts speaking, spewing directions that I try to follow, occasionally glancing between the road and the phone propped on the dashboard. As I knuckle-grip the steering wheel, hunched forward in my seat, I drive down the lane, craning my neck to look at the side when I need to switch lanes.

"Can you drive just a little faster?" Harlow whines. "It's been ten minutes and you haven't killed anyone, but you might if you keep driving *this* slow. Sometimes, you can even get a ticket for driving too slow."

I panic, pressing my foot harder on the accelerator, and the car revs as it suddenly lurches forward. Looking in the rearview mirror, I glare at Harlow before adjusting my hold on the accelerator. This time, I make sure it reaches the speed limit.

In the end… driving on the main roads is not *as* much of a scary experience as I expected. I might even say it's fun as I get it right, becoming gradually confident in switching lanes and increasing the speed.

I imagine it'll eventually get boring when driving becomes a day-to-day thing for commuting or when I have to deal with traffic. But I don't think about that right now as I get onto a mostly empty road, rolling down my window and messing with the radio until I find the right song.

There.

Driving doesn't seem so mediocre now. Harlow lets out another cheer, rolling down her own glass and sticking her head out.

"You're driving, Layla! Finally!"

At least that's what I think she says, since she has to scream over the wind. I laugh, increasing the volume and pressing my foot harder on the accelerator. It's late enough in the day that the sun is ahead of us, slowly setting down the sky.

I was right. It *is* freeing to press my foot just right on the accelerator until I feel as though I'm *flying* down the road, but not in mortal danger. The wind whips my hair around my face and I watch the sun sink into the horizon.

I'm laughing and I'm crying. Tears of joy and sadness because I wish my mother could see me. I wish I could turn to the side and see her sitting in the passenger seat, cheering me on, but even though she's not, I know she'd have been proud.

"You *are* coming, and that's final!" Harlow screeches, and I can hardly believe it, but she reaches for a shoe.

"No, Harlow, I'm not coming."

"Nope. You're an adult in college—you need this experience!"

What is *up* with her? "Sure, going out on a weekday is the *perfect* experience. I'm a college student with classes and exams! No staying out late!"

She marches up to me until she has to tilt her head back to keep glaring at me. At one point, she sighs.

"Stay here."

I do as I'm told, staying outside my room, and watch as she grabs a chair from the kitchen, bustles into the hallway, plants it in front of me, and climbs on top of it until she's at least three feet taller than me.

I raise a brow at her. "Yes, *you were saying?* Should I start calling you 'Mom' since you want to boss me around?"

She snatches my glasses off my face and I sigh. That's the second pair she's stolen, and I *like* those glasses. At this rate, I'm going to have to get contacts, and I doubt I'll be able to afford it in this hellscape. I regard the blurry blob of colors that is her, unable to discern anything, as she starts speaking. "Mothers don't encourage their daughters to go out on a weekday. I, as your best friend, am encouraging you to let *loose.*"

Walking around the chair, I go to my room and start hunting for clothes, because I need to go to class, and if I keep listening to Harlow, I'm going to be late. She follows me, still trying to convince me to come and advertising the place she has in mind.

"We'll continue this conversation after classes, Harlow," I tell her, snatching my glasses back.

Taking a step back, I check my outfit, pleased. Today, I'm *not* wearing pajamas, but a fitted shirt with a square neckline and straight-cut jeans. I even did my hair.

She should commend me for all my efforts and stop insisting on getting me to go out tonight. Instead, she grumbles something under her breath as we leave the apartment, slamming the door behind her before getting into the car.

Well, our discussion after class is certainly going to be interesting.

Today's class, per usual, is uneventful. I spend nearly every class learning something I love, and yet, I'm always relieved when the lecture ends. As I get ready to leave, the professor moves around the podium, packing away her things.

"Layla," she calls. "Don't forget to put your part on the class projects."

Oh, right. The one part of class I dread, and at the same time, look the most forward to. The anonymous artist hasn't left any more notes, and hasn't responded to my latest question.

It's the one answer I want more than anything else, but at the same time, don't want at all. It's confusing, and while I want to find this person and throttle them, I also want to run in the other direction, away from the memories they elicit.

By now, my board looks like something typical of a wall of graffiti—a medley of art styles all crammed together but still breathtaking. I take my time pinning my latest piece, avoiding looking for a new piece from the mystery artist. I don't last long, and by the time I find it, my body freezes, breath hitching. In a haze, I step closer to the drawing, reaching out to touch it.

There is no color, and the lines, while they were clearly drawn with a careful hand, are not that detailed. Yet, I know exactly where this is. If I close my eyes, I can see it perfectly, filling in the color that is missing from the sketch. I can see trees bordering a lake, choppy waters, and the slight blur from the rain. If I go a little further in the memory, I'll turn to the side and see a boy with a quicksilver smile and eyes as dark as night.

Before I look, I already know what the latest note says. In the familiar-not-so-familiar handwriting, I see a five letter word. The one word I know better than all others. Because it's my name. *A girl I knew. Her name is Layla*, it says.

I stare at the note, shock-still, in disbelief, sure that my mind has finally given up, that the edge between reality and imagination has blurred beyond recognition, and this is merely a hallucination. *It's not real*, I want to scream. Worse, I want to cry and laugh as my emotions volley between stupid hope and cold anticipation.

But I *know*.

And I have absolutely no idea what to do about it. Briefly, I entertain the idea of grabbing the sketch and the note and crumpling them, because *damn it*, I was just moving on. But more than that, I want to pull down the drawings and study them closely. I want to keep them and hold them close and stroke the words and drawings like they're a piece of my heart.

"Layla? Layla? Earth to Layla."

Snapping my head to the side, I see my professor looking at me, dark brows drawn close, lips thinned. "Are you alright?"

I nod, clearing my throat, embarrassed. "I'm fine. Sorry. Something just took me by surprise."

She studies me for a beat longer. "Go to the student health center if you need to."

Sheepishly, I nod again, and rush toward the door. When I leave the lecture hall, it's not with the note *or* sketch, but with my phone in my hand.

I open my messages to Harlow's contact, and not thinking twice about it, text her.

> Changed my mind

> Want to come after all

> Oh, and I need heels

Cazzo, how do people manage to strut, sway their hips, and *dance* in heels? What magic do they use? Worse, how have I completely forgotten what wearing them feels like? Stumbling over my feet, I right myself before following Harlow, shivering as we step inside.

Immediately, the difference in temperature is stark. Here, it is stuffy, nearly humid, and I can understand why Harlow insisted against a jacket, why she caked my face in waterproof makeup.

I have to resist wiping my palms as I stare at the scene in front of me. It's impossible not to notice the loud drum and bass of the music, the loud thumps immediately filling me with the urge to cover my ears. Then there's the smell, the way the thick scent of sweat and perfume permeates the atmosphere, chokingly so, until I want to turn around and leave.

Instead, I wobble to what is maybe refreshments and food, with bodies occasionally bumping into me, and the overhead flashing lights make it hard to see, but I don't sprain my ankle.

As I lean forward on the counter, I try not to grimace at the band playing on the stage. The song's not bad exactly, but do they have to be *that* loud? And that repetitive with their lines?

Harlow leans beside me, looking at the stage. "I'm getting up on that today, you know."

Ever since we met and I first heard her sing, I've been nagging Harlow to showcase her talent. That she'll finally be doing so makes being here worth it, and I squeal, hugging her. This place may make me want to crawl out of my skin, but I'm too excited to see her on stage to care. "You'll do amazing, and I can't wait to hear what you have prepared!"

She hums, tapping her fingers on her thigh nervously, eyes on the stage. "I need to go to the back and prepare. Will you be fine?"

I think I nod hard enough to break my neck. "Go break a leg! Well, knowing you, you might actually do it, so… go have fun."

"Why just one leg, why not two? Anyway, text me if something comes up, and if anything gets… too much for you, step out and get a breather." She sighs. "Sorry Aaron didn't come."

"That's okay."

I don't tell her I'm not upset at all that he couldn't make it, a little glad for the space and to not pretend. Frowning, I think over that, because when did I consider being with him to be pretending? And pretending what?

I already know the answer as I watch Harlow. She frets with her hair before deciding to leave it as is. Reaching over, she gives me a hug, tells me to "behave," and saunters off. In reality, I know she's thrumming with nerves.

Turning back around, I catch sight of an employee, the logo emblazoned on his vest. He's in the midst of handing off something to a patron when he asks me, "What can I get you?"

"Can I get water?"

A few moments later, a cup slides across the counter toward me, perspiration dripping off its lid. Lifting the cold glass, my grip slightly slippery from nerves or the wet glass, I can't tell, I bring the cup up to my nose and take a sniff. I wonder if places like this back home are where my father would operate, having his people slip things into unsuspecting patrons' drinks to get new customers for another drug. It's scared me enough that I'm paranoid and already, I regret coming here.

"Didn't slip anything into it, girl," the bartender grunts, glaring at me as he wipes the table.

Sheepishly, I mutter an apology and look away from him, bringing the glass to my mouth. I take a sip, hoping it cools my heated skin.

It's cold enough that I can feel it slide down my throat and my stomach churns, probably from all the nerves of today. *What are you doing here?* a part of me screams. Here, and not on campus, blindly searching every building until I find who left the note.

To distract myself, I look toward the stage, waiting for Harlow to go up, but it's still the other band, and they're still so loud.

Before me is a sea of faces flashing in and out of focus as the lights change color and strobe. I'm here as support for Harlow, but as I fidget in my seat, alone, and the bartender keeps coming back asking if I want something else, I wish again that I stayed home. Or that everything here could calm down a little, because I can feel the sweat sliding down my spine and beading across my forehead, and my skin itches with the urge to turn everything *off*. Few things overstimulate me, but I wonder why I'm shocked that this kind of scene does. What else could I expect?

Next to me, the bartender leans over and plucks the glass out of someone else's grip. "No more till you pay. That's your sixth one, and you better not be an alcoholic. One thing to get drunk, another thing to be addicted."

Addicted. His words play over in my head, and if I was mildly uncomfortable before, now everything's hazy in a bad way. Like my mind is messing with me even without the help of alcohol. I try to steady myself and push back the memories. *Stupid, stupid, stupid.* Why did I think this was a good idea?

My hand shakes, and I try to take a deep breath, reasoning I'll just find the bathroom and wait until I hear her go on the stage. The reasoning does little against the way I'm trembling all over, breath hitching, and I know I'm moments away from a panic attack. I can sense it, hating that I still get triggered so easily, and stumble to the bathroom, pushing past some people until I make it inside and to an empty sink.

Later, I'll probably register that the bathroom smells horrible, like alcohol and another heavier, musky scent. Now, I just breathe over the sink, shoulders hunched over, and will the spots in my vision to go away. *Air,* I think, *I need air.*

Instead, I wash my face, the water frigid against my skin, but it grounds me, and I wet a napkin and dab my neck and chest too. The cold water helps, but the urge to go outside, away from the noise that hasn't entirely dulled is still strong, so I take another breath and leave, pushing through the crowd until I get to the exit.

As I step outside, the fresh, cold air is refreshing, like a cool balm against my skin from the chaos of inside. Next time I'll be more adamant about not going, and I definitely didn't "let loose" in there.

Instead, I'm just dizzy, have a headache, and feel slightly feverish. Grumbling under my breath, I pull out my phone and open Harlow's contact, not sure if I can go back in to hear her. I'll just stay out for a bit and ask her to text me when she's about to get on the stage. I type out a message as I walk away from the noise, my heels clacking over the pavement.

I'm too absorbed that I don't keep track of my surroundings, and on the next step, I stumble into someone, my phone falling from my grip.

Hands settle over my shoulders, steadying me, and I notice their size before they're gone as the person leans down to pick up my phone, hidden from view. "Are you alright? I'm so sorry, I didn't see you. I'll pay for any expenses if it's broken." The voice is smooth, masculine, and vaguely familiar.

Swallowing, I smooth my dress as he stands up, hand outstretched with my phone. I avoid looking at him as I take it, beyond embarrassed. I laugh weakly, even though I want to run away, mortification coursing through me. "No worries. I'm the one who bumped—"

My voice dies down as I finally tilt my head and look at him, shock mirrored across our expressions. The blood drains from my face as my hands shake, and I'll probably drop my phone again.

Unbidden, I remember how sometimes, when I was a child and would want something I thought impossible, my mother would whisper, like it was a secret, "You know, I think if you want something badly enough—if you *really, really* want it—and it's good for you, it'll come to you. Or, I suppose, you'll find it and take it."

Is that what this is? Have I wanted this for so long, and so badly, against all reason of time and human emotion, that I finally get to have it? Is this even real, or has my mind hallucinated it, crafted up the perfect illusion that's too cruel to be fake?

"Layla?" he breathes, incredulous, voice a whisper.

I open my mouth to say something, but my voice chokes off. Instead, I just stare. His voice is deeper, more gruff and kind of raspy. No, it's more masculine. *Everything* about him is more masculine, from the stare that's more penetrating, to the hair that's— impossibly—darker, to the broader shoulders, angular face, and other details I hastily notice. I knew he'd have changed, but the entire time, the image of him in my mind had been of what I'd remembered, and all my imagination has not done the real him justice. But some things, like the necklace around his throat with his mother's ring, are still the same.

He's right in front of me and I'm frozen, still expecting this to be a trick of my mind. But I know it's not when he grabs me by the shoulder and pulls me into him.

"My Layla, it really is you. I finally found you. "

He squeezes me tighter, body shaking, and after a while, automated, I wrap my arms around him too, my body softening into him like it recognizes him despite all the time, despite all the changes.

The previous shock slowly wears off and my breath shudders as my eyes grow wet and I laugh brokenly. In the recesses of my mind, like a secret, I'd imagine this. I'd imagine meeting again and what he'd say and how he'd feel, but none of it measures up to the real thing.

His embrace is familiar, but different. He's taller, his scent more intoxicating, and his body is harder, too. I don't dare move, I don't even want to think, because then maybe this will last forever.

"I missed you," I rasp, my voice thick. "I missed you a lot."

He pulls back, cradling my head gently in his hands, and it's so *right*. It's been years since I've seen him and now, it seems perfect compared to then. Like this time, the timing is right.

He runs his gaze over me, before kissing me on the forehead, then my nose, lips soft against my skin. I wrinkle it and he laughs. "I missed that so much."

"I'm surprised you remember."

"Of course I remember," he insists, holding me like no time has passed at all, but I shouldn't be surprised. Jaxon has always been an anomaly. "Every day, I would remember. I would see you every time I drove by a lake, I would hear your laughter every time I passed a painted alleyway. I see talismans of you everywhere I go that I'm half sure this isn't real, that I've conjured you before me."

His eyes land to my lips like he wants to kiss away the last few years, and I can't help but think that he's rushing. I might feel like no time has passed, but the reality is that it has. I don't know anything about who he might be now, and he doesn't know anything about me either. We could be two entirely different people.

He grins again, still looking shocked, eyes a little wet in a way that makes me want to kiss all the hurt away, but I know I can't. When he leans in, to hug me tighter or do something else, I blurt out something I probably should have brought in more delicately.

"I have a boyfriend."

Chapter 8

Then

Apparently, one of our classmates tastes like "moldy garbage." Aaradhya's words, not mine. And it's actually, "moldy, rancid, garbage." I can't tell whether she enjoys laying it on thick with the adjectives, or if the taste is actually that bad. Then again, she scrunches her nose, squints, and downright grimaces, so maybe it really is horrendous.

"You don't know what garbage tastes like, so how does she taste like garbage?"

She looks at me as though I've insulted her. "I just *know*. Everyone knows what cardboard tastes like, but it's not like we go around eating cardboard." She fake-gags again. "I'm telling you, she's *filthy* on the inside."

The girl is a few tables away, and there's the drowning noise of the cafeteria, but I still pray she doesn't hear Aaradhya. For someone who's normally quick to forgive and excuse everyone's behavior, insisting they were just having a bad day, Aaradhya is oddly adamant on hating her.

"Now you're just being mean. You don't know if the 'tastes' have anything to do with personality. I think it's that you just don't like her. And won't the taste leave if you just stop looking at her?"

Aaradhya *really* doesn't like her. Her name's Lily, and just like her name, she's downright flowery—she's cheerful, optimistic, and apologizes when she doesn't need to.

"And you're probably focusing on her too much," I add, pointing at her with my spoon. "I mean, you're only getting her taste in your mouth and not anyone else's?"

"I'm telling you, appearances can be deceiving," she insists.

"I doubt she's *that* deceiving. You need to get over her dating... you know."

If I say his name, she'll turn beet red and glare at Lily again. Letting out a defeated sigh, she slumps over the table.

"Besides," I say, doing my best "mom" impression, "you wouldn't want to end up with him anyway. Now's the time for focusing on your studies, not boys."

She raises a brow. "Who said I can't do both?"

"Not the point. I'm suggesting you wait, maybe figure yourself out. You know, do good in school, be confident about yourself, and then *maybe* when you're eighteen you can give it a shot."

She raises *both* brows now. "Look who's talking. You know who skipped school a few days ago? You *and* Jaxon. That's who, miss hypocrite."

I shrug. "Okay, and? We're friends."

"You don't want to be."

"Woah, woah. Let's go back to talking about you. If you're so determined to 'have experiences' before the age of eighteen, at least go for someone who's single and knows you exist."

She opens her mouth, rebuttal ready, before a commotion at the entrance pulls our attention away. Somehow, the room gets even louder as more people enter, all guys, and they come in laughing and pushing each other.

I recognize some of the faces, simply because I may or may not spent the weekend finding videos of the swim team's past competitions. For... educational purposes, and not a certain tall, dark-haired, dark-eyed player. At the thought, I notice that he's here too, laughing alongside his teammates and receiving congratulatory slaps on the shoulder. It's different, seeing him with his teammates.

I've gotten so used to the way he is with me, during our morning meet-ups, library visits, and other times, that I forget how different he is with others, the mask plain only to me. Again, I wonder what happened to him, if it was in the foster system or before, and if his guardians treat him right.

"Yeah, and you were saying?" Aaradhya taunts. "You couldn't look more infatuated if you tried."

"Shut up."

I grumble under my breath, pulling my hood lower over my face even though I smirk.

"It's warm in here, the seats are soft, relaxing, and the day's young," he calls, teasing

The car speeds until it's right beside me, and if the sidewalk were bigger, I'd scoot to the other side. *No, you wouldn't.* The window rolls down, and I keep my gaze ahead, but from my peripheral vision, I can see that he's leaning toward the right, one hand on the wheel.

I'll be turning onto a main road soon, so he better quit it. "Eyes on the road."

"Layla, please get in the car. It's cold and the sun will set very soon. I'd be so worried, I'd follow you to your home, and then I'd accidentally follow you *into* it, cause I'm clumsy like that." I can't help it, I turn to stare at him incredulously. What the hell is he saying? "And to keep myself from getting caught, because I'm sure your dad would freak out if he knew you brought a *guy* home, I'll have to hide under the bed and spend the night. Please don't do that to me."

Now I can't help but *want* to get home faster now, the idea of him in my room, in my space, filling me with heady excitement. Maybe it'd make the house feel less like a tomb. But I know I need to keep him far away from my father and that side of my life.

Instead, I sigh like it kills me before stopping and facing him. He stops the car and grins wide, a genuine smile that draws my attention to his mouth and eyes, and I ignore how it makes things flutter and my brain go blank. I'm beginning to realize I have an unhealthy obsession for his smiles.

Instead of taking my phone out and taking a picture like a fool, I get in the car. "This better be amazing."

"Oh, it is. Trust me, your mind will be blown by how amazing the place is—it'll amaze you so much, you'll start following *me* home."

You already amaze me, I want to say. Who knew I had it in me to be sappy?

"You brought me to a secluded, old part of the city. To an *alleyway*. Are you going to hide my body here or something?"

He flicks my nose. "No."

I rub my nose even though it doesn't hurt and glare at him. "What is it with you and my nose? Jaxon, we don't touch people's noses."

"You have a cute nose. We're not having this discussion again."

He sounds so serious, I can't help but laugh, and he grins, eyes darting down to my mouth. Going to the back of the car, he grabs a duffel bag before holding my hand and pulling me after him.

His excitement is nearly contagious as we turn around the corner, and I can tell why when I see the amount of paint on the wall. The graffiti covers almost every surface of the wall, and the pieces have been layered over one another so many times that it's hard to tell where one painting begins and another ends. While I often view this city, especially the Loop, as full of skyscrapers and a sea of gray buildings, when there is color, it is *bright*, stark and loud, like here.

Placing the bag on the floor, he leans down and unzips it. Peering over his shoulder, I see that it's filled with bottles of spray paint, brushes, and tubes of paint. I was prepared to spend another half-hour studying the graffiti, analyzing each piece that's beautifully done, not a crude figure in sight. I didn't think we came here to *do* graffiti.

"You want us to vandalize property? I hate to break it to you, but orange isn't your color."

He places a hand over his chest in mock horror. "You really think I brought you here to break the law? And everything is my color." He gestures at the wall. "A graffiti artist bought the building a few years ago for the 'aspiring artists' in the city, and lets anyone paint on it."

He throws me a can of the paint, and I manage to catch it before it can clatter onto the floor. "Come on 'aspiring artist,'" he teases. "Paint."

"I don't do spray paint," I tell him, reaching for the brushes, but he shoos my hand away.

"I'll show you then. It's fun."

He pulls out other cans, shaking them before popping the lids off. "If you could have any superpower, what would it be?"

I will never understand his ability to change topics at the drop of a hat, but I go along with it. "I guess flying," I answer, looking up at the sky, thinking about it. "Not like Superman flying, obviously, but like with wings and all."

It still sounds weird, but the idea of flying with large avian wings sounds thrilling to me. The ability to just get up in the sky and *go*.

"Why?"

He's moved closer, and I like how whenever he talks to me, he takes me seriously, even if the topic is silly.

I shrug. "I guess it would feel... freeing."

I look away from the sky to him, watching the way the wind lightly tousles his hair, and his dark, dark eyes that regard me. I'm not thinking of avian wings and superpowers any more, and if I didn't know any better, I'd think that he isn't either.

Clearing his throat, he decides, "Let's do that then."

He moves to the cans, sorting through them for the right colors before settling with dark red, rusty orange, and a burnt sienna.

Grabbing one, he stands up and looks at me. "How much do you like the hoodie and the pants?"

I look down at my clothes. I've had the hoodie for years, and it's only recently started fitting, but I've worn it for long enough that the color faded in certain spots.

"Like I need a reason to get rid of them."

"Well then, is getting them dirty with paint good enough?"

I nod, and he steers me to the wall, tilting my body to the side like I'm a marionette before he pulls the hood lower over my face and tells me to tuck my hands into my pockets. I ignore the way my breath hitches at his hands on my arms, the warmth of them bleeding through my clothes.

I've got it *bad*, don't I?

"If the paint gets on your skin, I have a soap that can make it get off easier, but you're probably still going to have to wash that area a million times."

I nod and he grabs a can, shaking it hard, until it makes a *clickclickclick* noise before he positions the nozzle right above my head and starts spraying, moving his hand as he outlines my body. As he gets lower, he crouches until his face is level with the side of my hip and I try not to pay much attention to his proximity. Instead I listen to the paint spraying, the *shhhhh* sound it makes as it drips onto my clothes.

When he's done, I release a pent-up breath and step away from the wall. There's a side profile empty silhouette that's the same height as me, the paint dripping down in certain spots. Jaxon places a can of red paint in my hands as he grabs another.

"If you keep the can still, the paint will drip, but if you keep going, it won't. And treat your arm like it's the brush."

"Makes sense." It doesn't, but I shake the bottle anyway. "Anything else?"

"Probably, but there's no rules to art, so if there's a specific technique you want to do, I'll try to show you if I know it."

I turn to the wall and position my hand to spray before frowning. "How did you know I do art?"

"I snuck into the office, stole your file and found out that it's a hobby."

I whip my head around and look at him. "You did *what*?"

"Kidding! I'm kidding. No, you had a flyer with you for art classes the other day, and your hands always have paint on them."

Well, then it's obvious. I shove my shoulder against him and mock-huff. "I don't *always* have paint on them."

Before I can pay much notice, he reaches over and sprays my hand, the paint wet and cold. I squeal and jump back, shaking my hand as I glare at him.

"Well, now you do."

Instead of spraying him back, I huff and turn back to the wall, pressing on the nozzle and starting to outline the wings. Painting, like it always is, even if it's with spray paint instead of a brush, is calming. But instead of enjoying it, I'm focused on Jaxon, who hasn't started yet and looks at me like he's waiting for me to spray him back or scream.

I start humming, ignoring him, and when the paint starts to dry on my hoodie, making it stiff, I pull it off, hoping that the paint didn't get to the top I'm wearing beneath it.

"Layla?"

I hum louder, putting down the can and picking another, lighter color.

"I'm sorry. We'll wash the paint off your hand right now. I'm really, really sorry. I won't do it again, I promise."

I stop humming like I'm considering his words even though I want to double over in laughter. Eventually, I sigh and look at him. He is evidently nervous, like he's treading on dangerous grounds, and I can't hold it any more. The laugh bubbles out of me and I cover my mouth with my hand as I snicker. That was *easy*.

"Fine. You're forgiven."

He comically lets out a sigh like he's relieved before he shakes the bottle again. "You know, you shouldn't cover your mouth when you laugh."

I stare at him. Is this another one of his weird things? "Um, why?"

"Because it's a pretty laugh. I like hearing it, and I'd like to see it."

I can't tell if this is just him, or if this is him around me. And I wonder how much he means by that, because he's just turned my insides into jelly, and I'm sure that when I remember this conversation later, I'm going to *swoon*. If Aaradhya could see me now, she'd be rolling on the floor in laughter.

He's watching me, waiting for me to paint or say something, and I clear my throat. "Um. Thank you."

Nodding, he positions the can, reaching up to paint something overhead, and his shirt rides up just enough to reveal his flat, slightly toned stomach and a slight trail of hair that starts at his navel and disappears into the waistband of his pants. I stare for one, two seconds before flitting my gaze somewhere else, face heating.

When I look up, cheeks hot in embarrassment, it's to see that his eyes are on me. Shoot, did he catch me ogling him? Well *that's* bad.

Since I'll say something stupid if I keep meeting his gaze, my eyes move down, snagging on the bump beneath his shirt.

"What's that?"

Reaching in his shirt he pulls out whatever is at the end of the necklace he wears around his throat. The necklace is thin enough that I've never noticed it before, and a ring dangles at the end.

"It's my mother's ring. My biological mother, I mean. I don't like taking off." He laughs as he lets go of it, letting it drop onto his chest. "I used to wear it to swimming practice too, but I lost it one time and had the entire team search for it with me. They all wanted to kill me for it, but we found it. But other than that, I plan on having it around my neck until I die." His eyes get that intense look in them again, heating up. "Like when I'm sleeping, or eating, or in the shower."

Great. Now my mind snags on the word "shower." And I'm a lost cause. Because in my mind, I remember how he looked in the rain, water sluicing across his features, clinging to his lashes, his wet hair pushed back. *Do I need to be put away in an asylum?*

I shake my head, forcing the fantasy away. Since when do I fantasize about a guy I'll never have? I've spent enough time with him, and he's seen enough of me that he's crawled his way into my mind, slowly becoming an obsession. I've grown to look forward to seeing him, imagining what he's up to, and worse, wanting more. This is setting myself up for heartbreak, because I'll fall in love and then he'll get in a relationship with someone perfect, maybe someone like Lily, and I'll be miserable. I'll be in a club with Aaradhya.

"I can't do this anymore," I blurt out, abruptly. "Spending time with you, I mean."

The idea of it almost physically hurts, but I should be used to pain by now, used to the way it inks its tendrils across my mind and heart. He steps closer until it would take nothing at all to reach up and touch him, and something cracks in my chest at the pained look in his eyes because I put it there.

"What? Why?" He almost sounds panicked, but I tell myself that that's my imagination, or he just really needs a friend he can be honest with, which now makes me feel like a jerk.

"I just can't."

He shakes his head. "Don't do this. You have to give me a reason. Give me a reason at least, please."

My fingers wind around the hem of my shirt, words a dam in my throat, but I've already let go of so many inhibitions with him, what's one more?

"Because I like you, okay? I don't see you as a friend, and I don't want you to only be my friend. And if this keeps on going on, if you keep on noticing things about me, and caring about me, and *being* around me, and saying sweet things to me, and flashing one of your heart-melting grins—you blind *dimwit*—it won't be me *liking* you, but it'll be me *loving* you. And I'm not going to set myself up for heartbreak like that."

My gaze has long since darted away from his, and I can feel the flush stealing across my face, the mortification making me want to run away. We're even close to downtown—I'll just go hide in the Pedway, in the underground pedestrian walkways, and become a street musician.

But his finger comes beneath my chin, turning my face toward his and he grins, and I know it's my favorite grin of all. I want to take a picture and print it, because it deserves to be put in a frame and hung in my room. But now he's just being mean, as though he's trying to melt my heart on purpose. I just said all that, called him a dimwit, and he's *grinning?*

"It's funny how you can be so confident to say what you think, yet you always doubt what people feel for you."

"What?" I rasp, baffled.

He doesn't answer me, instead stepping closer until he's all I see, and he steps closer still until he's all I *feel*, impossibly warm. Confused, I look up, meeting his gaze, a question on my tongue, but he captures my mouth in a kiss, silencing my question.

My eyes widen in shock, body frozen as I register everything. He has two hands on my face, fingers on my cheeks, warm and long. My chest presses against his stomach, and his lips are soft against mine. My own lips are open in pure surprise, so it's not hard for him to deepen the kiss, tilting his head to the side. All my attention is zoned down to him against me, around me, and I wouldn't at all be surprised if I've stopped breathing, my heart a wild thing in my chest. In all of my imagination, I never imagined my first kiss would be like this.

When he moves away, dragging in a deep breath, I'm still stock-still, blinking slowly.

He takes my stillness for something else, and panic enters his expression. "I'm sorry, I should've asked first. I didn't think, I didn't mean to—"

Placing a finger over his mouth, I shush him. "No, I wanted it and liked it."

He smiles in relief. "Still sorry I didn't ask first—I'll make sure to do it next time. But, does that answer your question?"

I clear my throat, settling for a lame nod, unable to deny I like the idea of a next time. "You're, um, a good kisser."

Though it's not like I can compare his kiss to others, and I don't want to, but as for myself, I'm probably a woefully horrible kisser. Jaxon's *had* to have kissed someone before and in comparison, I'm probably a horrible downscale. I look away to the art on the wall, and then somewhere else.

"Layla." He holds my chin again, until I look back at him. "You can't spend all your time doubting everything. Let me be more clear. I like you too. I like teasing you, I like complimenting you, I love it when you smile, and I want *you*."

"Okay."

He smiles. "So I'm a really good kisser, huh? I take it I am, seeing as you were shocked."

I grab his collar and pull him back down to me. "You better kiss me like that again."

His arms move around me, warm and safe, as he does exactly what I asked for.

Chapter 9

Now

As it turns out, figuring out life is clearly harder than I thought it would be. Well, figuring out men, that is. Having had a brother, one would think I'd have some idea on how they operate, but other than knowing they're human, I don't have a single clue on how to deal with my current dilemma.

On the one hand, I have Jaxon in my life again. The words alone always shock me, and sometimes I have to double-check my contacts, click his profile photo, and contemplate calling him to make sure it's all real. On the negative side, I have no idea what to do. Do I introduce Jaxon to Aaron? Or would that be weird? Do I even *want* to introduce them? As much as I like to think I've been getting better through the months, that the regret and guilt have become manageable, ugly possibilities rear in my head.

Everything always becomes ruined. Is this how it will happen this time? *You don't deserve any of them*, a part of me always believes, no matter how hard I try to reason with myself that it isn't true, that my past is not my fault.

If I decide to spend the rest of the school year with no social life, I can't exactly blame myself, can I? I'll just convince myself that I'm busy with school, and change my voicemail to something like, "Layla has forgotten how to interact with people beyond her professors or read texts beyond her school books, please text and call back later."

Nope, that's too lonely. I mean, there's a *reason* I left that house, and one person from my past isn't going to change anything, nor my odd hesitation with Aaron.

My phone chimes with a text notification. It's from Jaxon, and I press the contact, already smiling.

> **Question**
>
> Do you still pick out all your vegetables out from your meals, or are you less of a vegetable-hater?

I think back to the night I re-met him. Jaxon, being Jaxon, first looked shocked, then depressed, and then finally determined when I told him I have a boyfriend. As much as I have my own problems to go through when I think of my relationship, it's not fair to dump Aaron over someone I knew years ago and just re-met, and I'm glad Jaxon keeps his texts platonic. I'm glad for it even if, as the days go by, the indecision grows.

That day, he just asked, "Does he make you happy?" When I nodded, he continued, "It may have been years, but I still want you happy, and if he makes you happy, then I'm glad for it. But you can't deny that when it comes to us, we just get lucky."

Then he plucked my phone from my grip, got the password in the first try, and put his number in. The entire time, I stared in a daze, puzzling over his words and the ease with which he behaved, like the years apart were nothing.

"Over five years—I think that's a lot of catching up to do. And I plan on doing it *well*," he added, and I think I sputtered, my mind veering in entirely inappropriate places.

Then he grinned that fiendish grin, curled my phone into my hands while I stood dumbstruck, still processing everything.

His grin disappeared, and he leaned closer, his next words a whisper. "You've consumed my thoughts so effortlessly that I doubt a day has ever gone by that I haven't thought of you. Now that I found you, I want to be a part of your life, if you'll have me."

I nodded slowly, mind slow to puzzle his words, but heart racing until I was sure it would beat its way out of my chest. By the time Harlow got out, looking for me, we still stood there, and I mumbled that I guess I'd see him around. When I turned to leave, I could've sworn a panicked, but also deranged expression crossed over his features, like he was seconds away from snatching me, dumping me in his car, and driving away.

I don't know why the idea didn't freak me out as much as it should.

Shaking my head, still unmoored even though it's been days, I answer his message.

> You're so weird

> I don't HATE vegetables you drama queen

> I just don't like them with certain foods

I don't need to wait even five seconds before he texts back.

> Who said I'm dramatic?

> I'm just stating facts

> Sure, let's call it that

> Anyway, just making sure so you don't hate your surprise then

I think I give a gasp and a happy shimmy at the thought of food. Already, I wonder what it is. Something Italian? Over the years, I've tried to replicate my mother's few recipes, like her *pasta alla norma*, but none of them have ever hit the mark. Am I just not good at cooking, or is that the fate of being an Italian-American almost three generations removed from Italy?

Over the years, "American" never fit, and neither did "Italian," like I've become a watered-down version of my ancestors, and when my mother passed, I didn't want to learn more from my father. Not when learning from him meant having it tainted. With him, everything is associated with the cosa nostra.

Pulling myself from the path my thoughts veer in, I text him back, still wondering if the surprise is food since he was talking about vegetables. At this point, it better be food.

Food? 🍽

I'll be open to seeing you if it's food

Jeez, Layla

At least pretend to want my company

He has no idea how much I want his company, eager to discover all the ways he's changed like he's my very own puzzle. For how long can I say that this is alright before I cross a boundary? If not in reality, then in my mind? But I refuse to be that person, the idea of it filling me with a sickening nausea. *Then do something about it, Layla.*

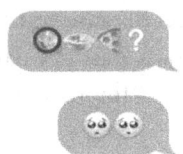

😄

Yes, it's food

You little gremlin

By the time Harlow hollers for me from somewhere by the door, I realize I'm smiling a full-blown grin as I stare at my phone. And it's always that way whenever he texts. Sometimes, I'll just see his name flash across the screen, and it's like someone has flushed happiness into my veins. Well, he would call it dopamine, and probably cringe at my butchering of the way hormones work.

"Layla! I'm leaving! You better hurry if you don't want to take the transit!"

"Coming, coming," I promise, stuffing my phone away and joining her by the door.

"And we're picking up Aaron on the way since his car is in service or something. Or maybe it's his excuse to see you, since you've been ignoring him lately."

Though she doesn't look at me, I imagine that if she were, she'd be glaring at me. Or her face would read *What are you doing?*

At her words, guilt churns its familiar acidic, shameful taste, and I cringe and bite my lip. "I haven't been ignoring him."

"We both know only responding when someone reaches out first counts as ignoring."

For a moment, the frustration surges until I want to direct it toward her, because why does she know anyway? Why is she meddling? Immediately, I deflate, because knowing Aaron, it's probable that he thinks something is wrong and messaged Harlow asking if I've been feeling well.

"I just don't know what to do anymore."

"I know, Layla. I'm just saying, don't use Aaron as your safety net because you're scared. And not to mention how you've improved these past few days."

"Improved?"

"You've been... happier. You don't zone out as much. And we both know what you used to be thinking about when you'd zone out."

I stare at her in shock as she pulls the car out of the lot. Is she insinuating what I think she is? For someone so happy when Aaron and I started dating, she's oddly adamant now that I... what? Dump him?

When we pick up Aaron, he holds my hand the entire time, which puts my arm in a sort of awkward position since he's sitting in the back, and I tell myself I enjoy his touch, that I like the way our hands fit together. And even if I don't, I could, right?

I miss being single, I whine in my head.

So of course, when we reach the school, I grab his arm before he goes to a separate building. "Are you free afterward?"

His eyes light up with excitement and the guilt grows. "Of course."

He probably believes it's my way of apologizing or making up for lost time, when it's actually the opposite.

"Great," I force with fake cheer.

He pecks my cheek with a kiss, lips feather-soft before disappearing. "See you later."

"Toodles," I mumble, lame, but he must think it's not, because he laughs as he walks away.

For all of ten seconds, I stand there lost in my thoughts, rehearsing what I'm going to say later before I sprint in the direction of where my lecture hall is.

And I almost curse. I've been distracted enough today that I forgot this lecture is for my other humanities class, the one with the hardcore disciplinarian professor and homework assignments that I haven't been doing as well on as I should. Heck, I almost failed the last one, which is annoying because the course should not be as hard as it is. What is up with the GE course professors making their three unit classes feel like a five unit one?

"Layla. How nice of you to join us. You missed your name on the roll-sheet, but lucky for you, I'm not done calling attendance."

From the seats, eyes turn to me, some sympathetic, others bored. At least I'm not the only one making it in the nick of time, so I don't shoulder the embarrassment alone as I mumble an apology and walk up the stairs to an empty seat.

A semester hasn't even passed and I already want a six-month vacation. But because I'm—sadly—disciplined, I pull out my notebooks and spend the rest of the lecture answering questions and taking notes like everyone else.

When the class is finally over, everyone snaps their notebooks and devices closed, clearly relieved before they slow down their movements since the professor technically didn't end class yet. When he finally dismisses us, we all stand up, almost tripping over our chairs to get down the stairs and to freedom.

"Layla, Josh, and Elizah, please stay back for a few moments."

We all freeze for a moment, our footfalls halted before we turn around and try not to die of embarrassment at being singled out. Wincing, I walk to where the professor shuffles through papers on the podium. Eventually, he hands out the papers separately, and I stare at the previous assignment he handed out. One that is now littered with blaring red marks. The perfectionist in me with a harsh thirst for academic validation wants to cry at the score on the top of the page.

"You all have a test coming up, and while I should just be giving you a fair warning that the state of your assignments will mirror the state of your test, I've done you all the next best thing. Some of our grad student teacher assistants will tutor each of you, at the time that works for them, so"—he looks to one of my classmates—"Josh, please go to the office and ask for..."

I zone out his voice as I stare at the paper in front of me, panic crawling through my mind. I *can't* fail this class. I just *can't*. I'll meet at whatever time the tutor's available and even become their personal errand-runner. I'll sell my *soul* to get all A's this semester.

"Layla." I snap my attention back to the professor, watching as he examines the list in his hands. It's no doubt a list of some of the graduate TAs in the department. I mean, how do they have time to be graduate students, adults, *and* teacher assistants? Their time management must be amazing. "You have Mr. Alyaan. He's in his first year of graduate school for psychology, but since this is a common GE class, he'll do fine in tutoring you. Please go to the Peer Support office, and they'll arrange your first meeting."

I nod, turning around before frowning and stopping, the name familiar. It's one thing for the both of us to move here and then meet outside one of the most crowded bars. It's another thing for him to be my tutor as well out of all the others.

I clear my throat. "Can you give me a first name? And, um… how were the tutors assigned to us?"

He looks up from the paper, expression borderline irked at my pestering. "Jaxon. And the supervisor probably randomly assigned you three to each available tutor. If you know him and him being your tutor will make you uncomfortable, please tell me now so I can get you another tutor, and we'll take necessary cautions against Mr. Alyaan. Harassment of any kind is not tolerated on this campus."

Great. Now I might be getting Jaxon black-listed. "No," I quickly correct. "I was just curious about the first name."

I leave the room, not sure whether to feel angry or relieved. Pulling out my phone, I open Aaron's contact and tell him we'll need to do a rain check for later. Grades-wise, I know Jaxon will be a great help, but this means spending more time with him. Time I know I want to spend, but don't think I should.

Because I know that when it comes to fighting my emotions, that's a losing battle.

I find him easily enough, in one of the break rooms in the Peer Support Building as he makes himself something. For a moment, I pause by the doorway, studying him, from the hair that brushes across his forehead to how he stirs whatever is in the cup in front of him, until he notices me. He beams at the sight of me, and I remember all the ways I would obsess over every smile as a teenager. It seems they have a similar effect on me as an adult. *Uh oh*, I think. *This is not good.*

"Hey, Layla. Couldn't wait and want your surprise now?"

I still, thinking, until I remember his texts from earlier. Answering, I snap, "What? No. How are you my tutor?"

He grabs his cup and walks over to lean against the doorway, regarding me. Instead of matching my tone, he's all ease as he says, "Oh, right, that. Odd coincidence, don't you think? But most of the other tutors are already booked for recurring one-on-one sessions, so there weren't many names for them to pick from anyway."

I don't buy that for a second. "I can take care of myself," I retort. "I don't need you to feel responsible for me."

"Layla, this isn't about feeling *responsible* for you. I'm trying to help, that's all. Consider it a platonic thing. No motives on my part beyond helping out a friend."

Already, the arguments I came with melt away, but then again, wasn't it always that way before too? "Fine. But you can't go snooping for my grades or anything else about me behind my back."

Who knows, maybe he can. "I don't sneak, Layla, you know that." He levels me with a serious look. "I have no problem being straightforward."

He straightens before heading past me down the hall, beckoning with his head when I don't immediately follow. "Since you're here, and I have a bit of a break, do you want to start the first session now? I'll put it in the system if you're getting a grade for seeing a tutor."

I watch the way his soft sweater stretches across his back, long legs easily covering the distance until I have to hurry after him. When he notices, he slows down, but now I can turn my head to look at his face, to catalog the subtle ways his features have changed. The faint stubble across his face today gives him a rugged appeal, almost making him seem older.

"Layla?"

Oh, right, he asked me something. "Yeah, we can do the first session now and get it over with."

Nodding, he pauses and opens a door, revealing an empty room with a desk, four chairs, and a board across one wall. To the opposite wall, there's a tinted floor-to-ceiling window, and I think I see the administration building past the shrubs and walkways with students milling about.

Pulling off my backpack, I step inside, cataloging everything in the room, but know that his eyes are only on me. I know it on a physically visceral level, my skin heating, goosebumps spreading across my skin, and I shiver.

Taking a seat, I pull out everything I need from my backpack.

"That's a *lot* of markers," he murmurs, eyeing the pouch with my stationary supplies. "Though the boba one is cute."

"They were all on sale. When you have a weakness for something, and it's on sale, you go all out. And you know, they're also good for pesky tutors."

I lift one of said markers and toss it at him. He catches it with ease and pockets it.

"Hey! That's my marker."

"Is it? I assumed you were gifting it to me. And I'm not a pesky tutor, I'm a very good tutor, you'll see." And he's still not humble, either. Pausing, he frowns. "First off, have you eaten anything?"

I'm in the middle of flipping through the pages of my textbook while organizing my homework papers when he asks that, and I look up at him. "What does that have to do with *tutoring*? Are you one of those 'study with a full stomach' types?"

He stands up, long limbs unfolding, and heads to the door. "No," he calls. "I'll go grab you something from the break room. Because if I remember correctly, you're not the best at eating and drinking water."

Before I can refute that—we both know it's true—he's gone. When he comes back, it's with a granola bar and a ramen cup. I've quickly learned that the idea of college students surviving off ramen isn't that far from the truth. Eagerly, I take the food, the warm, spicy scent of the ramen noodles making me happy. Opening the bar, I take a bite and hand him my textbooks, notebooks, and assignment papers.

"There, my tutor, now work your magic on me. In-smart me."

He laughs, the sound again familiar to all those years ago, except it's more husky and deeper, his Adam's apple bobbing.

I look away, and remind myself that I need to meet with Aaron. At this point, for him, and not me.

"Hate to break it to you, but that's not a word, Layla. And you're already smart anyway. I'd say your brain is your most attractive feature."

He starts sorting through my notes and flipping to another page while I muse, "So my smartness is attractive. Are you hinting that it compensates for my plainness?"

He looks up, and while in the past, he would've joked for forgiveness, he only arches a brow, regarding me coolly until I shiver.

"I said *most* attractive feature, not *only* attractive feature. The rest of you is very beautiful, too, like your eyes, and the way they seem to be different colors in the sunlight."

He looks back down and then starts explaining a concept as if he didn't just render me speechless. I make sure my mouth is closed before I pay attention to what he's saying. And soon, it isn't hard. Looking at him now, it's easy to see him as a teaching assistant. Heck, he's making a subject I practically hate seem interesting because now it makes *sense*.

When he flips to the mini assessments in the textbook, he asks me a few questions here and there, and the ones I don't get, he explains again, voice easy and smooth. Maybe the only reason I'm suddenly so confident in my lesson now is because he's teaching it to me. If it were anyone else, it'd be awkward, and I'd be too lost in my head. I don't want it to be anyone else.

I don't even notice the time until he looks at the clock and stops. "That took much longer than expected. Sorry."

I shake my head. "I enjoyed it. A lot."

His gaze strays back to me, and he looks like he wants to say something, something that I know isn't related to tutoring, but he doesn't. Instead, he closes my books, organizes my papers, and pushes them toward me.

Before we can do the awkward "I guess I'll leave now" thing along with that shuffling that accompanies it, I blurt out, "Does the break room have coffee? I know it's for you guys, but I think I should get some benefits as a friend of a tutor."

It's late for coffee, and we both know it. But the last part, where I dropped in how we're friends, is more for my benefit than his. And I do mean it. My emotions and my head are like a see-saw, fluctuating left and right, but I wouldn't do anything crazy. It's just that every time he leaves, I feel it'll be the last and one of us will disappear again.

"Okay. There's some decaf too, if you want that instead."

We make our way back to the break room, the lights overhead brighter now that it's dark outside. I watch him rummage around, heating the kettle, and before I know it, we're talking, and it isn't awkward—it rarely ever is with him. We talk about the past, about what we plan on doing, and we talk about each other. Words that we string into sentences, each one of them making me more and more comfortable, more and more needy for something I can't name.

At moments like these, I can pretend, but not in the way I would pretend before, when I was there.

There, I would pretend there weren't strange men coming to the house every few weeks, their voices filtering through the walls as I'd refuse to leave my room. I'd pretend that my father was entirely normal and the only reason I couldn't leave the house was due to a disease I had. I would pretend, pretend, pretend.

But this pretending is different. Pretending I don't catch the way he swallows thickly as his gaze traces across my features, will save me now. It'll save me from falling in love with him again if given the chance.

But then again, did I ever fall out of love with him?

Chapter 10

Then

It's said that regret is more genuine than gratitude, and that's why hospitals witness more genuine confessions than wedding halls. We cherish something best when we believe we are losing it. When I wake up with a start, screaming, and my door slams open, I believe it.

I've been avoiding him for the past few weeks now, ever since I told him he doesn't need to take me to therapy anymore and that I'd just stay in my room when he has "guests" over. I hadn't said why, and the brief eye-contact was the only sign that he heard me in the first place. His usual demeanor since the accident is a sharp contrast to how he is now.

His appearance is rumpled and wild, sheer worry written across his features, etching his face into an emotion I haven't seen in months. But at the sight of me alive and whole, no burglar in sight, he returns to that apathetic man.

When his breaths even out and he moves to leave, I'm mad all over again. He used to always be there for me whenever I had nightmares. Sure, when I started getting older he wouldn't lull me back to sleep with lullabies or tickle me to get my mood back up, but he would still *show* that he cared. We used to have a tradition; whenever my brother or I would have a nightmare, he'd bring a gallon of ice cream to our rooms, and whoever could savor their ice cream the slowest would win.

In hindsight, it was a smart way to get us to eat slowly and appreciate food better.

Right now, he's still physically the same person, with the graying hair and wrinkles around his eyes and mouth, but he doesn't *look* the same. It's as though a stranger's taken his place. With every day that passes, it's like a false skin sheds away, revealing a ruthless man, and I wonder why I was ever shocked at what he does. It's become increasingly clear that my mother and brother were the only ones to convince him to keep himself in check, to pretend to be a socially acceptable man. *Why am I not enough? Why am I not enough to have my father?*

Sometimes, a part of me believes he deserved to lose my mother.

Not because he ignores me, but because it's karma. Karma for what he *has* done almost his entire life. And somewhere along the way, I have developed a deep-rooted fear of becoming like my father, of turning into everything I promised myself I wouldn't be.

"Every time I'm in this house, I wish I died, too," I spit, and it comes out angry and venomous, like I hope that every single one of my words are thorns that hit him and *pierce*.

He turns back around, looking at me, but I don't meet his gaze, terror churning in my gut. But the anger keeps me going, stopping me from breaking down, and curbing the ache that comes with missing them.

I've come to associate him as two people. The man broken over my mother's and brother's deaths, and the man who's the reason my mother was too worried to think straight and see the light turn red.

Recklessly, I add, "Do you not know *why* she didn't see the red light? She was scared before she died. *Of you.*"

If he had any doubt before that I know, and for how long I've known, I'm sure it slowly erases. But every word is a jab that seems to only break *my* heart more, because I'm the reason she found out anyway. *I'm sorry, Mamma,* I think. *I'm so sorry.*

I don't stop, my words the only thing holding the tears at bay. "It's all your fault. I hope every filthy piece of money is worth it."

I need him to say something. Anything other than *Why did it have to be* you *who made it out?* He slams his hand on the door frame, hard enough that the walls rattle, and a part of me wants to cower behind the blankets. How long does it take before you can't hide your true self anymore?

In my realization that I don't know my father anymore, that the man to gently bandage every skinned knee is gone, nothing seems improbable anymore. When the nightmares claw their way through my mind, and I wake up thinking, *My father isn't like that, he wouldn't do that to people,* I have to correct myself, because I don't actually *know* anymore.

"Enough," he rasps, slamming his hand against the door frame again. "Stay out of my business, you hear me?"

He turns around, leaving, but I catch the vaguely muttered, "He needs to live."

I try to say something, but he's already gone, leaving behind nothing but more unsaid words and riddles. Who needs to live? I fall onto my pillow and scream into it.

I will not cry. I will not cry. I won't cry, because I don't care anymore. Giving him my hate right now, however extreme, would mean that I care. In all my life, I don't think I've ever *hated* anyone. Sure, there have been stuck-up snobs and bullies, but I've never *hated* them. When I got to a certain age, I just shrugged them off. They weren't worth hating.

But it's always hard to be indifferent about the people who matter. And when it comes to him, I know that seed of venomous anger grows and poisons me like something toxic.

But the blame poisons me worse than anything else. For the millionth time, I wonder how different things would've been if I never told her what I found, if we never got in that car. It wouldn't have changed who he is, but everything was fine before I found out and told her, and maybe it would've continued to be that way.

I wonder if my mother would still be here, not dead, but just a room away. If I would wake up to hear her lightly humming through the house, if I would go downstairs and have her ask me, "Good morning, sweetie, sleep well?"

I wonder if a boy with eyes like mine and an insatiable curiosity would be sitting by the table, short legs swinging. Perhaps worse than the memories of my mother are that of my baby brother. My baby brother with his toothy grin and wide eyes and fear of the dark. The brother I said I would always be there for and always protect. But I broke that promise. And now I'll never see either of them ever again. *I'm sorry,* I think, I shout, into the recesses of my mind. *I'm so sorry you're gone.*

Nothing stops the heaving gasps or tears this time, and I curl into a ball, clenching my fists tight enough that my palms hurt, my chest aching in pain until I want to reach inside and rip my heart out.

"I'm sorry. I'm so, so sorry," are the only words that circulate in my room, over and over again.

But in the depths of the machinations of my mind, a cold resolution settles, like hardened scales. I slip into the idea of doing something reckless, something there's no going back from.

My breath heaves, tears tracking down my face, a yawning blackness of grief where my heart should be, but now I know what I need to do.

There are some people who, sometimes, I just want to run them over with a car and then throw their body in the coldest, dirtiest river I can find. They would spend their afterlife in a sad, watery grave. A part of me knows I'm just latching onto the anger to have anything to hold onto other than the despair I've nose-dived into these past few days.

"Contemplating killing someone again?" Aaradhya asks, feigning boredom, but based on how she picks at her rice, I know that what happened earlier is bothering her too.

"I'm so mad at them, Aadhi. So what if you're Indian? So what if you have synesthesia? There's nothing 'weird' about who you are, and they're jerks for saying the kind of things they do."

Normally, the insults are veiled, but sometimes, like today, they'll play on stereotypes and generalizations, doing things like making fun of her hair or food. Because of course, when she oils her hair, it's "greasy," but when others do it it's a cool "slick-back" style. I want to throttle our classmate now. He can take his stupid face, and rude comments somewhere else. Like the bottom of a river.

In truth, I know Aaradhya *wants* to give them a piece of her mind, but she bites her tongue each time and looks down instead.

She shakes her head. "You don't understand."

My bad mood has nothing to do with her, but I still snap, "Well you don't tell me anything."

She doesn't miss the bite in my tone and hurt filters over her expression before it's gone. I sigh and have the urge to slap myself for being so snarky, the hypocrisy in my words obvious to me. Apologizing, I hand her some of my sandwich as repentance.

She stops schooling her features and smiles, accepting the peace-offering. Nibbling on the sandwich, she stays quiet before moving on to her rice. Like the little rice grains are the most interesting things in the world, she messes around before sighing. Maybe I'm getting some information from her today after all. If I'm lucky, I'll even convince her to march up to one of the jerks and punch him square in the chin, or knee him in the groin. I'm not picky; either one works.

"I don't say anything," she starts. "When they call me names or tell me to 'go back to where I came from,' or ask if I 'come to school on an elephant,' because according to their rules, they're right—I'm not a citizen, and so to them, I don't deserve the things they do. There's so many horror stories of things happening to immigrants, and I'd rather not experience them.

"I am proud of my ethnicity. It's a part of who I am, and I'm lucky to say I want to see my home country again, many, many times, but this is my home too. It's not perfect, but I've never seen my sister happier, because some people just find home in places far away from where they were born."

Her words are low, and she keeps glancing around her, and I wonder what it would feel like to live with the kind of fear she does.

"So every time someone insults me because of my condition or my race, I want to talk back, but all I can think is that maybe if I do, things will get worse and there'll be attention on me and they'll force us to leave. Yes, their words hurt, but they're just words. Like, what if I do talk back, and one of them looks into my background harder? Or follows me home? Or hurts me? I don't want to get the police involved, not when I can't trust that they won't involve the immigration officers, on account of being 'disruptive,' that they won't put my family and me in detention centers."

Before I've registered it, I'm across the bench and hugging her tightly, never wanting to stop. My own family may not date back more than a century here, since my father's grandparents immigrated here, not without challenges since racist profiling was different then, but today, I don't live with the kind of fear she does. I've never been deemed unworthy of living here to the extent she has, even though at the end of the day, despite the boundaries we draw over land and in our minds, we're all human.

I've never had someone accuse me of stealing their jobs or driving up the cost of living. I've never been used as a scapegoat to divert the attention away from a system that widens the disparity between the poor and rich, always serving the interests of those who have more than they know what to do with. I've never had someone explicitly say or behave in a way to say, *You don't belong here, because I was here first.* When really, were they?

"I'm glad you felt comfortable telling me, and I'm sorry you have to be hyper-vigilant. No one deserves to be scared their family could be ripped apart any day. I know it's not much, but you can talk to me. Because so what if you're different? That doesn't mean they can attack you."

"Yeah, well not everyone thinks like that, Layla."

I squeeze her harder, and with an *oof*, she returns my hug. "Too bad for them, then. We'll just figure something out. Maybe your synesthesia powers will kick in and you'll think of something."

She laughs, body shaking, and as much as I take her words seriously, I know the jokes ease her. "Doesn't work that way."

"Shame. And I know it's your choice, and you can take care of yourself, but if you ever want me to punch someone, I got you."

She laughs again, awkwardly patting my back before pulling away, and already, she looks relaxed compared to earlier. It's all going to be okay, I think. It has to be.

Even when I want to live in the moment, it's easy to plan ahead, if not by days, then by years. What kind of a person I hope to be, what wishes I want to fulfill, and who I aspire to become. And then there's when I blatantly plan it, aloud and with someone else. Like including a person into my goals and saying, *You, you are my milestone. Being with you will always be my milestone.*

"So you want to study on the other side of the country?" I ask, frowning a little because that's so far away.

But if he gets in, I know I'll be happy for him. I guess I'll just savor the months until then. Most good things end, anyway. I panic at the thought, and I draw my attention back to his gaze. His eyes are soft today, the black in them less intense, though the effect he has on me is the same.

"Yeah. Maybe do a few years here and then transfer."

Twisting on the bench seat, uncomfortable, but not wanting to leave yet and start heading home, I eventually give up and go down, resting my jacket on the grass and reclining over it until all I can see is the blue expanse of the sky above. With it being November, it's been cold, windy, and raining most days, but today's a clear day, the cold less biting.

"You know what we should do, JJ?" I say, changing the topic. "Stargazing. Think about it. Lying down on top of your car would be perfect."

Too bad it's probably half a day's drive to leave the light pollution.

He stands up, leaning over me, hands on his knees, head upside down from where I am, before he joins me on the grass, hand reaching over to play with my hair. The park is quiet right now, with only a few joggers passing by on the trails every now and then, and it's serene in a way I don't want to leave.

"That would be nice." He frowns. "JJ? Where did that come from?" Shuddering, he adds, "Please, please don't use it again. It reminds me of peanut butter and jelly."

"Your last name's Jonathan. Jaxon Jonathan, so JJ. But fine, I won't call you that again."

The sky is pretty above me, but my eyes are on him, until I can see the way something shutters behind his eyes, a muted kind of despair. "I plan on changing my last name one day anyway. Maybe my first too, since they changed that as well years ago, insisting everyone else also use it, and eventually I got tired of correcting people who wouldn't listen."

I stare at him, and he looks up toward the sky, body language almost casual, as though he didn't just share something astounding. It's odd to learn that the name I've been calling him, is not really his but a tool used to erase his identity. What would it feel like, I wonder, to lose a name? Worse, who does that to a child?

From what Aaradhya's been going through to this, I want to get up and scream into the sky, I want to find the people who revel in causing pain and make them *hurt*, and I haven't even lived their experiences.

Instead of screaming, though, I ask, calm in a way that's a lie, "What do you want to change it to?"

"Anything other than my guardians' last name. But I think I want to change it to my mother's last name—Alyaan."

I can tell it's Arabic from the way he pronounces it, the first "A" softer before the next vowel stretches.

"Is that why you study Arabic? Because your biological mother is Arab?"

When he nods, it's slow, and I can tell I've lost him to memories. His eyes have a haunted look in them, both sorrowful and shocked, almost like the look I'd barely noticed the first day I met him.

"Was Arab. And yeah. That's why I learn the language, even though they hate it."

It's clear that his mother, no matter who she was or what happened to her, is one of his most favorite people. I wonder why his adopted parents don't want him to learn a language so dear to him, a language part of his blood. I shift a little closer and settle an arm over him, and I can swear he melts into the grass.

There can be an unspoken bias that guys are all stoic and not the touchy-feely type, but everyone needs a hug from time to time. I can't help but be reminded of my younger brother, of the way he always needed to touch someone around him, even if just through a brushing of hands.

Jaxon's body is wound up tight, but he loosens a little, and with a sigh, wraps his arms around me, too. "What happened to your mother?" I venture. "And why don't your guardians like you learning Arabic?"

He's quiet for a long time, and I wonder if he didn't hear me or if it's too much for him to open up. Eventually he speaks up in a choked tone, and I wonder if this is how an anger that has culminated over years sounds like.

"They don't like it because they know I do it for my mother. And they don't like my mother because they're *racist*," he spits. "As for what happened to her, a drunk, angry neighbor barged in one day and shot her in the head." His body shudders beneath mine, flinching, like he's heard a gunshot, and I stare at him in horror, stunned at what he saw. "I was five or six at the time, but I remember the bang, and then the blood. He kept on calling her a terrorist and that if she wouldn't go back to her 'blood cave' then he'd have to take measures.

"And the thing is, he didn't kill me even though I was her kid, 'spawn of a devil,' and all that. He acted like he did a heroic act, saving me from being raised by her. Sometimes, they all acted like that. The case workers, the officers, and my guardians."

His voice breaks off, and I can't believe I'd never asked him earlier. I squeeze him tighter and tighter, my heart breaking for the little boy who watched his mother die out of nothing other than hate. A child doesn't deserve to grow up in a world with a media that vilifies a people so thoroughly that someone murders an innocent mother.

"The worse part?" he continues. "Years later, I... I don't know, I guess I just wanted to learn more about it, see what happened to him and if he's in jail. And you know what I found? There were barely any news reports of it at all. When someone from a minority group commits a crime, it dominates the headlines for weeks, but only a handful of news anchors bothered at all to talk about what happened to me. And they lied so implicitly and explicitly, you'd think the murderer was innocent. One headline even said 'Arab Woman Orphaned a Child.' They shoved all this racism down my throat that growing up, I would believe it, until I'd internalized it so much."

"And I-I can't *remember*," he rasps. "Which country we're from. She was so careful not to speak Arabic, even in the house, that I can't remember which dialect she spoke, and even if I did, who would I ask to know where it's from? I have my guesses, but how would I check? I can't remember what she looked like, just that she loved the color blue, because it was the color of my father's eyes. I can't remember, and for the longest time, I didn't care. Sometimes, I oscillate between being Arab and being American until I don't know who I am at all."

There's something heartbreaking about his sadness, until a protective urge surges so that even if I've never met those that have hurt him, I already hate them. I cup his face, a thumb swiping beneath his eye.

"You're kind," I tell him, but he looks at me like he doesn't believe me. For a moment, it makes me want to cry, but I keep listing things until he softens, until a tentative smile breaks out. "You're sweet. You're compassionate and diligent and intelligent and—"

"What about handsome?"

Rolling my eyes, I lift myself up so that I am looking down at him, until I am all he can see. "And such a *nerd*." My words have their intended effect—he tilts his head back, laughing, until his mirth is almost a tangible thing. "Seriously, you never shut up about psychology or a concept you learned in physics or history or whatever that you *think* is cool."

"Hey, they're all very cool."

Sobering, knowing that I've just been trying to distract him, I add, "I wish I knew the right thing to say to make you feel better, but

I know that you'll also always mourn the loss, and that it's so much different for you. You never should have gone through that, and as unhelpful as it is, I'm so sorry." I hold him tighter. "Thank you for telling me, and I wish I could have met your mother. But no matter what happened, I know she'd be proud of who you are today, and that you're going to keep on making her proud."

His eyes grow teary as he returns my hold, body bending around mine as he shakes.

"Thank you," he eventually gets out and pulls me even closer until I'm practically on his lap before he drops his head on my shoulder and stays like that.

I have my head on his shoulder, too, and even though my hip is screaming at me to shift positions, it's still comfortable being like this with him.

Eventually, he stops squeezing me so tightly, drawing his knees up. "I guess we're both damaged, huh? In need of serious therapy and all?" he says, joking.

I move up until my face is hovering over his again, and with one hand, he reaches over and undoes my bun, until my hair falls around us. The park is already quiet, almost private, but the added curtain of my hair adds to it even more until there's just him and his dark, dark eyes.

"So broken. You'll have to pick up the pieces and tape them together," I whisper, going along with the joke.

He fails first, bursting out into laughter, and dropping my forehead onto his, I burst out into giggles as well. I don't know who kisses who first, but his lips brush against mine, soft and sweet.

Being with Jaxon now, I'm not thinking about the nightmares or my father or how much I miss my mother. I'm not thinking about what the future might hold for either of us, and I'm not thinking about how messed up the world is. I don't think of any of that. And maybe it's unhealthy, because I might come to depend on him to always lift my mood up, and I know that won't help me or us at all.

But I savor this moment anyway.

When we break apart, I know I have the goofiest grin on my face.

He grins back and wraps his arms around me when I tuck myself under his chin and snuggle into him. It's warm, cozy, and having him hold me is my personal heaven, enough that I shudder at the idea of getting up and walking home, since I refuse to let him close enough to my neighborhood.

Eventually, he pulls me back up to him and frowns, running the pad of his thumb over the underside of my eyes.

"Have you been sleeping well?"

I stiffen a little and look away, mumbling, "It's better."

He clears his throat. "And not to come off like a parent, or an overbearing boyfriend, but do you still have some pills at home?"

"I do," I answer, still not meeting his gaze even if I thrill a little at him calling himself my boyfriend.

He stiffens beneath me, and when I glance at him, I see the worry in his gaze. "For my sake, can you bring them all tomorrow? I trust you, but I'd feel better. Please?"

"All?" I ask, and he stiffens even more underneath me, until every line of his body is drawn taut. "I've been trying really well. It's only one every other day instead of two every day."

At first, I'd tried cutting it all out, but the nightmares and sickness that came with that drove me to a desperation I didn't anticipate, and I decided to wean myself off instead. That has to work, right?

"Two *every day?*" he nearly jolts upward but tries to relax when I freeze at his tone.

"It used to be the only thing that would get me to sleep," I whisper. "The nightmares are back, but I haven't broken that rule I set, Jaxon. Soon I won't need them at all. And I'm only taking the prescribed stuff."

"Okay," he says eventually. "I hate to say this, but more deaths are from perfectly legal medication than illegal medication. And the weaning off can sometimes be as hard as giving up completely."

"No, it won't. Not for me."

We both know that's the drug talking.

Chapter 11

Now

Harlow glares at me again. Immediately, I look away and want to shrivel up and plead that I don't deserve to have someone look as though they want to kill me. Eventually, I cave and meet her glare, trying not to shudder or wail for forgiveness. She's at least half a foot shorter than me and a few years younger than me, but she is *menacing*.

Like how bees are small, but their stingers are the stuff of nightmares.

"Harlow, come on, don't look at me like that. You know I'm your bestest friend in the whole widest world and that your glares scare me."

"Yeah," she says, voice thick with sarcasm. "My bestest friend in the whole widest world who is also my stupidest friend in the whole widest world."

Placing a hand over my heart, I blather, "Ouch. That cut deep."

My attempts aren't working, because she's still glaring. I think she even wants to reach up, grab my ear, twist it, and give me a tougher lecture.

"Seriously. This isn't smart at all, Layla. You need to break it off, because you're *clearly* not happy, and as much as you think he is, no one wants to be with someone who's pretending."

I still can't believe what she's suggesting, considering I thought Jaxon was on her hate-list.

"I don't get what you're saying, Harlow."

"No, what you're doing is looking a gift horse in the mouth. Not with me, but with Jaxon. And it's so sad. He looks at you like you're his world, and he's been handed a miracle, and you look at him in the *same way*."

I frown. "When were you watching us?"

Now she *really* looks like she wants to slap me and maybe even yank my hair out. "That's not the point!" she practically screeches.

"I'll figure it out, eventually. There's no impending doom."

Immediately, I know I've said the wrong thing. Harlow's always been an advocate for taking chances and seizing life. Minimizing regret is her motto, but I know much of it is from the physical and mental toll of her illness. The other day, she opened up to me a bit, explaining a few things, but left when I started to ask questions, stammering that she had somewhere to go.

"Life's too short for you to think like that, Layla. You know that anything can happen"—she snaps her fingers—"in a blink of an eye, and it's all gone."

I think back to the accident, shake away the memories, and find myself agreeing with her. But her tone is serious, more serious than it usually is when she's talking about life and how short it is.

"What's wrong?"

Moving around me, she goes to the living room and plops down on one of the gray, cloth couches. Her shoulder-length hair is ruffled, more than usual, and her trademark sharp eyeliner isn't quite so sharp right now.

"I'm moving out in December."

She says it like she's talking about the weather. Or like she's going to wash her hair with a new shampoo tomorrow. She says it like it's a very small deal.

When it's not—it's a big deal. A very big deal.

I throw myself on the couch beside her, and she's already trying to cover her ears, but I'm faster. "*What?*"

She winces and scowls, nose wrinkling and lips puckering like she's tasted something sour.

"I'm moving out in three weeks, in December," she repeats.

"I heard you the first time. *Why* are you moving out? Where are you going?"

The edge of hysteria sinks its claws into me. What am I going to do without her? I'm going to need to find a new roommate, because I can't afford to pay the rent by myself—she already covers more than half, cause her dad's loaded like that—and on such a short notice, how am I going to find someone who isn't shady and probably a drug lord?

But more importantly: what am I going to do without her? Easily, as easily as breathing, I've grown used to being her roommate, used to sharing her space, used to making sure, when she doesn't know I'm looking, that she takes her medication.

"I'm going to San Francisco for a while. It's for... treatment."

My panic somehow grows. "Things are getting worse?"

Previously, many years ago, most with Harlow's degree of illness didn't survive past the age of thirty-three, and some past the age of eighteen. Now, with the medical advancements, it's no longer considered a terminal illness, but Harlow explained that with the addition of her immune system and other health problems, it could very well become terminal or affect her health more than it already does.

She always carries herself with such ease that it's easy to forget, or easy to refuse to believe, that the day she stops taking her medication and stops going to the doctor could very well kill her or incapacitate her.

The person she presents herself to the world as, sure and fierce, is not the person beside me, deflated in a way that speaks to a bone-weary tiredness. I'm angry at myself for not noticing it sooner, for being so stuck in my own head that I haven't been a good friend. *That's because you're not a good person.* I shut the thought away and pay attention to her.

114

"Kind of. But it's for treatment, they're coming up with new medication and such, and I volunteered for some of the clinical trials."

"Hold up. You're going to be a guinea pig in a bunch of experiments? No way."

"Yes, way. And they're not dangerous. Either they'll work, or they'll have no effect. And I've been feeling... worse."

Immediately, I touch her, like her sickness is a fever I can feel, one I can chase away with ease. "What, how? What is worse? But I thought if you just took the medications, you'd be fine. You said—"

"Layla. You need to calm down. I'll be back before you know it. And it's not as simple as just taking medication. It's having to arrange my whole *life* around it, catering to it, and still having it win sometimes. But we all suffer one way or another, and I've made peace with this part of me. Sometimes, I'm kind of proud of it. Of who it's made me."

She hugs me, patting my back like *she's* consoling *me*, ignoring my trembling hands, my body suddenly frail. "When you get back"— when, not if—"you're going to find the apartment smelly and the kitchen is going to be full of packets of drugs, and my body will be somewhere in the sewers because I'm going to accidentally get a drug lord to room with me. But hey, I don't think they'll do any torturing at this location, so there won't be blood stains for you to clean."

"Nope. I already found someone who's renting out the whole thing."

Clearly, she's been planning on moving out for a while now. It sends a stab of pain and bitterness in my heart, because couldn't she have told me earlier? The news of her leaving and worsening health is a whiplash, but I know I'm more angry with myself for not having seen it earlier.

Then I register her words better. "Wait, the *whole* thing?"

"Layla, we both know that you won't be able to room with anyone without hiding away or attempting to murder them and get their blood money to pay for the bills, so they're getting the whole thing. It's not like we own this anyway, I'm just on really good terms with the landlord."

"That's considerate and all," I muse, sarcastic. "But where am *I* going to live?"

"I've reached out to someone we both know, they have more than enough room, and you won't even need to pool in money for the bills." She narrows her eyes. "Though I doubt you'll listen to that, like how you didn't listen to me."

I would deny it, but she probably has a point. I didn't let her pay for the whole apartment, even when she insisted it's her father's money and he wouldn't miss a penny of it—in this economy? That's lucky.

I mull over her words. We don't both know many people. And she knows I'm barely comfortable with any of them, so I can just stay here. In this familiar apartment with its familiar scent of Harlow's cooking, and the occasional scent of burnt food—from my attempts at cooking.

"And who is this person?"

She grins, and it's one hundred percent fiendish. With it, she is transformed from melancholy into having an almost childish, pure delight. As much as I'm glad to see her smile, it's scary, and I want to cower under the blankets and pray that someone will save me from her evil plans. I know who she's going to say before she does.

"Jaxon."

By the time my tutoring session rolls around, I'm a bristling mess, hair not secured right in its braid, and my glasses in major need of cleaning, but I'm too busy fuming to actually stop and wipe them.

Too busy thinking of all the ways I'm going to yell at Jaxon, and then Harlow for playing matchmaker. Matchmaker when I *have a boyfriend!*

Rounding the hall, my body practically vibrating with rage, I'm a few steps away from the tutoring center when I stumble right into who I'm looking for, my hands steadying on his chest. Perfect.

I don't even have to look up, because I know it's him. It hasn't taken long to grow aware of him in an instinctual way that concerns me half the time. Half blind with anger, the kind my mother would warn me about but also joke comes from my father's side, I reach up.

My hands fist into his collar, yanking him down, and his eyes widen in shock before lighting up with nothing short of excitement and amusement.

"There she is," he murmurs, like my anger is a *joke*, like this is all a grand *joke*, and they can all step all over my boundaries and I won't turn rabid.

"You going behind my back and trying to get me to room with you is *not okay*," I hiss. "I'm not your charity case. I'm not *yours*."

For a second, my anger veers into shock at the expression that crosses over his face. There's a deranged gleam in his eyes similar to that I saw when I first met him again and thought he wanted to put me in his car and drive off. Except now, he looks like he's going to find Aaron and rectify my words.

Quickly, as though it was never there at all, the look leaves his gaze, but I still stare, floundering. In any case, he's not looking at me with excitement anymore, but with something akin to hurt.

Having my hands in his collar and bringing him down to my level was probably a bad idea, because now he's close, too close. I can count every single one of his lashes if I wanted to, and I can see the dark amber of his eyes, easy to mistake for black from afar.

"You've never been my charity case, and you're never going to become one either. Is it really so hard to believe I still care about you? That I want you in my life with a desperation that would scare you?"

I open my mouth to say something and close it again, his eyes searing into mine, my thoughts side-tracking. "Why do you still want me? It's been years. Long enough for you to move on. I can't believe that you haven't."

My hands fall from his collar, and he stands up to his full height, taking a step back. Because while there may be a depraved edge to him now that I cannot place, he has always been the gentleman, the one to think over his words and apologize when he doesn't need to.

"I tried to, Layla, but a part of me always knew I'd see you again, even if I had to wait my entire life. And while I want to be more than friends, I'm not going to do that to you, or push you for something you don't want. After looking for so long, I'm just glad I get to be in your life."

My throat gets thick, until I am certain there is an emotion I cannot swallow, a yearning I cannot quench. I want to hug him and never let go, because all of those years are catching up and telling me that he'll be out of my life again before I can blink. I try to joke it off and say, "Clearly, you're still a sweet-talker."

He laughs, even though it doesn't reach his eyes. "Of course. I need to sweet-talk to get away with things."

"What are you getting away with now?"

"My stalker tendencies and conspiring with Harlow."

I raise a brow and realize that he *has* been the stalker. "You're right, we actually need to talk about that. You've been stalking me since *before* you met me again."

He shakes his head, a smile tugging at his lips. "Have not. The day I met you, I wasn't going to be there, but one of my friends threatened to douse my notes in gasoline and set them on fire if I didn't."

I snort. "Still a nerd, too. But what about the art board? Those notes were from you."

"Were they?" he muses.

"Jaxon."

"Alright, yes, but I was there for a weekend seminar in that room one time, and I saw your art, and I hadn't realized it was yours, just that it was familiar. Odd coincidence, don't you think? Almost like it means something."

I roll my eyes. "Big deal. You found the art. It doesn't mean anything."

He taps my nose. It's a familiar gesture that has my heart clenching and tears burning in the back of my throat. "No, I was right. Out of many art students, I found *your* art. And that didn't even have anything to do with how I found you that day. I *happened* to be a teacher's assistant this year, and my friend happened to threaten me out of studying on *that* day. It *is* serendipity."

And that's what's scary. It's scary when it seems as if fate does so much, as if there are so many coincidences pushing two people together, and in the end, they aren't right for each other at all. Maybe you can feel as though you're meant for someone, but you're not necessarily right for them. And eventually, it'll almost feel like falling out of love for the same reasons you fell in it.

"Serendipity doesn't always mean something. It's just a chance."

"It's a chance given. If you decide to un-friend me, you're going against fate, and I will be badly hurt."

Unbidden, a laugh bubbles out of me, and I remember what Harlow told me earlier. That he looks at me like I'm his world. When I laugh, his face breaks out into a grin, and I'd bet on all the money I own that he has that look on his face again.

But the grin slips off his face as he looks behind me. "Your boyfriend—he's a redhead?"

Mutely, I nod. My throat is thick again, but this time, it's partly out of dread, even though we haven't done anything. Maybe because it feels as if I have.

"On the average-height side with wide cheekbones?"

If he's noticing his cheekbones, then he's close. Probably close enough that he can hear us.

"Uh-huh."

"Well then, he's behind you and doesn't look too happy." His gaze, warm and dark, slides away from him and to me. "And Layla? Don't do anything for anyone else's benefit when it comes to your heart. Not for me, or for him, or for anyone. As cliché as it sounds, follow your heart. Do what *you* want."

With that, he's gone, even though I know he wants nothing more than to stay and make sure I'm alright. Swallowing past the lump in my throat, I turn around and face Aaron. I can't read the look in his eyes and step closer.

"Hi," I say, my voice high and emotions probably written over my face.

In my bid for time, my indecisiveness, I never realized how things might look, and already, I regret not listening to Harlow, I regret delaying things, even if nothing happened. I am always, inextricably, full of regret or self-sabotaging myself. Like my mind has come to crave the toxicity of my emotions, until everything is purposeful.

"Not to sound like a jealous boyfriend, but who was he?"

"Uh, my tutor."

He sounds resigned when he asks, "And?"

I expect anger, I expect accusations, but don't see any of that, and it only makes me feel worse, because he's a good person, sure to assume a thousand good possibilities before the worst, and deserves better than me. His lack of anger only adds to my guilt, because he deserves to be angry. I may not have done anything, but that hasn't changed the way I feel.

"He's a childhood friend."

"Best friend?"

"You could say that."

A humorless smile pulls at his lips. "It's always the best friends, huh?"

"Listen, Aaron. We were close, but he and I... I would never... be with him, I'd never—"

"I might not know you that well, but I know you wouldn't do that to me. And besides, anyone can see how he looks at you the way a partner should."

"What?"

He smiles, and it's soft. "This is what you've really wanted to tell me, isn't it? Well, you don't have to make a choice anymore."

"I still don't get it. I do care about you, Aaron. I'm not trying to be with him."

This time he laughs. "I'm breaking up with you."

"But—"

"We both know it wouldn't have worked anyway, so why delay the inevitable? Though I hope we can stay friends. It is fun being around you, and while I would've appreciated it if you told me how you really felt earlier, I can understand needing a push sometimes from someone else. Consider my breaking up with you to be that push, whether or not you end up with him."

Words stuck in my throat, I reach out and hug him. My head meets the underside of his chin, and I'm surprised at the relief I feel, at my relaxed shoulders and easy breathing. Can things really be this easy?

"I hope you don't think this means that you're not worthy of anything. Or that you're not enough."

He pats my back. "Don't worry. I don't think about it that way."

"Thank you."

We both know for what. For being my comfort zone, no matter how short. For bringing humor to my life when I was down. Pulling back, he smiles, already slipping into the easy role of a friend, perhaps because that's all that had ever been actually easy between us.

"Of course. Go seize your chances, Layla—sometimes you only get them once."

Chapter 12

Then

I have a plan. I haven't given it a name yet, or much thought—lie—but it's in the works. But if I get caught, it'll probably land me in a hell of a lot of trouble and maybe even an early grave.

In truth, I've wanted to do this idea for almost a year now. And if it works, I'll finally find out the extent of how deep the "family business" runs. For so long, I've wondered if it's even worth it to find out more, but the itch to at least know has grown with every day. Worse, the need to keep my father in some semblance of an innocent light fades.

I just don't know what I will do with the information I may or may not find. But really, it's the *not knowing* that has driven me this far, the need to put the puzzle pieces together.

Moving those thoughts to the back of my mind, I finish getting ready. I just want to go to school the way I'm dressed, but I change into jeans and a sweater before wrapping a scarf around my neck. All of this takes me longer than it should, limbs trembling, and that's probably a sign, but it's one I ignore.

These days, I'm more cold than I used to be, and it always takes more effort to do or remember things like combing my hair or cutting my nails.

On the way, my legs feel weak, but I disregard it as I walk to where Jaxon's car will be, and then he'll drive us to school. When he said he could pick me up and drop me, I teased him and called him my own personal chauffeur. Now, with how I'm feeling and how perceptive he is, I'm not sure if I want to see him.

But I sit at the bench anyway, and with the mirror from my pocket, I check my complexion and face. My hair isn't a mess, and with the half-hour spent caking my face with concealer, I don't look like a sleep-deprived skeleton either.

I should be getting better, but I already know why I'm not.

But when Jaxon's car pulls up to the side of the road, and I see him through the window, I don't have to fake the grin that breaks over my face.

I open the door and step inside, laughing when he immediately grabs me and kisses me. The feel of him so close still has butterflies erupting in my stomach and my nerves thrumming. I wonder if it's just that teenage love is an ephemeral thing, or if this is something real.

I so badly crave a future with him; sleepy mornings, the both of us automatically reaching for each other with rasped, "good mornings." Surprising him at work, and having him say, "There's my Layla." I crave it like I'm missing something I've never had.

"We're going to be late," he says, face flushed as he pulls away, but comes back again for another kiss.

Only after he steals another and another does he pull back for good, taking away the warmth of his body. The chain around his neck gleams a little in the sunlight, and the rest of it is hidden beneath his shirt, the ring lumping his clothes. As he drives, I trace his features with my gaze, noting his swollen lips and flushed cheeks.

"Ready for winter break?" he asks, and from the small smile on his lips, I know that he has some things planned.

I nod as he parks the car, and like he always does when we reach school, he grabs my hand, winding our fingers together as he shoulders his backpack on and locks the car. This close to winter break, the hallways are less crowded than normal, with a few students having gone out of town early. The semblance of peace is a blessing as we make our way to my locker.

"I should get you a cat for your birthday next week," Jaxon muses as he slams my locker door closed.

Like always, I wince at the loud noise. This year needs to move faster so I can get a new locker. I doubt I'll remain rational if they give me the same locker next year, but then again, I'm already irrational, so there's not much to lose.

"Getting me something is sweet, but I don't think I'm ready for a pet. What if I'm allergic? And how would I—"

He lightly pecks my forehead. "I was teasing. Something I love to do with you. No cat then, for now. Maybe a pretty dress? What are your thoughts on a tutu?"

"Buy me a tutu, and I will make sure you wear it to your next swim competition."

His eyes widen in mock fear. "No clothes for gifts, then. Got it."

"I don't want a birthday present."

"Well too bad, Layla. Why wouldn't I get you a birthday present? That'd make me a horrible boyfriend."

I still smile a little goofily whenever he calls himself that.

"And," he continues, "I care about you, a lot, if you haven't figured it out already. So of course we're going to celebrate the day you were born, because it's one of the biggest reasons you're in my life."

I try not to let the effect of his words show, but my throat is thick with emotion, and if he keeps talking like that, I might start crying. It's abysmal that he doesn't come with a warning label, and distantly, I can sense myself slipping into that space of obsession, while everything else in my life corrodes.

Will there come a time, I ponder, when he's the only reason I bother getting out of bed? The idea dampens my mood, and so I tell him, "Why are you so perfect?"

"I'm not perfect, Layla," he insists, shaking his head like the idea is outlandish. "I just say what I believe, and anyone who cares for you, romantically or not, would say and believe the same. I don't say it to be sappy or to win you over."

With that, he gives me a small smile and turns down the bend in the hallway. I stare at his retreating frame, smiling, even if a part of me doesn't believe I deserve the words.

I have maybe three hours to find what I'm looking for, figure out what to do with it, and then put it back. And I'm rounding that time, not counting all the minutes it'll take to get back home, or the possibility that he'll come home early.

"What are you thinking about now? How to murder someone and hide the body well?"

Jaxon faces me, body tilted at the waist with one hand around the steering wheel, fingers drumming on the leather. We spend a lot of time in his car, I realize, but don't really mind. I study him, noting his hair, still wet from his swimming practice, and the car faintly smells of chlorine. His fingers keep tapping on the wheel as he regards me, head tilted to the side and a small smile pulling back his lips.

"Light's turned green!" I exclaim, and he whips his head back to the front, pressing on the accelerator until the car lurches forward.

This has become a day-to-day occurrence. He never keeps his eyes on the road when the light turns red. Soon, he'll start to fidget, either drumming his fingers on the steering wheel, or reaching over and playing with my hair. But I've given up telling him to keep an eye out for the green light and do it for him instead.

"And no, I'm not planning a murder." Just a mild form of robbery, and snooping. "I was just thinking."

"You practically live in your head. I wish I could join you sometime."

"You kind of do, since I think about you a lot."

He grins as though I've handed him his heart's greatest desires, and the butterflies that have taken a permanent place in my stomach flutter. I almost don't notice when we stop at the park we agreed to meet at. He hasn't pushed wanting to drop me off at my house, and I haven't offered, knowing I don't want him anywhere near my side of the city or near my father.

Gripping the handle, I open the door and reach for my backpack on the floor, but a hand grabs my collar, pulling me back into the car.

"Can I have a kiss?"

I nod and the next thing I know, soft lips meet mine. When he stops, I almost complain.

"What was that for?"

"I need my good-bye kisses, and my good-morning kisses, and my in the middle-of-something kisses, and—"

I kiss him again, laughing, and it makes it hard to kiss him, our teeth awkwardly clashing. Before he can take advantage of it, I pull away and step out of the car.

"See you tomorrow," I murmur as I close the door, trying to shake off the foreboding sense that I might not see him again.

"See you tomorrow," he repeats. "Don't miss me too much."

I laugh lightly, waving as his car pulls away. Once I'm sure he's gone, I head into the direction of my neighborhood, trying to stay in that buoyant mood, thinking about him.

It doesn't help much when the door clicks open and I step inside. The inside of the house is beginning to seem more and more haunted since it's always quiet and dark, the both of us having long since given up on opening the curtains everywhere.

I make a beeline for my room, trying to think. I've been planning about what I want to do all day and definitely all week, if not longer, and while I have a general idea of *where* to look, I don't really know *how*. There are probably code words and secret messages, and some might even be in Italian. I know it to an extent, but with parents who preferred English, and a family that has lived here for decades, I'm always sad to admit I can't carry a conversation far.

Though the house is empty, I still step carefully, every footfall quiet. I'm definitely paranoid, since he's not home, but that's far from my mind as I pass another room and reach the twin closed mahogany doors.

I try to convince myself I'm dizzy and cold from the anticipation, and that my body feels sluggish because I didn't sleep right last night. Blinking past the headache and the stomach pains, I twist the doorknob and step inside.

The study is dark, with only a faint glimmer of light beneath the drawn curtain and I don't switch on the light. Shivers begin to wrack my body, and I pull my jacket tighter around me, even though the cold doesn't make much sense. I set the thermostat high, and I'm not *that* nervous. Maybe going for a walk afterward will warm me up.

Trying not to disturb anything too much, I move around the study, walking past the dark leather couches on one end. It smells faintly of cigarettes and thick cologne, and I frown, because my father doesn't smoke. But if it's not from him, then it's from a guest.

Rounding the desk, I sort through the files on top, my heart a wild thing in my chest, as though I will be caught any minute. But even though I *know* I'm nervous, I seem to have a hard time *feeling* it, my mind hazy and fingers shaking. As though this is an out-of-body experience, and everything is sluggish with dull pains.

Looking at the papers on the desk, they look like what you'd expect to find from someone who owns or partakes in a shipping company. But I know that's only his alibi.

I start opening the drawers, though I know it's futile. If something here could easily give away what he does and his connection to it, then the door would at least be locked, or the drawers would be.

Giving up, I turn on the monitor. It's passcode-secured, like expected, and my fingers hover over the keys as I try to think over my pounding skull and cramping stomach. Of all the days to try this, why did I choose today, when I'm beyond out of sorts? Though yesterday was a similar story, and so was the day before.

Eventually, my fingertips clack over the keys as I try my mother's name. The little box slides left and right before the borders flash red in error. I try my brother's name next. It doesn't work either.

With every combination I try, the screen flashes red. I groan from the headache and irritation, glaring at the monitor as I try to think of something. Eventually, I even try my name. But as expected, it's wrong. The only logical option is something related to my mother, since any phone password I figured out over the years has always been related to her in some way.

It's always been clear how much he loved her, but it was evidently never enough for him to change that one part of his life. At least she never knew about it until the very end.

I try to think of other combinations, but I disregard them, knowing that if it is her name, it's going to be more complicated than a couple capitalized letters.

No, knowing him, it might as well be in a different language.

I snap my fingers, my mind snagging on the thought. *In a different language.* Of course. My mother's name, Rosa, translates to rose in English, and I go further than that and translate it to Arabic, the language she loved to study.

After a few variations of the name in Arabic, with a couple added numbers and symbols that take forever to test, the laptop locking sometimes for a few minutes, I finally find a combination that works.

Resisting my excitement, I continue searching, trying to find out more about the contact he met with all those months ago. After all, that was how I'd originally found out about almost everything. I admit, I feel guilty for snooping, and the feeling is acidic, making my heart thrums and breaths come in pants, until I want to shut everything off and scurry away, but the will to find out more is stronger.

Continuing to snoop, I close the contacts tab when it's clear that they message in code too.

I bite my lip a little harder than I should as I open something else, and I know it's because the shivers can't seem to go away. With the lights in the study off, the screen is too bright, and my headache grows worse.

Eventually, I find something on the "shipments." Not any hints on the codes, but what seems to be routes. It almost looks like a tracking system for packages, and I know it's wishful thinking to hope that that's all it is—harmless packages.

The *cosa nostra* is definitely not that simple, or that harmless.

And as I read deeper into this, I realize it's also very smart. If one doesn't pay close attention to this, it seems like a simple shipping site for a businessman to track his products. But I can find the different routes, and when I find one destination, a place at an abandoned storage site a few blocks away from a bar, I go in deeper. These "routes" have to be the passages different people take, all acting as "mailmen." I wonder how much they get out of it.

Shivers wrack my body as I search up the name of the bar, and any news on it. Perspiration slowly drips down my back and neck even though I'm so cold, but I blink and focus on what's in front of me.

Since the club is in a shady part of the city, I'd expected *something*, but I hadn't expected *this*, or what it means. If I had doubts earlier about my "snooping," now I wish I were back in the bliss of ignorance.

The club always has cases of overdose hospitalizations, but in the past few months, that number, along with those who have died, has increased. Eventually, thinking I found something, I open a news article, hands trembling, and read that someone was recently arrested when they found him sneaking drugs into people's drinks and then later selling it to them. When I go back to the "shipping site," the name of the person arrested, and one of the "mailmen" matches. Granted, they're anagrams of one another, but still.

Cross-checking everything and the local news sites for information, surprised I can through the pounding of my skull, I find that the person was recently murdered in his jail cell. He was found dead one morning by the guards, who dubbed the incident a miracle.

I know it's not a miracle, but a way of the *cosa nostra* keeping their secrets buried and themselves safe. Safe while they run their mafia, selling substances, get people killed, and I am filled with a venomous *hate* for my father.

I try to puzzle out the other "shipments," not seeing how the sporadic warehouses across the coast could relate to selling drugs, especially when the dates are far apart. Until I check the articles for a city with one warehouse, and a missing child report comes up, the dates matching. I cover my mouth, staring at the correlating dates. *No*, I think, pleading in my mind. *He wouldn't have his hands in something like* this.

I can't find more on this particular line of their *business*, on what the numbers mean and where they've gone, but it's enough to piece the puzzles together. It's enough to make me shove my hands through my hair, roughly tugging at the strands until my scalp burns, a hysteria clawing through my body.

All this time, despite everything, nothing would kill that hope that he's still my father, still the man who loved my mother to pieces, still the man who made sure we were never hurt.

There was always that hope that my father was nothing more than a pawn, unwilling in the business. The amount of information here, though, with his name on everything, proves the opposite. I already know there's a hierarchy system that he's on top of, but he's not a detached, passive leader.

I want to vomit and destroy this room, as though that will erase what I've just learned, as though it will stop what's happening. My breath comes out in wheezes, spots dancing across my eyes, and I know if I don't distract myself, I'll soon be lying on the floor, struggling for breath.

On a whim, I open his email. Most of it is neat, without any new messages, and I know that he's probably already read them from his phone, that there's nothing useful here. But before I can quit the app, a new message slides down, from a "Giovanni De Leone." I click it before I can think twice about it, and I hate the way my father and his men are skewing my idea of what it means to be Italian, the categorization that now blooms in my mind every time I see an Italian name.

Will I one day automatically equate my culture with the *cosa nostra*, forgetting everything else it has to offer? I know every country has organized crime, but after months of reading crime fiction—not the best source of information, I know—I've come to realize that crime literature has an abundance of mafias, and they're almost always Italian.

Shaking my head, as if it'll dispel the internal racism, I read the message.

Glad for our arrangement, Mr. Delaney-Rossi. Can't wait for the wedding, and say hello to your daughter for me.

Frowning, I repeat the name until I've memorized it, deciding I'll look him up later. I doubt he'd message my father about a wedding unless it's important—maybe it's a code for something else? Or maybe he's an innocent friend, with nothing to do with the mafia.

When I hear a noise, I spook, almost jumping, and realize that I don't have much time. This isn't as important as what I found earlier, anyway.

Fumbling in my pockets, my body shaking, teeth clattering and mind hazy, I try to find the USB. *Store the evidence*, I keep telling myself. *You need to store it, then you can sleep till this wears off.*

The idea of a bed doesn't make the headache even marginally better, so I try to think of something else to calm me.

I've plugged the USB into the computer when I hear the front door slam shut. My breath comes out in even shorter pants, and I watch the files and pictures upload onto the port. Body jittering, I move back and forth out of nervousness and so I don't accidentally slump onto the floor.

"Come on, come on," I whisper, though it comes out in gasps as I push back the nausea.

I'd been feeling ill for the past few days, but nothing like *this*, and as I pull out the USB after the files upload, I wish I paid more attention to it.

Stuffing it in my pocket, I try to discreetly get out of the room, but I stumble more than once, catching the furniture or the wall to steady myself.

Now I hear steps, hurried, coming closer, but I'm not overly worried. I left everything the way it was. Or did I? It's hard to be sure, but I can always make up an excuse, like I was looking for medication. With my face sticky with sweat and how I gasp for air as I find it hard to see straight, I know the lie will be believable, right?

The door to the study opens before I grab the handle, and I blink against the sudden light in the hallway, pushing back bile.

I think the figure in front of me is my father, the *don* of the *cosa nostra* in the flesh, but my vision is too distorted for me to be sure. I sway on my feet, and the next thing I know, the world isn't upright anymore, and I'm on my back.

I can hear shouting, and someone shakes my shoulder, but it seems distant, almost like I'm underwater. The sounds get farther and farther away as I slip into the darkness and welcome it.

Chapter 13

Now

Harlow is too excited for someone who is kicking her best friend out of a sanctuary.

"How long are you gone for?" I ask her for what has to be the millionth time.

The hallway is almost entirely full of boxes, a testimony to the answer I'm already expecting. "At least a few months. Probably more."

Knowing her, she's going to be gone for the rest of the school year. Now who will I rant to? Like my hair, makeup, and the horrible cramps from my time of the month? Who's going to be on my case to dress my age and try to teach me how to cook? Worse, when she gets home and curls on the couch, who's going to bring a blanket and cover her?

When we get the last box to the parking lot, I grab her tiny frame and crush her into my slightly less tiny frame, squeezing her tight. When I hear a bone crack, I know that I'm squeezing her right.

"I'm going to miss you so much."

"I'm not going that far, for crying out loud."

"But still. I'm clingy and need my people. Who am I going to talk to now about all the weird stuff that goes on in my head? Who's going to cook me food and scold me for holding chopsticks wrong? Who's going to get me to dress right? And even worse, who's going to keep you from committing homicide? It's a crisis, Harlow."

She laughs—mission accomplished—before wrestling out of my grip. I narrow my eyes at her twitching lips. "You can speak your heart's desire to Jaxon, and don't worry, I'm sure he'll feed you."

A car pulls into the parking lot, and squinting, I see it's him—talk of the devil. Harlow full-on grins, the little evil matchmaker that she is. She started shimmying in excitement when I told her a few days ago that Aaron and I broke up, but pulled my hair when she found out I didn't start something more with Jaxon. As if I should've run right into his arms and kissed him senseless. There are some who cannot stand to be single, and then there are some who cannot stand to see their friends single. Harlow is the latter.

"He better do more than feed you," she murmurs when Jaxon steps out of the car and comes toward us.

He's wearing jeans today, with a hoodie that accentuates his shoulders, arms, and tall body. I think Harlow even says, "Yummy."

"He's not food," I hiss at her, jabbing my elbow in her rib as I try not to play with the hem of my shirt.

"Someone's already possessive."

"Who's possessive?" Jaxon asks when he's within earshot, and he's already reaching for one of the boxes.

"No one," I chirp, trying not to pay attention to the way certain muscles flex as he picks up the box.

Bad, Layla, my consciousness scolds, *don't look at him like you want to eat him.*

I don't want to eat him. That's just… strange. Though it would be nice to get close and maybe… bite certain spots. Just a little nibble.

My face flames in embarrassment at the thought, and to busy myself, I pick up a box, following him to his car to place it in the trunk. As we load the car, Harlow continues trying to play matchmaker, and from the way Jaxon laughs, it's clear that he knows what her attempts are for.

He picks up another box with an *oof.* "What's in here? Bricks?"

"Yes," I say. "They're my weapons. I like throwing them at my mean friends." I look pointedly at Harlow. "Why do you think Harlow is barely five feet? It's because I've hammered her down with bricks."

Jaxon's brows dart up in worry, eyeing me warily, and he laughs dryly when Harlow punches me in the arm. I yelp and rub the assaulted spot. "Respect the short people, Layla. Respect us. We're so tall and mighty on the inside, that God made us short on the outside, otherwise we'd be too powerful."

She turns to Jaxon, adding, "They're not bricks. They're her babies."

Grunting a little, he puts the box in the trunk and grabs another. We watch, because we're creeps like that. "I am so confused right now."

"Books," Harlow amends. "They're filled with books—her babies—and if you crease the spine of even one, she will know, and she will hunt you down. It's not pretty."

He looks at me, eyes bright and lips stretched into a smile. I want to taste that smile. I look away, clearing my now burning throat, knowing I want someone I won't even reach for.

"I know. I've seen it before."

He has seen it before, that and almost everything else about me. Harlow is beyond herself with joy, and she looks like she wants to grab our hands and glue them together—fingers interlocked. Heck, she probably wants to glue all of me to him.

Scary little minx.

"Okay, Layla, I'll be back before you know it. Try not to freak out, and I trust you'll dress like you're in your twenties and not eighties."

Harlow hugs me, and I try not to cry at the reality of her leaving. She'll be back soon enough, and these things happen all the time, I tell myself. I pat her back, and hope I've cheered her up enough. She's been mostly quiet since she broke the news to me, and I hope it's not because she thinks the tests will do worse than fail, or that it's not worth it anymore.

When she breaks away, her tone is morose in a way I don't like as she says, "Grab life with both hands, Layla, and you're one of the best things that's ever happened to me. I don't really know what life you left, but I hope you let yourself heal from it."

Throat tight, confused at the finality of her words, I nod and watch as she gets in her car and drives off, eventually leaving my line of sight.

Fighting back a sigh, I climb inside Jaxon's car. With him beside me in the front seat, it's so reminiscent of my past, of when I'd climb inside his car welcomed by the sight of him.

It's not the same car, and we're not the same people or in the same place, but it's still like coming home. From the look he shoots me as we pull out of the parking lot, I know the familiarity isn't beyond him either.

"I've missed this," he murmurs, gaze on me when we reach a red light.

My chest tightens as I watch him drive, and everything, from the way he holds the wheel to his posture, is similar to years ago, but also different. I want to reach over and kiss him with a desperation I don't think I've ever felt before. At the red light, his fingers don't drum against the steering wheel, and he has all of his attention on me instead, dark eyes boring into mine.

"I've missed this, too," I say, though I want to say *I missed us too.*

Unconsciously, I lean a little closer, and he does too, as though there's an inexplicable pull about him.

Like this, he's close enough that I can see the small specks of gold in his eyes, the lashes thicker than they were a few years ago, and when he tells me gruffly, "I missed all of you, every day, sweetheart, even if we've changed," I'm reminded of how much deeper his voice is. It does interesting things to me, my stomach tightening and breath hitching.

His words make my throat thick and my chest tight, and for every moment that I don't lean in, I'm punishing myself. Like he can hear my thoughts, his eyes fall to my lips, and mine fall to his. They're close, so close, pink and soft, the bottom one fuller, and I'm inextricably *aware* of everything about him, from the crescent moon of his eyelashes to the stubble across his chin.

A horn blares, jolting us both, and I nearly jump out of my seat as my gaze swings behind me. The person in the car behind us yells something. Probably cursing, but I can't hear it. Jaxon guns the car, pressing the accelerator so hard, I almost fall forward.

"Sorry," he rasps, and I think it's over the jolting of the car until I see the visceral regret across his features. Did he not want to kiss me?

"Horrible driver," I breathe. "You, not the guy who horned."

He laughs, though it's thick and slightly forced. My body slightly trembles even though we haven't done anything.

"Well, I'm all you've got for now."

"I got my driver's license a few weeks ago, so I might just steal your car."

This time, when he laughs, it's a true one, and it's as though I've won some sort of award. I want to hear that sound again. I want to record it and play it on my bad days until they're not so bad anymore.

"It's not stealing if I let you borrow it whenever you want, Layla."

Smiling softly, I look out the window, and when we stop at another red light, I refrain from turning around and finishing—or rather, starting—what we were doing. "Keep your eyes on the road, Jaxon."

There's a pause, and then he says, "Can you say it again?"

"What? Keep your eyes on the road?"

"No. My name. I don't think you've ever said it since I've seen you again. It sounds nicer."

I know I must have, but I still murmur, "Jaxon." Knowing the bad history he has with the name, if I can help make it fit better until he makes a decision on whether to change it or not, I repeat, louder, "Jaxon."

I can almost swear that he sighs, and I fiddle with my hands, resolutely looking out the window. I can't help but wonder how our lives would be if we never... lost each other years ago. I undoubtedly wouldn't have turned out the way I have, but what else would be different? A part of me wishes that we never parted, but maybe we wouldn't be like this, here and now, if it hadn't been for that.

But I still hate the way it happened, and that familiar anger and sadness burns in me again as I watch the people crossing the road. My eyes snag on someone who stands still on the sidewalk, staring at the road, facing us. He's too far away for me to tell what or who he's staring at, but I could almost swear that it's us, and everything about him seems both familiar and... off.

Turning to Jaxon, I point at the window. "Is it just me, or is that person being creepy?"

"Who?"

"The man, over there—" I start, turning back around, except no one is there now.

Like an apparition, he disappeared, and I don't see him anywhere on the street or in the crowd. As if the temperature just plummeted, I shiver, goosebumps breaking over my skin, and a sense of fear and *wrongness* settles over me, cloaking me like a blanket.

The light turns green, and soon the car moves. I turn around and look to the front, chills still skating over my skin.

"Maybe they went into a building," I murmur.

"Probably. But I'm sure you weren't imagining it."

My mind stumbles over the image of the person repeatedly, like a broken tape, and I push the most feared possibility out of my mind. "Or maybe I was."

By the time we reach our destination, I'm still skittish as we start unloading the boxes, but when he unlocks the door to his apartment, the worry pushes to the far recesses of my mind. Dropping the box on the floor, I unabashedly turn around in a circle, taking everything in.

I think I immediately fall in love.

In front of me is the living room area, with black couches and a fluffy black carpet, and there are some pictures hanging over the beige-colored walls. Farther in, there are glass sliding doors that open into a balcony, and I can make out a couch and some plants. To my right is a short hall and then a kitchen, and to my left are the bedrooms.

It's small, but cozy, and I already know how easily a place like this can go from an apartment to a *home*, how easy it would be to come here and shed every layer presented to the world.

This is where Jaxon lives, I think. *Every day he comes home from somewhere, and this is where he comes. It has his touches and his traces, and I bet his room smells only of him.* My thoughts are probably creepy, but it's not as if I can stop them. And now I'm going to be living here—with him.

I kind of hope he doesn't have any spare bedrooms. But even if that is the case, knowing him, he'd probably take the couch. Now I wish that he doesn't have spare bedrooms *and* that he doesn't have any couches.

But then he would sleep on the floor...

"You've been staring at that wall for the entire time I was getting the boxes?" His voice startles me from my thoughts, and I notice that all the boxes litter the hallway.

Yes, I think. *While you labored away, going back and forth, carrying boxes—my boxes—I was thinking of all the ways I can share your bed.*

He smiles. "You daydreamer."

"Yep," I answer, ignoring the urge to run my hands over him. The idea of touching him has me melting into a pile of butter, because he hugged me earlier today, and his hugs are still amazing, and my greedy, evil soul wants *more* of them.

I'm beginning to think Harlow slipped something into my morning coffee now. To do something with my hands, I reach over, and start sliding the boxes farther into the apartment.

"You want my help unpacking?"

That would be a hard no. Knowing me, I'll hand him the wrong box to open and then he'll be awkwardly asking me where I want to put my lingerie. Though now that I thought of it, would that really be a bad idea? I let that thought trail off and end.

"No. I'm good."

His gaze lingers, and I know he's disappointed, but really, if he stays in my presence for longer, I'll end up pouncing on him, and that's not how I want to do things.

He gives me a tour of the place, showing me where the basic utensils and dishes are in the kitchen. I learn the left stove must never be used at all costs, and the black spot on the ceiling is not a bad paint finish, but testimony of how he learned not to use the left stove the hard way. Next, he shows me the master bedroom, and I want to linger, because it's evident that it's his room, but he's already moving on to the next room.

"And this is the bathroom. There's only one, and it's connected to the master bedroom and has a door that goes out into the hallway." As if to emphasize, he opens the door, and I see a clean bathroom with another gray door inside on the left wall, next to the shower.

Lock both *doors*, I tell myself. *Or not, if you're taking a shower.* Wouldn't that be fun? What is *wrong* with me today?

"And this is your bedroom." He pauses. "Unless you want the other one. Please take the other one if you want, I really don't mind. It'd make me happy if you took it if you wanted it."

He's kind of rambling, and if it wasn't so endearing, I'd laugh. "I don't want it. I want this one."

He opens the last closed door, to a mostly empty room, much smaller than the rest. "I think this is for storage." Now that he says it, it is like a closet, just slightly bigger. "But I never used it anyway, and thought you could, uh, use it for your painting, if you wanted."

Not thinking, I reach up and peck his cheek. He's tall enough that I have to brace my hand on his arm, the muscle not yielding at all, and his skin is soft beneath my lips. "I love that, thank you."

Before I can gauge his expression, I open the door to the guest bedroom. "I, uh, guess I'll unpack now."

He nods, the earlier contentment from when we first entered his apartment ebbing away into disappointment before he smiles. "Alright, let me know if you need anything. I'm really glad you're here."

Mutely, I watch his retreating figure until he steps out of the hallway.

Despite the days that have passed, and the ease with which we've slipped into a routine, carpooling to campus together and then back, it's still nerve-wracking living with him, having the intimacy of the domesticity I craved as a teen. But back then, I always imagined living with him and *being* with him. I wonder how much longer I'll hold myself back, how much longer before I throw away all the reasons I crafted in my head to wait. They seem silly now.

Every time I see more of him, learn more of who he is now through living with him, my resolve cracks a little further.

It's hardest when I catch sight of, more and more, that slightly deranged, obsessive gleam in his eyes, his hands fisting like he wants to reach out and crush me to him, and every time, I shiver.

"Is the pasta good?" he asks me from across the counter, his own bowl finished in front of him.

Nodding, I take another bite, having to stop myself from sighing in joy. Every bite of the garlic penne pasta is delicious, the blend of the cream, herbs, and garlic an utter delight, and just from the taste, I know he added pasta water to the sauce.

When I notice him watching me, I blush and say, sheepish, "Sorry I'm a bit of a bore today—the food's really delicious. I'll, uh, make something tomorrow, if you want?"

My mother would be aghast if she knew just how little I pulled my weight around here, and how I've practically made Jaxon into my manservant since he cooks and chauffeurs me around. The idea of her being alive to scold me sends a pang through my chest, even if it's grown bittersweet over the years.

Shaking his head, he gets up to make me another serving and ladles a bit more into my bowl. "Not at all, I'm glad you like it. And I like making things for you and knowing you enjoy them."

I nod, too jittery to say anything, my heartrate slowly increasing at his proximity as he adds to my bowl, and like this, with me seated and him standing, he seems larger than he is, until he's all I see. Any other moment, and I would be embarrassed at how quickly it takes for my skin to flush, how little it takes for my breath to hitch and stomach to swoop.

There's a cacophony of fireworks in my blood when I'm around him, and I haven't even touched him. When he moves the spoon away, putting it back into the pot, I worry for a moment that he's going to add even more, and my hand shoots out to clasp over his.

"No more," I insist.

"I know," he answers, bemused. "I was taking the pot away."

Except I don't move my hand back, his skin warm beneath mine. I'm transfixed at the sight of my paler hand atop his larger one, and the veins that run across the back of his hand, up to his forearm.

I find myself wanting to trace them, and my gaze tracks up his arms—disappointed that his shirt has sleeves—up, up, until I meet his gaze. I'm only touching his hand, but that hunger is written across his gaze until I think I'll combust. Immediately, I yank my hand back as though I've been burned.

"I, uh, just need to go to the bathroom," I murmur, making my escape.

"You don't need to keep running, Layla," he murmurs. "Is that what happened back then too?"

Going down the hall, I round the corner until I'm tucked away from view of the kitchen, and lean against the wall, heart racing a wild tempo. I place a hand over my chest, noting the rapid rise and fall. If I look in the mirror, will my expression match the hunger I saw in his?

As embarrassing as my reaction is, I calm down quickly enough, and his words come back to me. Maybe I do have the proclivity to run, but that's not what happened that day.

No, what happened was much worse.

Chapter 14

Then

In all my short life, there has only been one other time where the line between being awake and asleep was so blurry I couldn't differentiate between reality and hallucination.

I vaguely register it's happening again as I struggle to open my eyes, but everything is too muffled, and do I really want to wake up? I know there's a coarse pillow beneath my cheek, that my stomach twists and tightens with ache, but the sounds around me are so far away.

I can't be sure if I hear correctly as I'm pulled back into sleep, but I think someone murmurs, "And how long has this been going on?"

I want to know who's talking, who's asking, what's going on, and why. But my head is so, so heavy, and sleep is a thing that engulfs me and drags me under, making the world silent again.

It's the pain that wakes me up the second time, and I can't register anything except the pounding in my skull, the nausea, chills, and the way my stomach tightens with every breath. I don't know what's going on around me, what all the muffled sounds are, but I wish I could go back to sleep. Not only because of the gut-wrenching pain, but because I've never been so tired. Depleted, almost, but the pain is keeping me conscious while not allowing me to actually *wake up*.

Everything is a pendulum of sensations. One moment I'm too warm and sweating, and the next I'm freezing and shivering, each clack of my teeth resonating in my skull. I can almost *feel* the headache behind my eyes, making them burn, and the skin beneath my nose feels wet and sticky.

I want to wrap my arms around my stomach and writhe, to do anything to get the pain to go away, but I can't. It's as though every part of my body has given up except for the expression of the pain. Of the pins-and-needles sensation that's *nothing* like the tingling of a sleeping limb.

One prick is especially sharp in the inside of my arm, but when it fades, the pain reduces a fraction, to a throbbing soreness, and as my awareness evanesces, I think it might've been a needle.

I don't get to find out.

For what might be the hundredth time, I gradually pull myself out of the clutches of sleep. This time, the pain isn't acute, and I manage to open my bleary eyes, and almost immediately close them at the bright light. It burns the back of my eyes, and everything is too white, as though someone scrubbed every surface with bleach. Wincing, I try to move, wondering how long I've been here, and why.

"Layla?"

I freeze, every limb locking up as I almost forget how to breathe. Like if I pretend I don't hear him, I won't have to deal with this now.

The irony of it doesn't escape me—a few weeks ago, I would've given anything for his attention.

I clear my throat, as though to say something, but I don't want to. I want to ignore him, but I also want to scream, because the memories of what I was doing before I blacked out come rushing to me. I remember the blood money, and just what he does in his alleged "business," and it makes me sick all over again.

"Why am I here?" I ask, my gaze sliding over the machines beside the bed and the drip attached to my hand.

"You're here because of a near overdose."

I freeze, but the words pass over my head. That can't be what happened. My gaze slides back to him. "Why are you here?"

For a moment, he stares at me with such shock, I'm sure it's actually real. "You're my daughter, who was a few pills away from dying from an overdose, and you're asking me *why am I here?*"

"Yes, I am. After all, out of everyone to make it out, why did it have to be me, right? I don't want you here. Not when you live off of the blood, death, and addiction of others. It makes me sick to know that everything from you my entire life was paid for with *that*."

I'm shaking, and it makes my head hurt, but it's nothing like how my chest constricts until I'm sure I cannot breathe. I've never spoken like this before to him, and that alone makes me terrified. I am so sure, that in moments, his anger will become a visceral thing, an explosion of rage.

"Enough, Layla. My only mistake was not keeping a closer eye on you, one I won't make again. You won't cost me him."

I'm still shaking, body brimming with something violent. "That's a lie. If you truly cared about her, about me, you would've *given it up*."

"The doctor said you'd be very irritated," he starts, glancing at his watch, like he has somewhere else he needs to be, like I'm an inconvenience he's had to pencil in. "She said you're still going through the effects of the withdrawal, to an extent. But I know I should've been there for you, and I promise I will from now on."

I want to scream and throw something at him, frustrated at him for ignoring everything important. My upper lip pulls back into a sneer as the desperation and anger dig their claws into my mind.

"I can't believe I ever looked up to you." The words are a low blow, though they could be worse, and I feel a mixture of wretchedness and nothing at all as I spit them out.

It's almost ironic how the one thing he couldn't give up operates on selling drugs and people, and here I am, hospitalized because of a near overdose.

He is the king of an *empire*—if the amount of revenue and number of lackeys is any indication—one that he built almost all of his life in effort and blood. He used it to claw his way up life, to reach where he is now. It's practically a part of him, and no matter his reasons for starting, he never tried to get out of it when he could. I suppose it would be hard to let go of something you practically gave pieces of your soul to.

After all, we're all addicts in the end.

His expression changes to one I cannot read. "Layla—"

A doctor walks into the room, a pair of glasses sticking out of the breast pocket of her pristine white lab coat. "I'm going to have to ask you to leave, Mr. Delaney-Rossi."

He nods his head once, jaw tight, as he leaves the room. After that, she comes to stand beside the bed, giving me a smile, and asks how I'm feeling.

Tired, I want to tell her. *Angry,* I want to scream.

But eventually, her questions give way to more probing ones, until I wonder if she's trying to see if she needs to call CPS. Maybe she already has.

I already know my father will make sure I'm out of here long before they come. Or maybe he won't have to. Maybe it'll only take a little bribery or blackmail and we'll walk out in broad daylight. The thought fills me with such a bone-weary disappointment, I slump my head against the pillow.

"When can I be discharged?" I ask anyway. "And how long have I been in the hospital?"

"You've been here almost a week, it's the twenty-eighth today, and after the nurse checks all your vitals again, you should be good to go maybe later today or tomorrow."

I knew I must've been here for a while, but the date still throws me off. It's well into the break, and my birthday has passed.

146

"Wait," I blurt out when she starts leaving. "Has anyone come to see me?" She shakes her head, and this time, I can tell she's apologetic. "No visitors."

It's a while after she leaves that the nurse comes, and I zone out, staring at the wall as she checks on my vitals, and everything seems to fall apart a little more.

"What did you tell him?" I try not to hiss as soon as we're in the car.

For all of his dodging and ducking his head in the sand when it comes to talking about his mafia, he doesn't beat around the bush with this. "That nuisance of a boy? He was blowing up your phone."

"You didn't answer my question."

He sighs. "I told him to buzz off, like any father would."

"And?"

"Caught him walking around, getting close to my side of the city, and called the cops."

"You did *what*?" I shriek. And *my* side of the city? Just how crazy is my father? But then again, I suppose it's an addictive thing to believe you've accumulated enough power to stake a part of a city as yours. Does it hurt him, I wonder, that he can't put his name over it with a signboard? Like a child declaring *Mine!*

Also, it seems a little stupid for him, of all people, to call the cops. But then again, maybe half of them are on his payroll. My father shrugs like calling the cops on minors is a daily occurrence for him. "He got away as soon as he heard the sirens."

"And?"

"I made sure I got the message through. And before you ask, no, he's not dead."

I feel sick as I sink further into my seat. Is Jaxon in a hospital somewhere, barely alive? What did my father do to him? I imagine him lying in a bed, body broken, and have to bite my lip to stop myself from crying. And while I know I didn't do that to him, the

147

words *your fault, your fault,* circulate in my head. If only I'd stayed away.

What I wouldn't give, I think for the millionth time, to have never found out about my father all those months ago. If I close my eyes, I can remember the day I first found out. It had been a game—I shouldn't have been in his study that day, hiding under his desk with the last slice of cake, and I shouldn't have stayed quiet when he came inside to answer a phone call. But I had been in his office, and he had answered the phone. And I had heard enough of their conversation.

The other pieces to the puzzle came together. At the thought, I dig my fingers in my pocket, searching for the USB, but of course, it isn't there.

A muscle thrums in his jaw. "You can try to worm your way out of it, but you aren't seeing him again, and you're not going back to that public school again. I was stupid enough to think you were mature enough for it"—more like he was too broke to afford anything else, since I've long since understood his "success" has been declining—"but then you went and got yourself on a drug. And frankly, a person who couldn't be able to see what was going on with you, especially if he was your boyfriend, isn't good enough."

I shake my head and lean back into the seat. The doctor was right. The irritation and anger coursing through me right now *burns*, and I want to punch the window and yell at him.

"You're such a hypocrite. I really don't know what Mom saw in you."

"Watch your mouth, Layla."

The car reaches our address, and I'm out before it even stops, ripping the door open and lurching out. Punching the code to the garage, I rush inside, even though I have nothing to do. My head is strange, lightheaded in a way that tells me the doctor put something in the IV drip—something that will wear off.

What am I going to do? I think. When I think about my future now, it seems bleak, full of having someone always breathing down my neck, and always knowing that every time my father gets a call and goes to his office, it's because of a "shipment."

It's years in this too-big, empty house, with someone who is barely a *person* anymore. It's years with no more Jaxon, and no more days spent in parks and his car, and no more Aaradhya.

Immediately, my throat closes, chest aching as something squeezes it painfully, as though to say *you won't even get the air you need to breathe.*

"When's the rehab?" I wheeze, trying to distract myself.

"You're not going to rehab."

I stare at him in shock as he calmly moves around the kitchen, making himself a cup of coffee. "What the hell?"

"Manners, Layla." I've wanted him to talk to me for so long, and now that he actually is, I think I'm going to yank my hair out in frustration. *Manners? From me?* When he *runs a mafia?* I think I laugh hysterically, and his mouth draws into a tight line as he continues, "It was hard enough making sure no one knew about your stint—you cannot go to rehab, because they *cannot* know. They will hurt him if they know what you've done, do you understand? A doctor will come here every few weeks, and you won't have access to... *it.*"

He tugs his hair, almost yanking at it, and the silver strands stand in disarray around his head. Sometimes I forget, but he looks as though he's aged ten years in the past few months, though it doesn't distract from the pure deranged insanity that's come over him. Not when he sometimes mutters things that don't make sense. Like right now.

"They will back out if they find out, and then he'll die," he insists, almost to himself.

"*Who?*"

Shaking his head, he moves as though he hasn't heard me at all. "I found a way for you to finish school online," he continues. "And you will stay inside, where I can make sure you're safe. And then— and then everything will be okay."

"No," I blurt out, panicking at the thought of being in here, in this empty house, all day, every day.

Without even realizing it, my hand is already sliding into the pocket in my pants, a desperation in my limbs, my first instinct to tell the person I know I can tell everything to, except I remember my pockets are empty.

"Where's my phone?"

It's a useless hope to think he's actually going to give it to me. Useless, stupid hope. I hope, anyway.

"I got rid of it. And no, it's not hidden in my study. It's broken and thrown away."

I keep shaking my head, scrambling to figure out another way I can contact Jaxon, even if I don't have his number memorized by heart. I used to, but my memory became really botched before I got hospitalized. It still is.

I know my father, and I know how thorough he is. There's an increasing chance—one that's becoming more and more apparent—that I'll never see Jaxon again. That just like that, that day will be the last I'll ever see of him, without even getting to say a proper goodbye. I guess things really are as ephemeral as I first thought them to be. There will be no more lunches in the library, no more shy kisses, no more mini-lectures on psychology, no painting days in a secluded alley, and no more him.

And it *hurts*, as though in a short time, my mind and heart have grown hooked onto him, convinced that they cannot survive without him. How quickly one can grow passionate for someone to the point of addiction, until they've re-written their own chemistry to crave a person.

"I have to see him," I wheeze out. "Please let me see him."

I sound pathetic, and I know it. Throughout my life, he always hated it when I reduced to begging to get him to change his mind. He'd tell me to bend for no one, and grovel for no one, even him. Maybe—most probably—it's because of the ruthless way he runs his mafia. Like he wants me to turn out just like him.

He shakes his head. "You'll see that it's for your own good. You nearly died, Layla, you need to stay at home now." He sighs, like the next words pain him, and I wonder if he's even talking about me anymore, or about him and Mamma. "And your worlds are very different. To force them to coexist, to force them to collide, will only result in heartbreak if you're lucky, death if you're not."

I realize I'm shaking my head, any semblance of reason slipping into the panic, and I remember why I never let Jaxon drop me off anywhere near my house. Then again, do I even deserve to see him again? Do I even deserve him after everything that happened to him because of me?

I think of my mother, of my baby brother, dead. I think about what would happen if I saw Jaxon again, if my father saw him again. And I realize that one way or another, I lose those I love. I lost my mother and my brother to death, and I lost my father because the man standing before me is not the man I idolized, not the father I loved. And now, from my own mistake, I've lost Jaxon.

Looking at my father, I almost think that he's sorry. "If Mom saw you now, would she even recognize you?"

His hand slams against the counter, a man knowing his control is fraying at the edges, and that sooner than later, everything will come crumbling down. "You have no *idea* what it was like to watch you fall like that, your skin so pale, you looked *dead*. Do you even know what I'd lose with you dead, you *stupida bambina*?"

"You're going to regret everything one day," I promise, turning around to leave. "And I'm going to make sure that that day comes sooner than later."

As I leave, I think I hear him say, "I already do."

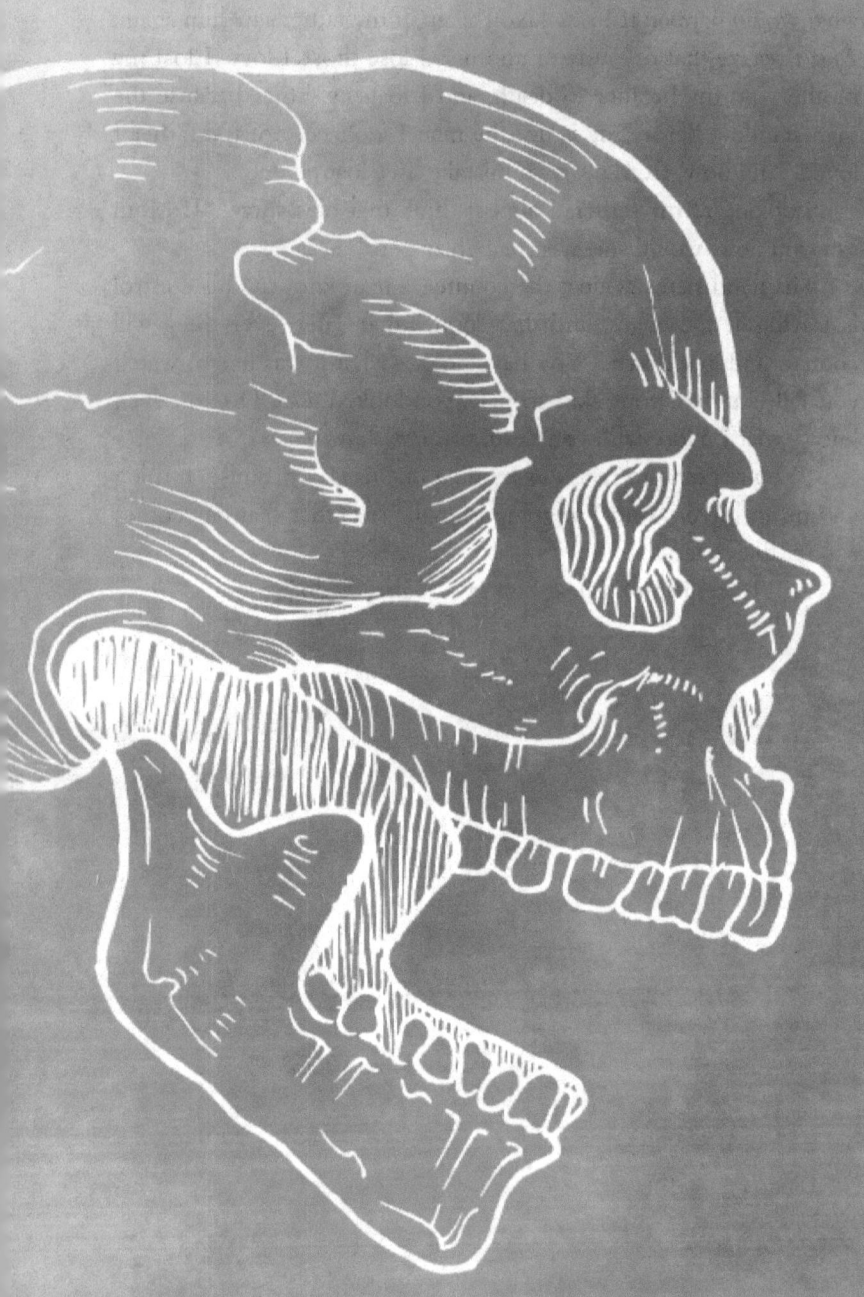

Interlude

The boy wakes up in pain, until he is delirious with it, as though it is sentient and has crawled its way into his mind, into his bones, until he can swear he can hear the whisper of a voice. *It'll be alright, ya habibi.*

He doesn't know if the voice is even accurate, if his mind actually remembers the way she sounded, but he can't help and think, *Mama? Don't leave me,* ya ummi.

Except when he opens his eyes, he's alone in a room, every limb covered in casts as white as the walls, and his mind spins with the pain and the screaming machines beside him. They scream until he is sure he will go mad, until people rush into the room, trying to push him back on the bed, insistent and rough.

For a moment, he is not in a white room but a stale, shadow-covered one, with men holding him down and screams clawing through his throat until can taste blood, the pain through every limb incendiary.

And above him, a man with moss-green eyes, so similar to those of a girl he wants to love, sneers down at him, except his are full of an arcanity he cannot comprehend. The boy is familiar with hate, with the way it seeps into a person's veins until nothing—no slur or hate crime or attack or ethnic cleansing—is unjustified, but he's never had someone do *this* to him.

"You will not keep looking, you hear me? You will not even think *of her."*

But the boy has never been obedient, and is sure he has only lived as long as he has out of pure, unadulterated stubbornness. So even when the pain fades away, his mind dragged to sleep, he knows he will never stop. Worse, he knows he doesn't *want* to. That in a life full of pain and people only interested in erasing who he is, he finally found someone who *sees* him, and he can never give that up.

So he will never stop. And for the next six years, even when he knows he should, he never stops looking for her.

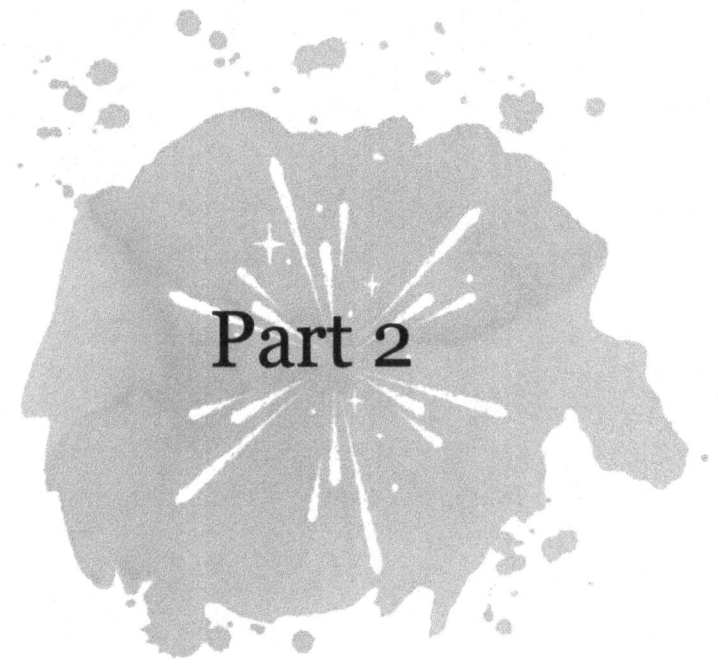

Part 2

Chapter 15

Now

The banging and hammering noise has been inconsistent for the past half hour, but when it picks up again, I close my book and take a breath. When I first heard it, I could've sworn my heart stopped, mistaking the banging for a headboard hitting the wall, and even though I didn't hear a guest come in, acidic jealousy filled my veins so quickly, I was half-shocked.

Then the drilling noises picked up, and it didn't take long to piece together that he's building something. Now, the sporadic noise just elicits curiosity and the occasional annoyance when it distracts me from my book. Eventually, it quiets down again, growing too faint for me to hear anything, and I wonder if I should go see what he's up to. But I haven't been in his room yet, and I'm not sure I can keep my hands to myself if I do. A room is personal, and the idea of being in his, especially with him there, and seeing all the pieces of him, seems almost intimate.

But curiosity bites at me all the same, until I'm too distracted to read.

Eventually, I hear something moving across the carpet, almost dragging, toward my room, and I can't help it anymore. I hurry to the door and pull it open to see Jaxon standing in the hallway, hand up and poised as though he was about to knock.

He regards me silently, and if I didn't know any better, I'd say he shifts his feet from side to side out of nervousness. Past him, there's a tall, thin bookshelf standing in the hallway, the whiteness of it a stark contrast against the gray walls.

"I don't know about you," I start. "But I don't think the hallway is a good spot to keep it."

He rolls his eyes. "Funny. It's for you."

"You got and built me a bookshelf?"

Rubbing the back of his neck, his eyes dart inside my room, and he tilts his head toward the stacks of books over every surface. "The sight of all of those books like that is just sad, and with a bookshelf, you could get to them easier and actually have access to your bedside table."

Almost instinctively, I reach up and peck his cheek, knowing I shouldn't be so comfortable with touching him, but the sight of him every time fills me with an inexplicable emotion that overflows, until I must touch him. I reach for the shelf, and it's a simple thing, but the sight of it pulls at something beneath my ribs until I cannot breathe. There was no *Do you want a bookshelf?* No *I'll get you a bookshelf, would you like that?* He just saw I needed it and got it.

"Thank you, that's sweet of you."

I've slowly been getting used to living with him, but sometimes I wonder what things will look like in the future, when Harlow gets back, thinking he wants this to be a temporary arrangement. And maybe he does, but getting me a bookshelf feels like more, as though the act of changing around his apartment for me, no matter how small, is him telling me that I belong here.

He helps me move it into the room and into an empty corner, and I stare when he leaves only to come back with another shelf. At my incredulous expression, he only says, "What, you didn't think I'd only get you one thin measly bookshelf, did you?"

After they're both up, he rubs the back of his neck again, eyes glinting with a hopeful look. "Do you like it?"

"I love it."

He smiles, dimple coming into view, and like every time he grins, I want to kiss that smile and taste his happiness like it'll be an ambrosia. No doubt I've been staring for a while when he clears his throat, smile falling away, and lingers by the doorway.

"Well, have fun putting the books away."

Rolling my eyes, I grab him and drag him back inside. "You can keep me company."

He sits on the bed, watching as I sort the first stack, and I try not to get distracted by the sight of him sprawled across the sheets. Taking the rest, I put them across the bed, since it's closer to the shelves, and work from there. Some books he picks up and paws through, and I think I nearly die when I see his hand hover over one of the more risqúe books before he picks something else up.

It's almost like old times as I move around, talking to him while he's stretched out on the bed, shirt wracked up and one arm behind his head. I don't know how much time passes before he glances at the clock, mutters something, and tells me he has things to do.

Even though the apartment is on the small side, I don't hear anything beyond his door open and close as I continue moving around the room, putting the books onto the shelves, enjoying myself.

Eventually, I take a step back and examine the room. He didn't need to get me two shelves—I don't have that many books, sadly— but the half-empty bookshelf now gives me a reason to buy more books. The shelves stand across from the door, closest to the bed, and I'm glad he picked it out in white; it matches nicely with the white duvets and beige curtains. Sure, the dresser on the perpendicular wall is black, but that's why I got black throw pillows and a black fluffy carpet. Eyeing the empty walls, I come up with ideas for paintings, color schemes already in mind.

A task nags at the back of my mind, one I know I need to do but have forgotten, and I slide the curtains shut since it's dark enough, before going to turn the light on. Stepping on something that crinkles, I frown as the light flickers on, and glance down.

"Oh, that's what it was," I murmur to myself as I look at the bag full of the toiletries I bought earlier today.

Grabbing the bottle of shampoo and conditioner, I open the door and step out into the hall. His bedroom door is closed and the apartment is quiet. I ignore the small pang of disappointment that stabs me, because what did I expect? That he'd wish me goodnight?

Shaking my head, I open the bathroom door in the hall, and reach for the light switch in reflex, except the light is already on. I freeze as the realization settles over me. Well, I guess I know what he's doing now. Somewhere in the far recesses of my mind, I internally scold myself. *There are two doors to the bathroom, Layla. Two! And when did you stop knocking?*

I should step back, but my eyes find him, a towel wrapped around his waist. I abashedly look away, but a few seconds later my gaze slides back to him. There's the light gray towel, but everything else is in clear view—from the breadth of his shoulders to the chain necklace that he still keeps on. Rivulets of water run down his tan skin, over the well-defined arms, chest, and hard stomach. Looking at him now, it's impossible to ignore the ways in which he's changed over the years. Unbidden, my gaze travels to the dusting of hair that starts at his navel and disappears under the towel.

With *that*, I snap out of it. My eyes dart up to his as I blush beet red, and I find him already looking at me, eyes dark.

"I don't think that's a smart idea," he eventually says, voice slightly rough.

"What is?" I ask, voice a whisper as though there's someone else here.

"Looking at me like that if you don't want me to do something about it. And since I'm not entirely sure if Aaron and you are still a thing—don't make me into the person who doesn't really have you."

Has he really thought this whole time that I'm still in a relationship? The regret I would see every time he looked like he wanted to touch me makes sense, and I shake my head, gnawing my lip in guilt.

"We're not together, and I'm sorry but I… I wouldn't be with you the way I have if I still was, and I would've never… let myself want you as much as I do."

"I don't think I heard you well, can you repeat that?"

My cheeks flame as I look at the wall and refuse to meet his gaze. "I want you."

He comes closer, until I can smell the musk and cedarwood of his body wash, and it does odd things to me. "Since when?"

Forever, I think, but I know he's asking how long it's been since the breakup. "Three, maybe four weeks ago?"

He's closer, close enough that I can feel the heat radiating off of him and it'd be nothing at all to reach over and touch him, to trace the dips and valleys of his skin, and oh how much I *want* to.

"Why didn't you tell me?"

"I… I don't know."

"I really don't understand. You look at me like you want me, you *say* things like you want me, but then you break up with Aaron and don't tell me. Did you not want to break up with him?"

"No!" I rush. "He did break up with me, but I'd wanted to, so I guess you could say he beat me to it. We both knew we weren't right for each other, and my only regret is being a coward and not breaking up with him sooner."

"And why weren't you two right for each other? Why wasn't he right for you?"

He already knows the answer—he has to. "He… he isn't you."

That little frown is still on his face, the unguarded confusion, and I want to reach up and wipe the lines away. "But I don't understand why you wouldn't tell me if you want me."

"Coward, remember?"

He steps closer still, hands coming up to cup my face and brush across my skin with such tenderness, I wonder what good I've done in my life to deserve this.

"You're not a coward, sweetheart."

"But I am, and I-I think I got scared every time you looked like you wanted me—"

Immediately, his hands drop like I've seared them, and my own twitch with the urge to reach out, to erase the hurt and shocked look across his features. "I would never do anything you don't want, I would never… God, Layla, I wouldn't *force* a relationship on you."

My words are so wrong, it's like I'm digging my own grave, and I shake my head, confessions tumbling from my lips. "It scared me because of how much I wanted it. And I've grown used to losing what I have that I guess I thought it would be safer to want you than to have you only to lose you."

I want his hands on me again, but when he stands there, my own hands go to touch him, settling over his face like this is what the curve of my palms were made for. Water drips from his hair over my fingers, but none of it can take away from the warmth of his skin.

"I want you more than I've ever wanted anything. And it scares me. It scares me how quickly my heart latched onto you, now and then, like an obsession. Did you know, I would think of you over the years? I'd imagine what it would've been like to still be with you, what a future would've looked like, and now that there's the possibility, I think I've made all of this up. I don't want to find out it's real only to lose it again."

His hands settle over mine, holding them tighter against his skin like he wants to crawl into me. His eyes tell me he knows he already has. "Sweetheart, I'm not going anywhere. What do I have to do to convince you of that? To take the fear away?"

"It's not your responsibility to soothe the chaos of my mind."

"What if I said I want it to be? What if I say I already do?"

"Jaxon—"

"Because you already have me. You say you're scared to have me out of a fear of losing me, but you already have me. You've had me for far longer than you can possibly imagine, sweetheart."

His arms curve around me, pulling me into a hug, and I think I melt into him a little, even if the water from his shower seeps through my clothes. It's innocent enough, until my arms grow tired of reaching for his face, and I settle them lower, over the warm expanse of his chest. His hands tighten around me, that depraved, yearning look written across him again, and I shiver.

"And there's that," I murmur.

"What?"

"That look you get in your eyes. Like you're going to do unspeakable things for me, and then unspeakable things *to* me."

"What kind of things?"

Devour me, I think, wondering what that would look like. "Like kissing me." Except that's wrong—kiss feels too light a word to describe what it looks like he wants to do.

"Like this?"

Leaning down, he kisses the far corner of my lips. My breath hitches, and I shake my head. He tilts his head until his mouth is only a few spaces away from mine, and that *want* pulses fireworks through my blood, filling me with a desperation I know he can see in my eyes.

"Like what, then? I think you need to show me."

Dark amusement glimmers in his eyes, and I realize this is my punishment for not telling him, for teasing him. And it's a challenge, too. He's not going to give me anything until I *take* first, take what he's giving until no doubt remains in my mind.

The challenge calls to me like nothing else, and I want to win it. I want to erase any doubt he has that I cannot do this. Boldened, I slide a hand down, across his skin, reveling at his shock, until my hand rests over his abdomen, and I can feel every tremor of breath, every twitch. I steady myself as I reach up, pushing myself higher on my toes, and cup his face with my other hand.

"Like *this*," I murmur, and bring my mouth to his.

Chapter 16

Desperation

When I slide my lips over his, we both let out twin sighs. It's as though there have been too many moments where we've wanted to kiss and touch and hold each other, and now that we *finally* get to do it, we're relieved. But he threw a challenge, and I plan on answering it. His bottom lip is between mine, soft, and without warning, I nip it. When his lips part on a gasp, I use it to deepen the kiss further, until I can taste him and *take* and *take* and *take*.

Each kiss slides into the other, with us moving closer and closer, until I'm arched into him, both arms around his neck, fingers splayed into his wet hair, and his hands are around my waist, skimming over my ribs.

I'm shivering as I kiss him, wanting to burst. I don't know if it's from happiness, or relief, or the way every nerve ending seems to sing and hiss. It's both like coming home and everything daring and exciting I've ever done, and maybe this is what I missed most about him. How he could be my rock and my anchor, but also the one to set me aflame.

He shudders as my hands roam over his skin, over the dips and valleys of him, flushed from the shower. As I touch him, my hand to his heart, I want to laugh and cry.

"I missed you," I mumble in between kisses, my words coming in pauses and abrupt stops between soft breaths and greedy moans.

I know he likes my words, because he kisses me harder, one hand unraveling my hair so he can fist it. Moving my head to the side, I'm prone to his advancements, and I grip his arms as he moves his tongue against mine. The soft, wet glide is a sharp contrast to the solidness of him, and I whimper, body arching, unable to focus on anything except all the places we touch and press against each other, his interest unmistakable against my stomach. It's everything and it's too much and it's not nearly enough.

When we break apart, he drops his forehead on mine, panting. "Are you panicking about this yet?"

I shake my head. "Never."

His face is tinted red from kissing, and his lips are swollen and mauve. I know mine are in a similar state. Cupping my cheek, he swipes his thumb back and forth across my face, and it soothes me, my face tilting further into his hand. *This, right here*, I think. *Is where I'd like to say.* Ever since I left *there*, I've been trying to find a place that feels like home, and I can see how easy it would be to experience that with him.

"I'm sorry I didn't tell you sooner," I murmur after a while.

"Don't apologize for doing what you think is best for you."

"It hurt you, and I don't want to hurt you."

He smiles, teasing, leaning closer to murmur over my mouth. "I can think of a few ways you can make it up to me."

"Oh yeah?"

"You know it." Moving back a little, the smile fades away, until he regards me seriously. "But I don't want you to ever doubt that I want you or that you can tell me what you're feeling."

"I know, I've been getting better at it over the months, but sometimes the communication skills are a little worse for wear."

It wasn't like there was someone to talk to during those years, anyway. Well, technically, there was, but I'd rather chop my own arm off than deal with the men my father worked with. At my words, his eyes darken a little, and I know that this time, he's going to ask the question he's probably wanted an answer to the most.

"What happened that day?"

I freeze, every bone in my body locking up as I remember what happened, and then everything after. I remember what—or more accurately, *who*—I ran away from, the fate I was only a few months, at best, away from facing. But even if I did leave it all in the past, or tried to, the way Jaxon has wedged himself into my life again—and the way I eagerly let him—doesn't remind me of everything I ran away from.

"I had a near overdose and lost my phone, so I couldn't contact anybody, and then I had to… leave for a bit."

When I put it like that, it sounds so horribly down-scaled and as though I didn't really try to look for him. I did, in the ways I could at the time, but nothing came up. Eventually, I'd given up, just like my father wanted me to. I was young anyway—what Jaxon and I had wasn't supposed to mean anything, I would try to tell myself. But that never stopped me from latching onto the idea of seeing him again like an eight-armed tentacled octopus and refusing to let go.

He stares at me with something I cannot decipher, and I wonder if he remembers. The memory of what I did, of how desperate I was and what happened as a result, always fills my mouth with a bad taste. *That wasn't me*, I'll insist in my mind, except it was, and I wish I could go back and help that girl deal with her demons better, help her to not feel so alone.

"I'm so sorry for what happened when you looked," I continue. "That never should've happened to you."

He frowns, eyes far away. "What never should've happened to me?"

Staring, I puzzle out his words, remembering how my father said he "dealt" with him so he'd stop looking. Had that all been a lie?

I shake my head, wondering if I should tell him what my father said he did, but then think better of it. That would only lead to more questions I'm not willing to answer. "Me disappearing like that without at least a goodbye."

"I never would've accepted a goodbye anyway."

Shaking my head and laughing, I expel a breath and hug him, relieved. I'm sure he has questions, and I have my own, but it's probably better to leave it in the past. In the back of my mind, a voice insists that the coincidences of meeting him again are too odd, that there's more to dig up, but I don't want to. Not now and maybe not ever.

Maybe it's because I don't want to tell him anything else. That a few months ago, he probably wouldn't have recognized me, reacting as though everything was a novel experience. Being outside, seeing streets bustling with people, knocking into someone, and *touching* people again had all been so shocking. I'd never realized the importance of touching others, until it'd been taken away for years.

As he wraps his arms back around me, I sink into his warm embrace, welcoming it, loving how he smells and how he plays with my hair. He's still a little wet from his shower, the water seeping into my clothes, but I don't care.

"What about you? What have you been up to?" I ask the question I've been wanting to for so long, as though finally allowing myself to learn more about him.

"Made some poor life choices here and there, and some good ones, changed my last name, am deciding if I want to change my first name to my birth name too, went no contact with my guardians when they couldn't respect the name change, and you know, started my phD."

My finger traces patterns across his skin as I absorb everything, trying to imagine how he must've felt through doing all of that. "I'm so, so proud of you. What's your birth name?"

"Shu'ayb."

The syllables roll over his tongue, some soft, while others are harsh, like the "a," his Arabic fluent. Or at least, I'm sure that's what my mother would've told him. I test it out, though I can tell from his expression that I get it wrong. He laughs and shakes his head.

He presses a point on my throat, the skin-to-skin contact brief and soft. "'*Ayn* is a mid-throat letter, it comes from here, when you say the 'ay in Shu'ayb. You sort of tighten your throat but make it a deeper... 'a'? I don't really know how to explain it. And then after that, it's more soft with the 'y,' like you make it less harsh."

He repeats the name again, taking my hand and placing it on his throat so I can feel where the *'ayn* is coming from. I try it again, and after a few back and forths and me doing it wrong enough that I hurt my throat, I finally get it right.

"Shu'ayb."

The name is definitely different from Jaxon, and I imagine him going through with changing it. It would certainly take some getting used to, but in the end, they're both him. The difference is that one was a name given at birth, the other one fitted over him like an ill-suited mask until it eventually became his.

"I could get used to that name again if you keep on pronouncing it like that. Makes it sound special."

"Everything about you is special." I yawn against his chest, wondering if I'm sleepy because it's late, or because his voice rumbling against me lulls me.

Which is a shame, because I want to ask him so many things. I want to know how he changed his last name, if he felt people treated him differently afterward, and all the nuances of his birth name. I want to find and collect the grander and minute details like a hoarder.

"Is that all the romance books talking, or are you just trying to get me to kiss you again?"

I slap his arm, though it comes off more like a pat, and my glasses are awkwardly tilted with my face against him. He's still very much only in a towel, though neither of us mind. I wouldn't mind *at all* if he chooses to spend the rest of his time around me in only a towel.

"Shut up and accept my sappy compliment," I mumble, sighing when he laughs.

Grabbing my shoulders, he steers me out of the bathroom, and I register that he's taking me to my room. I grab his hand and shake my head, pointing to his bedroom.

"Can we share tonight?" And every night afterward, I don't say.

Brushing my hair from my face, he kisses my forehead, like touching me is easy. Like the entire time, he's held himself back, and now I've let him loose. "Of course. Though I should've known you have a naughty side."

I roll my eyes and push him to the bathroom—he doesn't so much as budge, of course, body too big for me to manhandle him. "Go put on some clothes."

Laughing, he slips into the bathroom, not bothering to close the door, and I go to my room, quickly changing into something more comfortable. Staring at my pajamas, I realize I can just wear the baggy shirt, and no sweatpants. He *is* warm, and I would hate to wake up tomorrow all sweaty and bothered. Before I can think too much about it, I pull down the sweatpants, toss them on the bed, and make a beeline for his bedroom.

He's in his bedroom, opening a drawer in the armoire, and I take his distraction as an opportunity to dive under the covers.

"Hi," I squeak.

That he's only wearing sweatpants doesn't help either. Even though it's more clothes than the towel, my eyes roam over him, enjoying the way various muscles in his back ripple and flex as he looks for something in the dresser. My hands itch to touch him, or reach for a brush, paints, and render his likeness on a canvas.

When he turns around, it's with a raised brow at my evident nervousness, and I look away, taking in his room. It's similar to mine, but bigger, with a closet, and a few paintings and sketches on the walls. The style is familiar, and I know that those are his pieces. In the corner of one wall is a hazel-brown desk, and I can see the titles of his textbooks and a few pens neatly tucked to the side.

His entire room is like that—neat and organized, with everything having its place, no doubt. The desk, armoire, and bedside table look like they're all from the same specific line of furniture, the styles matching, everything in colors of hazel and moss green. The only out-of-place thing is the bright lava lamp he has perched on his desk.

"You are *not* going to decorate the bed with throw pillows tomorrow," he murmurs as he slides under the covers.

I try to keep my breathing rate normal. *You're a mature adult in your twenties, Layla,* I tell myself. *Not a hormone-controlled teenager. You will not attack him over the night.*

I inch a little closer to him, wanting him to wrap his arms around me and become my personal pillow and bed. "But they're *throw pillows.* They're a needed decoration."

"With twenty little pillows, it'll be a headache making the bed every morning."

"Not twenty, more like four. If we're going to share this bed, said bed needs throw pillows."

His arm snags around my waist and drags me closer until my front presses against his. My breath catches even if my body relaxes, still sleepy. He tangles his legs with mine, and the sensation of his clothed legs over my naked ones makes me feel simultaneously exposed and comforted, the material soft against my skin until I want to rub my leg against it.

"I don't care if you want to paint the walls a neon yellow that'll blind me every time I come into the room, or if you want us to have nine cats. As long as you're with me."

"I'm always with you."

Feeling bold, I prop my head on my elbow and lean a little closer, squeezing my hand on his shoulder before moving it across his chest, enjoying the way his muscles tense under my touch. His breath hitches, and he leans closer, his teasing long forgotten as he grows enthralled. I lean a little closer, and can't help the grin that spreads over my face as I firmly plant my hands on his chest... and shove.

With a shocked yelp, he topples over the bed, disappearing from my view for a moment. "What was that for?" he moans from the floor. "I didn't think you'd kick me out of my own bed when I invited you."

Laughing, I peer over the bed at him. "I didn't really think you'd fall over."

A few seconds later he crawls back onto the bed, grumbling under his breath, and grabs me by the waist, firmly squeezing me against him, giving me no room to do things like shove him. Hooking a leg over my hip, he draws me in even closer, cocooning me like the best blanket there is.

Sliding my hands across and over his waist, I snuggle in deeper, sighing deliciously at his heat. I hope he doesn't expect me to go back to my own bed after this—I will never give up this newfound heater.

Chapter 17

Causerie

I wake up to someone… tugging my hair? The movements are barely there, the hands in my hair gentle, but tugging nonetheless.

Blinking my eyes blearily, I take in the white ceiling above me before moving my gaze over the room. I frown at its unfamiliarity, from the lack of a black carpet over the floor, and the new pictures on the wall, before remembering where I am.

The memories from yesterday rush back—Jaxon in a towel, the kiss, and my insistence on sharing a bed. In the light of day, it's easy for mortification to crawl its way into my veins, and a flush takes over my skin.

Distracting myself, I look around and notice that he's right beside me, awake, but the sight of him is a blur and I fumble for my glasses.

"Good morning," he murmurs.

"Good morning," I rasp back, trying not to crawl out of my skin.

I notice the tugging again and realize my hair isn't around my neck mostly. Hadn't I kept my hair down last night? Jaxon drops his gaze to his fingers, and I do too to see that he intently and perfectly braids my hair. He doesn't let go when he's done, and instead continues to play with it, twirling the strands around his finger and unwinding them.

I stare at the braid. It's perfectly neat, all the strands in place, and even the parts look perfectly proportionate. Heck, it looks way better than how I do it.

"You know how to braid hair?" I ask the obvious. "Did you have a phase where you grew your hair long?"

He laughs. "No, though I've sometimes wanted to try for a man bun. I know how to braid hair because of the army of little girl cousins I have. If I didn't braid their hair, or the hair of their dolls just right, they'd have a full on tantrum. It was scary."

I laugh and snuggle deeper under the covers before glancing at the clock. I can stay in bed for just a little while longer. Sighing in bliss, I murmur, "You can braid hair. You should be warned that I'm keeping you now and never letting go."

To instill my point, I wrap my arms and legs around him and nestle my head in the crook of his neck, half surprised at the ease with which I touch him. I try not to moan at how wonderful it feels to be this close to him, our bodies pressed close and his body heat better than any blanket. The spot where his neck meets his shoulder is perfect, and I sigh into his skin.

"I guess it's a good thing I want to be kept, then," he rasps, arms banding around me.

Not able to help myself, I kiss his collarbone, and then higher, to his pulse. My earlier embarrassment is gone, and I explore leisurely, because he's *here*, and he's *holding* me, and I can touch him, and smell him, and taste him, and kiss him.

He skims his fingers lightly over my skin, and I shiver. "I shouldn't be able to feel that," I mumble, almost like I'm blaming my skin's sensitivity, and he does it again, skimming his hands over my back, so lightly it's almost like a feather of sensation.

He laughs. "You can thank your Meissner's corpuscles, or tactile corpuscles, for that."

"My what?"

"Meissner's corpuscles—that's a type of receptor that is responsible for sensing light touch, and it has encapsulated nerve endings."

I shake my head. "Of *course* you know that. I don't ever need a search engine if I have you. Tell me more."

"What do you want to know?"

Teasing, I kiss the corner of his mouth. "Why I want to kiss you for the *whole day*, everywhere."

He laughs, though it's rougher than normal, body shifting beneath me as he adjusts himself, and the sound vibrates into me.

"Prepare yourself for a rundown of one of my psyche lectures. The scientific reason would be because of the release of certain neurotransmitters. Dopamine is like the 'happy' neurotransmitter, or more commonly known as a part of the 'reward system.' It's one of a few that's associated with feelings of pleasure and happiness. When you do things that make you excited, or bring you pleasure, or make you happy, the neurotransmitter is released more. Like when I do this"—his hand travels from my back to my front, inching up slowly—"you're getting excited, and your body is responding, and now more dopamine, along with other neurotransmitters, like oxytocin, are released." His hand inches higher, and I think I've forgotten how to breathe. "Though certain amino acids can also influence their production, and your dopamine can be transformed into the brain chemicals norepinephrine and—"

I cut him off, kissing him smack on the lips. He growls low in his throat, his hands moving to cup my face as he tilts his head and kisses me back deeper. His lips are soft, but he kisses me hard, thorough, until every nerve ending is aflame, little fireworks going off in my blood. Fireworks in my mind, fireworks in his eyes.

When air becomes a need, I pull away, breathing hard. "That was irresistibly attractive. Keep spewing interesting facts and I'll be on you in no time."

He shakes his head a little, smiling softly, before rolling over to the other side of the bed and getting off, robbing me of his delicious scent and heat. I pout, and he smooths my lips with a frown.

"Are you *trying* to make us late?" he admonishes. "Don't look so tempting in my bed."

I laugh as he goes to the bathroom, stretching across his covers before reaching for my phone. My first inclination is to tell Harlow that her wish has been answered.

I wonder how she's finding the city so far, and how her visits to the hospital are going. Tapping the call button, I make the bed while the phone trills. She picks up after the fourth ring, her voice breathless.

"Hi, Layla. Are you going to tell me that you two are planning to make me an aunt?"

She's quiet, and I can practically see her smile when the pieces click. I roll my eyes.

"So that's what all this is about. You just want me to get with Jaxon so you can be an aunt. Honestly, now you're acting like a mom who wants grandkids. It's creepy."

She laughs, and I don't miss the voice in the background that... cheers? And then there are the whispered words, "I *knew* you could laugh. It's a pretty cute laugh, like your five-foot-tall self. You should know that I've now taken it up as my personal mission to make you laugh. I could bottle the stuff and sell it."

I almost choke on my own spit. And not because someone just used words that would melt any normal woman, but because she hasn't punched him. At least I don't think so—not yet. But someone's clearly trying to charm Harlow. The same Harlow who dragged a guy out of a club, twisting his ear, because he was hitting on someone aggressively. And when she's the one being catcalled? I pity whoever is stupid enough to do that.

"Don't you dare," she starts, as if she can hear my thoughts. "We're still on you."

I open my mouth to argue, but she's already talking again. "Now, since you're calling me at this time, when you're usually dead and getting ready, I can only assume that you have news for me. *Great* news. Jaxon-related news."

"Who's Jaxon?" the person in the background asks, a tint of envy in his tone.

I move the phone closer to my mouth and holler, "Don't worry, Harlow's not interested in him."

She growls. "Men. They'll get jealous over their own kids if they feel that their partner is spending too much time with them. My dad got jealous over my mom's *plants* one time. Her *plants*. Anyway, update me on the Jaxon-and-Layla status. Can I make a ship name at least, if you're not going to let me plan your wedding?"

She's probably planning the baby shower already. I take a deep breath. "We talked, and I think I... moved into his room? We kissed," I say it in a rush, the words meshed together, and I sound like I've swallowed a helium balloon.

She catches it all anyway, and is quiet for a whole minute before she squeals loud enough to break my eardrums.

"I *knew* it. Welcome to the light, you sorry, sad human."

I roll my eyes. "Harlow. I gave you details. It's your turn now." Since she's a tough nut to crack, I holler into the speaker, hoping whoever he is can hear me, "Hey, what are your intentions with my non-blood-related sister?"

There's some jostling, a shriek, and then I know the phone's no longer in Harlow's hands. "Hi, Layla. I'm Damon McKnight." *Of course* it's someone with a hot name. I mentally high-five Harlow. "My intentions with your best friend range from gentlemanly to fantasies your grandmother would probably faint at."

"Nah, my grandmother was pretty wild."

"Okay then, she'd *love* the fantasies I occasionally have about your best friend."

"You're so dead," I hear Harlow hiss in the background. "So very dead. If you were wise, you'd go and start digging your own grave, because you won't like what I will put in it."

"See?" Damon says. "Harlow likes my fantasies, too. If she didn't, she'd have kicked me already."

Whoever this guy is, he's figured out Harlow well. She looks and talks like she's a razor-sharp knife, but in reality, she's a cinnamon roll. A bitter, plastic cinnamon roll, but still. "When did you two meet?" I grill.

He hums. "Maybe four hours ago?"

Well that's *kind* of worrisome. "And you want to... what? Harvest her organs? Get in her bed?"

"No, I only have the best intentions with your best friend. I'll make her like me, you'll see. She's so… *feisty*, even though she barely reaches my sternum."

Thanks to the *Ow* I hear, I know she's punched him.

"I'm giving you the standard speech now. Hurt her, I'll hunt you. Use her, I'll hunt you. Treat her badly, I'll hunt you. I'll make you rue the day you were born."

Jaxon exits the bathroom, looking a little worried at my threats, before pointing at the clock. "Want to ditch?" he mouths, though I know he doesn't want to. I doubt he's ever skipped classes, and I'm not going to on my first term either.

I shake my head. "Alright Damon, good luck on winning the demon over, and Harlow, try not to kill him."

I hang up, kiss Jaxon quickly on the lips, and dash to grab a change of clothes. From what happened yesterday, to Harlow potentially getting in a relationship with a guy she hasn't chewed up and spat—yet—I am sure I am in a dream; one I don't want to wake up from.

"Dirt-track racing doesn't seem that crazy for you."

Side-eyeing me, he narrows his eyes, but quickly looks back to the road at my glare. Laughing, I ease farther into the seat, my hand tracing over his knuckles. It's like I've had a pent-up need to touch him, and now that I can, it's all I do. I'm always touching him, either tracing his skin, or kissing his cheek, or squeezing his hand.

"So, how did you and Harlow meet?" he asks. "She's scary but almost in a cute way sometimes. Don't tell her I said that."

I puff out a laugh. "We met online, some group thing," I answer vaguely. "We hit it off after talking about songs, books, and the cruelty of the world."

"What about Aaradhya?" he murmurs. "You two stayed in touch?"

I freeze a little at her name, wondering like I occasionally do of what she thought when I suddenly disappeared. "No. The last I saw her was right before winter break that year."

"Do you still miss her?"

"Sometimes."

I miss her in the way one misses their childhood—nostalgic, but aware that they've grown out of that skin. When did it change from missing her to having a nondescript nostalgia? For weeks, in that big, empty house, I'd miss how she always had remarks about someone "tasting" like day-old expired milk, or sweet as fake perfume, and then that one time one of our classmates was apparently "spot-outlined." I miss stealing her lunch sometimes, *biryani* and *haleem*, and how she would try, but promptly give up, teaching me Hindi.

"I have a friend who's really good with tech stuff. And Aaradhya Navaid is a pretty original name, so he shouldn't have a hard time finding her. She could just be a phone call away—for tying loose ends' sake. If you want to."

He means I *could* talk to her, if I really wanted to, that it's not that hard. I could at least tell her that I didn't fall off the face of the planet when I disappeared.

So I nod, and file away the idea.

"Back to you—tell me more."

Like everything when it comes to him, I'm hungry for more. I want to know what keeps him up at night, what brings a smile to his lips every time, and what he's obsessed with. One would think too much time had passed and we'd be too different now, but I love the ways in which he's different.

He's more confident, more sure of himself, and I can see it in everything. But there's still that pain that lingers behind his eyes sometimes, and something new and dark in them, something that tells me he went through something. I don't push, knowing it'd make me a hypocrite.

"I joined a band once, on a reckless whim, and one time, I was coerced enough that Mike, a friend of mine, got me to get a tat."

I frown, remembering last night when he was in a towel. I didn't see the tattoo then. Before I can ask, he notes my expression and says, "On the hip bone, low."

Well that explains it. "What is it?" I ask.

We're almost at the school campus, and I take a greedier gulp from the coffee cup in my hands. It's not strong, but delicious all the same—because of course he makes great coffee too.

He's silent, and I fight to keep the grin off my face. Now I really want to see it if it's making him embarrassed.

"Tell me," I urge.

I can swear his cheeks tint pink. "As strange as it sounds… It's the outline of a bird in flames."

"Why a bird in flames? And that's not too bad."

"It's a cartoon bird," he mumbles. "The angry one."

"Oh."

Unable to help myself, I laugh, imagining an over six feet, ripped Jaxon with a little cartoon bird on his hip. From what I *clearly* remember last night, he has the kind of body that one only gets from dedication, hard work, sweat, and pain. Pair that exterior with a cartoon bird and it's no wonder that I'm struggling to keep my laughter in.

He scowls at me a little before looking back ahead of him as he pulls into the parking lot. "Why is it more expensive to get rid of a tattoo than actually get it?" he mutters, mostly to himself.

Still laughing, I reach over, pecking his cheek with a kiss after he turns off the ignition. Turning to the side, he rasps, "Can I get a proper kiss?"

At my eager nod, he kisses me, tilting his head and roughly deepening the kiss, devouring me. I'm not laughing or thinking about cartoon birds now. Instead, my hands reach over to fist his shirt, fingers grasping as though I might reach into his chest and touch his heart.

Every rough roll of his tongue against mine has me moaning and the muscles low in my stomach clenching, and I am reduced to a creature of *want*. He's making wicked promises with every glide of his tongue and every nip of his teeth… until he abruptly pulls away.

He gazes at me with a dark hunger that elicits a shiver before glancing at the clock. "I have a feeling that you and your lips are going to do very bad things to my punctuality and grades. Very, very bad things."

I think I actually pout, even though I also have classes I need to get to. With a growl, he leans over, harshly nips my lower lip like he can't resist, and practically hurls himself out the car.

Grinning, I follow, glancing around the empty parking lot. The campus is practically dead at this time of the year, and I can almost count the cars on this floor. In any case, I'm glad there's no one to witness my embarrassingly smitten expression.

But when I spot a silhouette dressed in black, in the back of the garage, almost entirely concealed, my grin falls.

Chapter 18

Track

Some say that when it comes to dread, or the acute feeling of being watched, it's because your subconscious is always one step ahead of you. And that sometimes, you just choose to ignore it. I'm not ignoring it right now, and somehow, that makes it worse than just pushing the gripping dread away.

The figure isn't exactly familiar, at least not in the way they look. From here, the figure seems to be male, tall with broad shoulders, but the clothes are baggy and dark. He knows I've caught him staring, but that doesn't seem to stop him, and he continues, head tilted to the side. But the acute sense of fear and dread that pull at the expanse beneath my ribs until I am sure I cannot breathe are not from his staring—I'm familiar, unfortunately, with the nature of some creeps. It's not even that he seems to be unstable, constantly shifting on his feet, as he sways a little from side to side.

No, it's because of the phone in his hands, and how he nods and talks to whoever's on the other side. He's far away and the parking garage is dark enough that I cannot see him properly, but for a moment, my mind twists, sure that he says, "Found you."

I choke on my next breath, even though a part of me insists that I am just being paranoid. I *know* I imagined it, and I know I'm imagining the danger—no one from the *cosa nostra* has found me. They *cannot*. In the face of everything from yesterday, my mind has found new ways to show me why this cannot last.

"Layla? You okay?"

I blink and see Jaxon waiting a few feet away, twirling his keys around his finger as he regards me, head tilted. I quickly grab my bag from the seat and close the door, hearing the click of the car when he locks it.

As I walk to him, I whip my head around, looking for the creepy starer only to see that no one is there. The parking lot is entirely empty, as though I imagined it all. Letting out a breath, I tell myself to calm down, and when I'm within arm's reach of Jaxon, he grabs my hand.

"You look like you've seen a ghost. Everything alright?"

I can tell he's trying to distract me, to pull me away from the thoughts that want to drag me under their ink-black tar. It doesn't work. I open my mouth and close it, trying to say something, but the words *I found you* repeat over and over in my head, even if they are not real. The familiar urge to run worms its way underneath my skin, and I want to cry, because it finally felt like I found home.

Jaxon pulls me against his side, rubbing a hand over my arm, and I can feel the heat of him through my clothes.

"Want to talk about it?" he asks as we walk toward the school buildings.

"Just a little paranoid, is all."

We both know it's more than that, but I'm not going to voice out my thoughts. That would make them seem more real, and in my head, it's easier to convince myself it's all fake. And to explain my fears would mean explaining my past, something that also needs to stay in the recesses of my mind.

He shoots me a worried glance, one I pretend not to notice, but I tighten my hold around his waist. When we're in front of the Arts and Humanities building, he quickly kisses me, so abruptly that our noses bump once and my glasses press against my eyes.

I laugh when he leans down to nip my neck, his hair tickling me, and I can feel his grin against my skin. When he pulls back, he takes my glasses with him, and I squint at his suddenly blurry image. I'm half-blind without my glasses, and probably wouldn't be able to tell a tree from a pole.

"You can't make me go the whole day without my glasses," I mumble.

In answer, he props them back on my face, sliding the bridge over my nose until I can see him again.

"Don't worry, I was just cleaning them."

Before I can thank him—and maybe melt at the gesture because I am easily enamored—he presses a quick kiss to my forehead and hurries to class. In a daze, I turn around and head into the building, unable to stop the blush that spreads over my cheeks and the grin that tugs at my lips. Already, the parking lot incident is long forgotten.

Apparently, we can't spend the winter break here—at least not all of it—according to Jaxon. He insists we should plan a getaway, and is indecisive between the beach, a recreational park, or someplace with snow.

I can't believe the semester has passed so quickly already, nor can I believe that I'm still living with him. With winter break right around the corner, our conversation acutely feels like *deja vu* from all those years ago.

Everything went to hell then, and if that one judgment heuristic is any indication, it's easy to believe there's going to be a repeat. With my fears from earlier today, it's even easier to think that way.

"This is the place of beaches and long, lazy days," he insists, pulling me from my thoughts.

"Pretty sure that's somewhere else. The beaches here are *cold* right now," I say, tapping my hands against the glass pane. "We should surprise Harlow, and then we can do whatever. Besides, aren't you spending a whole week prepping for the next semester?"

"I'm a creature of routine and vigorous study habits, let me be. And it's not like I spend the *whole* day studying. I run too. And swim. And go to the gym. Fun stuff. Not to mention, Mike's in charge of dragging me out of the apartment so I can, and I quote, 'touch grass.'"

I bark out a laugh, tipping my head back a little, trying to control the giggles that burst out of me and resisting the urge to kiss his scowling face. It goes away when he glances at me, and he grins. "What?" I ask, quieting down.

"I don't think I've seen anything more beautiful than you laughing. Well, you're beautiful all the time, but when you laugh, it's… it's *radiant*. I like seeing you comfortable with being happy around me."

Though a part of me is sure he doesn't know what he's saying, that he couldn't possibly mean it if he knew more of me, I do understand. Because every time *he* smiles or laughs, I can feel myself growing a little obsessed, a greedy desire settling in my heart.

"Okay, wow. Do you want to change my contact name to 'radiant sun' then? Radiant Layla? Do you want a picture of me smiling for the contact card?"

He side-eyes me before muttering, "I'd actually like the picture, thank you very much."

Snickering, I reach over and peck his cheek for the millionth time, smiling when the edges of his ears turn pink. "Okay. But thank you, I think that's the sweetest thing anyone's ever said to me. And I find your smile *addicting*. Especially the dimple."

Smirking, he highlights said dimple, and I peck his cheek again, right over it.

I don't even notice that we've reached the apartment until he turns the car around and starts reversing. And I only notice because he moves his hand to the back of my seat with the other on the steering wheel. For some unknown reason, there is something so wonderfully, effortlessly attractive about seeing him reverse the car with one hand. The way his hand splays across the steering wheel, body half tilted toward me and arm close to me as he looks behind him does *interesting* things to me. It's one of those anomalies and things men can pull off without even trying.

My new weakness is Jaxon wearing hoodies or reversing the car.

He still smells like his shampoo from the morning, the scent stronger than his cologne, making it a mix of musk, cedarwood, and what I think is sage. Whatever it is, it's stronger now that he's closer, head turned as he looks behind him, one hand gripping the back of my seat. He's all ease and concentration, broad shoulders and sharp jawline.

I'm kind of disappointed when all too soon, he looks back to his front and turns the ignition off.

His jaw is slightly clenched, grip tighter around the steering. "Layla. You can't keep looking at me like that. I can only imagine what's going on in your head right now."

I blink innocently. "I don't know what you're talking about."

Turning to look at me, he raises a brow, seemingly unfazed, even though that hungry look is back in his eyes, making me shiver. "You sure you want to play that game?"

Leaning closer, I trace the edge of his collar, close enough that I can see the dark amber in his eyes, mesmerized at the way they grow hooded, head tilting to mirror mine. Just as I am about to lean in further and kiss him, I abruptly pull away, grabbing the door handle.

"What game?" I call over my shoulder as I open the door.

He practically lunges for me and with a shriek, I'm out the door, bag in my hands, and running for the apartment room. I don't even bother with the elevator, instead taking the stairs.

I hear the door open behind me when I'm halfway to the next floor, and when he calls my name, a warning in his tone, I let out another shriek and run harder.

By the time I get to the apartment, I'm laughing and shaking, quickly rushing inside, dropping my bag onto the floor. I don't even get to close the door behind me before Jaxon shoulders inside. Grabbing my waist, he pushes me against the wall, body firm and warm against mine, his gaze piercing.

"I didn't realize this was the game," I murmur, still smiling.

His hands move higher, brushing over my ribs, thumbs swiping beneath the curve of my breasts, and I suck in a breath before his hands move to my arms and then my hands. He grips them and moves them up to the sides of my head, until my back arches a little.

I'm definitely not laughing now, and my eyes grow hooded, my breathing coming in shorter breaths, excitement making my body shake. He leans his head down until his breath fans the side of my neck before his lips brush against my skin as he speaks.

"That wasn't very nice, Layla."

They're innocent enough words, but his scent and voice alone, husky and deep, makes my body tighten further.

I gasp when he nibbles my skin, lips soft and teeth hard, the sensations at war with each other. He trails higher and higher, until he's at the corners of my mouth, and I'm wantonly shivering in anticipation over a *kiss*. What has this man done to me?

He keeps teasing me though, as if punishing me for my earlier antics. I still don't regret them. Even when he presses against me closer, a knee sliding between mine.

"Jaxon," I beg, tilting my head to the side and trying to capture his lips in a kiss.

He evades me, the grip on my wrists tightening, and I can practically feel his grin against my skin. He hums in reply, the sound reverberating into me. "Hmm?"

"You can't do this to me and then *not* kiss me."

"I can't?"

Apparently, he thinks he can, since he keeps doing it, the leg between mine spreading them apart before pushing up.

"No. You're making me all hot and bothered and not doing anything about it."

He tsks. "Shame. We wouldn't want that now, would we?"

I wait, my chest brushing his with every deep breath I take, and wait some more. "Jaxon," I practically whine.

"So greedy," he praises, voice low, but he doesn't disappoint.

His lips crash against mine hard, and instantly, he draws my lower lip into his mouth and nips it roughly. I moan in approval, shaking from the position, my feet arched as I'm pushed against the wall, hands still above my head, and kiss him back just as fervidly. His hands drop from my wrists to cradle my face, holding me gently as if I'm precious, even as he ravages me.

My calves hurt from standing on the tips of my toes to reach him, and the effect he has on me only makes it worse. I'm wound tight everywhere but melting at the same time.

I love how he presses against me, until he is all I can feel, but I love it even more when he grabs my waist and slides my body higher up the wall, urging me to wrap my legs around his hips, bringing him closer.

There are countless places of contact between us, and each one has me plunging deeper, lost to the world.

I can't get enough, I never want to get enough, and he growls when I free my hands to plunge my fingers into his hair, but the hands on me are gentle.

"So beautiful," he rasps when he breaks away to breathe, one hand moving to cradle the back of my head, fingers splaying in my hair. "You always seem so innocent with your wide eyes and large owl glasses, but I know better, don't I?"

He nips my ear when I don't give him an answer. "Do I?"

"Maybe." It comes out low and scratchy, like I haven't used my voice in a long time, and my heart beats a wild crescendo.

He strokes my hair and I lean into him more, my hands sliding from his hair to over his biceps as I drop my head to his shoulder. He's still pressed against me, making me ache and tempted to writhe, but I like this moment too much. I like the way it makes my heart fuller, as if it'll burst apart at the seams.

"You know, I would think about you a lot, but I never thought it'd be like this," I murmur as he pushes off from the wall, his arms traveling down, one encompassing my waist, and the other curving under my hips as he walks to the couch, settling with me on his lap.

"Like what?"

Wrapping my arms around his shoulders, my legs on either side of his waist, I settle into him. "Easy, I guess? I don't doubt, not with you, and wanting you and being with you is as easy as breathing."

He smiles that smile again, and I kiss his dimple, because I can. Eventually, he smirks, that crooked incisor coming to view. "You would think of me?"

"More than I probably should have, until I'd imagine things."

He hums, moving closer until his lips brush against mine, and I worry I've awakened an insatiable part of him, that he will now find every excuse to put his mouth on mine. I find that I do not mind.

"What kind of things?"

In the end, I'm the one who needs any excuse to touch him, kissing him just like I imagined I would.

Chapter 19

Sarnies

Minutes or hours later, I lie over him, and shiver as he rakes his hands across my ribs, fingers light before becoming more insistent. Eventually, he's just full-on tickling me, and squirming, I yank his hands from under my shirt.

"Behave," I admonish, leaning back down to rest my head against the nook of his shoulder.

He does, for a while, before he starts to shift with that restless energy of his. Giving up, he sits up, arms around my waist as I wind my legs around his, and strolls to the kitchen. "What's your take on a grilled cheese sandwich with some jalapeño?"

"Sounds amazing. But I'm not hungry, you don't need to make anything. I'd hate to... impose."

More than I already have, I don't say.

He raises a brow as he sets me on the counter, stepping into the space between my thighs, the ease of his proximity pumping languid excitement into my veins. "You slept in my bed last night, I've kissed you more times than I can count, you've unofficially moved into my bedroom, and you're worried you're going to *impose?* Do I need to kiss some sense into you?"

I like that idea. "Yes, please."

He shakes his head, though he can't hide a little smile, and moves to the fridge. He rummages around, cursing Mike under his breath, before grabbing a few things. Kicking my feet lazily in the air, I watch him cut a slice of butter and put it on the pan.

Instantly, it sizzles, and the oily, rich smell of the butter permeates the air before he places the bread flat on the pan. I alternate between watching the food and watching him cook— admittedly, I do the latter much more. The way his long fingers deftly layer everything as he cooks, with his sleeves rolled up, leaving those strong forearms with their slightly raised veins and evident tendons on full display, is sublimely attractive.

I almost don't notice when he's done, scooping the two sandwiches from the pan and placing them on plates. I moan a little at the smell wafting from them—the perfect aroma of melted cheese, sharp spices, and starchy bread. But mostly, I moan because I don't miss the way it makes him tense up a little.

After diagonally cutting the sandwich in half, he places the plate in my lap. "Eat—you don't eat enough. Or drink enough water either."

I roll my eyes. "Why does everyone keep saying that? And I'm an adult, thank you very much, who eats fine."

"Eat the sandwich, Layla."

"You first."

He rolls his eyes, cuts a piece and eats it, movements perfunctory. I watch as he swipes his lower lip with his tongue, watching me look at him. He has his hands braced on the counter at either side of my hips, body angled toward me, making him a little more at my level.

"Your turn."

I hum, watching his lips that are still a little swollen from my kisses minutes ago, and he bites his lower lip. He can't expect me to *not* kiss him, looking like this. "I have a better idea."

It takes no time at all for me to put the plate aside, wind my legs around his hips and crash my lips against his. He tastes like the grilled sandwich and his signature taste, and this is infinitely better than eating said sandwich.

I pull away before he can take control of the kiss, mainly because I'm sure the front door just opened. At his bewildered expression, I say, "This is a lot more fun, no?"

"Jaxon, why do you have someone wrapped around you like a monkey? And why in the *kitchen*? I mean, anyone could just *walk* in here."

We both turn to see someone standing in the doorway of the kitchen, and I know I should probably unwrap my limbs from around Jaxon, but I really don't want to.

Jaxon rolls his eyes. "That's why we knock, Mike. Knocking is key. And it's not like you live here. You just like to randomly barge in since you stole a key set and made a copy of it. Psycho."

Mike glares at him, eyes narrowed threateningly as he pockets the key and then pats it. "Keep at it and I'll tell the frat house that they can come here."

Grinning, he shifts his attention to me. Jaxon tries to move out of my grip, but I still have my legs wrapped around his hips, and he doesn't give much of a fight.

"So you're the famous Mike. Jaxon's told me about you."

He grins wider, revealing white, straight teeth and a dimple on his chin. He seems to be of mixed heritage, eyes reminding me of Harlow's with the epicanthal fold, but at a better glance, have a more tear-drop shape to them, light tawny skin, a lean but swimmer's build frame, and an afro with gold and red streaks. "All despicable things, I hope."

"I thank you for your service of making sure Jaxon touches grass and competing with him at the gym."

He gives a mock bow. "Of course. Had to make sure he has the kind of arms a girl likes."

I glance at Jaxon's biceps and appreciate them a little, my ogling obvious. "I'm one lucky girl then."

"Really?" Jaxon drawls. "It's my arms that make you lucky? So it's all at body value?"

"I knew you when you were a scrawny teenager, remember?" I say, tugging his hair.

Mike fake-gags. "Keep the cute mushy stuff to the bedroom, okay?"

"Go away. I don't have any food for you, okay?"

"Whoa, whoa. Be nice, or else if the IRB approves your study in the future, I'll do an anonymous report that your study has a conflict of interest, and that you're causing your participants undue harm."

Jaxon grows still. "You wouldn't *dare*. It'll take *weeks* for them to approve the protocol. If I have to stay another year to finish my dissertation, I *will* shave your head."

They go back and forth, until I raise my hand. "Undergraduate here. What's an IRB?"

"You're dating an *undergraduate*, Jaxon? The horror. The travesty. I didn't know you preyed on people like this." He turns to me. "An IRB is every research student's pain and nightmare. Are they necessary? Yes. If I want to study the rate of internalized racism for one or both heritages in bi-racial children—cool stuff, I know—I need to submit a protocol for IRB approval. But do I want to rip my hair out just looking at the process? Also yes. Also, I can take you to the title nine office, if you want, to report Jaxon, because—"

"There's barely a two-year age gap between us, shut up. But, I am her tutor," Jaxon interrupts. "Anyway, an IRB basically approves human-subject research, which is *very* necessary, for ethical reasons."

"Her *tutor*?" Mike screeches.

At that, a heated discussion starts, centering on how Mike is adamant that Jaxon is a predator and won't leave until he cooks something for his deprived friend.

At one point, I give up on following the argument and excuse myself when my phone rings. I grin when I see that it's Harlow, even though there's practically no one else who'd be calling.

"You're a godsend, Harlow," I start. "Mike, Jaxon's—"

"Ma'am," an unfamiliar voice cuts me off, dripping with professionalism and a clearly prepared apology. "I'm Anna, a nurse at the UCSF Medical Center."

Immediately, my fingers start to shake, breath stalling, even as my mind scrambles to pick up her words, as though my body already knows what I refuse to believe. I want to tell her I don't care who she is, or where she works. I just want to know why she *called me.*

"I'm calling you because you're listed as an additional contact, and her parents are not picking up."

I want to tell her, again, that I don't care. That I hate how she's pausing, like she's waiting for me to brace for the news or process everything when I just want the bandage ripped off. *She can't be dead, she can't be dead.* She was supposed to be getting better. She went to San Francisco to make her fibrosis *less* serious, not to—

"What happened?" There's no hiding the snap in my tone, one that hides the desperation.

"She almost died," the nurse said bluntly. "Possibly dying, the doctors aren't a hundred percent sure, though. She's in a critical situation."

Now *that's* ripping off the bandage.

The *not knowing* is the worst thing in all of this. Not knowing if Harlow will survive is like hanging on a precipice while holding on to very little. It's hoping and dreading all in one, and there is nothing worse than building on hope. Adding to it and keeping a tight grip, squeezing and grasping vainly, only to find out that you were holding onto nothing all along.

It's not really realizing what "she almost died" and is "possibly dying" could mean.

"Layla, breathe for me. Come on, deep breath."

I don't even realize that I'm panicking until Jaxon shakes me out of my stupor, and I'm glad again that he managed to get me to sit in the passenger seat and not drive.

I try to do as he says, taking in a deep breath and then another, but what does it really matter when she could be *dead*?

"Layla, breathe, we're almost there. She'll be fine."

"But she's still in a critical situation," I rush out, counting on my hands. One, two, three, four. One, two, three, four.

She, quite literally, saved me. She made sure I had the means to come here, away from my past. She gave me a new life, and she could be *dying*.

The back of my eyes burn with unshed tears, and my throat clogs up as my chest fills with a medley of emotions, making my lungs heavy.

Every joke, every time we stuck up for each other or she bossed me around or we made each other laugh, plays in my head as Jaxon gets off the highway and into the denser part of the city.

The GPS voice is monotonous and automated, filling the deafening silence, and I vaguely notice that we've reached the hospital.

As soon as the car halts to a stop, I'm hurling myself out and running to the building. I hear Jaxon lock the car before hurrying after me, though I'm already at the hospital, the automatic glass doors sliding open as I bound inside, almost bumping into someone.

Calming down, I compose myself and walk to the receptionist's desk.

"How can I help you, ma'am?"

"We're here to visit Harlow Arita. She was admitted sometime today, I believe, in the ICU," Jaxon says as he stands next to me, getting the words out much more calmly than I'd ever be able to.

Reaching over, he grabs my hand and squeezes it reassuringly.

The receptionist nods. "And you are...?"

I don't know if we have to be family to visit, since it's within the visiting hours right now, but I still say, "I'm her sister. Her half sister." The half part should explain why we look nothing alike, right? I wave my hands to Jaxon. "He's my boyfriend."

The receptionist looks to the screen in front of him, and I hear the clacking of the keyboard as he works before looking back at me.

"You can't visit her now, as the doctors and nurses are still with her, but you can wait in the waiting room outside of where she is. Her room is number two-one-four on the second floor."

Jaxon thanks him, his hand tightening on mine as he turns and tugs me to the elevator. The ride in the elevator is quiet, but Jaxon has me pressed to his side, no hesitation as he wraps an arm around my shoulders and rubs a hand up and down my arm.

Once out of the elevator, the sterilized smell of the hospital that seems to cling to everything, the nurses, the machines, the chairs, makes everything so much more real. Everything is white and overly lit, the lighting reflecting off of the shining tiles. It's almost blinding.

A hospital can always seem to be a somber place despite the miracles that happen here every day. Some lives are saved, and others are born, yet no one's ever really *cheerful* to be in a hospital. Everyone is somber, nurses and doctors working, families visiting, and of course, us.

After finding Harlow's door, we go back to the waiting area down the hall. There's a low table in the center of the room, scattered with magazines and other things to entertain people while they try not to tear their hair out with worry or throw a chair at the television with a *way* too cheerful spokesperson trying to sell an insurance plan.

Or maybe that's just me.

I plop down on one of the chairs, pulling my hair away from my face and taking off my glasses even though it makes the world blurry, turning all the edges and details into nothing more than fuzzy shapes. Now I won't be able to pay attention to anything specific and contemplate breaking it.

Instead, I can stew in my thoughts.

I wonder what happened to her to warrant a hospital visit. How bad was it? Did she start having breathing problems? Did her airways block? I can't believe that before today, I never *really* knew the full extent of her illness.

She never seemed like someone who has to deal with that every day, and with all of the advancing technology and medicine that saves her health, I never really thought it'd take her away from me. Surely she had visits to the doctor over the months, frequent enough that they were monitoring her closely, or did she not? And where was Damon?

Unable to sit, going slowly mad in my head as I wonder about Damon and her, what could've happened, and how I should've been there, I get up, placing my glasses back on. At Jaxon's inquisitive glance, I tell him I'm going to the vending machine.

It doesn't take me long to find it, my shoes squeaking over the tiles as I walk down the halls. The machine is slightly whirring, and behind the glass, it seems that all the healthier foods are nearly out, while the soda and chocolates are stacked.

It just means more chocolate for Harlow and me. I take out four bars, one for me and three for her, because when—not if—I see her again, she's going to demand chocolate.

I almost choke on a sob that threatens to break free, but push it back down, focusing on the chocolate. She better get better, because no way am I eating more than one bar of the candy when it's not in my favorite flavor. The false bravado doesn't help much, but it's enough for me to pay for the chocolates, pocket them, and head back.

Again, I'm so lost in my thoughts, my head filling with answers only Harlow can give me, that I accidentally bump into someone, their shoulder pushing me back roughly.

I'm about to murmur an apology before the hands, large and abrasive, grip my forearms, and even though he's probably only steadying me, I rear back, fear suddenly wrapping its icy fingers around my throat. Everything slows down in the face of it, that familiar mantra repeating in my head. *Hide, hide, hide, and don't let them see you.*

Humored, but wild eyes peer into me, the pupils blown wide enough that I think he's on something. "Emergency, princess?"

As quick as he grabbed me, he lets me go and saunters past, whistling carefree, that I almost think I imagined the whole thing.

Almost.

As I catch my breath, I head back to the waiting room, trying not to run or glance over my shoulder. I can't help but catalogue his accent, sure that it is similar to mine.

Except I tell myself that my mind is playing tricks on me and bury it all inside.

Just like I always do.

Chapter 20

Hospitals

It's as though forever passes, the minutes excruciatingly long, before a nurse comes into the waiting room, asking if I'm Layla. As I stand, my "yes" is rushed, until it's obvious that I'm brimming with nervousness.

The nurse, a man who almost seems fresh out of nursing school, smiles, telling us that yes, Harlow is alive and well—or recovering—and that she can see us now.

He doesn't need to tell me twice, and as I leave the room, Jaxon grabs my hand again, easily tugging me close. I haven't been with him for long, and yet, it's as easy as breathing to lean into his warmth. I take a deep breath, finally feeling like I can calm down.

Now I can throttle her for scaring the life out of me.

When we walk in, the doctor is finishing off with Harlow, telling her that after they monitor her for a few more hours and take another blood and saliva sample, then they'll discharge her.

On the medical bed, dressed in a hospital gown, she looks somehow tinier than she actually is. The pillows behind her swallow her small frame, with the blanket wrapped around her huddled body, encompassing her.

Her face is paler than normal, making the few freckles she has over her nose and cheeks more prominent, her collarbones protrude more than I think is healthy, and she looks achingly bone-weary in a way that goes beyond the physical.

Harlow grins at me, despite how tired she is. The first thing she notices is Jaxon holding my hand. She cheers, and it ends in a raspy cough, but she keeps the fake bravado. "I've been shipping you two for forever! So—I want details."

"It doesn't work that way," I say, trying not to snap.

She nearly died, and then she tries to joke it off. And some things aren't adding up.

"So, are they giving you any different treatment?" I ask.

She waves her hand dismissively. "Nope. Same thing."

"And are you going to the Cystic Fibrosis Center here afterward?"

"That fancy center a few miles down? No way. I'm not going to be their guinea pig."

Harlow's always been so paranoid, I almost roll my eyes. Almost. Instead, I grip the railing on the foot of her bed.

"So then why did you come here if you've never set foot in the Cystic Fibrosis Center and would never be their 'guinea pig,' when you told me that you're coming here for better medication and to participate in their clinical trials?"

Jaxon slowly starts backing out of the room, and I figure that's probably a wise move. Harlow's face pales a little further as realization dawns on her. But I'm not done yet.

"You had a feeling, didn't you? You didn't come here for any test treatment they 'offered' you, which they didn't. You came because you had a feeling, or worse, you *wanted* it, and you always said the closest place you'd want to die in would be in a big city, overlooking the bay."

Hysteria and panic at the thought of her dying have set in, until I don't care about the venom in the words I spew, even if she's alright. I imagine a world without her in it, my closest friend, and all I can think is *no*. Worse, the insidious part of my mind tells me that this is my fate in life—to always lose those around me, and even though she doesn't know my history, the hysteria morphs into reproach, into *How could you let me lose you too?*

"You came here to, literally, *die*. Were you never going to tell me? What if you *did* die, Harlow? Were we all going to never know until we got a call or a death certificate? Why is it that you're always advocating about the normalcy of death, yet don't ever let anyone really in, or tell them what's going on? How could you do that?"

How could you do that to me?

And if in the face of what she's done I've grown bitter, so has she in the aftermath of my words. Every muscle in her body is drawn tight, hands desperately fisted over the blankets until her knuckles bleed white, and her sable eyes radiate such broken anger, they shine.

"Stop," she spits. "*Making it about you.* About what my death would've done to *you*, and how it's not fair on *you*, and how it's such a damn inconvenience for me to be so *inconsiderate*. Because you *have no idea* what it's like to live this way. You're always so sick of being in your head, doubting, when you don't even realize how *lucky* you are.

"And I tell you and everyone that I don't really care, that it doesn't define me, but you have no idea what it's like to live with this. I'm *tired*. I'm so tired of wondering when it'll be. I'm tired of all the medication, all the time. I'm tired of *wanting* to do so many things, but being in a body that can't. I'm tired of being in pain. I'm tired that out of all of the chances of having a chronic illness *and* something else, *I* have it. I'm just *tired*."

Her voice wavers, eyes growing wet, and I don't think I've ever really seen her cry before. "You don't know what it's like to finally *want* someone," she says. "But you can't have them, because it'd be so unfair to do that to them, and no one sticks around."

She places a hand over her eyes, brokenly sobbing, like someone who's lost the one thing they've ever wanted, and I think my heart breaks. In the back of my mind, I wonder if this is how Jaxon felt in the aftermath of his cold righteousness all those years ago when he'd found out what I'd been doing.

"And now I'm being a horrible friend. I'm sorry, Layla, you don't always make everything about you."

Rounding the bed, I take a seat on the thin mattress and quickly grab her, the curvature of her body trembling, and murmur over and over that I'm so terribly sorry, that I didn't mean it, and I'm glad she's okay.

I let my insecurities get in the way and say things I shouldn't have.

"I'm so sorry I hadn't realized, Harlow," I murmur into her hair. "I'm sorry I let my own insecurities push me to say things I never should. I-I just don't think you've realized how much you've saved me, and while losing those you love is a part of life, the idea of a world without you in it feels like someone is reaching into my chest and ripping my heart out."

Harlow's always so infallible, blazing through life, and never seems to be bothered by anything, that it's almost ineffable to see it finally taking a toll on her.

Her arms wrap around me, hands cold against my back, and she sniffles against my shoulder. She keeps blubbering apologies when I'm not, shoulders shaking. Eventually, she calms down, and I'm still patting her back, not wanting to say anything or even move, lest she puts that facade on again, or feels awkward.

"I think your shirt is all wet and icky," she whispers eventually, throat a little hoarse. "Sorry, not sorry."

I laugh a little because, of course, Harlow and sarcasm go hand in hand. "What happened, Harlow?"

She pulls away from me and leans back into the pillows, letting out a sigh. It's evident she must still be exhausted, and probably wants some sleep, but she answers me anyway. "I realized that I was getting attached and would probably need to tell him"—I don't need to ask who "him" is—"about things. Had another realization that I really wasn't going to tell him, which would be unfair of me, so naturally, I left. Fast forward, I got sick, and had a bad episode, probably 'cause I started skipping on treatments, and then here we are."

While I'm upset over her condition getting serious enough she had to come to the hospital, the rest of it isn't really a shock. I'm surprised she let Aaron and me get as close to her as we are, but then again, we're not romantically involved. And any attempt I make to hug her again only gets me a punch to the arm.

"Tell me something, Layla," she says, as she sinks back into the pillows, letting out a yawn.

She keeps on zoning out, staring at nothing in particular, a wistful expression taking over her features, making me want to ask more about what happened. Instead, I distract her like I know she wants me to, even though I want to ask her what happens from now on. Is she going to keep on skipping her treatments, or is she going to start going to therapy?

"Well, it's almost winter break, and Jaxon wants to make plans, but we don't really know where to go. Well, he does, I don't."

She smiles softly, her eyes closed. "Don't worry. I'll be out of here by then, and then I can give you two many, many ideas. And I knew my wish would be granted. Laxon has been made! Or maybe Jayla? Point is, you two have a ship name. It's non-negotiable."

I shake my head as she yawns again, pulling the ratty, thin blanket over herself. With all the money insurance and hospitals take, one would think they could afford to give better accommodations. I don't say anything, thinking that she's asleep, but she frowns.

"I swear to God, if you keep staring at me, I'll throw my shoe at you."

Before I can plead my innocence and point out that she can't reach her shoes, she's knocked out, lightly snoring, her head already buried deep into the pillow as she hugs it like it's her soulmate. Deciding that she might throw said pillow at me if I keep staring, I get off the bed with a sigh, wondering what's going to happen now.

As I leave her room, I remember the gut-wrenching worry that thrummed beneath my ribs on the way here, the *what-ifs* circulating in my mind, incessant. I think about the ways we grow inextricably close to one another, but that in the face of our fears and cowardice, it's easy to cut ties and downplay things.

Did Harlow downplay what it meant to come here? Did she reason to herself that we would all move on and eventually stop caring? I remember how that's what I did, all those years ago, except while I know Harlow is alright, someone else never got to know that about me when I disappeared.

As I walk back to the waiting room, I pull out my phone and start searching. I never found her when I first looked online years ago, and then eventually, so much time had passed that I figured it was useless to try again. That even if I did find her, I wouldn't have anything to say. But this time, it doesn't take much time to find the right person.

She has a few social media profiles, most mainly consisting of pictures of various sceneries in nature, sharp and vibrant until they are evocative. When I see that they're in a few galleries, I couldn't be more proud. She has a business email on all of her profiles, and I compose a message, my thumbs hovering over the screen. I have a hundred things I want to tell her, and yet I have no idea what to really say.

"Are you alright?"

I look up from my phone as I enter the waiting room to see Jaxon looking at me, brows drawn in concern as he beckons me to sit on the chair beside him. I take a seat, and reaching out, always grateful that I can hold him, I smooth the furrow between his brows.

Nodding, I say, "Harlow's fine. She's been through a lot, but she's going to be okay." It's both a reassurance to myself and a message to him. I wave my phone. "And I'm emailing Aaradhya."

"I'm proud of you." He says it as if I'm taking a big step toward something in my future, as if I'm making the effort to do something monumental. Although, I suppose, it is very important in a way. It's an effort to say that goodbye, that apology, and then, maybe, *I still want you in my life.* "And how are you feeling?"

"I'm fine." At the nudge he gives my shoulder and a probing look, I add, "Still a little shaken, I guess, but happy that she's alright and alive. Also nervous, I guess, to email Aaradhya after so long. It seems silly."

"It's not silly. You'll tell me if you're feeling upset?"

I roll my eyes. "Yes, my shrink, I'll tell you." Unable to help myself, I lean forward and lightly, quickly, kiss his lips before pulling back. "Fine. I'll always tell you."

Okay then, tell him about why you left in the first place, the cynical, accusatory part of me whispers. *He definitely deserves to know about the deal.* The words claw across my mind, but what is there to tell if I left it behind? No deal matters when I'm not even there for *him* to hold it up.

"You're miles away."

I mentally shake myself and right myself as I pay attention to him again. Smiling softly, I take his hand and kiss his knuckles, staying there for one, two seconds, pressed into his skin like I can crawl my way into his veins. Sometimes, I wonder if I already have. Is it from ease and affection, or an anxiety to accumulate everything with him before it can go away?

"Nothing, just thinking about what I'll tell Aaradhya."

Lies, lies, lies. His eyes darken, as though he knows more than I'm letting on, and I'm reminded again that in the years apart, something has happened to make him cynical in a way he hides. Looking down at my phone, I tell my consciousness to shut up, and push the guilt away.

Soon enough, Jaxon stretches his long legs as his fingers play with strands of my hair and then trace the edges of my ears and cheek. It's distracting, and I try to focus on the screen in front of me, my thumbs over the screen.

After a multitude of attempts that all involve typing, deleting, retyping, and then deleting again, I finally come up with a decent email that will convince her it's me and isn't only filled with apologies.

It wasn't my fault what happened years ago, but it's still worth sending, and a vindictive part of me wonders if there's any point in reaching out when it's not as though she has either. Then I remember the lengths I've gone through to make it impossible to find me.

I hit send, and even if my email is a little somber, and she could never reply or even see it, a serenity settles over my skin. I got to say goodbye, at least, and not bury my past completely.

Harlow's alright and she's *going* to be alright, and I've finally worked up the courage to talk to—or email—Aaradhya. It's like admitting to myself that I still have a long way to go, but that I *am* becoming the person I've always wished to be. Someone who isn't only free of the world of my past, but *behaves* as though free, not laden with guilt.

But then I remember my doubts around the strange men I see, from the parking lot to the earlier encounter in the hall. I remember how I dodge Jaxon's questions and lie instead of outright telling him that there's something—someone—I'm hiding from. I remember how, technically, he can never be mine and I can never be his, if he doesn't really know me.

So, not really any less of a coward, then.

The drive back seems much shorter, as though the distance has warped and shrunk, though it's probably due to the lack of eroding worry and fear. Harlow is in the backseat, lying down against all three seats horizontally. I don't think she's tired, because she *always* lies down and uses all three seats as her own personal bed whenever she's the only one in the back.

Her parents' car practically tails us until I can see the setting sunlight shining on her father's glasses and the glossy black surface of their car. Jaxon, for his part, doesn't seem too worried with how close they are as we head to the suburbs to her parents' house, where they demanded we all would go. Her parents are a slightly scary bunch.

Her father, from what she says and my brief interaction with him, is slightly intimidating. According to Harlow, he can murder you with a glare, and has a knack for getting the truth out of anyone. But what *really* makes him formidable is the way he screams "sophisticated." Everything about him, from the way he walks to the way he holds himself, disseminates the image that he comes from wealth—wealth that he worked for. The similarities between Harlow and him, from the midnight-blackness of their hair to their facial features, is almost eerie.

Her mother is almost the complete opposite of her father—sentimental and genial where he is stoic, smiling where he is grim, though whenever she smiled up at him, even in the hospital, his mouth always quirked in a mirror image.

When she first saw Harlow, asleep on the hospital bed with an IV drip attached to her wrist, she broke out in tears before promptly yelling at her husband for not getting to the hospital soon enough. They're opposites in their coloring, too, until Harlow looks almost nothing like her.

In the end, Harlow probably gets her soft heart—granted, some have to dig a little for it—from her mother, her no-nonsense attitude from her father, and her mean punches from all of those self-defense classes she took when she was younger.

"So," I start. "How long are you staying at your parents' house?"

She groans. "After this episode, my mom is going to try and convince me to stay with her forever and finish school online. I mean, I love my mom, I really do, but I'm not going to complete my bachelor's online." She pauses, mulling over her next words, one of her feet lazily swinging in the air. "I suppose I *could* technically finish it online, but that won't do it for me. I mean, how can I punch you if I'm online? And how can I check on Aaron and ship him efficiently? Speaking of, you better not have cut him out of your life because you broke up with him."

Lifting herself up, she mushes her head between the head of my seat and the side of the car as she glares at me through the side mirror. "When's the last time you've talked to him?"

Jaxon's quietly laughing, no doubt at her scolding me, and I shoot him a half-heated glare, mouthing *traitor*.

"Sometime this week," I answer. "We have the same humanities class."

She gives me one last glare before lying back down against the seats, one leg crossed over the other. "Well, then you won't mind that I invited him over and he'll be here soon?"

"Nope."

The automated voice of the GPS spews the last directions before Jaxon stops the car in front of her parents' house. It's in a quiet, gated neighborhood, well into the suburbs, and after hassling with San Francisco's traffic, the differences are almost jarring. But unlike other neighborhoods, most of the houses seem brand new with different models, obviously personally designed.

It makes the neighborhood a medley of various houses—some are in a Mediterranean style with flat roofs and large patios, while others are more Western, with the kinds of homes I am familiar with, like the red tiled roofs and small front yards. One house almost resembles a castle with what I can only think are turrets.

Harlow is out the door first, stretching and yawning before groaning when her parents' car stops and her mom rushes out, telling her to take it easy and ushering her into the house. Practically all of Harlow's belongings are already there, the ones from her childhood and our old apartment. Her father parks their car in the driveway before getting out and making his way to the front door.

Jaxon and I glance at each other, obviously both confused. Do we go inside? Or does he clearly want us gone?

But her father turns around, gives us a look, and with a slight sigh and a tilt of his head, we know we're invited.

"This is going to be interesting," Jaxon murmurs.

And it was.

Three hours later, kicking my shoes off, I'm still reeling from the visit. Who knew Mr. Arita had humor? And good humor, at that. It was all very nice until he challenged us to a game of chess and was aghast when he realized that Aaron and I had no idea how to play. I quickly realized that Mr. Arita is the kind of man that grows on you, intimidation becoming clear as shyness, and despite his offended shock, he was patient in teaching us how to play.

The biggest surprise might've been the ease between Jaxon and Aaron. There were no side glances from Aaron, no subtle "How is life with my ex that you stole from me?" behavior or anything similar. If anything, there was a glare from Jaxon, but otherwise, dare I say it, they seemed to get along.

It wasn't long after dinner that Harlow went to bed, waving her hand when I said I'd call, and that was our cue to leave. But Mr. Arita did challenge me to come again for another game of chess, so there's that.

"Thinking about chess?" Jaxon asks me as he drops the car keys onto the table beside the door.

"Sort of."

He stretches his long body, arms above his head, letting a sliver of his skin show as his shirt rides up, and I have a delicious, tempting view of his flat stomach and the dark line of hair that disappears into his jeans. I don't really know why, but I'm beginning to realize I have a bit of a fascination for the sight.

He tsks, as if he can hear my line of thoughts, before bending down and dropping a kiss on my forehead from where I'm cozied up on the couch.

"I've been sitting and driving almost all day, so I'm going for a swim." He always needs to have some form of movement, I noticed, so of course he hates sitting still, even when driving. "Unless you need me for something?"

"I always need you," I tease. "I'd join you on that swim, but it's getting late."

He nods, and I bury myself deeper into the couch before remembering that I probably have assignments to do and exams to study for. And then that I have class tomorrow, and I think I want to cry.

No, please, I beg in my mind. *I don't want to go.* But in a couple of days, finals will roll around, and then it'll be winter break. While I'm not looking forward to the finals, I can't help but get a little giddy over the break. The thought of getting to sleep in and staying in bed all day reading fills me with pure, unadulterated joy.

I missed you, long nights of sleep, I think forlornly.

I yelp when Jaxon suddenly picks me up, arms banding beneath my legs, and I cling to the solid breadth of him as he carries me to the bedroom where he promptly dumps me on the bed.

"Try not to think about me too much," he whispers, eyes shining with his contained laughter, a smile tugging at his lips, and I wonder if this feels as easy to him as it does to me. As much as my mind can twist in on itself, as much as my thoughts spiral down a negative loop with proficiency, I will always be grateful he bumped into me that day. "You can survive without me, sweetheart, as depriving as it will be."

I scoff, but laugh a little. He might get cocky at times, but he's also funny, so it's worth it.

Shut up, you know everything about him is worth it, you infatuated idiot.

Closing my eyes, I listen to the sounds of him moving around the room, grateful in a way that eases me. I marvel at how quickly feelings can change, the calm of right now dichotomous to the pure fear of a few hours ago. And while there's the uncertainty of the future, the fear that my past has not let me go, and worry for Harlow's health, I let myself appreciate what I have right now.

After all, no one can fully grasp how quickly it takes to lose everything.

Chapter 21

Deceived

The shrill sound of my phone ringing jars me awake from my stupor, and I fumble for it, groaning in the dark. Reaching, my body half stretched off the bed, suspended in ways it should not be, I yelp when I fall off. Cursing under my breath, I look around the room, noticing that Jaxon isn't here, and the clock tells me it's only been a little over an hour since I fell asleep.

Still.

I kind of want to murder whoever is calling. That is, until I answer the phone and a familiar voice immediately asks, "Layla?"

My entire body freezes as I process who I'm hearing, and can't stop a smile from breaking across my face. "Aaradhya?" I ask, disbelieving.

I had no idea hearing her voice again would be like this. It brings back memories I thought I'd forgotten and nostalgia I believed I'd gotten over.

"Oh my God," she shrieks. Yep, definitely her. "It is you."

I laugh, climbing back onto the bed, before deciding that I'd rather go make something in the kitchen. And by "make" I mean scour the fridge for any leftover food Jaxon has already cooked.

"I'm so glad you reached out. Gosh, how have you been?"

And with that, we somewhat catch up to date on our lives. After deciding on an apple—today, I shall reward you, my body, with healthy food—I multitask. I eat, listen and talk to her, and rummage around what's *supposed* to be my bedroom. Occasionally, I have to hold my side from laughing too hard at the comments she makes.

I'd worried that even if she wanted to talk again, things would be too awkward to go anywhere, even if I'd at least have closure. In reality, while she's definitely different in certain ways, she's still the bubbly, eager-to-share girl I was friends with years ago.

By the time she hangs up, explaining that she has an early flight tomorrow and promising to call me when she's at the airport, I learn the important markers and details of what happened. She's studying in New York and joined a synesthesia awareness program. Not like it's an illness, but she's with other people who understand her better, and the program focuses on raising awareness and clearing up myths around it. After all, when you have people who can see the world in an entirely different way, they usually have the most to show you.

After propping a canvas on the easel and selecting the paint colors and brushes I want for the project I have in mind, I leave the spare room that I've turned into a mini art studio, deciding I should change my clothes.

I hear the front door open, and am a little surprised when I hear Mike's voice too. He still wants his food? I stand right beside the wall behind the living room, able to hear them clearly, before I pause, deciding I'll go back to the bedroom and wait till he leaves. It's late, and I'd rather not socialize right now.

"Michael, it's kind of late for this, don't you think? Layla's asleep, try to keep it down," Jaxon says, voice tired.

So that's his full name. Full name usage never means anything good.

I'm about to head into the bedroom and away from any potential eavesdropping before I hear Mike snap, "I took care of the one that

209

followed you into the city. I don't want to have to do it again. I thought you covered your traces?"

"What are you saying, Michael?" Jaxon's voice is low, the baritone dangerous in a way that reminds me of men with a facade, and I remember the new edge of darkness in him, the hidden ruthlessness that occasionally filters through his expressions.

Mike senses it too, and his next words are careful, a surrender. "Just be careful, okay? And remember what you promised me. I don't want to assume the worst, but I hope she's worth it, for your sake."

"Everything and more," Jaxon snaps. "Now get out."

"Come on, man. Don't be that way. We're friends, remember? And you're a nice guy who likes to cook me food and joke, remember? Damn, you can be so nice and calm that I sometimes forget you can also be a mean bloke."

"Bloke?" Jaxon's tone is incredulous. "What are you? Sixty?" Even from where I'm hiding, the tension visibly calms down, and he huffs a laugh. "Besides, that's because I *am* nice. Now go, before you wake up Layla with all your drama."

"Okay, man. Sorry about that earlier. I know you have it under control."

There's the unsaid, *you better,* and I wonder what Jaxon has been up to, why they would be worried about people showing up to their practice. More than that, I wonder what it has to do with me, if the "she" who is worth it is me.

"Of course I have it under control." He sighs. "I just can't let anything happen. Not now that things are finally looking up. And she doesn't need any of that worry, okay?"

"I'm sure I was just being paranoid. Anyway, love the heart-to-heart, Jaxon, but I'm clueless when it comes to romantic relationships. Just buy her chocolate in abundance. I heard that's good."

Jaxon laughs a little, and I know that Mike said all that to get him to relax. They remind me of Harlow and I in that aspect—the rare kind of friends who understand the parts of you no one else will.

When Mike says something random again, and then the front door opens again, I make a beeline for the bedroom, throw myself under the covers, and relax my body to give off a semblance of sleep.

It's only a few moments later that Jaxon walks in, the swishing sound of his swimming shorts making it very hard to fake being asleep. Imagining him in swimming shorts, my earlier curiosity is pushed to the back of my mind. Besides, I trust him, don't I? Now, I just wonder what he looks like, if his hair is still wet from his swim.

Don't you want to at least check?

No. I make sure my breathing is regulated, and my body is lax. I don't even tense when I can sense him right beside the bed, standing above me, the sound of his moving clear, a slight warmth radiating from him.

My eyes are closed, but my fingers tighten into a fist under the covers, radiating with tension because I can viscerally *feel* his gaze on me. It traces over my skin, and I have to fight to stop from shivering, to stop from biting my lip.

I want to reach out and touch him, but I worry if he'll know I was eavesdropping then. I'm not ready for that, not ready for the confrontation, not ready for the likelihood that his world and mine, here, is messier than I hoped.

When he leans down, his breath fanning over my cheek before a feathery-light sensation runs on my cheek, I almost gasp. He kisses my forehead too, and there's no way I can hold out for longer. Something will give me away soon, I just know it.

His gentle kisses across my face are sweet, but my body wants to shake as though his lips don't skim across my face, but the inside of my wrist, the curve of my waist. My efforts to pretend I'm asleep turn his touch into something different, until tension curves its way through my limbs.

Just as soon as I think I'll lose this battle of mine, he moves away, and then the shower starts running, saving my facade.

As I remember his earlier words to Mike, I want to go into the bathroom and demand answers. More than that, I want to give my own. But these past few days, he and I have been in a decadent bubble, the normalcy too sweet to give up. I don't want to be the one to ruin it.

My thoughts twist and turn around my head, repeating over and over like I'm a hamster subject to run forever in a little round wheel.

Eventually, Jaxon finishes taking his shower, joins me in bed and wraps his arms around me, his embrace familiar and becoming more and more like coming home as I'm lulled to sleep.

The mind is a fickle thing—easily deceived and easily led to craving. Compared to the months and years of having my own space, my own bed, the days I've spent with Jaxon are few in comparison; a drop in a bucket.

And yet, I've grown used to waking up with him wrapped around me, as though physically removing the cobwebs of loneliness around my heart and in my mind, and crawling into my very veins to settle. In the span of a few weeks, my mind has become convinced I cannot live without him, and I know another word for that is *addiction*, is deep-rooted *obsession*.

I've grown so used to him that when I wake up, I'm already frowning before I realize what's different, mind stumbling in panic over what could be wrong, disoriented, until I notice that he's not wrapped around me like a monkey. The reprieve is minute, before senseless hysteria sets in, with the unmistakable belief that something is wrong, that *they* came and took him.

Blindly, I grab my glasses, searching the room, only to see that he's still in bed, asleep, with his arms beneath the pillow like a child rather than around me. Shaking my head, almost disappointed in myself, I relax back onto the bed, wondering when the paranoia will leave me—*if* it'll ever leave me. How ironic it is to escape physically but not mentally, to have them win even from across the country.

But in this little haven, in this hazel and green room that's slowly morphed from his to ours, there is no *cosa nostra*, there are no nightmares. Slowly, I settle further, nerves settling. I wonder if we can become addicted to stress—to cortisol, as Jaxon puts it—and that's why I continue to conjure demons when there are none. Once something becomes normal, it becomes a necessity, no matter how toxic it is.

Evening my breathing, I stare at him, gaze tracing his features, soft in sleep, mouth slack, the draw of his brow almost innocent. The blanket reaches up to his midriff, revealing the expanse of his back, the arch and dips of his shoulder and spine. He must have been really exhausted if he didn't move at all throughout the night, and I remember how crazy this past week has been with finals.

The day we went to see Harlow, and then the conversation I overheard between Jaxon and Mike, seems like forever ago, when really it's been barely over two weeks.

Between his finals, research project, having to grade papers for the classes he's TA-ing in, and being a tutor, I'm surprised Jaxon hasn't dropped dead. Even in his sleep, he looks exhausted, the skin beneath his eyes deep and dark. I could—should—get up and do something since I'm awake, but I'm content to lie down, faintly tracing his brow and the line of his nose, watching the sunlight flickering across his features as the curtains rustle from a faint breeze.

I stay like that until he stirs awake, body stretching, sinews pulling taut, and eyes slowly blinking open. When they focus on me, he smiles sleepily, all soft lines and half-hooded eyes, hair thoroughly missed. I wonder if he'd still be smiling if he knew just how long I've been lying here, staring at him like a creep.

"Good morning," I whisper as he rolls onto his back, the sheets pulling around his ribs, and languidly stretches his limbs, oddly reminding me of a cat stretching in the sun.

Reaching out, he slides an arm beneath me and pulls me into his side, until my hand settles across the warm skin over his heart, my head resting over his shoulder. I pull a leg over him, luxuriating in the soft feel of his pajama pants. While few things about a six-foot-something male with a body built from work and sweat scream "cuddle-able," his soft sweatpants and hoodies always do me in.

"Good morning," he answers, his voice all husky and deep edges from sleep, the timbre sparking an ember in me. "Dream about me?"

"You wish."

"You know," he starts. "Now that finals are over and you're off from work, I have the perfect opportunity to just keep you right here, or take you somewhere far away, and no one will know."

"Promise?" He laughs, the sound rolling into me, lighting up all the dark recesses of my mind. "You've got the kind of laugh that makes me stupid."

"Oh yeah? How?"

I trace patterns across his skin until he shivers, arm tightening around me and a hand settling over my knee, thumb rubbing back and forth across the bare skin. "I love hearing it, and it makes me want to do crazy things to hear it again and again."

He groans as though I've pained him, and pulls me over him entirely, until my legs are on either side of his waist, and I look down at him, tendrils of my hair hanging down around us. "You can't say things like that, sweetheart."

"Why?"

"It makes me want to kiss you senseless."

I lean down further, smiling, and like he can't help himself, he mirrors it, until his dimple comes in view. Tilting my head to the side, I kiss it, hand coming down to skim around his ribs, and when he smiles harder, almost laughing from the sensation, I kiss that dimple over and over.

"You *should* kiss me senseless."

I have no doubt I look like I want him to, and he groans again at the sight, but instead of kissing me, he tightens an arm around me and sits up, the other leveraging against the bed. "Come on, let's have breakfast first—I'll make some eggs."

I think I actually slouch in his arms, wilting at the mention of eggs. "I don't like eggs."

"But you haven't tried *my* eggs yet—I make them nice. I'll even teach you."

As it turns out, I do like his eggs. And his teaching, but not as much as his cooking. It's decided—I'm keeping him.

Jaxon is smug, chin lifted and a small smirk tugging at his lips, and I roll my eyes at him playfully. "Fine. You win."

The smile morphs into a full-blown, conceited grin before his attention shifts to the clock. "Oh, we're going to need to hit the road soon."

I frown, narrowing my eyes. "Hit the road? We're going somewhere?"

"You want to go see a lake for the weekend?" He phrases it like a question, as though he hasn't already made the plans.

"Where is it?"

He shakes his head, lifting me off my chair like I'm a sack of potatoes before heading to the bedroom. After plopping me on the bed, he leaves, and returns with two small suitcases.

"Lake Tahoe—it's east from here, great for holiday getaways, and since I'm not doing this explaining thing well, you'll just have to see for yourself."

I eye him skeptically for a while, but have to hide how excited and relieved I am at the idea of getting out of here. Normally, I hate spontaneity, but the idea of it, right now, with him, is one I don't mind. It's only a while after I pull him down onto the bed, my arms around his neck, fingers in his hair, lips on his, do we actually start packing.

And it's only after I do it again do we actually hit the road, and for the first time, I don't feel like this is too good to be true.

I spend an hour talking to Harlow on the phone, and of the most random things, of course. Jaxon whistles by the time I hang up and hands me a bottle of water jokingly.

Rolling my eyes, but leaning over the console to peck his cheek, I take the bottle. "Don't lie, guys have weird and random conversations, too."

I remember Mike's conversation with Jaxon a few days ago—his input was definitely bordering on random.

He looks at me, aghast, before sobering up. "Yeah." He sighs. "We probably do."

I snicker, and slap the hand that is sneaking toward me. "Freeway, Jaxon. You're on the freeway. No red lights, so no playing with my hair."

He pouts. "You could always drive."

"I could, but then you'd be touching me while *I'm* driving, and then we'd have a car accident. Besides"—I glance at the ETA on his phone—"we're almost there."

He mutters something under his breath that is positively filthy and my breath catches a little. Catching my reaction, he smirks, lips pulling back enough that I can see one canine.

I almost don't notice when he parks the car and climbs out, stretching his arms above his head. "Finally," he mutters. "I hate driving."

I join suit, sliding out of the car before stretching too. The four-hour drive was tiring, but at least he chose this place and not another popular landmark that's seven hours away.

Not bothering to open the trunk, he locks the car, and reaches for me. I always enjoy his need for physical affection, but lately, it's as though he holds me close out of a worry I'll disappear, his grasp sometimes desperate.

Joined together like glue and paper, Jaxon and I walk to the motel, his arm around my shoulders. The receptionist behind the desk tells us we're a cute couple, and Jaxon beams like she's handed him the sun before I nudge his hip and he accepts the cards she slides over the desk.

"Breakfast is nine every morning, but sometimes they'll start serving the waffles before that. Oh, and every Sunday, they go all out and add muffins to the menu."

We nod, thanking her one last time before we begin to head back to the car.

"Oh! And one last thing," she says. "I hate to do this, but there's a 'no loud noises after ten PM' policy, and it's always the adults breaking that rule. So, the walls are thin, and please don't make me have to deal with complaining families."

As we head back to the car to grab our luggage, I ask, "But why would it be the adults breaking that rule? Who throws ragers at a motel?"

"She didn't mean ragers, Layla."

"Then what—" I pause. "Oh."

Jaxon laughs while I simply stare ahead, face flaming.

"I keep forgetting you're a little prude. But I guess we'll just have to be quiet, sweetheart."

Rolling my eyes, I shove him, even if I wish a little that he wasn't teasing. For as quickly as we got together after I moved in, he's been moving at a snail's pace when it comes to other things, insisting we take our time.

And while I can appreciate it, there's no hiding the needy frustration that courses through my body on mornings when we wake up tangled together.

"I doubt you'd have an easy time keeping quiet," I tease as I open the trunk door and grab some of the luggage. I'm wearing two layers of sweaters, and a beanie, but my face still feels cold, my nose no doubt red.

"Guess you'll just have to find out," he whispers, nipping my earlobe before grabbing everything else and shutting the trunk.

Inside, we ignore any looks the receptionist gives us as we walk past the lobby and hunt for our room. The hallways are carpeted red, and immediately come off as old and well-worn, with some of the threads undone at the edges. The walls, a dull beige, carry on and on as the hall continues, and the doors have an old-motel-look that's clearly intentional. Rather than being plain, they resemble what I imagine I'd find in an eighteenth-century castle, from the doorknob to the skull door-knocker. The only touch of modernity is the keycard swiper above the handle.

With a swipe of the card, the door opens first to a living room area, the room slightly dark since it's late. The room is small, but has a TV facing the couch and its side tables. Above the furniture is a collage of photos of the lake and snow, so white it almost blends in with the walls. The TV rests on a rustic cabinet with drawers, and there seems to be many other places to put your things in—enough that I'll probably forget something. The living room also branches off into a mini kitchen that consists of more cabinets, a sink, and then a mini fridge.

I don't really care about those too much. In my opinion, the most important feature in the whole hotel experience is the bedroom.

Once there, I switch on the light and, stretching my limbs wide, jump onto the queen-sized poster bed, with a loud, "Weeeeee!"

The bounce is just right, and as I get back down, I survey the room. The walls are painted two different colors. One wall, the one the bed is against, is a light, robin blue, while the rest of the walls are oyster white. The colors complement nicely with the rest of the room, and I like the ambience they went with.

There's a TV in front of the bed, sitting on a low armoire, and to the side of that are a few closets. There is a small balcony, and I get up to close the curtains, wondering what the view will look like in the morning.

Jaxon enters the room, placing our bags on the cabinet, before heading to the bathroom, and I join him. It's a little early, enough that a few places in town might still be open, but we're both so exhausted from the drive that we change into more comfortable clothes.

"I know it's a bit small," he starts. "And not a state of the—"

I shut him up with a kiss. "I like it. You know I'm not with you because of what you can do for me but because I want *you*, right? I don't care if the room is small—I just want to be with you."

For a moment, he looks like he doesn't believe me before grabbing me and reeling me in, planting a kiss on my head. What must it have been like, I wonder, to always have to give and give to be seen as someone worthy of being loved or cared for?

As I stretch in the bed, burrowing into the pillows, I imagine a younger Jaxon, a little boy constantly having to prove he's not dangerous and is someone worth loving. With an unyielding conviction, I know I want to ensure he has the kind of love that's freely given, that's soft instead of harsh with expectations.

Beside me, he has his phone on, and with an expectant look, lifts his arm so I can nestle at his side. He has a journal article open, reading something about the biological markers of DID, and I give up trying to read it when I don't understand even half of the terms, like "amygdala" and "hippocampus."

"Nerd," I say affectionately. "If I didn't know any better, I'd think you're in your fifties and not twenties."

"Keep that up and I'll prove just how young I am."

While his words could mean anything, they carry a seductive hint, his hand squeezing over my hip, and I have to bite my lip from goading him to do just that. The hand I have over his stomach starts drifting down before I've even realized it, and Jaxon gives me a *look*, the screen on his phone going dark as he stops paying attention to the article.

"Go to sleep, Layla."

"You're not tired or sleepy."

I hear my phone let out a little ring from the bedside, a distraction I take, which tells me all I need to know about what I want, about how far I'm actually willing to go with him right now. Rolling over, I grab it, thinking it's Harlow.

Except it's not.

Instead, it's a text from an unknown number. It's only two words, but it reminds me of all the growing dread and problems I left, and I *hate* it. I hate that it's controlling me even when I'm gone and the past is states away. I hate the way it pierces the assurance that I successfully made it out.

But the words, *come home*, aren't going to put fear in me. Instead, they blaze me, and I ignore it. *It's not the end of the world*, I tell myself. It doesn't mean anything. If they really did find me, they would've taken me back long ago. This is only a means to make me panic, to make me slip.

Double checking, I make sure that all the methods I put in place to avoid a potential tracing are secure. With relief, I note that they are, but I'm still going to change my phone and number when I get back.

The fact that *he* can't trace me, wherever he is, proves that the message is a taunt. It's a way to mess with my head more than he already has, and I won't let him.

And it's not going to take away what I have *now*. I have everything I wanted and craved for during those years, and I'm going to *keep* it, crime organizations and syndicates be damned.

Chapter 22

Promises

After many, *many* failed attempts, Jaxon and I discover, much to the instructor's peeved dismay, that we royally suck at skiing *and* snowboarding. With the biting cold and our large mittens, neither of us have pulled out our phones to check the time, but by the hazy trek of the sun through the sky, I imagine we've been trying for a couple of hours at least.

With his goggles off his face, there's no hiding the instructor's tired exasperation, and he attempts to cover it up with a smile. "How about a break, yeah? You two can try on your own for a little, and I'll be back in a few."

The words are barely all out before he peels off, surprisingly fast despite the dense snow. I look at Jaxon, his own goggles off his face, and he's already an adorable shade of red from the cold. How are we both so bad at this when we come from a city that has heavy snowfall?

"Yeah, he's not coming back," I tell him. "He seemed like he'd rather go look for a bear in the mountains than attempt to teach us for another five minutes."

"Honestly, after I accidentally wacked him with the stick, I don't blame him."

I snort, remembering that. It'd been an honest mistake on Jaxon's part, but there was no hiding the instructor's baffled, "How do you even *do* that?"

Though I suspect Jaxon isn't as bad as he's letting on, and is just trying to keep me from feeling singled out. Narrowing my eyes at him, I lean down and scoop some snow, feeling the cold even through my thick gloves.

"Are you faking it?"

"Faking what, sweetheart?"

Wagging my finger, I raise the snowball threateningly. "Uh-uh, you're not going to 'sweetheart' your way out of this one. Are you faking being this bad at skiing because you don't want me to feel bad?"

His pause is all the answer I need, and with a shrieked, "Jaxon!" I toss the snowball at him. To his amusement, it misses him by a wide margin, pathetically splatting onto the ground.

"I just didn't want you to feel lonely!" he insists.

The plea falls on deaf ears, and I reach forward to tackle him in the snow. Except my feet are still attached to the board and all I succeed in is tipping over, arms flailing as my gravity shifts before I plant face-first into the snow.

"*Cazzo*," I mutter into the snow, the cold instantly chilling my face until I'm sure I'll never feel it again.

Struggling, I glare up at Jaxon as he laughs, mirth written across every feature, and the sight almost makes me forget my annoyance. When he sees me looking at him, no doubt plastered with snow, he laughs harder. Reaching behind me, I struggle for the button that will release my feet from the board, except my mittens are stiff and give me the finesse of a stumbling drunk.

"You're not going to help me?" I ask, looking up at him.

He leans down until his face hovers over mine, nose near enough to brush mine, and answers, "Say please."

Stubborn, I keep reaching behind me for the damn button, and mutter, "*Stronzo*."

221

I'm contorted far enough that this time, I tip backward, awkwardly on my back with my knees folded beneath me, and sigh, deciding that he'll get some manners after all.

"That's not very nice, sweetheart."

Since when did he learn Italian and not tell me? I narrow my eyes up at him, pulse slowing with wariness, that paranoia stealing my thoughts in a way I hate. Because so what if he did? "How would you know that's not nice?"

"I imagine anything you say in that tone is quite... colorful."

"Fair enough. Okay, can you *please* help me?"

He hums, considering. "What will you give me for it?"

"A kiss? God, you're such a haggler."

"Sounds like a deal."

Reaching down, he deftly pulls the board from beneath me and finds the buttons and clasps, freeing me from my torment. Taking his outstretched hand, I pull myself up, dusting off the snow, though it's futile.

"Come on," he prompts, tapping his cheek. His no doubt *cold* cheek. "Plant it here."

I do, chuckling despite myself. "You're such a weirdo."

"Your weirdo."

"My weirdo," I acquiesce, and he smiles like I've given him something precious.

It might be over something silly, but I can't deny that it's comforting to have someone to call my own and vice versa. It's even more of a solace to hear it aloud, as though voicing the words makes it more real.

Reaching down, he picks up my board, stubbornly refusing to let me carry anything before we head back to the ski equipment shed. After we've returned everything, I start to tug off my outer gloves—because of course it's cold enough I need to wear two—thinking we're heading back. But Jaxon grabs my hands, keeping them on.

"Not yet," he says, tugging me back toward the snow. "We're not leaving yet."

I wonder if he genuinely still has something planned for us at the ski resort or if he just doesn't want the moment to end. Whatever his reason though, I follow.

"Come on, let's go find a spot that's less crowded," he murmurs, his hands a little fidgety in a way that's endearing. The rest of him is calm and collected, and I wonder at what point I grew so used to him and his body that I can now tell his cues and quirks. It exhilarates me in a way that almost steals my breath, the passage of time that almost, foolishly, promises more. It quiets the fear that I'm on borrowed time, that soon enough, I'll have to lose everything I've come to love.

I raise a brow, wondering why he's nervous. "Why? You need a good spot to hide my body?"

"What?" he asks, aghast, shooting me a bewildered look. "No."

Laughing, I nudge his shoulder as we walk away from the crowd, up the slope, closer to the trees in case someone is skiing down. "Relax, I'm just teasing."

Before I can fully process what he's doing, he reaches down, rolls some snow in his hands, and pelts me with it, the ball thudding against my stomach, surprisingly solid. I stare at him, baffled, and narrow my eyes at his self-satisfied expression. With a huff, I make my own snowball, but when I throw it, he ducks, laughing, and it misses him.

"Come on, sweetheart," he teases. "You'll have to do better than that."

Like a game of dodgeball, he evades each and every pelt of snow, lithe body curving and ducking until with a shriek of indignation, I jump, pouncing on him. It takes him by enough surprise that when I collide into him, he falls backward, arms coming around me as we fall to the ground and he lets out an, "Oof."

"Ha!" I announce triumphantly, staring down at him in the snow. "Got you."

Except I grow distracted, despite the cold and the snow, lying above him. With only endless white surrounding him, there's nothing to take my attention away from him, from the way snow clings to his lashes and the sight of him beneath me.

My distraction costs me, and when the hands that have traveled up to my hips tighten and his body shifts, I don't realize what he's planning until he's turned me over.

"Did you?"

Now, his body presses mine into the snow, and I don't care that it's soaking my hair. It's cold against my back, and I sink into it, with him above me, until I'm almost entirely cocooned. I can't say I hate it. "What?" I ask.

Laughing, he shakes his head. "So easily distracted by me, are you? Did you get me, I mean."

I blush, because he's right, and it seems that this weekend, I have a one-track mind. *Very* one-track mind. "I suppose not."

Even though the snow is freezing behind my back, I'm still disappointed when he moves, standing and pulling me up with him. But I take the opportunity to finally, *finally*, pelt him with snow.

He freezes, hands stilling over his knees where he was dusting off the snow, and looks up at me, one brow arched. With an "Oops," I bolt farther up the slope, laughing.

Bolt is a generous word, considering how thick the snow is up here, and I half-stumble, half-scramble away from him, shrieking with delight.

The rest of the climb up the slope is a blur of laughing and teasing as we throw snowballs at each other and shove one another into the snow. As we stumble up the slope, sludging through thick snow, it doesn't matter to me that our plans of skiing were derailed; I'm having just as much fun doing this. And maybe, a part of me delights with smug glee at behaving similarly to a child, in a way "unbecoming" of who I am, in a way I know my father and his men would hate.

When we finally get to the top, I collapse over the ground, panting and laughing, my breath misting over me. I don't care that my face is cold but the rest of me is too warm beneath my jacket from the running, or that my hair clings to my neck, wet. I can't remember the last time I had this much *fun*, the last time I laughed this hard.

Pausing, I think over it. Could it have really been years? When things had been "normal" and my family was whole, not a splintered portrait? The thought sobers me, and I wonder how much fun my brother would've had if he did this. He'd always been so competitive, I have no doubt he would've tried his hardest to reach the top first, little legs stumbling through the snow. Except he wouldn't have been little. If he were still alive, he'd probably be taller than me.

My heart bleeds at the image, but I cannot imagine how he would have looked as a teenager. I cannot even fully remember how he looked as a child.

And that's the thing with grief. Sometimes, it's easy to forget it, it's easy to move on. And other times, even years later, it surges like a wave, dragging me under the water, until I am sure I will never breathe. Though just like my memory of my brother, even the harshest waves of grief have lessened over the years. But perhaps worse than the grief is the regret and guilt. Unbidden, there's the thought, *What am I even doing? I don't deserve this.*

The sentiment has always been there over the years, lurking like a shadow, and I hate that it's surfaced again.

"Hey," Jaxon says above me, shocking me from my thoughts. "Everything okay?"

Throat thick, I nod, smiling, and pretend it isn't fake. "Yeah, just got a little winded."

We both know it's a lie, but he doesn't push, instead pulling me up and kissing my forehead. I cannot shake the thought that I don't deserve this, that nothing good will come from hiding parts of me, but I am selfish.

I am so selfish that I lean up and kiss him, holding him harder. His lips are cold against mine, but his shocked exhale is not. I'm about to deepen the kiss before he pulls away.

"As much as I'd like nothing but to kiss you, look."

Turning, I look toward where he's pointing, and blink, my jaw going slack. The vista stretches before us, all snow and trees, and my breath catches at the sight. Lower, I can see the outline of the winding road that led us up here, resembling a black stream, the cars on them ant-like from up here.

With thick clouds overhead, the sky seems to mirror the pure white snow in its brightness, until white is all I see. The only interruption to it are the trees that scatter across the mountain range, their leaves and pines laden with snow. In the distance, I can make out a lake, maybe frozen over. While all the white is almost blinding, there's no denying that up here, everything resembles a winter wonderland.

Most of all, there is a perpetual stillness that comes with this monotonous beauty, as life hides away for the winter. It adds a haunting element to the sight, and I shiver beneath my clothes, wondering what it would be like to be lost in this cold and silence.

Turning up, I look toward Jaxon to find him already watching me, dark eyes assessing. My breath catches at the intent in his gaze as I wonder what he's thinking about.

"Do you like it?" he asks, and there's no hiding the edge of nervousness in his voice.

It makes me smile, and reaching over, I grab his hand. "I love it. It's very beautiful; one of the most beautiful things I've ever seen." Turning my head, I point to that lake. "Like that. Have you ever seen something more beautiful?"

Still looking at me, not even turning to the lake, he pulls me closer. "I have not."

When I catch his meaning, I blush. I've read enough romance novels to recognize what his words mean, but never, in all my grandest dreams, did I ever think someone would say it to me. Worse, I never thought I deserve them, never thought I am worthy of love, worth it to say those kinds of words to. And here he is, saying and doing the sweetest things as though caring for me is as easy as breathing.

I want to go back to my younger self, to the hopeless romantic so sure she would never experience what she read in books, and hold her close. I want to tell her everything will be worth it one day.

Leaning down until his body curves around mine, a marionette perpetually strung toward me, Jaxon fills my vision. Reaching down, he takes off both his gloves, a hand coming up to brush my hair off my face, and murmurs, "As much as it was fun climbing up here, I didn't bring you here just for the view."

"Then for what?"

His smile is quick, but his body is frozen in a way that radiates tension, throat bobbing anxiously, and I remember his earlier nervousness. "I know I said I plan on keeping this around my neck until the day I die..." he starts, and reaching behind him, he finds the clasp of the thin necklace with his mother's ring and undoes it.

He cups the ring in his palm, the chain trailing around it, and I stare at the dainty jewelry in his hand. It's a simple band, gold, with a red stone in the center and two smaller white ones beside it, the prongs wrapped around the main stone in the style of a rose. It's small, but undeniably beautiful, and I wonder about his mother.

Did she pick that ring, or was it the father Jaxon never got to meet? I wonder if she is where he got his dark eyes and thick lashes from. Whenever I think of her, and how Jaxon lost her, my heart breaks a little more for him, but now, it breaks a little for me too. I would've liked to meet her, and maybe she would have grown into a mother figure for me, easing the edges of pain from the loss of my own mother.

But the sight of the ring in his hand and not around his neck stills me as questions slowly rise, and my gaze darts up to his. Maybe he can see my fear, because he grows even more tense, the nervousness practically a live wire wrapped around his every limb. If I were not so shocked, it would be cute.

At my expression, he takes my hand, while the other holds his mother's ring in between us like an open flame. "Don't worry—it's not what you're thinking. I said I would never take this off," he repeats. "Because it symbolizes the memory of my mother, and has always meant more to me than words can describe. Like if I kept her ring on this chain around my neck, she'd always be close to my heart."

Taking a deep breath, he looks at the ring, and I know that regardless of what he will say or do, this is the kind of moment one doesn't come back from. It's the kind that rewrites a script, that pulls two people either inextricably closer or pushes them apart.

Regardless of what will happen, I will always remember the sight of him, backdrop all snow and trees in a winter wonderland, his eyes brimming with so much emotion, I'm sure I can practically taste it.

"And I know that I'm butchering this, that you deserve more than a bumbling confession on a cold mountain, as beautiful as it may be. But for a long time, longer than you can imagine, what mattered most to me was not close to me, not resting around a chain over my heart. Because slowly, but stubbornly, *you* became everything that mattered to me. You mean more to me than my past, more than my demons, more than my wishes and dreams. And so I'd like to give you"—he slides off my glove until his hand curves around mine, skin cold—"the person that means the most to me, this ring, the item that has meant the most to me for almost the entirety of my life."

I watch, breathless, as he slips the chain out from the ring and then slides it over my finger. It rests like a confession and a promise, even if he says this isn't what I was thinking.

Cold hands cup my face, tilting my head up so I look at him rather than his mother's ring resting on my finger. Every word I can think of, every question, dies on my tongue at the utterly *raw* display of emotion across his features. I imagine this is what a man would look like after having found salvation, eyes full of unbelieving hope and the kind of relief that only comes after years of having something you've wanted for years.

"When I do this again, one day, it'll be with the prettiest ring, *ya qalbi*," he promises. "But as much as I am known to have no patience, this isn't a proposal. I know we're not there yet, so I'm making you a different kind of promise today, with my mother's ring, if you'll have it."

I wrap my arms around his waist, grounding myself, and I don't realize I'm crying until he swipes his thumb across a tear. This might not be a proposal, but I know the severity of what having this ring means, the kind of promise he just made with giving me something he's held close his whole life. If there was any doubt over our relationship, over my importance to him, it just disappeared with the simple sliding of a band over my finger, and it's not even an engagement ring.

He's taken every sinister, dark thought, every *You're not good enough*, every *You're unlovable*, every *You're not easy to care for*, and every *All you'll ever know is heartbreak and cold men*, and cast them away.

"I'll have it," I acquiesce, throat thick. We both know what is unsaid; *I'll have you, all your demons and your wants and every dark part of your past, and I'll cherish all of it.*

@lyyzis_art

With a smile that rivals the beauty around us, he pulls me closer until his forehead leans against mine and seals his promise with a kiss. His lips are soft, the kiss gentle in a way opposite of our pasts. We've taken the stories we've been given—a girl running from the mafia and a boy surviving his demons—and rewritten them into something better. Something *ours*.

From somewhere behind us, a throat clears, and I jump away... or at least try to, but Jaxon keeps his arms around me and with a lazy sort of confidence, lifts his head up to look at whoever it is. His gaze is hard, unamused at being interrupted, and I wonder how he can pull that off when he's normally all smiles and teased words.

"Listen, I hate to be interrupting just as much as you do, but I work here and have to ask—where are your skis?"

Since Jaxon doesn't seem like he'll give an even mildly polite answer, I do, turning around in his arms so I can look at whoever it is. "Um, we don't have them. We walked up."

The worker, someone wearing a red safety jacket, gives us a deadpan look as though we're joking. Jaxon and I glance at each other, confused. Are we missing something?

"You *walked* up the slope?"

"...yeah?"

Shaking her head, she mutters something like, "They don't pay me enough for this job," before turning back to us. "I'll assume they forgot to tell you when you were coming in, but climbing up the slope is not allowed, whether on or off the trails. On the trails, there could be skiers going down very fast and there might be a collision. Off the trails, well, this is a mountain, and we occasionally get bears or wolves wandering around. Now, please go to the gondola and catch a ride down."

She points toward the gondola with the seats coming up, and we head over. With the interruption, I'm harshly reminded of the cold, and frantically tug my gloves back on. When Jaxon's eyes are still narrowed, I nudge him in the ribs and tug him behind me, practically bolting toward the gondola.

Once we're strapped in and descending, I can't even marvel at the view below as the car moves down the line, our feet dangling in the air. Instead, I keep my face buried in Jaxon's shoulder.

"That was so *embarrassing*," I whine. "They're probably going to blacklist us."

"Worth it. Besides, it was an honest mistake—no one told us we couldn't climb up."

"But *still*."

The rest of the way down and then to the car, he tries to reason with me that it's not worth being embarrassed, and when that doesn't work, he distracts me with a game of "Would You Rather?"

In the car, I'm finally spared from the cold, and I take off my beanie with glee as he starts the car and we begin moving. When I rip my gloves off, the sight of the ring greets me, and I raise my hand in front of me, unable to resist admiring it, his gesture stealing my breath.

As Jaxon stops at the stop sign, I reach over, pulling him in for a quick kiss, my hand over his chest. He grows distracted for a moment, kissing me back before pulling away.

"No distracting the driver," he admonishes, taking my hand and placing it over my lap.

I'm excited the whole drive, either glancing at the ring or at him, hands inching toward him every chance I get.

A small eon later, the car finally stops, and I turn away from him, opening the door. "First one to the room—"

My foot pauses on the ground as I finally notice my surroundings. Whipping my head back to him, my eyes narrow and I accuse, "This isn't the motel."

With a simple, "Nope," he gets out and rounds the car to pull me fully out of my seat and lock the car. He laughs at my shocked expression, grabbing my hand, more relaxed than I think I've ever seen him, and tugs me toward the entrance of the quaint bookstore he's brought me to.

"You didn't think a—failed—ski and snowboarding lesson and a mountain slope was all I had planned for the day, did you?"

And it really isn't.

Chapter 23

Nightmares

"You've killed me," I moan into the couch. "I'm so *tired*."

The ski resort was apparently only the tip of the iceberg in terms of what Jaxon had planned for today. His reasoning was that we were only here for a few days, but I think he overestimated how long I can be out for and with giving me the ring, he really wanted to go overboard.

And there was no room for a deviation from the list of places he wanted to show me. Not even for some light kissing in the car, which was an utter travesty.

At one point, after maybe the third place we'd gone to, but before dinner, I'd leaned over and kissed him in the car while we were still in the parking lot. It was finally dark enough that I reasoned I could climb over the console and straddle him, desperate to just have him press against me, to melt into him.

Instead, he'd put me back in my seat and said, "Keep those grabby hands to yourself, Layla. Trying to debauch me, are you? Corrupt my innocence?"

Shocked, I'd only been able to sputter, "You're the furthest thing from innocent!"

If it wasn't for the heated glances he kept shooting at me throughout the day or his white-knuckled grip on the steering wheel most of the drive, resisting the urge to reach over and touch me, I would've thought he just wasn't interested in having me that way.

Instead, it's been proven that Jaxon is a stickler for following his schedules, down to the last minute, and cannot be rushed. I remember all the grand plans of seduction I had earlier, but now that I'm face-down on the couch, legs aching miserably, I wonder if I'll even have it in me to get up and brush my teeth.

Jaxon, on the other hand, hums happily as he moves around the room, too energetic for someone who was just out for the whole day. My derailed plans and tiredness aside, I can admit that I really enjoyed myself, and Jaxon is not one to hold back on spoiling me. From the carefully selected places and sights to the delicious dinner and his sweet words, he's ruined me for any other man.

But then again, he did so long before today, anyway.

With a dreamy sigh and probably still in a food coma, I roll over, watching him move around and get ready for bed. He smiles when he catches me watching, but there's no hiding the way it slowly morphs into something heady and dangerous, the insatiable side of him coming to play.

Of course, he'll not take me up on any of my advances for the whole day, but start sending signals the moment I'm tired. Despite that, disappointment surfaces when he looks away. I really don't have any sense of self-preservation, do I?

My phone chiming pulls me away, and I grab it from the side table. Since yesterday, I've been wary about every notification, but that never stops me from quickly checking my phone. Is it human nature, I wonder, to be drawn toward danger and the things that hurt? Or is that just me?

The whole day, every text and notification has been safe and not from someone trying to chase me across the country. Except every safe notification lulled me into a sense of complacency until I slowly began to hope that maybe that one message was a fluke.

But that's not the case, because this is another text very obviously from the people I ran away from. This one is from a different number, the words, *Do you really think I can't find you?* staring at me, and this is so much worse than yesterday's.

Yesterday's was almost like a plea, but this is a taunt, warning, and gloat all in one. It's more than a question; it's an ownership. An ownership that resembles a noose around my neck, even thousands of miles away, until I am sure I cannot breathe. Any moment, and I know my thoughts will spiral, I know the *what-ifs* will start to haunt me until they're all I know.

Perhaps it's from a lack of self-preservation, but again, I delete and block the number, refusing to be the girl that takes every veiled warning and catastrophizes it. Every part of that world, every part of him and the men around him is a game of wiles and cunning, and I refuse to play that game. My past can come knocking as much as it wants, but I won't let that door budge even an inch.

Because I made it out. *I made it out* and it's going to *stay* that way. Right here, right now, my father is nowhere near me, the mafia is nowhere near me. It's just Jaxon with me, and the only ring on my finger is his mother's, and the only promises on my tongue are for him.

So when I change into pajamas and go to the bedroom, finding him on the balcony, and he tugs me down to his lap, mouth finding mine, I kiss him back. I kiss him like he's air and I'm desperate to breathe; like I've been denied it for long enough, and I won't ever stop now.

I kiss him like he's my drug, my safe place, my heart. I kiss him like he's everything I want right now and everything I need. And from how his hands travel beneath my shirt, rucking my shirt up, I know he enjoys it very much. His arms are my haven, his heart my home, and I melt into him, not bothering to support myself, because I know he'll catch me—that he'll always hold me in a way no one else ever has and ever will, rendering me into a person simply content to *be*.

I remember all our moments together years ago, who he was then and who he is now, from every sweet gesture to every addictive grin, and I fall into him a bit more. I wasn't lying when I thought it would be easy to fall in love with him. I always doubted whether I could be loved easily that I never realized how easy it could be for me *to* love. Wanting him is as easy as breathing, and filling up every inch of my heart with him is addicting.

His hands are around me and my hands cradle his face, my legs on either side of him, and he tastes like everything I've ever wanted. "I want you to be my everything," I tell him in between kisses and moans and with a heart that won't stop pounding.

"You're already my everything," he promises, pulling back far enough that his eyes tell me more than I ever need to know.

Before I can even let out a shaky breath, he draws me closer, a hand in my hair tugging my head back until he fills my vision, and while my body shivers with excitement and hunger, I've never had so much raw hope for the future.

He kisses me softly, and it's a caress, a promise, a tender thing that burrows into my heart. He does it again and again, a little deeper each time, and even though there's nothing urgent to them, I tug at the hem of his shirt.

"Off," I plead, when he pulls away again.

Instead, he abruptly stands up, and I feel the muscles beneath my hand flexing as he grips me harder. I tighten my legs around his hips, watching as he slides the balcony door shut, now holding me with one arm. The display shouldn't do much to me, but it does, and I know I could easily become addicted to the strength in his body, the ease with which he carries me.

Carrying me to the bed, he arranges us much like we were before, with him sitting and me above him. I almost forget my request until he reaches behind him, grabbing the back of his shirt and tugging it off.

Before I can look my fill of his moon-kissed skin, smooth over the curves and ridges of his body, he tugs me closer, mouth slanting over mine. I kiss him back, hands settling over his chest, luxuriating in the solid feel of him, the way his body doesn't give at all, hard where I am soft. His heart hammers a wild crescendo beneath my palm as I touch him. I am distracted by his hands roving up across my waist before dipping down to grab my hips, as though he cannot decide where he wants to hold me.

He kisses me until I cannot breathe, until I cannot think, and I shift with yearning, lean into him with desperation. Pulling back, I pant, and almost sigh at the sight of him, all flushed skin and swollen lips, half of him cast in moonlight.

"I want you," I say, my meaning clear.

Pushing off the pillows, he braces himself with one arm behind him, and for a moment, I grow distracted by the sight of certain muscles across his shoulders and chest rolling beneath skin. He cups my face, the soft gesture dichotomous with his next words.

"The first time you'll have me won't be in a motel room where I need to worry about stifling your sounds," he rasps, voice a rough timbre, as though the self-control it took to say those words is moments away from shredding.

As much as I'd like to taunt him, to test how far that self-control can stretch before it *snaps*, I can see the reasoning in his words, and I tell myself to shake off the impending worry that this is all borrowed time anyway.

Even then, I must make a face of petulant disappointment because he laughs, head tipped back, the bold column of his throat half-visible, that dimple peeking out to play. "Oh, sweetheart, you're going to be *bad* for my self-control."

Like it always does, his blatant mirth brings out my own, and I settle back against him, smiling into his skin. "Better kiss me good then."

And he does, until I can almost convince myself that we'll get to stay in this bubble for a little while longer, that every worry, from the texts to my fears, doesn't exist.

Almost, but not quite.

It's so quiet. Too quiet. And everything around me is dark as I struggle, trying to push past the barrier that blocks my senses.

When I do, I wish I hadn't.

There are flashes of red and white light, and everything is disoriented as sirens blare. I vaguely register that I'm being moved, with masked figures above me. There's a dull pain everywhere, pulsing throughout my body in hot bursts as I slowly remember the moments before I passed out, as I remember what we were running from.

I'm trying to jerk off the surface, tugging at the mask over my mouth, ripping at it as panic overtakes me. Everything is blurry, but I know that there were only two people with me. There's a gurney a few feet away, with people moving around it, almost frantic.

I throw the mask off, breathing in pants as I try to get up. Rough hands grab me, but I scream and yank.

I just need to see.

I just need to see.

Running, body tripping over itself, I reach the mass of bodies that are probably fewer than they seem, and I squeeze through, managing to get a look even though someone grabs my arms and tries to yank me away.

Dark brown hair so similar to mine is splattered with blood, an ugly, jagged mark slashed across a forehead. The blood is everywhere; across her hair, dripping from her mouth. None of that compares, though, to the eyes staring blankly above, and it's the one sight that finally does me in, searing itself into my brain.

Your fault, your fault, your fault, the darkness chants in my mind.

There's a shrill noise piercing my ears, a heartbroken keen, and I realize it's coming from me. Even when they pull me away until she disappears from sight, I don't stop screaming.

Even when a lone figure steps out of a familiar car, his body freezing at what he sees, car keys dropping from his hands as though he already knows who he's lost, I don't stop screaming.

And I don't think I ever will.

I wake up to someone shaking my shoulder, repeating my name. Blinking my bleary eyes, my heart pounding hard enough that it hurts, I see Jaxon staring down at me. Though I can't see him properly in the dark, I can hear the worry in his voice as he repeats, "It was just a nightmare."

Immediately, he arranges me to lie over him, arms wrapping around me, but I shake my head, because it's not enough.

"On top," I mumble.

I need to feel him over me, the weight of him pressing me into the bed until the demons of my mind are soothed once more. He does as I ask, hesitant to crush me, but I tug him all the way down until he presses against me, infinitely better than any weighted blanket, and gradually, I even my breathing until it matches his. Everything is obscure without my glasses, but my inability to focus on anything only helps to calm me down further, the contours of my panic becoming blurry until it fades away.

"Want to talk about it?"

"Just a nightmare," I mumble.

"You haven't gotten them before with me. Is this a one-time thing, or has it been happening frequently still?"

When the nightmares and night terrors started becoming infrequent, and stopped altogether with him, I really hoped that they were over. That as the days morphed into weeks, the surprise of waking up slowly to a morning and not abruptly from a nightmare became acceptance, became something I now expect.

"They used to be pretty frequent but got better recently. And stopped altogether for these past few weeks."

And even though he doesn't say anything, I know there's the question of *what prompted one now, then?* I know the answer—that texts not only drudged up fear, but dug into my subconscious, burrowing in like a parasite until a nightmare surfaced once I slept.

"I'm fine now," I lie, even as weary frustration settles in my veins, curling into my mind, and I wonder what else will surface. Will my mind twist and stumble on itself again, my thoughts once again veering into a dark fascination with everything that can harm me?

My throat burns, and I want to cry. I want to cry because I thought I was finally getting better, and I hate this relapse, even if it could be momentary. I hate it because I don't want to feel that way again, I don't want to find out that to heal isn't so easy.

"I'm fine," I repeat, but there's a tremor in my voice, and an ache in my chest.

He knows, as he always does, and murmurs, "Oh, Layla," into my hair. "It's okay for things not to be fine." I grasp him tightly, body shaking, mind crumbling, and he lets me, a hand alternating between rubbing up and down my arm or sifting through my hair, the movement drugging. "It's okay, sweetheart. It's okay to stumble, it's okay to break, and when you can't pick up the pieces by yourself, that's okay. I'll pick them up for you."

But I don't want to cry, and I don't want to break. I want to *forget*.

"I don't want to go back to sleep," I say into the dark. I don't want to relive that moment again, or the other slew of nightmares my mind likes to cycle through.

He pulls himself up just enough to see me properly. "Then what do you want?"

Reaching up, I cup his face, bringing it closer to mine, until my meaning is clear, and his voice, as low and rough as it gets, is still a warning when he says, "Layla…"

"Please," I rasp. "I want to forget. With you… with you, my mind quiets in a way it doesn't with anyone else. With you, I'm not someone who's scared, or paranoid, or haunted, I just *am*." And maybe it speaks to an unhealthy need to have him, but I want him all the same. "But I don't want to make you feel like I'm using you, because I'm not. You're never a means to an end for me."

For as much as he may think he has a moral obligation to make me process my emotions, he caves, dropping closer, until his breath coasts over my mouth, his lips tantalizingly close. "I know that, sweetheart."

"I love it when you call me that," I murmur, and kiss him.

With one arm braced beside my head, holding himself half-up until I can feel the way certain muscles stretch taut beneath my fingers, he buries a hand into my hair, almost spanning half my head until every sensation is of him. Of his body above me and his mouth against mine.

I'm insatiable as my hands rove across him, over his shoulders and chest, across his arms, delighting in the solid feel of him, the bulges and dips of his body, before I cup his face. When he pulls away, his breath practically heaves, whole body rising and falling like I've utterly unmoored him.

I reach to pull him back to me, but he traces kisses across my neck, alternating between featherlight sensations and deeper kisses, wet and hot against my throat, until I think I will combust out of my skin.

He nips my ear and my back arches a little, a whimper climbing up my throat. When he places his hand on my waist, I murmur senseless pleas, until I'm not Layla but a mindless creature made up of nerve endings and maddening sensations. Every groan from him and touch lights me aflame until I shake, desperate. His hand edges beneath my shirt, grip utterly possessive, and it's just his hand, but the skin-to-skin contact is divine enough I have to bite my lip, my senses jarred.

"Whatever you want, sweetheart." He'll never stop calling me that, and I couldn't be happier. "You tell me if something is too fast and I'll stop, alright? That's how this works, and how it'll always work."

I nod my head, a few seconds from begging him to just shut up and kiss me again, even when his careful consideration makes my breath trip and stumble. In the darker moments of my past, when I knew that *he* was visiting, and slowly came to understand the kind of life promised to me as a *don*'s daughter, I never believed I'd have a partner so careful to make sure I want him. So careful to make me feel wanted, so careful to only give what I also want.

Sometimes, I couldn't even be sure if I deserved anything other than what was promised to me, and with every day, Jaxon proves me wrong. Every day, he shows me what it means to be cared for, and better, he slowly, maybe unknowingly, makes me believe I deserve it too.

And maybe it's the bare minimum, but it floors me all the same, because for years, I never believed I'd get even that.

Unbidden, my hands come up to hold his face, to gently trace the arch of his cheekbones, the curve of his brow. His head falls into my hands, wordlessly taking what I offer until his throat bobs on a rough swallow, his eyes telling me the words I'm not ready to hear yet.

Slivers of moonlight filter past the edges of the curtains until I make out the edges of want in his eyes, his jaw tightening as his hands move over me. It's impossible to hide the ways he's changed over the years; his desire tastes dark, body shaking like he's holding himself back.

I realize that there's a lot I haven't told him, worried it might scare him, but I wonder how much he hides, worried he'll scare me. I want to tell him to bare all his demons, a hypocrite when I won't do the same with mine.

He draws my legs up to wrap around his waist, until I can feel him, and my bare legs rove across his sweatpants, my shirt bunching up around my waist.

Leaning down, lips rasping against the shell of my ear, he murmurs, "Want me, sweetheart?"

I shiver at the dark *want* in his voice, at the way it reflects in his eyes. He looks like a starving man placed in front of a feast, the *hunger* so raw, I shake my head sharply yes, and widen my legs a little. He grins a little, body pressing further against mine until my eyes roll back, body shivering in anticipation, in pure senseless want.

Unable to stop myself, I touch him, desperate, pulling him down to kiss his throat, his jaw, tasting and biting until he seals his mouth over me with a groan. Every slide of his tongue and nip of his teeth is echoed with a twist of his hips until my blood heats and body shakes, strumming higher.

Perhaps more addictive, though, is how he seems to slowly grow ravenous, body shaking, senselessly seeking mine, and I am only made of *want*. When he pulls away, it's to slide his gaze down to the sight of me beneath him, shirt racked up high.

"I want to see you," he murmurs. "But I'll save that for another day."

"Shut up and kiss me."

With a smile, he comes closer, lips close enough they brush against mine, his next words spoken directly into my mouth. "Whatever you want, sweetheart. Though next time, you'll have to specify where."

Shivering, I cling to him harder, almost needy. When he trails kisses across my neck, my head falls back onto the pillows, and I look at him through half-lidded eyes, murmuring, "*Mia vita*, I don't think I can breathe without you."

And then he *loses* it. A hand tunnels into my hair, pulling my head so he can ravish me the way he wants, the other coming up around me to pull me further into him. I gasp at the undeniable press of him between my legs, the sensation heady despite the barriers of our clothing.

I shiver, sliding my hands around him, one going into his hair, enjoying the feel of the strands before everything grows hazy as he kisses me. Except this time, he's not just kissing me, but moving as well, hips rolling and punching up. It's a promise and a tease of how different things could be if there were less clothes between us, and soon enough, I writhe over him, gasping and shaking.

His movements grow less finesse as he ravishes me, mouth moving against mine and hands strobing and squeezing until I cry out into his mouth. He presses and rubs until my body clenches, needy delight curling low in my stomach, but it's not *enough*. It makes me ravenous for more, and with every movement, he stalls from giving me what I want.

"Jaxon," I wheeze.

"What, sweetheart?"

"More." More of what, I don't know. Harder? Faster? Or do I want less? Less *damn clothes*.

"You have no idea how long I've wanted you, Layla. No idea how long I'd imagine you beneath me, wondering what you sound like. So no, now that I finally have you here, in a bed, I think I'll take my time. And you'll enjoy it, won't you, sweetheart? Do you think you can be good for me for just a little longer?"

They're just words, but my head falls back, neck arching. My breathing saws out in pants when he keeps kissing my neck, nipping and sucking, his hands everywhere, the breadth of them over my skin a heady thing, my shirt nearly at my neck now, and he keeps languidly rolling his hips.

"I think you like it when I talk dirty to you, don't you, sweetheart?"

I mumble something incoherent, twisting a little, as if unsure whether I want to move lower or escape.

"You know how I know you like it?" he hums, body working faster. "Because you have this pretty flush over your skin that reaches all the way down to your chest, your skin's almost as red as these cute as hell cherries on your bra. And I can *feel* your want."

If most of my senses weren't thrown out the window, I'd probably choke at how he talks.

"Is this what you like? When I whisper dirty nothings in your ear?"

He keeps rolling his body, faster now, continuing to whisper delightfully wicked things in my ear while keeping that steady pace, occasionally faltering as though he can't help himself. A flush spreads over my chest and cheeks as I spasm around nothing, and I know that it's *right there*. He can tell too, because he leans even closer, telling me to open my eyes.

I do, meeting his gaze desperately. It's feverish, like the flush that spreads over my skin.

"That's it, sweetheart," he murmurs, hands traveling across my skin, mapping all my sensitive places, before a hand settles over my mouth.

"Quiet," he gasps. "We need to be quiet."

With what can only be described as a muffled moan and a gasp, I come apart at the seams, breathing hard, filled with a languid sort of contentment. I watch, enraptured, at the pleasure that breaks across his features, his head falling back, a flush flaring across his face, his breath heaving and body shaking until he is a man undone. Someone who is all *mine*.

I don't know when I'll be able to form a coherent sentence again, but he drew it out for so long that I'm too sleepy to bother speaking at all.

Without looking at him, I know he's smirking, a satisfied gleam probably in his eyes. I don't bother rebuking it, just sigh softly when he wraps his arms around me and pulls me closer, plunging me into the world of sweet sleep that's not an abyss of escaping.

Chapter 24

Kaleidoscope

For the rest of our stay at Tahoe, it's easy to believe that we're a normal couple. *And when De Leone finds you?* I bury those thoughts away as the day carries on, and it's easy to. Because hurling snow at Jaxon is fun, and sledding even more so.

We spend the rest of the day laughing and sledding over the snow, purposely going over the rocks and bumps and then cursing when I go back up the hill. The snow is soft and wet, and the higher we go, the more we sink into it. By the end, I'm aching all over, cold from the waist down despite wearing the thick snow pants. And every time, Jaxon laughs as he hauls me back up, even though he's no better, the both of us tumbling like fawns learning how to walk.

At the end of the day, we collapse, exhausted, in the motel room, and the following morning, the aches hurt more.

Rolling across the bed, I climb on top of Jaxon, snuggling into his warm, hard body, drinking in the smell of him. I love the way we fit, the way I melt into him. "I want to stay here forever."

"Tahoe? Really?" he murmurs, voice thick from sleep, the edges of it husky. "I thought you said you'd be glad to be done with all the snow."

"I mean," I correct. "Stay like this forever. On top of you."

He laughs a little, and my body rises and falls with every breath he takes. "I wore you out very nicely, didn't I?"

The innuendo is clear as day, even if I'm worn out from a long day in the snow. He tries to sit up, but I moan and squeeze onto him tighter. "I'm not going *anywhere*."

"But we need to check out soon. We woke up late and still have to get ready."

With a sigh, like he's being utterly outrageous and unfair, I roll away, tangling in the sheets, and bury into the pillows. He seems disappointed that I've gotten off of him, brows momentarily slanting downward, hands reaching for me, but since his discipline is way better than mine, he actually gets up. I'm convinced that to him, checking out less than fifteen minutes early is egregious.

Grabbing my ankles, he drags me toward him, kisses my pouting lips, and pulls me off the bed. Sighing, I trudge to the bathroom to get ready too, and decide to take care of the mess that is my hair.

"You know," I tell him, "the faster we get ready, the sooner we'll be on the road. Imagine that—hours of driving, and you won't get to touch me *at all*."

His eyes meet mine in the mirror, a brow arched in amusement but gaze calculating, and I can already tell that I've won this round. I've barely finished rinsing the toothpaste from my mouth before he's grabbing me and backing me against the wall, kissing me and touching me like I'm his everything.

Outside, the morning is quiet, snow steadily falling across the parking lot, turning the world into a blur of white. I pause, dropping the bag until it thuds softly against the ground, and tilt my head up, the snow falling across my face like a soft, cold caress. As short as it was, the getaway was a reprieve I hadn't realized I needed, and now that I'm faced with leaving, I find myself slowing, trying to enjoy everything one last time before we go. We might come here again in the future, but that insidious part of me doubts, and with the texts, I almost believe someone is waiting for me back in the Bay Area.

"Your pretty face will get cold like this," Jaxon says, and even though my eyes are closed, I know he's standing before me, close enough to touch.

Mitted hands settle on my face, the soft cloth dotted with snow, the threads of his gloves tickling my skin, until I smile. I open my eyes to the sight of him, half-cast in white with the snow across my glasses. He dusts the snow away, giving me a sweet, small smile, almost as soft as the snowy world around us.

"First one to the car gets to pick where we'll stop on the way back."

I see it for what it is—a distraction from whatever has curled into my mind—but I take it. When he tries to grab me, as though to cheat, I dash away, bundled in my thermals and winter jacket. My shoes crunch across the snow, almost slipping, and stopping, I bend down to pick up a handful, laughing. Compressing it, I turn around and hurl it at him, and it hits him square in the chest before crumpling over his jacket and to the floor, white streaks left behind.

For a moment, he stops, dusts off the snow, and then looks up at me, a positively devilish grin spreading across his features. Similarly, my grin gets wider from pure glee, and I blink at him innocently before searching for the car and running toward it.

A laugh builds in my throat as I run, almost jumping every time I can hear him getting closer. I squeal when he grabs me, an arm snagging around me and hauling me up into him, mere spaces away from the car. He presses a gloveless, cold hand on my cheek, and I squeal again from the cold, laughing and trying to break from his hold.

"Jaxon! They're cold, get your hands away, or... or, no kisses!"

He pulls his roaming hands away only to pepper my face and neck with kisses—and of course, his lips are cold too. Though occasionally, his kisses are less lip and more teeth with how hard he's grinning.

"I love your laugh and your smile, you know that, right? I love it when you're happy," he murmurs.

His skin is paler, his nose is slightly red from the cold, and he looks kind of adorable. "You make me happy," I tell him.

"Good. Because I'll have you know I consider it to be my job. And if that ever changes, if I ever do anything to make you unhappy, I want you to tell me immediately, so I can rectify it."

As much as his words pull at something in me, giving it wings, urging it to fly and *feel*, I playfully roll my eyes. "Such a sap."

He leans down and nips my ear for my sass, before dramatically wrapping an arm around my waist and dipping me down. I laugh, wrapping my arms around his shoulder, and he passionately kisses me, but overly so, to the point it's playful.

With a dramatic flourish, he breaks away and, eyes gleaming wickedly, drops me. I fall flat on my backside, eyes wide, stunned, as I blink slowly, shocked at his audacity. Laughing, he helps me up, dusts me off, and after I demand it, gives me an apology kiss.

"So," I start, getting in the car. "Where are we going?"

"Where do you think we're going?" he ventures, reminding me of when we were younger and how he figured out to take me to the lake.

I want to see him flounder for a place to go. "Oh no, that's not going to work this time. I don't know what's on the way back."

"Well, it wouldn't have been a surprise anyway since I'll need to use GPS."

After putting in the directions, he starts the car, the wheels crunching louder since he's put the chains around them. For the entire drive, all we do is talk. With the heater on, and as I occasionally laugh at something he says, the atmosphere is cozy.

Eventually, he gets a call from Mike, and from what I can glean from Jaxon's side, it's cute to hear the two of them converse.

Leaning further back into the seat, I look at the scenery outside to give him a semblance of privacy, and also since their conversation reminds me of that night I overheard them talking.

And of course, it gets worse when I hear Mike yell, loud enough that his once muffled end of the conversation is now clear. "I am *so* calling a restraining order. They're *everywhere*. Creepy freaks. Don't they know I've *retired*?"

Jaxon sighs. "This again?"

I don't miss how his eyes dart to me, and then back to the road. Does he feel guilty that he's hiding something?

Well, I'm the daughter of a don, *with whoever holding my hand in marriage promised to be the heir to a crime empire, so your secret can't be too bad.*

But in the end, it's just both of us hiding things.

The drive back, after our pit stop, is mostly uneventful, the two of us lapsing into a comfortable silence, occasionally talking about everything to anything. I pretend I didn't hear their conversation, pretend nothing could ever be wrong. *Just let me have this*, I can't help but think.

Sometimes, when he isn't paying attention, I furtively take a picture of him, snapping it and storing the moment. *It's not so I'll have something to remember*, I tell myself. *I won't need to say goodbye.*

My mind aches for an escape, and I'm reminded that I haven't painted anything in a long time—almost weeks now. My hands itch for a paintbrush or a sketch pencil, and I already know what I want to paint.

Like a woman possessed, the artistic urge at the forefront of my mind, I'm only half-aware of my surroundings as we carry our luggage to the apartment, too busy planning what I want to create. Now, my mind and body are a medium for the conveyance of art, my limbs possessed.

Still, when the door finally opens and we stumble inside, the familiar sight greeting me, a smile breaks across my face, jittery urges settling. "Home sweet home," I murmur.

Jaxon's eyes dart to mine, and I pause a bit at my words. But it *does* already feel like home.   Home is where you're happy, comfortable, and safe. And in my—albeit very short—time here so far, I've experienced all of that in these walls.

He smiles softly, and unable to meet his gaze, my attention darts away. When he looks at me like that, and it's become more often, my heart almost wants to burst until I want to tell him words I'm not sure I mean yet.

Kicking off my shoes, I don't bother with changing my clothes or unpacking my suitcase, and head straight to the little art studio. Just being in here, with the sight of the easel and paints and cabinets full of art supplies, sunlight streaming in through the little window, is cathartic.

Humming to myself, I select the colors I need and the paintbrush for the first layer. One memory is still fresh in my mind, enough that I don't need to pull out a picture of it, and for the fuzzy details, I can simply wing it.

I start with the first layer, which is mainly just the sky, and then the background of the lower half of the painting. The sky is always my favorite part to do—blending out the colors, starting with a dark blue before lightening the tone as I go down—and soon, it's easy for me to lose myself in the painting. I add the layers as I go, occasionally humming to myself, and as my hands get messier and my back begins to hurt, I adjust the easel and shed my shirt.

Now, in my black tank top, I tie my hair on top of my head and let out a sigh. It's still not done, and when it is, it probably will be a plain piece, but with the stage it's at right now, like a set of bare bones that need fleshing out, I have a hard time liking it, a hard time seeing it for what it could be.

Sometimes, one of the hardest things about being an artist is trying to love your work, no matter what stage it's at and not obsessing over minor "mistakes" a viewer wouldn't even realize.

"You look like a hot mess."

I jump, startled, and turn around to spot Jaxon leaning against the doorframe, arms crossed, one ankle behind the other. His hair is slightly damp from a shower, falling over his forehead and curling slightly around his ears.

Looking toward the mirror on one of the walls, I see that he's right. My hair is put up in a chaotic bun, most of my fingers are spotted in paint, and somehow, a streak of it ended up on my face.

"Mess, yes. Not so sure about 'hot.' And just how long have you been standing there?"

He grins. "For ages. I've been watching you like a creep."

I fake-shudder, and he comes closer, a plate of food in his hands, a cut apple and a cheese sandwich. Wordlessly, he hands it over to me, and gestures to one of my unopened, smaller canvases.

"May I?"

Nodding, I grab an apple slice, and he sets the canvas up, starting his own project. Soon enough, once I've finished the food, grateful he brought it, otherwise I probably would've skipped lunch and dinner, we paint side by side. Occasionally, I steal glances at him, watching the sunlight turn his hair a lighter, almost gleaming brown. Like this, with the edges of his eyelashes almost a brilliant gold, his eyes a bright amber rather than an almost-black, he looks as though he's painted in sunlight, and it's the most beautiful thing I've ever seen.

Looking at him, my heart aches with a sweet kind of hurt, as though realizing it isn't mine anymore.

Chapter 25

Endearments

It's not often that I consider myself a perfectionist, except maybe when I'm staring at a painting on its third layer and it's still not looking how I want it to. And it seems I'm also a perfectionist when it comes to gift-giving, or maybe it's just that I want the gesture to be memorable.

I glance down again to the ring on my finger, wondering how whatever I give him can come even close to the significance behind his gift for me. But the longer I take to decide, the sooner until he shows up, and I'd rather have *something* than nothing at all.

He left with Mike around an hour ago, saying they wanted to do some swimming practice, that he'd be back in the evening, and that he'd text me if anything comes up. So far, it seems everything's okay, but he has been messaging anyway with little things like, *How are you?* And *Don't tell anyone, but I think Mike is jealous that I text you.*

His messages are heartwarming, especially since I know he has to get out of the pool and dry his hands first to send each one, breaking away from practice and whatever else they're doing. He left his car for me too, saying Mike would pick him up instead so I could go somewhere if I wanted to.

It might have taken very little effort on his part to simply hand me his keys, and maybe he lets everyone use his car if they need it, but I almost melted at the gesture. Maybe it's because of the girl in me that never knew a semblance of freedom over those years, or maybe it's because I see it as a clear sign of his trust in me.

That incessant, nagging voice surfaces again, telling me I'm not good enough, that I don't deserve this, that I don't deserve him.

And maybe it's true, but I *want* to. I want to be the kind of person that irrevocably trusts him as he does me and feel comfortable to tell him about my past, about what I left behind. I want to have faith that just as how I've always trusted him with my body and who I am, that I've trusted him to be nothing but caring, that I can also trust him with another part of me and he won't freak out.

But right now, I want to get him a gift. Sometimes, I feel he's the only one doing things for me—letting me move in, taking me out on dates, planning a weekend trip—and I want to make his heart trip too.

So with that, I grab his keys and head down, an idea slowly taking root.

As much as I enjoy walking through the shop-lined street with its bustling cafes and bulb lights strung across the storefronts, by the time I go into the last stop for the day, face still flaming from Harlow's suggestion, I'm exhausted and beyond ready to go home. Still, I wish I'd come to this part of the city sooner, with its cobblestone, narrow roads and miniature triangle banners criss-crossing overhead.

I've grown so used to the gray, almost industrial style of many buildings in this country, that to see something else is like looking at art, the similarities distinct.

As tired as I am, by the time I eventually leave, almost fighting for my life to exit the narrow parking spot, I'm disappointed. When

I get home, I nearly groan at the thought of everything else I still have planned, but then I imagine Jaxon's expression when he sees it all, and I'm filled with a giddy excitement. It fuels me as I paint the miniature canvas and then get ready in the few hours I have to spare before he gets back.

But what I saved for last—to make some semblance of a meal— is what does me in. I stare at the mess across every kitchen counter, at the various ingredients strewn over the surfaces along with the many plates and spoons. *Where the hell did all this mess even come from?*

Worse, the cute dress I put on, stupidly thinking I couldn't possibly get it too messy, has streaks of flour across it.

"No, no, no," I mutter as I move around, trying to clean up while keeping an eye on what's in the oven, not willing to risk burning it.

Frustration climbs up my throat as I try to clean the mess while constantly glancing at the clock. Stupidly, I have the urge to cry, frustrated at the long day, the sun less than an hour away from setting, and that this isn't turning out exactly how I wanted it to. I accidentally took a little longer with the painting project, and Jaxon texted ten minutes ago that he's on his way. I look at the clock again. Well, more like fifteen minutes ago now.

And I still need to clean everything, take the food out to cool, change my clothes, and wrap up the gifts or put them in a gift bag. I pause as I reach above the stove to put the flour and dry ingredients away in the cabinet above. Merda, *did I even buy a gift bag?*

"Okay, Layla," I say aloud. "Calm down. One thing at a time and take deep breaths."

Stilling myself, still stretched up to reach the cabinet, I take a deep breath, and another. Soon enough, it regulates me until the edges of panic seep away, but on the third inhale, there's a strange smell.

Sniffing, I try to puzzle out the smoky smell, glancing down when I finally put the ingredients away. And that's when I realize three things: I somehow left the stove on, the hem of my dress is on fire, and the front door just opened.

And then the smoke alarm turns on, and Jaxon rushes into the kitchen, calling out my name in panic.

When he catches sight of me rushing to the sink, holding the flaming edge of my dress away from my skin, the next "Layla?" is incredulous before he's helping me turn on the water and douse the fire.

We both stare at the charred remains of the hem of my dress, the blaring smoke alarm the only sound in the room. I'm utterly mortified, sure he's processing what he walked into and debating if it's worth it to leave me alone in his apartment again. I cover my face with my hands and groan, wanting to crawl under the sink. Better yet, I want a redo of the day.

Turning me around, he takes my hands and pulls them away from my face, his skin warm against mine, hands engulfing. His expression is concerned, brows drawn, as he says, "Hey, are you alright? Did the fire touch you?"

I shake my head, gnawing on my lower lip instead of giving an explanation, before realizing the stove is probably still on. "Uh, the stove is still on."

Immediately, he reaches over to turn it off, and then glances up to the smoke alarm. "I'm going to open up the windows to get the smoke out."

By the time he's done, a cool breeze blows into the apartment, and his earlier shock has worn away. If anything, as he comes back, tidying the kitchen while I stand there, I almost think the fire never happened and it was all in my head.

"I just almost set the apartment on fire," I say, wondering why he's not even a little bit angry.

Instead, he looks at me, body angled toward the pantry door. "You sure it didn't get you?"

I shake my head again.

"Layla, it's normal for accidents to happen in the kitchen, and you seemed to be handling it fine."

"But I could've set the apartment on fire," I repeat.

Shaking his head, he stops what he's doing to come to me and places his hands on my shoulders. "Unless you covered every surface in gasoline or got too close to the walls, you would not have set the apartment on fire. I'm not upset, Layla, if that's what you're worried about. It's totally normal to slip up in the kitchen, and I'm just glad you're okay. In fact, I'm happy you were comfortable enough to use the kitchen, since you haven't really been... settling in and treating this place as yours."

It's not my place, I want to point out, but I know what he means. Most days, I'm trepid against touching anything or opening cabinets, as though this is a dream I will be yanked out of if I overstep.

"I was trying to make you something," I grumble.

Immediately, his eyes light up, a smile pulling at his lips, and the next thing I know, I'm smiling back, utterly stupid with the sight of his happiness.

"You were?"

Nodding, I reach over and open the oven, grabbing a mitt to pull out the dessert. "I-I just wanted to make you something," I stutter. "But I don't think they came out right. They're apple turnovers."

"They're perfect."

"Jaxon, you haven't even tried them yet."

"Don't care. They're still perfect to me."

I let out an *oomph* when he grabs me and crushes me to him, squeezing me in a tight hug. "I can't wait to try them, sweetheart. And trust me, the fact that you made me something is more important than how they taste or look."

Wrapping my arms around him, I return the hug, sinking into him, burying my head into his soft sweatshirt, and joke, "You're this touched and I haven't even given you your gifts yet."

"You got me gifts?"

He sounds dumbfounded, arms tight around me, and I wonder if he's unused to these gestures, if no one really gets him gifts. The raw happiness and shock in his tone makes me want to gift him something every day, and I promise myself I will.

Whether it's small like an unexpected kiss or grand like the cooking machines and motorcycles I catch him sometimes looking over on his phone. Sure, I'd probably have to sell a kidney to afford it, but to see the soft, surprised smile on his face again would be well worth it.

Nodding at him, I pull back and run to the other room, gathering the items. With care, I lay them over the counter, the stutter back in my voice as I say, "I forgot to get a gift bag, but I hope you like them, and there's a—"

He rounds the corner and pulls me in for a kiss, shutting me up. A hand goes up to cradle the back of my head while the other wraps around my waist, and he lifts me until I have to balance on the tips of my feet, body leaning into his. He kisses me desperately, sweetly, like he can't have enough of me, and moans into my mouth when his tongue slips against mine.

Dazed, I don't fully realize when he starts backing us up toward a wall. Pulling away with a gasp, I complain, "But you haven't even seen what I got you yet."

Dropping his forehead to mine, he pants like I've made him undone. "Right," he rasps. "Right. Okay, let me see."

With an arm still wrapped around me, he peruses the items, lifting them and admiring them. I try not to wear my heart on my sleeve and show how invested I am in his expressions, wanting, *needing* him to love every gift.

"This is a lot, Layla."

"Keep looking."

And he does. He lifts the hoodie, opens the packages, hands stilling over the new food mixer I got him. I shush his plaintive, "This is *expensive*, Layla, you shouldn't have spent this much money on me."

I think I sigh dreamily when he laughs at the psychology meme cup I got him, the one that reads, *No, I can't read your mind, I studied psychology, not telepathy.* I found it hidden in the back of a crowded shelf at an off-price department store while looking for something else, and just knew I had to get it.

He reaches the last item, the painting of two silhouettes holding each other against a snowy backdrop, and stills, fingers reverently touching the strokes and dips of the paint. "You made this?"

At my nod, he turns back to tug me even closer, kissing my cheeks, my chin, my forehead, pecking my lips. "Thank you, *ya qalbi.* You have no idea how much your gifts mean to me, how thoughtful they are. You *see* me. I don't deserve you, but I promise I'll spend every day learning how to."

And I know what he means, because I've always felt that *he* sees me, no matter the demons in my head or the secrets in my heart. It's odd to hear him say aloud the words I believe about myself, and I want to shake my head. I want to tell him he's gotten it all wrong, that *I'm* the one who doesn't deserve *him*.

When he leans back down to kiss me again, backing me up against the wall, I cover his mouth and hold him back. "You haven't tried the dessert yet!"

"I know a better dessert I can—"

"Jaxon!"

"Alright, alright." Turning around, he grabs a turnover, taking a bite, and I watch him attentively, half-expecting a wince. I really should've tried it first in case it came out terrible, but when all he does is offer a beaming smile, I shake off the worry. "Now I get why you were so adamant to jump my bones when I gave you a gift."

"I was not," I deny, reaching for a turnover.

He grabs my hand, keeping me from lifting the turnover to my mouth. "You definitely were. But are you sure you want to have dessert on an empty stomach? Let me make you a sandwich first."

My eyes narrow. "No, I want to try this."

"Layla—"

Grabbing another with my free hand, I bring it up and take a bite before he can stop me. Almost immediately, I rush over to the trash can and spit it out, grimacing and gagging. What did I *put* in there? Poison?

"That was so *bad*," I whine.

"No," he reasons. "The pastry is quite nice and flaky, and I liked it."

"*Amore mio*, don't lie. That was the worst thing I've ever tasted. How did I even make it that bad? You were faking that smile," I accuse.

"No. I am genuinely happy you made something for me."

"It was bad, admit it."

Sighing, he grabs me and lifts me onto the counter, stepping in between my legs so I have nowhere to go. I shouldn't keep letting him move me around whenever he wants, but a part of me delights in it every time.

"I love everything you made me and got me, I promise. I love that you've been thinking about me the whole day and went out to get me something. I love that you put thought and care into everything you got and made, because it shows me how much you care for me."

"But it isn't perfect."

"It's perfect for me."

Still a little disappointed, I open my mouth, but he silences me with a kiss, only pulling back to say, "Let me prove to you just how much I love everything."

Chapter 26

Closer Still

It's easy to think "everything" means me too, and soon enough, I'm lost in his drugging kisses, hand buried in his hair to hold him closer. I want to crawl into his heart as surely as he's burrowed into mine, until no one can see him without knowing he's mine.

When he begins to lay me back against the counter, my dress riding up until the cold countertop presses against my skin, I pull at his shirt, gasping, "Off."

My head spins as he pulls me up and lifts me, and in any other instance, it would be endearing how he fumbles toward the bedroom, almost bumping into the walls when he can't stop kissing me. In the room, he lies onto the bed, arranging us so he leans against the headboard and I'm above him. I almost forget my earlier request, enraptured with the sight of him, his eyes hooded as he regards me, hands warm against my hips. For a moment, I am sure that I have conjured him, that this is all an elaborate dream I will wake up from, and my hands twist in his shirt, reassuring myself that this is very real.

259

Grabbing the hem, he tugs his shirt off, revealing his skin by inches of tantalizing expanses before I take it, ball it up, and toss it behind me. He laughs at the gesture, the sound tapering off when I kiss him, swallowing the sounds of his happiness, and I don't think I've ever had anything better in my mouth.

His hands are almost frantic against me, tugging my dress up, only pulling away from my mouth so he can lift it over my head. I shiver against him, blood rushing in my ears, expectations and nervousness pulling at the space between my ribs until I am sure I can no longer breathe.

I remember that he's never seen me entirely topless before, and my fingers fidget now that my dress is off, now that I remember the last thing I bought. Catching my nervousness, he keeps his eyes on mine, gaze never once straying down, the darkness of them so deep I want to fall into him. Reaching, he grabs my fidgeting hands and laces our fingers together, the press of his palm against mine a promise, saying, *I'm not going anywhere.*

"Can I look at you?"

I watch him, riveted with how the setting sunlight sets every feature of his aflame, revealing the amber of his eyes with ease until they look like twin embers. I may want him, and I may want this, but there's no hiding the way my body tightens at his question, nervousness coursing through me.

In all imagination, in all my *want* of having a "normal" life, of having the things most people do at my age, this would obviously come up too. Thoughts of being with someone and seeing him and having him see me, but in the face of it, I balk a little.

But I know that he would not look at me with anything other than adoration, that he would rather hurt himself before saying or doing anything to make me self-conscious, and it's a relief to know, without a doubt, how he would be.

So I nod my head jerkily and shiver at the dark *want* in his eyes, more so when his gaze drifts down. I'm still wearing my glasses, and I wonder if I should take them off. If dulling one sense would give me a semblance of ease, by not seeing him. But I know that would be hiding.

His gaze lowers, inch by inch. It snags first at my neck, and I wonder if my fluttering pulse is that obvious. I flush deeper, and I can tell he likes it because the heat in his eyes goes up a notch. His gaze travels lower, sensual, better than a caress, tracing my collarbones before he dips further. He stills, sucking in a breath, and in any other moment, the ease with how he reacts to me would almost be cute.

"Surprise," I whisper. "You like it?"

Slowly, his hands reach out to trace the lace, following the path of his gaze. "You wore this for me?"

Throat thick, body shivering, I nod. "I wanted you to like it."

"I do," he rasps. "It's so pretty on you that I just want to stare and not take any of it off." Gaze coming up to mine, he continues, "But you know I love the sight of you no matter what you wear, right? You're so beautiful, the word itself gives you injustice. You didn't have to—"

In response, or as a dare, my hands go behind me, and for a moment, when the sound of a clasp coming undone fills the room, I am sure that he chokes on his own tongue. I let the article of clothing slide off, the purple lace and tulle falling to the edge of the bed.

I'm a far cry from the person a few months ago who had forgotten what holding someone really felt like. I'm greedy and needy and crave to overdose on all the *touch* I've missed. I want to know what it feels like to let a person—let *him*—touch me and hold me and chip away at me with no words at all.

"Can I touch you?" he asks, voice a rough whisper, that familiar ravenous hunger spread across his features.

I marvel at him, this sweet man with the dark hunger he hides, and wonder what it would be like if it came out to play.

I slide my arms around him in reply, pressing us skin to skin, and it's the most exquisite form of content and torture ever. I'm close enough that I can see how blown out his pupils are, like a man utterly ruined.

His arms, in turn, slide around me, around my waist, and then his hands are traveling across my skin like I'm a treasure. My spine is his road to having me shudder, the skin around my ribs a place for his hands to roam. He grabs my waist, and I almost roll my eyes at how exquisite it is to have him just touch me.

The hands on my waist tighten, and he rolls us over until he's on top, his weight a delicious comfort above me, the glide of his skin against mine my very own heaven. We're a mess of gasps and shedding clothes until he presses against me, the heat of him a heady thing, and I reach for the bedside table, knowing exactly what I put there. He picks up quickly and grabs my hand, stilling me.

"I want you," I insist. "And we're home."

He groans at the expression on my face, like I'm unraveling all his self-control. "I want you too. More than anything. But I don't want to hurt you. Let me just…"

Showing me what he means, he kisses across my skin, mouthing at every erogenous zone he can find, leaving a trail of kisses and bites, until I can *feel* the flush spreading across my skin, unintelligible words tumbling from my mouth. Maybe later, I'll marvel at how easily he elicits a response from me, how artfully he teases.

Not to be outdone, my hands rove across his skin, starting at his shoulders, gliding over his arms, then his chest and stomach. The muscles of his abdomen contract as my hands map the expanse of his torso. He presses against me in all the places I'm soft, and I know he likes it, because he grows even stiffer.

When I pull back far enough to see his face, his eyes dark and sensual, brows knitted, jaw clamped down shut, and pulse hammering, he almost looks like he's in pain. I want to ask him if he can feel what I can. That with every passing moment, I'm convinced my heart will only beat if he's around.

"Can you feel how much I want you?" I whisper in between gasps. "Does it scare you?"

I don't know why I whisper. Maybe because what we have feels like a secret. Like a little bubble I'm afraid to burst. Or maybe he just makes me too breathless. He stops kissing his way across my skin, lifting his head to watch me, but not before tracing a mark he left across my skin, the love bite blooming like a flower.

"Scare me? Never. But Layla…"

And I can tell he knows where I'm trying to go with this. And Jaxon, always sweet and considerate despite the demons that rage behind his eyes, would never want me to do anything I'm not sure of.

"How much do I want you, then?"

"You want me like I'm your addiction, your salvation. Your eyes get all hazy and sweet, and you get so much more bold than you normally are. You want me like you've craved me for the entire time you lost me, and you want me like you *need* me." The look in his eyes has me beyond breathless, and I almost look away, sure that he can see every detail about me. His eyes lock on mine, telling me more than words how he feels right now. "I know because I want you the same. But you already have all of me, sweetheart, and I want you to know that before you do anything. I'd rather have you comfortable with the pace of things than feeling as though we're rushing."

He brushes my hair gently away from my face, and his words wreak havoc in me. He holds me like he cares for me, as if every smile or laugh has only ever been for me. I wonder how he can't see that *this* is what makes me want him. That when he leans down and kisses my lips tenderly, the want is everything. It's everywhere, seeping into my bones, into my nerves, setting off fireworks in my blood.

"I don't want you this way as a means to a goal. Or as a way to have you every way," I murmur. "I'll always want you, today, tomorrow, next year, every way. Whichever way."

"I should've known you'd be stubborn," he teases, as though his body doesn't practically shake with want.

Grabbing his nape, I pull him down to me and kiss him. He holds me delicately, but kisses me back fiercely, his head slanted, body insistent. Only when I roll my hips against his, releasing a whimper, does he pull away, loving my reactions. The Layla-let's-wait argument is quickly fading away, and I can tell that soon it's going to be Layla-scream-for-me.

"You wouldn't leave to deal with all that alone, would you?" I ask.

If he seemed as though he was in pain earlier, he looks like I'm torturing him right now, and I almost laugh.

"You're a little minx, and you're fooling everybody with your innocent wide eyes and owl glasses."

Then his hands are on me again, until I'm pliant against the bed, before I remember these kinds of things require conversations. I clear my throat, my words breathless. "I've never done this before. So I'm clean, but I'm not on birth control."

"What?" He nips my ear as he rolls his hips over mine, and I don't know how I'm supposed to carry a conversation like this.

I repeat my words, watching as he stills to look at me. There's no hiding the satisfied gleam in his eyes, and I arch a brow, wondering if I should be offended.

"Really?" I shove his shoulder mockingly. "It's that big of a deal to you?"

Understanding dawns across his features, and he shakes his head, blushing a little. "Not in the way you're implying. I've just wanted to be your last for so long that finding out I can be your first too is… exhilarating. Blame my lizard brain, if you must, but the way I want you wouldn't change, whether or not I am your first."

I don't blame him, because I get it, and I've never wanted my firsts to be with anyone other than him. "Well, you were my first kiss," I concede.

I laugh when his eyes brighten. Lizard brain, indeed.

"I've never done this before either," he admits. "So I'm clean too."

Immediately, I hate that my mind can never take things for what they are, instead spinning stories. His choices are his own, and yet, suspicion sinks its claws into me. Maybe I never wanted anyone, but I was stuck for six years with either silence or a megalomaniac for company. The alternative, to go downstairs during one of his parties and pick a man from the den of sharks, was one I never considered.

But that was not the case for Jaxon, and I can't believe that in six years, he never wanted anyone else. For him to have never done this before, but want to with me, hints toward something I cannot understand.

I continue to stare at him, the cynic in me, the one intimate with the nature of obsessions and crossing lines to rule a mafia, refuses to take his words at face value. He very well could have just not been interested in sex for his own reasons, but what if it's something more? What if he waited for me, and how could he when he never knew if he'd see me again?

"Why?" is all I ask.

Shrugging, he plays it off, and I wonder if I'm imagining the gleam in his eyes or if I'm just too paranoid to trust anything good in my life. "Never wanted to." His forehead rests against mine, body unmoored, trembling. "I don't think you fully realize how much I've only ever wanted you, but that's okay, I'd rather show you, over and over. For as long as I have known you, it's always only ever been you."

Before I can say anything, he rolls his hips, reminding me that he is above me, pressed against me, skin warm against mine, the entirety of him bare for me to explore. I should pull back, voice my worries, but the part of me that ran from my past, that deletes those messages, that avoids confrontation, cannot bear to pull away.

He kisses his way across my skin, and I almost whine in disappointment when he no longer rests above me, instead sliding down my body. With no effort at all on his part, I'm soon a mess, body shaking and clenching, my head turning side to side until my glasses are askew, and he takes mercy on me, plucking them off and putting them on the bedside table. And all he does is *tease*. Every senseless plea is ignored, my feet roving across his back in frustration, almost turning my body away entirely, until he grabs my legs more firmly, forcing them still over his shoulders.

Mindlessly, I blurt, "Take care of me before I find someone else who will."

As soon as the words are out of my mouth, I know they were the wrong thing to say. When his hands tighten around the inside of my thighs, and he looks up at me, gaze searing, hair an utter mess, I almost surrender and apologize.

I have enough self-awareness to know that regardless of whether I mean the words or not, they're not the right thing to say. Because if the roles were reversed, I'd *hate* it if he said something like that. But my self-preservation is not as advanced as my self-awareness, so all I do is arch a brow in challenge.

"Oh, you're going to regret that, sweetheart," he rasps into my skin.

For a moment, I wonder if I heard him correctly, because immediately, if anything, he *rewards* me, mouth intent against me as he catalogs everything that elicits a response, and then he keeps doing it until I shake. I'm his marionette, and he plays me like an excellent puppeteer, and I know it's only because it's *him*.

My words are jumbled, spurring him on and begging him both to stop and never stop. His moans of approval reverberate through me, making me impossibly more needy. He's a surprisingly quick learner, and all too soon, I can sense my body tightening, mind slipping into hazy pleasure.

Abruptly, he stops. With a cry, I whip my head up from the pillow, staring at him in disbelief.

"Whose house are you in?" he rasps against me, gaze hard on mine. I shiver at the sight of him, even if most of it is a blur, his hands rough on my thighs, so *big*, and his hair a mess from my hands.

Apparently, I'm a glutton for punishment, because I say, "Technically, the landlord's, since you're renting."

"Not desperate enough, then, I see. That's alright, sweetheart, I can remedy that."

And he *does*. If he played my body well before, he practically *decimates* me now, clucking his tongue at every "please" and senseless beg, only murmuring "Try again," my mind too hazy to even remember what I was supposed to say.

"Do we not share this bed? Are you not mine? Are you not absolutely mindless with want *because of me*?" he says against me. "Whose mouth is on you? Who gets to see you this way, all greedy and desperate? Who will only *ever* get to see you this way?"

Sweet Jaxon is long gone, and in his place is a man who knows what he wants and takes it—a man who can expertly torture.

"You," I gasp, I promise. "Only ever you."

"Good job, sweetheart."

I'm about to say something that will probably earn me another hour of torture before he climbs up my body, hand against me, fingers curling to find a spot that has me seeing stars. He swallows every moan and cry until I can't give him any more, dazed and drugged with pleasure.

"Layla," he murmurs, pausing and almost making me scream in frustration. "Look at me. Keep those pretty eyes on me, sweetheart."

I snap them open, fingers desperate in his hair. It's infinitely more intimate like this, until he slowly unravels me. He keenly watches me, so intent, I know he's savoring and storing everything away. Every look that crosses over my face, every light behind my eyes.

When I collapse, I worry that I'm spent, that he wrung everything out of me, until he settles over me, skin brushing against mine. Soon enough, I wrap my legs around him, pulling him into the cradle of my hips, shivering at the feel of him.

There's no hiding the satisfied gleam in his eyes, even as he clenches his jaw, the expression almost one of pain.

"That did wonders to your ego," I mutter.

"Of course it did, sweetheart."

"That sounded a little patronizing—maybe *I* should tease you a little."

We both know I'm torturing myself just as much, body shaking in a way I didn't know desperation could feel. With an expected look, I hand him the wrapper, watching—*melting* from—the way he rips it open with his teeth before reaching down to put it on.

"Sweetheart—"

When I move over him, in little tilting movements, his mouth snaps shut, hands desperate on my hips, but never taking control from me. The entire time, I watch how his jaw tightens with every movement, until his eyes go hazy.

Every move only seems to make him more unhinged, until he pants with the effort of holding himself back. He looks like a man in the midst of torture, even though I'm really just torturing myself too.

Taking mercy on the both of us, I move lower until he's right *there*. His eyes regain their focus, intent on me once again, hips twitching like he can't help himself.

He kisses me softly, sweetly, despite the way his body practically vibrates with the urge to move. I've read *plenty* of books, both contemporary and outlandish, to have a semblance of an idea of what intimacy means, but it's nothing compared to actually having Jaxon above me, to watching the way sweat beads across his brow and the desperate edge in his gaze.

But none of that hunger spurs him to rush, and he's slow, an inch at a time, his entire demeanor concentrated over my expression, noting every gasp and pausing at every twitch. By the time his hips meet mine, there's no pain, barely even mild discomfort, just the heady sensation of having him and the desperate want for him to move.

It makes me vulnerable in a way my nakedness never could, and I never realized that the entire time I was running away from the nightmares of my past, I was really running toward *this*. The entire time, I craved this sweetness, this unquestionable affection from him.

His arms are secure around me, one under my body, holding my waist, the other under my shoulder blades, his hand cradling my head. I brace my hands on his arms, and the both of us moan and hiss when he shifts, slowly coming to learn what to do.

"Jaxon," I gasp at the feeling, drawing him closer, but moan when he stops.

"Am I hurting you?" he asks, worried, tone tight, brow furrowed in concern even when his body shakes.

I shake my head, almost urgently. "No," I gasp. "No. I need…"

His gaze darkens knowingly, and then he *moves*. I close my eyes, pushing lower on him, loving the stretch of him, and every time his breath fans over my face or he whispers in my ear, his warmth encasing me, *falling* becomes physical.

"Layla, open your eyes," he rasps, words familiar, and I do, sucking my breath in, because now *falling* is becoming *plummeting*, and I want to ask him if he can *feel* it.

His arms move from around and under me to beside my head, forearms braced against the bed, so every time he moves, his skin slides over me, until nearly every erogenous zone ignites. I hold him closer, but he doesn't let me hide from his gaze, doesn't let me bury my head in the crook of his neck.

He finds a spot that has stars bursting in my vision and my breath quickening, and he hits it *over* and *over*. Already, he's memorizing my body and what I like in the span of minutes, seconds.

"Did you know," he starts, words rough across my skin, and I wonder if I've broken him since he's babbling during sex. "That your cervix shifts over the course of the month? So right now, in your ovulatory phase, it's higher and softer, which is why you like it more when I go deeper." He enunciates his words with a movement, and I think I choke on my own tongue. I think this is what will actually kill me. "But closer to the menstrual phase, it gradually lowers and becomes more firm."

"You're such a *nerd*," I gasp, pulling him down to kiss him, sure I am going to crawl out of my skin.

His movements grow jolted and less finessed, and grabbing my hand, he puts it between us until I get his intent. "I'm sorry, but you're so perfect, and I never thought it'd be this easy for me to..."

His jaw clenches and unclenches, brow furrowed, eyes getting hazy, Adam's apple bobbing up and down with every rough swallow until his movements become frantic. Sweat makes both of our bodies slide together easier, until we're all skin and nerves, and below that, dancing emotions.

I comply with my hand, riveted as he positively unravels at the seams before me, having to fight against the urge to close my eyes at how unquestionably addictive he is.

He watches me, just as I watch him, and I know that that's what makes this not just physical. What makes it more, because I've always been able to read him, and his emotions are laid bare for me. And all that I can see from him makes me want to cry, because I never knew it could feel this way with him. So utterly raw it's beautiful, and I want to fall into him.

He whispers words into my ear, dragging me closer and closer to the edge. "You're so pretty like this, sweetheart, taking me so nicely. You can't begin to imagine how utterly *good* you feel, because I'm not going to last at all."

I both blush and moan at his words. "Please," I whisper.

"Please what?"

I blush harder, trying to come up with a way to say it suggestively, but I can't come up with anything. "Give me what I want, please."

"Such manners," he teases, leaning down to nip my ear, the sensation making me pulse around him once, and he mutters an epithet before smiling against my skin.

"I should've known you'd like to be bitten."

I whimper, meeting his movements, until he's *everywhere*. I'm frantic, practically right there, and he can tell, because his mouth travels lower, planting open-mouthed kisses across my skin until he finds the sensitive space between my neck and my shoulder. My back arches, mouth opening on a silent scream as I pulse around him, like a string that has finally snapped, and I want to feel him shatter just like me.

And I do.

Before I even feel him, I can see it. See the intense burn of fire behind his eyes, the momentary blank. Breathlessly, he collapses on top of me, both of our chests heaving, breath mingling, and in my post-euphoria state, I wrap around him like an octopus, savoring his warmth. Around me, consuming me.

I can't tell how long it is that we stay there, though I whine when he pulls away.

"Layla?"

"Yeah?" I say, though it comes out more as a mumble because I've buried my head in the pillows.

"I hope you know there's no taking this back." His words are light, but his tone is serious, as though I've just signed away my soul. "If you ever want this to end, I will not be able to let you go. It would've been hard anyway, but now? Now it'll be impossible, and maybe that makes me unhinged, but now there's no me without you. There's no future in which it's not me and you. There never was anyway, but you've just done something funny to my brain, and so I'm finally telling you."

I always thought that with the nature of the men in my past, I would hate to hear such possessive words, that even the idea of marriage would freak me out. But to know someone—to know he—so irrevocably considers me *his*, doesn't fill me up with dread. Maybe it's because he's only ever tried to deserve to be mine, and he doesn't take without giving ten times over.

Cupping his face, I brush my fingers across his skin and tell him, "I'm not taking this back. And I don't want a future that isn't you and me. I know I don't really say it, and I don't really show it, but you were the light of my life in a time I really needed it, and you are now, too. Every time you laugh or smile, it's like it burns away all the things that haunt me, and when you're not smiling, I think of what I can do to bring it back. When you hurt, I hurt, and when you thrive, you light me up like the sun."

He curves an arm over me, leaning down to kiss my shoulder. "That's the sweetest thing anyone has ever said to me, *ya qalbi*, and I'll always carry your words in my heart."

Like always, I'm glad I know enough Arabic to understand him, to know that his other favorite nickname for me is "oh my heart."

He kisses me before turning me onto my front, and he pulls my hips up to slide two pillows beneath them. I look behind my shoulder to watch him tear another wrapper open, and shivering, ask incredulously, "*Again?*"

"I need you," is all he says, and I'm helpless to resist.

Hours later, he collapses on the bed beside me after having wiped me with a warm towel, and I barely hear him mumble, "Go use the bathroom so you don't get a UTI."

I do, a little glad that he reminded me, and try not to wince every time I walk, my legs shaking with slight tremors. *Damn, what did he do to me?*

By the time I crawl back into bed, I want nothing more than to reach over, shut the light off, and go to sleep. Instead, I study him for a little while, running my hands through his hair, smiling when he leans into me like a cat. The sun has long since set, until he is half-covered in shadows, the darkness settling across the dips and divots of his body, almost turning him into something ethereal, my heart full in a way that reminds me again of that sweet ache. I take in his features, the line of his shoulders, to the hand that rests on his pillow.

I'm drowsy enough that I almost don't notice his bruised knuckles, with one even cracked. Stilling, I stare at it, shocked I didn't notice earlier.

Maybe Mike and him just went boxing too, I try to tell myself, trying to reason that the bruises have to be for an entirely normal reason. None of my reasoning chases away the chill at the sight.

Chapter 27

Lies We Tell

It isn't until early afternoon that I bother to successfully get out of bed—and it's not my fault. Or Jaxon's, for that matter. He woke up bright and early, and the memory of it is still fresh in my mind, of blearily blinking my eyes to him gently sifting his fingers through my hair, his arms around me until there was nowhere else I wanted to be. My mind was hazy, head half buried in the space between his neck and shoulder, and before I registered it, I'd reached out to kiss his Adam's apple.

"I've always wanted to do that," I mumbled into his skin, too drowsy to be embarrassed. "I think I really like it."

"My Adam's apple?"

I nodded, and then he asked me what else I like about him. Hands traveling across his skin, I enunciated each spot with my words.

"These," I said, squeezing his biceps, tracing the veins across them. "This." And I ran my fingers across the valley and dips of his abdomen, the muscles clenching beneath my hand. "Your back." I reached beneath him to try to trace his spine. But then I skimmed my fingers across his ribs until he smiled, halfway to a laugh, and said, tapping his smiling mouth, "But this I like best." Rounding my finger around the dimple on his cheek, that little divot my biggest obsession, I added, "And this."

Eventually, he went for a run, got back, took a shower, tried to get me out of bed, failed, and then made breakfast.

I'm not lazy, I promise myself.

It's just that some days, I like to treat myself. I sleep in late, wear comfortable pajamas for the whole day, and forget things like bras exist. Then I paint or read and don't bother with responsibilities. *Especially* now that it's winter break. I fear I will have to be dragged to lectures once the break is over.

But he's moving around in the kitchen, and I come up with an idea for what to do today—cooking. Or, more accurately, him teaching me to cook.

Fifteen minutes later, when I burst into the kitchen with an eager grin on my face, he looks up and smiles softly before eyeing me warily.

"Why are you dressed in your least favorite clothes? You don't wear those unless you plan on making a mess," he asks, running his eyes up and down my outfit. He notes my hair, in a neat bun—out of the way—and that I've gone without socks even though I don't like walking around barefoot.

"You can teach me how to cook!"

He laughs, going along with me in my dramatic flair, and grabs my waist. Twirling me halfway, he dips me down and kisses me. When I wrap my arms around his shoulders, dive my hand into his hair, and lift a leg to his hip, he gets a bit more enthusiastic and kisses me more sensually, the glide of his tongue against mine more insistent. What was once dramatic and fakely enthusiastic quickly becomes serious and seductive.

"Well, good morning to you too," I breathe when he pulls away, grinning down at me and my paint-streaked clothes.

I bet I look ridiculous, but he doesn't seem to care. Pulling me up, he looks to the kitchen. "I don't know why you think I'm some amazing cook since I just know basic recipes, but we'll see." He looks at me as if an idea will pop up by staring at my face, or maybe he's trying to think of a recipe to try that won't result in me burning the apartment down. "Let's go with baking brownies. Can't go wrong there, and we have all the ingredients."

"Sweets," I murmur in agreement. "And chocolate. If I know how to make brownies, I'll never break free of my chocolate fascination, but I guess there are worse things in life."

He shakes his head, smiling softly, and moves around the kitchen, pulling out bowls, spatulas, and what I assume are the ingredients.

"We don't have an apron, but this shouldn't get too messy. Okay"—he looks to the countertop covered in measuring cups and ingredients—"first, we're going to melt the butter."

And then it begins.

By the time we get halfway done, I've managed to get myself covered in flour, and then Jaxon, because I smothered him in a hug. "Looks like I'm the one who needed an apron," he muttered, and in retaliation, dusted flour on my face.

For the rest of the baking process, we continue measuring and adding ingredients—who knew it'd be so much fun to mix the cocoa powder in?—while throwing some sort of ingredient at each other or shoving one another playfully.

When I'm done pouring the batter into the pan, and Jaxon turns on the timer, I'm a mess. Sighing, I look down at my clothes and touch my face to discover I'm covered in flour. And surprisingly exhausted from the baking. Who knew it could be tiring? Or maybe it's because we made a bunch of batches for the neighbors too.

Desperately needing to clean up, I run to the bedroom to change before remembering that Harlow has probably blown up my phone with texts, and that I haven't checked in on her in a while. From bombarding her with messages to a standstill of texts, she must think I'm dead.

After hunting for my phone, finding it, and turning it on, I see that she did, in fact, send me more messages than I can count.

Heading out, I recline on the couch, in clear view of the kitchen and Jaxon moving around, and I call her. For the next five minutes,

Harlow berates me in a mix of English and Japanese, my plea, "But my phone was off and I forgot to turn it on!" going unheard.

In the kitchen, Jaxon laughs, getting the gist of the conversation, and I mouth, "You traitor."

When she's finally done scolding me, I relax into the cushions as she tells me what her parents have been up to and how she can't wait to get back.

"Speaking of," she continues. "I'll be moving back in a week or two for the next semester... and I have to ask, did you want me to get the lease on that same apartment again? Or are you staying with Jaxon?"

I still, limbs locking. "Like move back?"

These past few weeks, with the break and with him, have been like a serene bubble, the rest of the world and responsibilities muffled. When I first moved in, I knew it wasn't a permanent thing, that he was doing me a favor until Harlow gets back, but I'd forgotten that. Even if that's changed, do I really want to stay? Have I been rushing things not because I want to, but because I think we have a time limit?

"I'm not saying I want you to, especially if you're happy with him, but I wanted to give you a heads up that it's an option. And don't consider moving back in for me—if you stay with him, I have options, don't worry."

"Let me... let me think about it."

"Of course. I'm sorry, I didn't mean to make you doubt or anything, I just wanted to let you know."

I nod before realizing she can't see me, and speak up. Eventually, she has to go, and we hang up.

Doubt festers like a sore wound as my thoughts spin. Is it even fair of me to stay without him knowing who might be after me? Is it fair to stay even if he does? I thought I took enough precautionary steps when leaving, but there's no denying that at any moment someone could find me, could find this place and hurt him. But if I were to leave and move in with Harlow, she wouldn't be safe either.

You idiot. Why did you stop running? Why did you ever stop running?

Jaxon comes over, sitting on the couch and tugging my feet into his lap.

"That was Harlow?"

I nod, not meeting his gaze, but he reaches over and tilts my face toward him. "You're not sure if you want to stay with me? I don't mind, if that's what you're thinking."

"That's not it. I just..."

"Have you forgotten what I said yesterday? That you're mine now just as surely as I am yours?" Squeezing my foot, he implores, "Tell me what's going on. What's holding you back, Layla?"

Everything, I want to tell him.

Though really, it's just me.

Frustration at having to understand that the real world doesn't stop for anyone, that I need to make choices that will hurt, threads its way into my voice, and there's no hiding my defensiveness when I snap, "Tell me why your knuckles are bruised then. Or what Mike is worried about, and if it has anything to do with me." Because I know it does.

Immediately, like my words have doused any fire in him, he sighs, lying back against the couch. He looks like a man who realizes that he cannot keep what he has—what he has wanted to have for years. It's etched across his face, across the lines of his shoulders, and I'm reminded of all the ways we don't really know each other.

"That's not a conversation you're ready to have yet, Layla. That much I know. I need you to trust me on that. Do you think you can?"

Not liking the defeated expression on his face, I tug my feet away to get closer to him, holding his face. *Just for a little while longer*, I tell myself. *Don't worry about anything else just for a little while longer.*

"I do. And you trust me?"

He nods, and we both know the smile I give him is broken around the edges.

"Okay," I whisper. "Then everything will be okay."

It has to be.

I don't know how long I stay in my thoughts, unsure of what to do. I leave the studio, unable to find solace at the ends of a brush and paint, and go into the living room. The air is thick with awkwardness and silence, and I hate it, because this has never been us.

I find him sitting on the couch, with books over the coffee table, his body bent over it, almost like a man bowing at his altar. I mill around for a while, watching him awkwardly, hands fidgeting in front of me, before I turn to the kitchen with the plan of maybe tidying it up a bit. Except it's already clean—of course.

With no other ideas on how to avoid this, I tentatively take a seat next to him. His body slightly tightens, sinews pulling taut, but he continues what he's doing, shooting me an indecipherable glance.

I wonder if he can feel it in the air like I can, the solemn stillness when good things end.

He tilts his face toward me, and I lean over him and kiss him— hard. In between kisses, I murmur, "Everything will be okay," echoing what I said earlier.

It couldn't be any more of a lie, and like he can sense this, when he kisses me back, it's punishing.

I kiss him urgently, and every kiss he returns is almost harsh, but I can sense it fading, because the kisses alternate between rough and gentle, like no matter what, he cannot help but be sweet to me. I climb onto him, grasping, and not only at him, but at something I know I'll never reach, because I'm the one holding myself back.

"Jaxon," I gasp in between kisses, needing to touch him, my hand slides below his shirt, landing over his heart.

It beats wildly below my palm, and it's enrapturing and heady to know that I'm the one who does this to him. But almost as punishment again, he grabs my arm, moving it away as he wraps my legs around his waist and stands up.

I can tell where this is headed, and know that it won't be like last time—soft and slow and sweet. But I kiss him harder, my tongue more insistent against his, and pull him closer. His kisses are raw, though his hands are caressing and caring, until he pulls at something within me. I want to cry, because I will miss this. I will miss him in the way a body never forgets a missing limb, in the way the earth hungers for spring.

My body tilts backward before I'm lowered onto a soft surface—the bed, no doubt—and again, I lower him onto me hurriedly.

I can tell that he's already slipping back into the Jaxon I know when he tries to slow down. But the urgency doesn't leave me. In the face of the fear that everything will come crashing around me, that they will find me, I rush.

He makes a noise in the back of his throat, half a moan and half a sound of frustration, and then he's on top of me, body pushing me into the mattress before he abruptly pulls away, eyes dark. I feel the loss of his heat keenly, and reach for him again, but he grabs my hands and pins them above my head.

A gasp tears out of my lungs as I shiver, and he holds the hem of my shirt with his free hand before slowly tugging it up, skin skimming over mine as he pulls it higher and higher. He briefly releases my wrists to tug it completely off, and before I can register it, his hand moves to my back, undoes the clasp of my bra, and tugs that off. His hold is back on my wrists before it even lands to the floor.

"Look at me." His voice is rougher, darker, though there's something behind his eyes I refuse to decipher.

Holding my gaze, he crooks a finger into my waistband and tugs off my pants and underwear in one pull. But I'm warm, too warm, and still hunger to have him press against me.

And he raises the inferno when his head dips down to kiss my skin. He doesn't build the pleasure like he did all those times before, taking his sweet time. Instead, his hands and mouth are insistent, almost rushed in a way that mirrors my movements, every nip and lick spinning me into something mindless, incoherent words leaving my mouth.

He makes a sound in the back of his throat. "Always so desperate for me, aren't you?"

His words helplessly make me want more, and in answer, his movements become more raw. He's insistent as he touches me, his mouth leaving marks across my skin, fingers deft against me, so that

I'm already desperately trying to push back the impending riot of sensations, against the heat coiling low in my stomach.

"You wanted it fast," he tells me. "You got it fast."

He wrings the pleasure out of me until I writhe and gasp as the sensations rip through me. None of it can stem the urgency that still lives in me, burrowed into every marrow, and I doubt the hunger will ever leave.

"I'll never get tired of watching you unravel. All for me," he rasps.

I watch him, watch the unburdened gleam in his eyes, that edge of danger coming out to play. Every line of his body above me is taut, with him braced on one hand, the other reaching up to run his ring and middle finger over the seam of my mouth. "I want to see it again, and again, until you scream. Until you scream my name."

I shiver as he leans down, breath fanning across my skin, his hair tickling the space below my sternum. I watch, riveted, combusting, as he traces figures across my skin, at the hand on my hip that grasps me desperately until I cannot so much as shift my body.

He starts at my midriff, kissing and nipping, making me hot and restless. I'm sensitive to every draw of his lips, every sting of his teeth, and everything he does with that tongue of his. He takes his leisurely time at my navel, swirling and carefully tracing my skin with his mouth. Eventually, I shake, my fingers threaded through his hair, body writhing and aching, his hands unrelenting as he grips my thighs, my feet against the middle of his back.

One moment I'm tugged mercilessly closer to the edge of release, and the next, I'm there, roughly and suddenly. An incoherent noise leaves my lips, back bowing off the bed like a marionette shoved up, extorted in mindless obsession. And even if he's been ravaging me incessantly, he gently kisses the inside of my thighs, the curve of my hip, the dip of my waist. It's always the soft caresses that do me in, and even though I am sure this cannot last, I'm helpless against falling a little deeper.

"Layla, you don't get to slip away now," he says gruffly, and then he's above me, arms on either side of my head, body warm and blanketing, his clothes on the floor. "You're staying with me right here, right now. At least give me that."

I wrap my arms around his shoulders as I swallow thickly. "I'm here with you."

His eyes search mine, his gaze soft and almost worried, and I don't like it at all. I don't like that I've put that there. Pulling him closer, trying to tell him without words what I mean, I wrap my arms tighter around him. Letting out a yawn, I open my mouth to say something, but he speaks first.

"Oh no, you don't," he admonishes. "I still haven't heard a scream."

He sits back on his heels, his body heat snatched away from me, and rakes his gaze over me leisurely, eyes dark, a depraved satisfaction in them. "You look thoroughly ravaged now. I can't imagine how you're going to look when I'm done with you."

He slides his hands from my waist to my back and pulls me up, until I'm on my knees. Swallowing from anticipation, I watch him curiously, glasses askew, my breath already quickening and blood thickening.

He leans down, until his lips brush across the shell of my ear, and a shiver skates down my spine. "Close your eyes."

Instantly, I do, and shiver again. Now all my other senses are alert, until I can sense when he moves away and around me, hands circling me the entire time before he stops behind me.

His body is close enough that I can sense him, but not enough that his skin presses against mine, and the anticipation builds until I almost open my eyes. His arms circle around my waist, almost in a hug from behind, while he leans his head down to my neck, his breath skating over my skin.

I shudder, drawing in a breath that doesn't help, and lean back into him, until my back presses to his front.

"You can open your eyes now."

I do, and without him in front of me, I can see our reflection in the mirror against the wall. I don't look like myself with my skin flushed, hair a mess, body shining slightly from sweat, and face rosy. My eyes are hazy and wide, my chest rising and falling unevenly.

I look lower to where he's left love marks all over my skin, and I flush further at the sight. The tawny skin of his arms stands stark against the paler skin of my torso, and I marvel at the sight of his arm around me, his hand spanning, stretched, from the underside of my breast to the lower edge of my hip.

I'm startled away from watching us when a foil rips, and my gaze jumps to him in the mirror. He has the foil in his mouth and grins wickedly at me as he drops the wrapper onto the bed, and the contents of the packet disappear. His hands glide from my waist down to my legs, drawing them apart.

I look down to see his hands on me, but he stops. "Eyes on the mirror, sweetheart."

I do as he says, and he's watching me, and I have nowhere to hide. I want to hate that he won't touch my body without making sure he touches my heart too, and I almost look away.

To make this anything other than mindless, anything other than two people seeking release, will make it hurt more later. He holds my gaze as he slides forward, movements shallow and back and forth instead of up. His arms band around my waist again to keep me still until I whimper as he continues the motion—until it's almost torture.

"Jaxon," I whimper, eyes imploring. "Please."

And that's all he needs. I can both feel and see when he finally gives me what I want, my legs shaking to stay upright, because his jaw clenches, and his eyes grow hazy. But he keeps holding my gaze in the mirror as he moves, and because there's still a height difference with both of us on our knees, he needs to draw me higher, until my back plasters to his front and my knees lift off the bed.

When he feels I'm at the right height, the tempo of his movements increase, until I can do nothing but hold on. I shake every time he draws back all the way only to slam back forward until I shake and gasp, sweat breaking out on my skin all over again. My head falls back against his shoulder as the familiar flush starts to break over my skin, and I can't get enough air as the sensations pull and *pull* at me.

Despite himself, despite the tense lines of his body against my back as he moves and holds the both of us upright, he kisses my forehead like he can't help it. The gentle glide of his thumb across the curve of my waist is dissimilar to the pistoning motion of his hips.

"Layla, sweetheart," he repeats. "Look in the mirror."

I comply, watching his expression, the desperate cadence of our breaths, and lower, to see the way our bodies join and meld together. I see my knees off the bed, his arms insistent around me, one banded across my waist, and the other around my ribs, body so much larger behind me.

The sight drives me to desperation, until I grip his forearms, nails almost digging into his skin. My head rests against his shoulder, the strands a mess, with his head tilted toward me, mouth against my hair, but eyes meeting mine in the mirror.

To both feel and see what he's doing to me pushes me closer and closer to the edge, and I futilely try to push it back, but he has none of it, a hand sliding down to my body to roll his fingers across where I desperately need him. And this time, I scream just like he's wanted, and it's his name, my body locking and head bowing back as I can't stop shaking.

Not with how he moves, and certainly not when his movements become erratic, helpless moans falling from his lips until he buries his head in the space between my neck and shoulder, almost like a lost man seeking solace, his frame shuddering.

He rasps, senselessly, "Sweetheart," and "You're so *good* to me," and "Can you feel that?" and "Please stay right here, with me, forever," into my skin until I want to cry. How can I not keep the one thing that has come to mean the most to me?

I stare in a daze, barely noticing, as he twists to the side and lowers us onto the bed, his chest rising and falling behind me in a rough, stuttered cadence. I do, however, keenly feel when he pulls away, and whimper at the loss of his heat, uncaring of how needy I am.

He returns soon enough though, with a wet, warm cloth, taking care of me, and then his arms circle around me and pull me close to him. I sigh and snuggle into him, that sweet ache settling like I'm right where I belong. He holds me tight, like I'll evanesce if he doesn't. There's no denying he ravaged me, like if he can't crawl into my mind, then he'll claim all the parts of me I have to give.

Chapter 28

To Crash

I wake up alone, still exhausted, to find the bed empty, his side cold. I tell myself it doesn't mean anything, even though my breathing slows and lungs grow a little tight.

Every morning so far he's been with me in bed, or woken me up with a kiss on the forehead before getting up, and I don't know why I need that more after last night. As if last night made me vulnerable, which in truth, it kind of did. It was different, but with everything from before that, I can practically *feel* my thoughts starting their tight spiral down, down, down.

I can imagine what my father would say, I can imagine what De Leone would do, and now I'm just thinking of the ways in which everything can go wrong. My thoughts oddly resemble a leash, tightening and tightening until my breathing becomes shallow. I imagine Jaxon finding out, and not trusting me anymore, and the leash gets tighter.

Why does the thought of losing him hurt and scare me so much?

I'd say it's almost like last time, when we were much younger, when I almost loved him. Except it wasn't truly because of who he was, but because of what he gave me—an escape.

This time, I can imagine how easy it would be to love him, even though the word is so inadequate to cover everything I feel for him.

And I know why the thought of losing Jaxon terrifies me now— I think I've always known. I don't really dare to say it aloud, but I know. I know it like it's a given.

It's something that's built and built until it stares at me in the face and I'm helpless to not notice it. And why would I not when I've *wanted* it? The epiphany should come with joy, with ease, but I know to hope is to break, and worse, to love something is to lose it.

So just like that, I know what I need to do. It hurts, even more so when I imagine the expression on his face once he finds out. But better betrayal and pain than death. Better than losing him just how I lost everything else. *And it won't be forever*, I try to reason with myself, knowing it's most probably a lie. *Just until they stop looking.*

But I'm selfish, and while the opportunity is perfect, I want to see him, I want to hold him again.

For most of the morning, the apartment is empty, and I restlessly try to stay busy, but I brim with anxiety and dread, because what if I'm making a horrible decision?

By the time the front door opens, I'm almost throwing myself in that direction, but check myself, knowing I need to be inconspicuous.

"Where have you been?" I ask as soon as he steps into the apartment, even though really, it's still early morning.

He takes one look at me and raises a brow at my outburst, but it's not humorous, and he doesn't make a quip like, "Missed me so much, *ya qalbi*?"

Instead, his eyes are dangerously closed off, darker in their intensity, and not with the intensity I love. It makes me expect the worst. And yet I can tell that he foolishly hopes for the best.

"Running, and used the apartment gym," he answers shortly, before striding past me and down the hall, where I hear the bathroom door close. His short, curt words, devoid of emotion, and lack of touching me are so different from normal.

He's never been able to look at me without wanting to touch me.

It's odd how quickly something can become normal, until I'm conditioned to it, and I've grown so accustomed to him touching me or joking with me that to lose it, if even for a few moments, shocks me. *I've been Pavlov'd*, I think, trying to find humor in it, except I can't.

A medley of emotions grips me at the exchange, and the biting words *it's over, he knows, he knows, he knows* chant inside my head, fear coursing through my system. *It isn't supposed to be this way*, I insist.

I tell myself that I'm being foolish. I'm being paranoid, and this isn't that serious; we just need to have a conversation, is all.

I know my reassurances are lies when he walks back into the living room, where I've been rooted the whole time, his hair wet from a shower, expression as equally stony as before.

"Jaxon," I murmur as I go to him, close enough to see the brown of his eyes, like I can read them better at a shorter distance. "Are you alright?"

He exhales slowly, and I don't like how he searches my eyes, as though everything is plainly written. To slowly watch myself lose someone—to know it viscerally—is again like slowly spiraling again.

"I'm here for you. If something's wrong, talk to me."

And I know I'm digging my own grave. It's the fear of being found out that sometimes makes one reckless.

"Why aren't you trusting me to take care of you?" He looks at me, the lack of emotions going away, revealing him beneath, until he is a creature of emotion, of *pain*. "Do you really not know? Have you really not known this whole time?"

Know what? I want to ask, but I know I'm not ready; I know I want to stay in the bubble a little longer. "I do trust you."

"Then *why*—" he starts, and the hint of anguish I hear in his voice, the one emotion he lets through before that's blocked, too, only makes everything tighter for some reason. For a moment, I think he wants to block the door, barricade it, and keep me here forever, before he realizes he can't, the shock of it fleeting across his features. "—are you planning on running? You're planning on leaving, aren't you? Not just me, but this city, maybe even the *country*. After everything, you want to leave."

With the truth out, my face blanches. I know it does, because my eyes widen, unbidden, and my jaw goes slack, as though I myself don't believe that's what I plan. Like this is just a nightmare I'll wake up from. And now that he's put it out in the open, I doubt again that I *would* have told him. Because he cannot know why. He can never know why.

"You don't understand."

He bites his fist, a bit of emotion leaking into the wounds across his eyes. "Then help me understand."

I shake my head, desperate, mumbling, "You don't understand. You *can't* understand. You can never understand all the ways in which I don't deserve you, and I can't lose you too. Not like how I lost my mother and brother. They'll take you away from me."

Like a dam, any barricade he has over his emotions breaks, and he pulls me in, arms wrapping around me until my head buries against his chest, close to his heart, close to my home. "You're still holding onto it. Layla, sweetheart, it wasn't your fault they died in the accident. It was never your fault—car accidents happen—and you can't carry the blame forever." I shake my head, almost adamant, because he does not know. I told him they passed, and how, but I didn't tell him everything. Not that I was the catalyst. "Then why must you carry that blame forever, *ya qalbi*?"

"Because I have to. Because whose fault is it then? He wasn't even there, and everything was fine before—before I found out." I know I'm rambling, I know that he doesn't understand what I'm saying, but it's cathartic to spill it all out, to bare the wound that has festered in my heart for over six years until it became a rotten thing. "If I don't hold onto it, what do I have to hold onto? And you don't even know the half of it; you wouldn't want me if you did."

"You have me to hold on to, sweetheart, until you don't need to anymore." Cupping my face, he turns my head to look at him, so I can see what is written there, plain as day. "And do you think I cannot want all of you? That I cannot love all of you? Do you really think that you need to hide your grief, your regret, and your demons? Do you not understand that every part of you is beautiful to me? Give me your sunshine, and I'll show you how I can bask in it. Give me your demons, and I'll show you how I can dance with them. Give me all of you, and I'll show you how much you deserve all the love I have in me to give. I said it before, and I'll say it again—I'm not going anywhere, sweetheart, and I promise you are worthy of being loved exactly for who you are."

I know what he's saying, even if he hasn't said it outright, and I want to cry at the sincerity of it, at how I'm so wretched I fooled him into thinking I'm worthy of being loved. "I'm still that girl," I whisper. "I thought I wouldn't be anymore, but I still am."

"That's okay, *ya qalbi*. You were stuck for so long those years, and even before that, that it's okay if it takes time to heal, Layla. You can take all the time in the world—I'm not going anywhere. But I want you to know, even if you can't believe it, that telling your mother about your father and there being a car crash afterward doesn't mean it was your fault."

His words are a balm, something I so desperately want to believe, something I've tried to convince myself of many times over the years, but have never really been able to. I settle further into him, lulled into his comfort, almost fooled into believing that everything will be okay.

Almost, until his words settle over me, like a bad taste in my mouth, like a nightmare I don't want to examine. Because I may have told him about the accident, but I never told him why it happened.

I rip away from him, jarred by the sudden cold, my lungs seizing until my chest hurts, and I almost trip over the carpet, just knowing I need to get *away*. The pieces come together in a way I don't want to admit, in a way I don't want to believe.

"How do you know?"

He squeezes his eyes shut once he realizes his misstep, his hands reaching for me, but I stumble back farther. "Layla—"

"*How do you know?*"

"Because I know everything."

There's very few ways in which he can know, and the possibilities all break me, until I'm sure the sound of my heart splintering will fill the room. It's an odd thing to realize that the person you thought you knew doesn't really exist at all.

I want to scream at him that he doesn't get to look heartbroken at the way my chin wobbles. But don't I deserve this? I thought the worst thing in our relationship was my secrets, but it turns out, it was his.

"*How*, Jaxon? How do you know everything?"

He's resigned as he says, "Because I worked for him."

"*Who?*"

And I think he's about to say my father. I dread the words, because what was real then, and what was fake? Instead, he says something worse. "Giovanni, okay? I worked for Giovanni."

The world mutes around me, everything growing hazy as my heart hammers in my chest, so hard it hurts. In all the ways I expected my past to come after me, it was never like this.

"I *trusted* you," I scream, voice raw, the pain so visceral I am sure it will spill out of my chest in a torrent of blood. "And the entire time, you've been working for *him*? Was any of it even real? Are you just here to take me back?" At the thought of it, at being back in that house, or worse, with Giovanni, with a ring I don't want over my finger and vows I don't believe, I want to get on my knees and beg. "Don't take me back. *Please*, don't take me back. You *can't*."

He comes closer, hands reaching out, and I scream again. "Stay away from me! Don't *touch* me."

Written across his face is what I think defeat looks like, what loss looks like. So, like a man with nothing left to lose, it all spills out of him, like a rotten fruit ripping open.

"You weren't supposed to find out this way. I was going to tell you, I swear. All of it was real, sweetheart—every part, I promise. I'm not taking you back. You will *never* go back there, he will *never* have you. Did I not say you are mine? That you've been mine for far longer than you can imagine? I worked for him, for six years, to find you. Every day, I was looking for you, getting closer to him so that I could find you, and when you left, he trusted me enough to task me with finding you. I promise, sweetheart. Everything I've ever done has been to find you. You have to believe me."

The last words are pleading, and I think I see his heart break when I say, "I don't. I can't."

Nothing makes sense, the realities I thought I had upturned, even though really, weren't the signs glaring in my face? The hushed conversations, the bruised knuckles, the men that randomly showed up, that I half-convinced myself weren't real?

Worse, how can what he says be real? How did he obsess over me, as a teenager, to the point that he joined a *mafia*? Though haven't I always known neither of us are "normal," that obsession exists in our very marrow until that's all we've become?

I always thought the messages were because I didn't hide my steps well enough, but what if, really, it was him?

He takes another step closer, and needing to clear my head, needing to think logically and not with my heart, I rasp, "Leave. Please, just leave. I need... I need to think."

Resigned, like it's the last thing he wants to do, he takes a step back, grabbing his keys. "Okay, but don't leave. It's not safe. Not yet. I took care of some, but—"

And I can't bear to hear another word, to know that everything isn't the way I thought it was, that he sacrificed parts of himself no one should ever have to. "Just leave."

And he does, until his apartment is silent in a way that reminds me of years behind locked doors with my walls and paint for company.

It doesn't take long for me to know I'm leaving too. At least this apartment. It isn't mine, and I *can't* stay here. Something screams in me to stay, but to stay is to have my mind turn in on itself, to obsess over every interaction and conversation. Every additional moment inside has the walls closing in on me, and I quickly pack a small bag.

I don't know why I don't bother with packing everything, but maybe it's because I refuse to believe that this is the end of us. Even though, regardless of what he said, I should still go through with my plan. Maybe more so now, because if what he said is true, any chance of Jaxon surviving once Giovanni shows up just reduced drastically. You don't run away from the mafia, and you certainly don't steal something they think belongs to them.

He said a lot, but questions still burn through my mind. How did he start working for Giovanni? Worse, what did Giovanni make him do? I imagine Jaxon, as a teenager and growing up in that environment, and my heart further breaks.

In the end, he isn't here to answer my questions, and unbidden, anger flares. How dare he make those sacrifices for me? How *dare* he hurt himself for me? Ignoring his earlier plea, I leave the apartment in a daze, needing to get away from all the signs that I live with him.

I don't even realize where I want to go until I search my GPS for a familiar name. After finding it, I call a lift, and sit down on the side of the curb, waiting.

The driver is young, and I'm oddly reminded of when I was leaving Chicago, and of the taxi driver who took me to the airport. Is that what this is? Will I change my destination to the airport instead, repeating history?

"Would you like to put the bag in the trunk?" he asks, leaning forward in his seat, the passenger window lowered.

I shake my head, opening the door and sitting inside. The bag is small enough that it fits between my feet, and I detachedly wonder if I'm going to go back to pack more.

When we arrive, the car stopping beside the curb, his eyes drop to my overnight bag, and he murmurs quietly, "This part of the city isn't really safe."

"I'm here to see a friend."

And frankly, it isn't any of his business anyway. I shove away the irritation, knowing that he doesn't deserve the brunt of my disgruntled emotions. After thanking him, I grab my bag and get out of the car.

Outside, I hesitate, mutely realizing this is not the best place to get a clear head—it's for the opposite. But the urge to escape, even if just for a few moments, is strong. Nothing good can result from being here, but I don't know what else to do, and it seems that every time life takes a turn for the worse, I always look to… losing myself.

Now hateful at myself, at the life and people I left behind, I shoulder open the door and walk in, not caring that I'll stick out like a sore thumb with my obvious travel bag. But when I step in, the sight is different from that night with Harlow.

There are no flashing lights, no grinding bodies, no loud music, no flashy clothing. I don't know if the almost somber tone right now is a regular occurrence during the day, and if the… revels only start at night.

I suppose it's easier to let yourself loose when the world is shrouded in darkness. And the night in itself is sometimes described as a time of seduction and danger.

It reminds me of my name, and then that day years ago when Jaxon explained it to me. He's inextricably a part of my life, a part of my memories, that I know leaving will be like ripping out a piece of me.

Pushing away the pang of pain and regret, I go to the counter. Despite the calmer atmosphere, it's still relatively dark, the overhead lights dimmed and colored, and there are some couples dancing. But the music is softer almost, and the place isn't packed at all.

Shifting my view away from the couples, I look to the bartender, who's in the process of making a drink for another customer.

Her hair is the first thing I notice, cut in a bob almost, shorter to the back of her head, and colored all the colors of the sea until my hands itch to paint her, the colors almost making her seem ethereal.

Eventually, she turns to face me, offering a smile. "What can I get you?"

She waits for my answer, regarding me with bright aqua eyes, the contacts shimmering in the light. I've wanted to escape my mind so badly, but now that the opportunity is here, my hands sweat, and my heart pumps lethargically.

After my incident, the thought of nearing any intoxicant, any mild hallucinogen, even if it's a medicine, fills me with a sort of dread, as though I fear I'll grow hooked on it too. In the end, I say, "A soda, please."

Seconds later, she puts a cup down in front of me, tells me to let her know if I want anything else, and goes to another customer.

The drink fizzles down my throat, nothing more than soda, and I relax a little at the taste, even if it won't shut off my mind. I can deal with the pain, I try to reason, because it's a part of life. What will I become if I try to drown my mind every time something disastrous happens?

I chip away at the peeling paint over the counter, morose in a way I didn't think possible, because what happens now? Do I still leave, thinking that will save him, or will Giovanni find him and kill him anyway?

As much as he shocked me, I don't want him to die. He *can't* die. Not when all he's done is look for me. I realize where that edge of darkness veiled behind his eyes comes from, that hidden desperation whenever he holds me.

It was obsession. Pure, cathartic obsession. My heart breaks when I now know where the despair comes from too. It came from seeing things no teenager, or person, ever should, from working for a monster wearing flesh.

If hope got me through the years, pure obsession is what helped him survive. He mainly lied by omission, but I know he also lied when he insisted every earlier encounter—like the art—were pure coincidences. They couldn't have been, not when he was sent to find me and did just that.

I barely pay attention when the bartender switches to another one, and I repeat my order to him. In moments, he puts down another cup in front of me.

"Enjoy," he tells me.

I lift the glass, swallowing down the soda, frowning a little when it tastes different than before. It's probably a different soda brand, I tell myself, since I wasn't specific. Except in seconds, it leaves a sour taste in my mouth, and my head grows fuzzy.

And it's only when the drink settles in my stomach, heavy almost, that I realize the bartender looked familiar. This time, I don't hesitate for a moment, I don't tell myself it's just a coincidence.

Eyes widening in panic, sweat dampening my palms, and my heart beating faster are the only signs of my panic that I can register beyond the growing fog pressing at my lucidity as I stumble out of the chair.

Black spots dance and grow in my vision, threatening to take me under, and a part of me wants to slip into it, where everything will go quiet and away. But I continue to struggle, staggering to the bathroom.

Everything is disoriented, my limbs heavy, and every time I put my legs down, they shake, knees wobbling, yet my mind is light. It grows even lighter, before dizziness sets in. Urgency becomes a faraway thing, and I laugh. *Isn't this what you wanted?*

When arms sweep under me, carrying me, and a ring slips onto my finger, I shake my head slowly. *Not like this.* Voices pull me away from the impending darkness for a little while, my eyes too heavy to open.

"Fiancée got a little carried away," I hear someone say, the voice vaguely—horrifyingly—familiar, his voice reverberating into me. I struggle infinitesimally at his words, and the grip on me tightens.

Never like this. And the world slips away.

Chapter 29

Old Memories

I'm slow to come to awareness. Odd sensations, muted but obvious, drag me to lucidity. I struggle to open my eyes, my tongue heavy in my mouth, my throat dry as if I've swallowed sand. Eventually, I register the awkward position of my body, limbs twisted uncomfortably.

I'm sitting down on a hard floor, and shifting my hips, I grimace at the pain in the small of my back. My legs are stretched out in front of me, with something wrapped around my ankles, constricting movement. But the deepest ache stems from having my torso stretched up and to the side, my hands bound to something cold and steel—probably handcuffs—somewhere above my head. I stretch my neck, wincing, trying to ease the ache, and open my eyes slowly.

Trying to shake myself from the odd stupor, I realize I'm in a neat bathroom, the tiles gleaming until the light harshly reflects off of them. The odd sterility makes me guess I'm in a hotel bathroom, something I confirm when I see the small, packaged toiletries. My ankles are tied together with zip ties, and I'm handcuffed to the towel rack.

As the reason for my prone state begins to sink in, so do the emotions, until the panic that had been pushed away because of the drug surges back in full force. I struggle against the handcuffs, chest tightening in frustration when I get nowhere.

It becomes harder and harder to breathe when the blind panic increases, dulling my thoughts into something senseless, into a cacophony of *I need to get out, I need to get out, I need to get out!* The words chant in my head, fueling my urgency, because it's not my tied-up state that really worries me.

It's when whoever brought me here decides to show up, and whether it's them or one of their men, I know I can't be here. If I can't get out now, then I never will. But I should realize by now that good things don't come to people like me, that to hope is futile, because moments later, the bathroom door opens, releasing a small click that seems almost foreboding. I freeze, as if he'll go away, because I already know who is standing at the doorway, here to seal my fate.

I wish I couldn't recognize him, but he's familiar in the way we're most intimate with our biggest fears. I've seen him before, mere glimpses in a haunted house, and will never forget the day he looked up, toward the banister where I was crouched, and smiled like a shark scenting blood in the water. Giovanni De Leone has always been a monster masquerading as a man.

I hold my breath as he stares at me, and the acidic, oily feel of his gaze nearly makes me retch. I want to struggle even though I know I should be still, an innate part of me recognizing it's vital to stay still in the face of danger.

Like maybe, if I still my limbs for long enough, I'll discover this is all a horrid dream. Because for the longest time, the thought of finally being tied to him and losing the tiny semblance of freedom I had was a nightmare.

It kept me up at night over those years, never failing to make my heart clench in dread and panic, my mind always stumbling over *What will he do to me?* I remember finding the contract and ripping it in a blind rage one time, immediately regretting it when I feared my father would tighten his leash in retaliation.

But ripping it never did help anything. A contract can be copied.

And foolishly, I thought that running away could finally make me free.

I want to scream and lash out, because I'd been *so* close. I almost had it all; everything that ever mattered to me, a chance to never look back. I swallow thickly, trying to fight past the lump in my throat, with the urge to say *I just want to go home*, but home is a man who'll walk into an empty apartment, full of everything I left silent.

I oscillate between anger at him being here and fear over what it means, until I keep my eyes glued on the floor beside his shiny, leather loafers. If I were to measure their cost in what he sells, then how many pounds of drugs did that cost? How many people did he have to sell? I imagine someone taken for their labor or organs or worse, and in the end, the money used for something as mundane as *shoes*.

In the end, the anger wins out, and I look up higher.

My eyes trail over the faded jeans, the numerous lighter spots and wrinkles a lie to who he is, contrasting with one of his greatest ticks—perfection. Higher, and I see a black dress shirt half tucked into his pants, his sleeves rolled up, hands lazily in his pockets. I know he could have them wrapped around my throat before I could even blink.

He's dressed simply, even though it all probably costs an entire year, if not more, of my school tuition. Finally, my eyes travel higher, to his face. His is a face that is almost nondescript, that would blend in at one of my father's parties, but with him, the look in his eyes is all wrong. I hope that the only thing he can see is my anger and defiance and none of my fear and regret.

His eyes are a startling, almost venomous shade of green, stark and demanding attention compared to the rest of him, a shade that would look attractive on anyone else but depraved on him. The dead look in them is his one outlier. I heard a rumor that the shade almost got him killed when he was born, that his father was certain he wasn't his. In the end, it was nothing more than a genetic oddity.

They pin me further to my spot, as if daring me to move so he can strike fast and hard, gaze penetrating in a way that makes me want to shed my skin and become the ugliest thing he's ever seen.

His lips tip up in a smirk, but an otherwise mischievous, playful expression is cold and calculating on him. Already, in seconds, I'm convinced there is no line this man will not cross, no sense of morality. That if he were to see a dying child on the street, he'd walk right on, or only pause to consider selling their organs.

But then again, on our screens, a lot of us see dying children from half a world away and scroll on with ease. Not only that, but we'll continue to support the organizations that fund that death.

When he stalks nearer, I reflexively draw my legs closer to me, and he catches the movement, no doubt filing it away to use against me. Everything is a battlefield, and Giovanni, a careful strategist, goes for the kill.

The bathroom is small, until he's near me in only two strides, towering above me. I refuse to tip my head back and look at him, and instead, glare at the walls. It's easier to be angry rather than afraid when I'm not looking at him.

Though it gets harder when he sinks into a crouch beside me. He huffs out a laugh, and he's close enough that it skitters across my skin, a thousand ugly spiders that *crawl*. "Layla, why are you so terrified? Am I a monster to you?"

I swallow, refusing to rise up to the bait, and continue to glare ahead of me. My answer is plain as day.

"Let me tell you a story then, maybe it'll ease up some… tension." His voice is soft and wrong, another counterintuitive thing about him. I know he's anything but soft and gentle.

"When I was younger, my brother and I used to play games. Games of promises. If I'd win, I'd promise him something, and if he won, he would promise me something. When we got older, it changed, but we still played it. Still played promises. That, in itself, became the game. To see who'd break their promise first. Who'd promise something too big, too precious."

He absentmindedly reaches for a strand of my hair and twirls it between his fingers, and I immediately yank my head away. Only Jaxon's ever done that, and Giovanni's hands on my hair are a violation. But his fingers tighten around the strand, yanking me back until my scalp stings.

"One time, he got drunk. Drunk enough that he lost his guard. We played our game, and he promised me his lover and his title as heir. Foolish, isn't it? But no promise was ever high enough. I won, and he never paid up. Do you want to guess what happens next?"

I keep my mouth shut, glaring at the finger that continues to play with my hair, since I already know where this will go.

"I took his lover, and had him watch as she screamed while her flesh burned. But I was kind enough to give him the urn with her ashes. And then, when he tried to have me killed to keep his title, I killed him. I think the dogs have developed a fascination with human meat ever since then, because they bite trespassers more viciously."

I shiver slightly at his story, wondering if it's true, hoping it's not. It's never been so obvious that while I come from that world, I am not of it. I did not grow up knowing what my father does, and that has made me soft in a way none of them are. It makes every part of his story revolting to me. Who kills his brother and feeds him to the dogs? Who burns a person alive and rejoices in it on the basis of pure sadism?

I imagine doing that to my brother, my sweet, baby brother, and want to throw up. How depraved do you have to be to burn someone alive because of a drunken promise? But I imagine setting *him* aflame, and for a brief, twisted moment, I delight at the idea.

And you thought wedding me to him would keep me safe, *Father?* I think bitterly. Or maybe he foolishly thought that power meant safety.

"The moral of this story, Layla? When I am promised something, I make sure I get it. And when I get it, I keep it. And I don't ever let go."

His hands move from my hair to my face, and he grips it roughly, forcing me to look at him, and my lungs tighten in my fear at the wild look in his eyes.

"Don't touch me."

"Ah, but you are mine. I can touch what's mine, no?" His grip grows firm around my jaw, hard enough that I wince, that I want to retch. "*E non dovresti desiderarmi?*"

I am slow to comprehend the last part, and his hold on me tightens further, until my cheeks press against my teeth.

"You can't even understand your own language anymore. You came here to live and submerge yourself in your American dream, and sully your time with that American boy." Jaxon is not American, and my family has been here for generations, but I don't point this out. "That you've forgotten who you are."

"I will never want you," I answer his earlier question. "And don't. Touch. Me." His eyes flare in anger, but I keep at it, my own anger fueled by his violation of *touching* me. "I have never forgotten who I am, but you have, you *pezzo di merda*."

His face flushes in rage, complexion taking a red hue, upper lip pulling back in a snarl. And slowly, I'm reminded that nothing stops Giovanni. How can it, when he doesn't have a conscience?

"Such an ungrateful *cagna*."

He delivers the words with a backhand I don't see coming, and I know it's a test, a tease, a promise for more pain. My head snaps to the side from the blow, skin stinging, and one side of my gum smarts when it pulls over a canine. The sharp tang of blood fills my mouth, and tears reflexively sting my eyes before I blink them away.

He viciously grabs my face again, forcing me to face him, and his hold is hard enough that it's sure to bruise, the pain heightened from the cut inside my mouth and my stinging skin.

"Do you think I take pleasure in hurting you? I wouldn't have to if you'd only cooperate."

I almost laugh bitterly, because of course a man's rage is always somehow the woman's fault, and spit, "You take pleasure in pain, *stronzo*. And you'll never get my *cooperation*."

He grins this time, and somehow, that scares me more than everything else today. "I never understood why Jaxon wanted to follow you so badly, but I see it now. The prickliest fruits are often the sweetest on the inside. Will you be sweet for me?"

"Keep his name out of your mouth."

"But he's mine just as much as you are. Alessandro was a fool to raise you blind, because now you really don't know how our world works. There is no leaving the mafia, not for you, and not for Jaxon. The only way you leave is in a body bag, and with what he's done? No doubt *touched* you? I'll cut off his hands before I make him beg for death."

"Touch him, and *you'll beg* for death." If I couldn't imagine hurting a person earlier, I know I would do everything possible to make him scream for *days* if he touches Jaxon. "I swear it."

Throwing his head back, he laughs, the threat amusing him, because what can I, the female heir of a dying mafia outfit, do to him?

"Is that how I get your cooperation? If I threatened to hurt him, kill him, would you be sweet? Sit if I tell you, stand if I ask for it? Become my own personal dog? It's nothing less than you deserve."

He says it in amusement, but we both know it's true. To use Jaxon is how he wins, and I can feel the adrenaline wearing off, the anger slowly morphing into that dark exhaustion, that urge to close my eyes and sleep forever.

"You're already a dog," I say, even if it doesn't carry half as much venom as earlier.

I try to draw away from him further, ignoring the multiple aches and sprains around my body from my still stretched and twisted position. The movement tugs at my handcuffs, but this time, it almost... gives. Not the handcuffs, but the towel rack.

He grows angrier, until I am sure he can somehow hear my thoughts. But I can't tell by any outward change—his face doesn't grow more red, and his snarl isn't more venomous. I can tell because he grows still, scarily so. As if when he does move and speak, it'll be the epitome of an explosion. That his anger is building, a storm brewing beneath the surface, ready to burst out at any given moment with no warning.

"I'm not a dog. I'm your fiancé, and it's about time you got that stuck in your head."

His words are steady, calm even. But his eyes are anything but, and I know this is a man who does not understand the concept of "no," the idea of "do not touch me." Or he does, but doesn't care.

The hand on my jaw travels down to my neck, and it's large enough that it encases the entire front, gripping hard on either side. He could probably kill me with that one hand, choking the life out of me, like I'm nothing more than a tiny, helpless child.

He leans closer, enraptured, as if the idea of my fear pleases him, and desperately, I use it to my advantage. I kick out my legs, hitting him in the knee. It gives me just enough of an advantage to lift my hips off the hard floor and twist my body to the left, where my hands are handcuffed to the pole. I latch onto the towel rack, heart hammering in anticipation and fear, and *yank*. On the second pull, it gives, ripping out of its place with a crack and a pop.

He's already recovered, shoving me back against the wall as I slide back down, but I swing the pole wildly, fueled by pure desperation, the disgust from remembering his hands on me making me insane. My ankles are still zip-tied and my wrists are still handcuffed, but I have the metal pole in my hands and more flexibility to move now.

Too bad it's all for naught.

It takes nothing for him to grab the pole on the third strike and rip it away, suddenly enough that my arms tug roughly before I have to let go.

I scream at him, frustrated, except it ebbs away into fear again when he grabs me and shoves me against the wall, my head slamming into the plaster, my back smarting in pain until I'm sure it reverberates into every bone.

I'm back to square one again, and I have no advantage this time.

He shakes his head at me, disappointed. "You have spark, *la mia sposa*, I'll admit that. Except it's getting old now."

"Oh, am I not amusing anymore?" Of course the defiance is amusing to him, until it's no longer entertaining, and then he realizes he wants something he needs to tame. I'll show him *tame*. "You'll regret taking me back," I promise. "There is nothing I will ever give you."

"That has never mattered, though it would make things better for you. You promise you'll make me regret taking you back? I promise I'll make you hurt. And don't think I won't enjoy every second of it."

He doesn't elaborate on his threats—I doubt he would've anyway—because something trills from his pocket. With a promising glare, he looks away, pulling the phone out of his pocket and picking up the call.

"*Che cosa?*" he barks.

Whoever is on the other end speaks too low for me to catch anything beyond muted words, but I don't like the interest that slides into Giovanni's features, the smug look of triumph.

Carefully, I attempt to gradually slide my body away from him, inch by inch, just enough that maybe I'll be able to crawl out toward the door. It's all probably going to be futile anyway, since my hands and ankles are bound, and there's no way he's the only person in this place. But maybe I'll hate myself a little less for getting caught if I keep vainly trying to escape.

I don't even get those few inches before his hand shoots out to clamp on my throat again, squeezing tight enough that the warning is clear as day.

"Bring him then, if he's so eager," he murmurs to the other end, not even looking at me.

He hangs up and tucks his phone away, an almost mad gleam in his eyes.

"Looks like we're going to have an audience. One I think you'll like."

Audience for what?

Don't, I want to scream, because I already know who's on the other side of the door.

But it's too late for that now.

Chapter 30

Blood in the Water

He cuts away the zip-ties on my ankles, and it's a small reprieve, one drowned out by the biting panic. I know why he's cut them off; to take me to whatever, *whoever*, waits outside. I want to go back in time, if even only by a few seconds, when things were slightly better.

I try to fight against him when he grabs my arm to pull me up to my feet. My legs and ankles are cramped from lying on the hard floor for a long time, so that when I stand, I cannot feel them and stumble, hating that I have to hold onto him for support, even when I claw to get away. My fighting does nothing, and he just tightens his grip, practically dragging me out of the bathroom.

I barely register my feet stumbling over the carpeted floor as I keep trying to wrestle out of his hold.

"Scared now, *dolcezza*?" The pet name is an insult coming from him, and a word that should be loving and sweet is now poisonous.

I try to school my features as the hall opens up into a room, but I know that to him, the fear is obvious. It's obvious a panic attack is near, that I have to hold back a scream, that there are vicious snakes wrapping around my ribs and throat, *squeezing*, until almost every breath is a struggle.

It only gets worse when I look around the room. I don't take in the closed window, or the exit only a few paces away.

No, I'm too focused on the person on his knees in the living room, his hands held behind his back like someone brought to heel.

Giovanni chuckles, endlessly amused, when a gasp chokes out of me. I don't care that his grip is hard enough to bruise, that he's pulled me into him like his own personal property. Not when all I can see is the bloody face, the red still wet and dripping down his chin, the beautiful eyes that are scrunched in pain.

No, all I can see is Jaxon bound and on the floor, his face a few punches away from being a mess. His lip is puffed and split at the corner, a purplish bruise covers nearly half of his face, and there's another forming across his forehead.

"What did you *do* to him?"

At the sight, it's easy for the panic to evanesce into anger, into the kind my mother would warn me of, and later, the kind my father said does not belong to a woman in our world. Again, I imagine making Giovanni *hurt* and *bleed*.

Whirling to him, all I know is that anger, breathing and pulsing in my blood, and I kick him, over and over until he tightens his grip on me to the point my arm goes numb, and I know what he does next will *hurt*.

I don't care, because all I can see is Jaxon's anguished eyes and how I was so stupid, because anger is a companion emotion. It rises to mask the helplessness from the disparity of this. Did I really think that I could escape? Did I really think he wouldn't get dragged into this mess?

"*I* did nothing to him. If you mean the bruises, that's courtesy of having him spying. Someone found him lurking outside, trying to get in. But I did bring him in, so he got what he wanted in the end."

I glare and raise my hand to slap him, but he backhands me, this time harder than before, on the same cheek, and I can hear it even afterward, the sound resounding in my ears. I hiss and squeeze my eyes against the instinctual surge of tears, pushing them down, fighting the urge to reach up and touch the smarting skin.

Another sound of skin hitting skin forces my eyes to open, confused when I don't feel the pain, until I see Jaxon forced back down, snarling at the guards and Giovanni, rabid in the face of what he's done.

One of them rears his hand back to punch him, and then *I'm* the rabid creature. "Don't you *dare*," I hiss. "Touch him and die. Touch him and you'll never see the light of day again, I swear it."

He punches him anyway, until there's the sick sound of a battering fist, and Jaxon's head snaps back from the blow. But when he lifts his head, he grins at the guard, teeth streaked with blood and a rivulet of it running down his chin, a maniacal gleam in his eyes. I realize that any hint of depravity I would see over the months was only a taste of how he's really changed. "That's all you got?"

His eyes dart to mine, and immediately, I look away, not wanting to study what I may find. Will there be regret for being with me? Anger for what I've put him through? Will I see him realize that none of it was worth it? *How could you?* I want to ask. *How could you want to be a part of this world for me?*

"I'm sorry," I whisper, humiliation burning me, and I know that Giovanni's won before he's even said his threat. Turning to him, hating his bored amusement, as though this is a regular occurrence for him, I say, "Let go of him. Leave him alone and let him go, and I'll come back with you and marry you willingly."

He runs the pad of his finger over my face, over the bruise no doubt forming across my skin. He caresses it lovingly, like the blatant sign of my pain brings him joy.

"I could tell you no, and still get what I want. I don't need your cooperation to take you back, or your willingness to marry you, but I admit that I like it too much—seeing you agree with me. Your father promised me a wife, and a wife is to be sweet for her husband, no?"

"Don't touch her."

The words are low, filled with malice, and I know Giovanni has killed men for less. My gaze jumps to Jaxon's, unbidden, but he's glaring at Giovanni. He's only going to make it worse. At best, he'll leave here scathed for life. At worst, he'll leave here in a body bag, lucky to have his body whole.

"Or what?" Giovanni muses. "What could you possibly do? You're bound and on the floor, and I can do *anything* to her, and you can't do a single thing about it. Not so fun, is it?"

"*Don't touch her.*" It almost comes out panicked, the aggravation clear, and I want to tell him no. You don't show emotion, not if you want to live. But he must know that already.

Giovanni runs a finger over my arm, all the way to the tip of my middle finger before going back up. Again, I'm reminded of a spider skittering across my skin, and I shudder in revulsion. "Again, or what?"

Pulling my foot up, I stomp it over his, hoping I stub a toe, delighting in his grunt of pain. "Don't touch me. *I* didn't say you could. And the 'or what' is that I bite."

I shriek when he leans down, closing his teeth over my ear and biting down *hard*. Hard enough that I'm shocked a piece of my ear hasn't ripped off, and I hiss in pain, hand twitching to reach up and cradle the wound.

"You're promised to me, so I *can* touch you. It's a simple concept."

I don't register Jaxon yelling, or the rising tempo of my heartbeat. I'm too focused on the movement of Giovanni reaching for something, the sound of a click, and then something cold and round presses against the side of my forehead.

A shaky exhale escapes me as I try to still my body, every limb locking. It's one thing to say I'd rather die than cooperate, and it's another to have the end of the gun pressing against my forehead. But perhaps worse is the way Jaxon's eyes blank, and I know he's lost in remembering when someone else in his life died by a bullet to the head.

"Interesting," he drawls. "I should've done this from the start— would've gotten you to shut up much faster."

He touches me, hand feathering across my face, across my hair. The barrel of the gun is unyielding, the danger of it almost toned down since I can't see it clearly, but the presence and feel of him behind me is *wrong*.

Don't touch me. Don't touch me. Don't touch me. Say something, Layla.

Somehow, I push past the paralysis pulsing through my body, the false promise that if I stay still and quiet, I'll be safe. I'll never be safe. "You're disgusting. You have to threaten to kill someone to get what you want? Doesn't that make you feel... inadequate?"

My words don't do any good at all, and the gun presses harder against my forehead. In my mind, I can see his finger over the trigger. It'd take just one pull. He could do it without even realizing.

This time, I shake.

And shake further when his finger traces the shell of my ear. My skin grows flushed in the way it does when I get a fever, and suddenly I'm too hot and too cold, and *I can't breathe.*

Don't touch me. Don't touch me. Don't touch me. Don't touch me.

He doesn't care about my wheezing breath, and I know soon, spots will dance in my vision, an invisible hand tight around my throat. I'm so lost in it, until everything grows hazy, as though I've become untethered from my body.

I vaguely register Jaxon yelling and the scuffle that's started again with him and the guards, but his yelling only makes me more worried. *Don't touch me, don't touch me, don't touch me,* has become *don't hurt him, don't hurt him, don't hurt him.*

The words are loud enough in my head that I don't fully notice when someone stumbles into the room. And I don't realize when Giovanni stops his taunting.

It'll get better, I promise, I lie, I try to trick myself. *It'll get better. Deep breath in, deep breath out.*

And maybe, it only helps because Giovanni removes his hand.

Only then do I notice who it is.

Even though he's not the last person I expected, this moment will always be a shock. A dose of fury, sadness, and hate, because *he* is one of the last people I want to see.

"Mr. Delaney-Rossi," Giovanni starts. "You're a bit late."

Sometimes, it can only take weeks to forget something, no matter how important it is. Or want to forget something badly enough until the edges of it blur and the hate becomes dull.

In the months since I've left, it's become easier and easier to forget the loneliness, the pain, and the never-ending *quiet.* It became easier to forget that house and him.

Now, seeing him like this, is as though I've gone forward a couple years. In my head, I always remember him as who he was back then, even if only a few months ago, and now, at the stark differences, it's like looking at a different person.

He doesn't look like a *don* anymore—he looks like someone a few steps away from his deathbed, someone moving forward to it himself.

The once strong features are now slack and weary, and his eyes, almost a replica of mine, are dull, until he already looks dead. And I know that all the incidents in these months—the stalkers and texts— were Giovanni's work, not his.

A man *he* tied me to, because nothing less than a legacy was enough. Alone, I'd never provide the security for a *don* on the brink of a collapsing empire.

"This wasn't part of the deal." Even his voice comes out older, rougher in a way only possible from certain uses.

Which Giovanni evidently knows. "Do you even remember it anymore? Or has using your own product messed up that memory of yours? You never use what you sell, every smart person would've gotten that down by now." A few years ago, Giovanni would have been tortured for that. "No? Well, I do. Her hand, the title of future *don*, and in turn, I strengthen the business until your natural death— nice job speeding that up, by the way, much appreciated—protect your daughter, and ensure your legacy lives. I've done and will do all that. How is this not part of the deal?"

The part where you have a gun pointed to my head.

I glare, but the both of them continue to act as if no one else is in the room, discussing me and their arrangement.

"Protecting her isn't holding a gun to her head."

"I'm protecting her by keeping her goddamned mouth shut since it'll land her in situations that danger her."

I hate you. I hate you. I hate you. I hate you. I hate you.

"Protecting me," I rasp, my head still clouded from the fear of the gun, the rush of memories that surface from seeing him again, and the unexplainable... tiredness. I can't believe how much I just want it to end. "Isn't this. Protecting me doesn't involve tying me to a marriage at the age of *fifteen*."

Maybe it wouldn't have been such a shock if I'd known about the mafia my entire life, that a marriage to someone not of my choosing would be all I could expect. But I'd never known about it. I'd never expected it, and I'd always thought my life would pan out... normally. Normalcy might be overrated, but it would've been *mine*.

"I can't believe you would sell me like a common animal simply to save your legacy."

My father shakes his head. "You don't understand. I had to save him. I had to choose, and I needed you both to live."

I know not to expect much from my father, to not expect that he's the same man who loved my mother and his family. But it still hurts, still claws at my chest, to know that a man—that *Giovanni*—is worth saving, but I am not.

"I think that's enough," Giovanni says. "You know what needs to stay hidden."

He wraps a hand around my throat, and immediately, I move to take it away, but then the safety of the gun clicks off. "Stay still."

I bristle, really lacking self-preservation. "With your dogmatic personality, someone will stab you in the back one day. Take me back, and that someone will be me."

Clearly, my "troublesome mouth" doesn't know when to shut up, and I almost expect him to tighten the pressure on my throat, but he takes the gun away instead, shocking me.

Only to point it at Jaxon moments later.

My breath hitches, and I have to bite my teeth to keep from screaming out. He won't kill him. He knows he needs him alive if he wants me to cooperate.

Giovanni chuckles, amused. My skin chills and nausea climbs up my throat when he leans his head down to plant a kiss on my skin. *Wrong. Wrong. Wrong. Wrong.* It's *disgusting*. The texture of his lips and his breath skating over my skin is all *wrong*.

I gag, and the hand over my throat tightens, my obvious disgust only angering him. I try to find it in me to push it down in case he enacts that anger on Jaxon.

"I could do more than this. I could do anything, and you'd come to *like* it."

You're sick. So sick.

310

Jaxon shakes his head, his face red from struggling against the men holding him, and it hurts to see him begging Giovanni. Every time his eyes meet mine, he shakes his head further in frustration and mutters "sorry" over and over again. Sorry for what?

His efforts only amuses Giovanni, and he laughs as he kisses my cheek, right over the bruise. "I should bring him back with us just so he can watch."

I can't hear him over the rushing sound in my ears and the loud beat of my heart, my breath wheezing. I'll never be able to get rid of the feeling of his hand on me. And it'll always make me sick. I can't decide if the kisses, the chasteness of them a lie, are worse than the thought of what will come if I go back.

"I'm so sorry, Layla. This isn't what I ever wanted for you," my father rasps, not *doing anything*. He's not a boss now, but a broken man who has lost the love of his life and still cannot cope. He's the man who lost one child through death and the other through betrayal. "My family is all I've ever cared about, all I've ever tried to save, and I have failed so badly."

When Giovanni pulls back enough to talk, I don't think twice about it. I don't even fully process it before I'm doing something stupid. I reach for the gun, thinking it's all I need to turn the tables.

I grab his arm, steering it away from Jaxon, and wrench out of his grip as I try to close my hand around the gun. At the sound of banging, I panic and freeze, thinking the firearm went off. My gaze darts to Jaxon, but I don't see him curl in pain.

And then the door breaks down.

Everything is loud, too loud. The door crashes against the wall, and many booted feet thud over the floor. I think that the rest of Giovanni's cavalry has arrived, but they're dressed in camouflage green military apparel, each holding mammoth-sized guns with both hands.

I don't have time to register the shock and bizarreness of it— one minute I'm hassling for a gun, the next a damn SWAT team breaks down the door—before they're moving, immediately going for Jaxon.

In seconds, they have the ones holding him down taken, grabbing them and shoving them against the wall. I stare, dumbstruck, at their efficiency and quick work, half surprised they're helping us and not Giovanni, that they aren't corrupt.

There are words circulating around the room, and the noise from the chaos is still there, but it's dull in my head. Why am I so slow?

Get away from Giovanni.

I know that I need to do this much, that he still has the gun in his hand. It may feel as though I've spent minutes rooted to my spot, staring at the event in front of me unfold, but I know it's been only seconds.

Seconds that I move away from Giovanni, seconds before the officers reach him, ordering him to put his gun down. And it takes less than that for Giovanni to react faster than me. To grab an officer with agility and push him into another, giving himself enough time.

Enough time to pull the trigger, the only sound I hear, until another firearm goes off and Giovanni curses.

And even though I'm pushed forward from the impact, my eyes seek out Jaxon, panicked. But he points a gun at someone behind me, shoving past the officers trying to usher him out, and screams something I cannot hear past the ringing in my ears.

Slowly, I register the wet liquid seeping over my skin, soaking my clothes, and then the pain that follows. Staggering forward, I reach to clutch at the wound, knowing I need to cover it to keep more blood from seeping out. But that heightens the pain, making it sharp until I gasp, a scream building in my throat because it *hurts*.

Everything around me mutes, from the familiar voice that screams my name to the arms lifting me.

I'm only acutely aware of how everything becomes *less*, every sense growing dull, and I can't figure out if it's from the blood loss or shock. I just want all the noise and jostling to stop.

But it doesn't, the movement jarring my wound, forcing me to stay lucid even though the blood loss is beginning to make me drowsy. The world grows bright behind my eyelids, and fresh air brushes my face.

Desperate hands grasp my face, tracing across the skin, as familiar to me as my home, and someone murmurs, over and over, "Open your eyes, sweetheart. Stay with me, please."

Everything shifts until I'm settled against something that moves, and I think I'm finally allowed the rest my body so badly wants. But instead, something closes over my nose and mouth, and instantly, I panic, eyes snapping open as I try to rip my head away.

Blurred figures hover over me, someone pressing something against my mouth and nose. I struggle against it, but when I take a breath, it smells cloying and sweet, and the urge to slip away comes back in full force.

And helplessly, I fall into it.

Chapter 31

Yours

Lucidity is a fickle thing.

Every time the monotonous beeping brings me to consciousness, something else drags me down until I give up on the idea of waking.

Someone holds my hand and occasionally speaks to me, but I can't understand them and don't know if it's real or just my mind playing tricks on me. Maybe this is all a dream and I'm reliving that day years ago, when I woke up in a hospital, similarly out of sorts.

Gradually, I realize a hand brushes my hair away from my forehead, repeating the motion over and over, and this can't be a trick of my mind.

There were no caring touches on that day. The continuous motion finally spurs me awake, my eyes blinking away the harsh light as I shake off the remnants of sleep, and the hand falls away from my hair.

My body is still disoriented, mostly numb everywhere, and as I remember the gunshot, I'm glad for it. The machine wired up to me beeps, and there's an IV drip attached to me, no doubt pumping me with morphine.

All too soon, I look at the arm resting on the bed railing, the masculine hand all too familiar. My gaze travels higher, until I'm finally looking at his face.

For the longest time, I simply stare at him, both relieved that he's completely alright, and downfallen as I remember everything from before. What happens now?

He's the first to speak, releasing a breath, his dark eyes searching mine. Everything about him is scruffy, from his hair to his clothes, and dark circles shadow his eyes, until I want to reach over and brush his tension away.

"You're awake," he breathes, the tense lines of his shoulders falling into something relieved, and I offer a watery smile, unsure what to say. In the end, he forges on, and I don't have to. "I'm so glad you're okay, and I'm sorry that happened, that I didn't get there soon enough." He swallows thickly, Adam's apple bobbing, and his hand slides over the blanket, toward mine, but he stops it a few inches away, looking almost pained to do so. "And I'm sorry for how you found everything out earlier, before that."

Reaching over, wincing when I pull at tender muscles, I cup his face, shutting him up, and my eyes mist with tears as I smooth the skin over his cheeks. In the face of everything that's happened, there's no hesitancy to my words, no hesitancy to my want for him, and the words flow out of me with ease.

"You don't need to apologize, *amore*. You're always so careful to apologize for everything, so careful to be the one to give, and I'm sorry I've been holding back, I'm sorry I've been scared to have you with both hands."

He opens his mouth as though to argue, and I tap a finger over his lips. "No, I have been. Whether it's been unsure to move in with you permanently, or tell you about my past, I always held a piece of me back. And I'm sorry I shouted at you to leave. I can't believe you worked for a twisted man for six years just to get to see me again."

Maybe there isn't the possibility of an us anymore, and we've finally reached our end together, a candle wick burnt out, but I keep speaking anyway.

"And I know it was a choice you made, but I also know what my father and the men of his world do, and I know how that environment can change a person, can twist someone into murdering his own brother for power. But that you let none of that darkness bleed into your actions? That you're still the caring person I knew from all those years ago? That's a hard thing to do. It's hard to stay hopeful, to keep that light of morality when everything around you is twisted, and I'm so proud that you did. I'm sorry I didn't see that, didn't tell you that I'm nothing but proud of you, nothing but honored to be yours."

He smiles, eyes a little sad, as though he doesn't believe he's worthy of love, and I know I'll have the time to prove him wrong. He kisses the palm of my hand, looking uncharacteristically nervous, the both of us purging every secret we've ever kept, every confession we were too scared to make.

"My life was so dark, and so lonely, before I met you, and you were like this... *light* I found, and I couldn't fathom not keeping it.

"I've loved your laugh since the day I heard it, and I've loved your smile since the moment I saw it and realized that I'd do *anything* to just get you to smile like that again. I love it when you reach for me first thing in the morning, even half asleep, like the need to hold me is in your psyche. I can't tell you when I fell in love with you, because all I can remember is always loving something about you, one after the other, until it built up and you became my best obsession—"

I interrupt him, remembering the ways that scared me. "I will admit I'm worried about that. Worried that I'm just your obsession, to the point you followed me across the country. And that you've wanted me for so long, that now the real thing will fall short." I remember his promises from earlier, that I deserve to be loved, that he would do everything to deserve me. "And you're always doing things for me, things I can never measure up to."

He shuts me up with a kiss before continuing, "Layla, I'm trying to do a sappy monologue here, and you keep interrupting me. Sweetheart, it's always been you. You've always been the only person for me, there's no way having you will ever disappoint me. And what I do for you is the bare minimum." When I shake my head, he frowns, carrying on, insisting, "No, it is. And I'll prove you wrong—that what I've done so far really is nothing—and raise your bar until the day I can say I deserve to be your husband."

I stare at him, shocked, because when did we start talking about marriage? He gives me a sardonic look, as though he can't believe my astonishment.

"You say I'm obsessed, and yet you don't really realize the depth of it, do you? The fact that you are not my wife bothers me almost every day because I *want* to be your husband. I want another ring of mine on your finger, and I want one on mine that I can look at throughout the day. Sometimes, when I call you sweetheart, I actually want to call you *wife*, and I hate having to bite my tongue to stop from calling you what you are not."

My exhale is shaky as he leans closer, a man of conviction, and I know every word he's said is true. His next ones are what I thought I'd never hear, and yet, I know they're the best thing I'll ever listen to.

"Every part of me is so utterly, desperately in love with you. If you were to find a window into my soul, into my heart, you would find every piece of it full of you. You can say you are my obsession as much as you want and nothing more, but is the greatest proof of my obsession not my love for you?"

My hand reaches toward his, grabbing it firmly before I yank him to me, even though it pulls a little at my wound, and he awkwardly stumbles onto the bed. I can't decide whether to grin or cry, and it's as though the incident hasn't happened at all, because how can a monstrosity survive in the face of my happiness?

He sprawls on top of the bed, over me, and it takes nothing for me to scoot and settle my head against his chest, where I can hear the wild tempo of his heart. He sucks in a breath, and I can feel the frantic rise and fall of his chest as I intertwine my fingers with his.

"Tell me again," I whisper, unable to stop from pulling my head back and kissing his chest where his heart is. Where my home is.

"I love you."

"Again."

He leans in to kiss my cheek, and it's *right, right, right*, telling me, "I love you, Layla, *ya qalbi*. Did you know that one meaning of your name is seductress? Everything about you always draws me in helplessly, and I'm keeping you now. Do you want me to?"

"I love you," I say in answer. "Sometimes, when I was in that house, I didn't think I'd ever find love, or that I'd ever *want* to, but loving you is as easy as simply being, until I cannot imagine ever stopping. Does that answer your question?"

I think the smile he gives me, sweet and hopeful and full of emotion, like it's helplessly spilling out of him, is one of my favorite ones yet. His gaze travels over my features as he resumes brushing my hair away from my forehead. When his jaw ticks, I know that my face is bruised, another stark reminder that the incident was definitely not a nightmare.

"How are you feeling?" he asks.

I open my mouth to answer, but a nurse walks into the room, clipboard in hand, one eyebrow raised at our position. Jaxon doesn't budge.

"Hello, Layla, glad to see you awake." Turning, she glares at Jaxon. "Your fiancé was quite adamant about staying by your side, and I'm sure he's relieved now that you're awake."

I freeze at the word "fiancé," my eyes widening until Jaxon squeezes my hand, drawing my gaze down to our entwined fingers where I see that he has a… keychain ring on his ring finger?

It slowly clicks in place. Of course, Jaxon decided to say he's my fiancé in order to stay past visiting hours. *He makes a much better fiancé,* I think, before shoving *that* thought away.

He told you that he loves you, not that he wants to marry you. Slow down, Layla. Except, didn't he sort of say that too?

"So, Layla…"

The nurse checks my vitals, telling me they'll keep me here for a few more days, depending on my condition.

"And how are you feeling?" she asks, and I wonder if she's trying not to laugh at our awkward position, with Jaxon and I squished on the bed.

"I'm fine, thank you. I'm just tired is all."

"Well, alright then. You need your rest. There are some guests who've come to see you. Is now a good time, or are you too tired?"

I frown, glancing at Jaxon. "Guests" can only mean Harlow. For a moment, I want to tell the nurse no, I will not be seeing any guests. When Harlow decides I'm fine, she'll probably put a bullet in me herself for scaring her.

But I miss her more than I'm scared of her. "It's fine, I'd like to see them."

She leaves, and not even a few moments later, Harlow bursts into the room, making a beeline for me, and Jaxon barely pulls back quick enough before she smothers me in a hug. I squeeze her back and squeak when she practically strangles me.

"You're hurting me, Harlow," I wheeze out. "Lighten up just a little."

"Serves you right for scaring me like that. Seriously? You got *kidnapped* and then got *shot*. Gosh, is this how you felt when I was in the hospital?" She eases up, pulling away, a frown marring her features. "What even *happened?*"

At the sight of her, and the relief of being here and not in a hotel with Giovanni's hand around my throat or the threat of going back, my throat tightens, eyes burning from unshed tears. They get harder to hold back when I notice two others entering the room, holding hands. One is Aaron, and I immediately know who the other is.

Aaradhya looks everything like an older version of the self I knew her to be, and I can't believe she's really here. My attention goes back to their intertwined hands. Just how long was I asleep for that I missed *this* development?

After Aaron gives me a one-arm hug and tells me that he's glad I'm alright, Aaradhya disentangles from him and squeezes me in a hug that rivals Harlow's. I don't ask when she got here, how long she's staying, or when Aaron and her clearly started getting to know each other. I wonder how long it took after giving Harlow her number for her to arrange the two of them meeting.

Instead, we simply hold each other, and everything about her, from her hug to the smell of her shampoo, is the same.

She's teary-eyed when she pulls away, and that's nothing new either.

I take in all of them, and my chest aches in a way that hurts from my gratitude to be here, alive and safe. As much as I put on a brave front—for the most part—when I got kidnapped, there was no hiding how it shook me, fear clawing into my being. Fear of going back, of being forced to be with him, but also fear of being alone in a big house with only monsters for company. With no one to hold me like they love me, no one to take the time to get to know me.

But looking at the faces of those who will always matter to me, who understand me and are there for me, only ever wanting my happiness, I know I'm not alone.

And I'll never be.

I remember the girl that craved normalcy for so long, how my entire teenage years were spent chasing what I had as a child, before my mother and brother died, before my life irrevocably changed. But I don't need normalcy or a "normal" past when I know I'm loved, when I know I'm not alone.

Chapter 32

Fireworks

I wake with a start, gasping, to a hand rubbing my back and another sifting through my hair, someone murmuring that everything is alright. Slowly, the worst of my panic from the nightmare eases, ebbing away, as though rescinding its claws, until I can soften into the body beneath mine, the planes of it familiar.

"A nightmare?" he asks into the night, resting his head over my chin.

Nodding, my arms tighten around him, tensing as I remember the nightmare, the sight of blood running across his face. Except instead of flowing from cuts, the nightmare spun a bullet wound onto his skin, until his eyes were lifeless.

There hasn't been an incident for months—no one has come to avenge Giovanni's death or to take me back—and yet, my mind will still find something to panic over, to let the fear feast on.

"It's okay, sweetheart," he murmurs into my hair. "Everything is okay—it's all over."

In the first few weeks, the police let us know someone had come snooping around, inquiring about Giovanni's death, and I'll never forget the cool malice in Jaxon's tone when he said, "You'd be wise to make sure they don't know anything about Layla or me. If they do, I'll know who to come to first."

A few days later, whoever it was "disappeared," and there's been nothing since.

And yet, I will find myself wondering over what could have been, until my mind is full of *what-ifs*. It's not just me either—some nights, I'll wake up to Jaxon jerking in his sleep, only to grasp me urgently when he wakes up.

"Do you think seeing your father set this one off?" he asks, bringing me back to the present.

I still wonder why I did it, but yesterday I went to see him in the rehab center, where he was on the long track of recovery from the cocktail of drugs he was dependent on. As much as I'll always miss my mother, I'm glad she never had to see him this way, broken and a ghost of the man he used to be. I doubt I'll ever forget the way he begged me to forgive him, or how wrecked he looked when I left.

I can't shake his panicked words from my mind, the mania in his eyes when he grabbed me and begged, "You have to find him. You have to save him."

A vindictive part of me was very pleased to spit, "He's dead. Jaxon killed him."

"No, he's not. He *can't* be dead. I did *everything* they wanted."

In the end, the nurses finally got him to let go, and I left, not understanding what he meant.

Now, I'm far away from everything, and we're safe, so in the space of our bedroom, the sweat from the nightmare cooling, I trace the edges of Jaxon's collarbone. "Maybe it did. But it's just a nightmare."

"Just a nightmare," he agrees.

For as long as I get to wake up next to him, I'll take the nightmares any day over what could have been. In the beginning, when the ceaseless panic wasn't getting any better, and I kept having panic attacks, I caved and started seeing a therapist.

Now, it's been months since the incident, with life and school having carried on, and I've been forced to either continue on with it or get stuck. Most days, I'll want to stay in bed, not doing anything, either gripped by a depleted tiredness or an anxiety that if I leave the apartment that day, something bad will happen. It's a battle sometimes, to convince myself to go out, and some days, I don't.

Sometimes, I'll let the bad days take their toll, but Jaxon and the mindful practices the therapist has been giving me help. At first, when I'd told her the extent of how bad it used to be, of the way my eyes wandered toward traffic, the thought of stepping onto the street—the want to do it—she'd give me terms like "intrusive thoughts" and "suicidal ideations." She gave the pain of my mind words I sometimes don't know what to do with, and insisted I needed a combination of Cognitive Processing Therapy and medication to get better and made me promise to let her know if I ever feel my mind slipping again.

That while being in a healthy relationship might have helped, the reason I still lapse sometimes is because it's the equivalent of putting on a bandage without applying a disinfectant—I can cover up the wound and ignore it, but it's still there. There's healing and then there's only avoiding the triggers, and I was doing the latter. While I've been unable to budge on taking medication, that fear still there, I've been seeing her weekly.

Often, it's a battle to get better and talk to her, to realize that there's a lot I've held onto for years, that the nightmares and substances from my youth were a sign of untreated PTSD from the crash and everything else. And yet, I know I'm getting better. The nightmares and panic attacks grow less and less, feeding that insatiable kernel of hope.

All too soon, and this semester will almost be over. But with the passage of time, I've learned more and get to experience the kind of love I only hoped for in my wildest dreams. With the panic attacks and everything else, Jaxon has seen a side of me he never has before.

I always thought knowing more of me would mean wanting me less, would mean loving me less, but he proves me wrong every time. There is a beautiful intimacy in knowing I could be any version of me, the messed-up girl and the haunted adult, and he'd love me all the same.

Kissing his pulse, I murmur, "I love you."

His arms tighten around me. "I love you, too."

And it really is the best thing I've ever heard.

Tears stream down my face in the art exhibit when the new year arrives with a bang, until the sky is a cacophony of exploding fireworks. But my eyes stray from the window back to the piece hanging in front of me, the strokes of paint as familiar to me as my own hand.

"You got this into an art exhibit?" I ask the man beside me, his arm wrapped around my waist, head resting over mine, always around me like a sunflower perpetually twisted toward the sun.

Softly, as soft as a promise of kindness, a thumb brushes over my cheek, wiping away a tear. "Yes, *ya qalbi*, and I promise they know as much as I do that it deserves to be here."

With the dry spell that lasted weeks after everything happened, and then the tireless amount of turned-down applications, I never thought I'd see my art hang up anywhere other than my school's exhibits or the small museums around the city.

But here it is, in one of the most renowned art exhibits in San Francisco, in a place I never even dreamed possible, and so I never applied.

I cup his face, and look up at the person with my heart. "I love you."

The declaration is quiet in the space of the exhibit, the fireworks lighting up the sky outside, and maybe it's just the start of another year, but I remember the symbolism my mother would love to speak about every new year. That I come from a place where the neon lights and loud bangs of fireworks are believed to scare away malevolent forces and usher in good fortune.

And maybe they do, because I've never had as much pure, unadulterated hope for the future as I do now, when he pulls away, descending, and reaches for something in his pocket.

"And I love you," he tells me, smiling softly as I cover my face with my hands and shake, like my happiness cannot be contained, like it has to spill out of me in confession. "I love you and I need you, and for however long or short, I want you to be mine forever. I want to be your last everything, like I promised."

When I find my voice, I answer, I promise, "You've always been my everything."

Somehow, I know I will always mean it. And that in the end, sometimes it can only take one person to light up your entire world.

Thank you for reading!

Want more? You can find Amal on social media at @amalkimalbooks or subscribe to the newsletter to learn more about bonus content and book two, featuring Harlow and Damon!

Scan the QR code below to read a bonus chapter from Jaxon's POV!

To subscribe to the newsletter

Amal's website

Acknowledgements

When I first set out to publish *A Light in the Arcane*, I never expected to receive the amount of support I have, and while this acknowledgment may be a few pages long, please know that my gratitude is ineffable.

First, I'd like to thank those who knew ALITA before it even became ALITA—back in 2021 when it was a very, very rough first draft, under an entirely different name *(Before We Lit It Up)*. Sara, wherever you are, thank you for being my very first writer friend. I don't know what you saw in my first drafts way back then, but thank you for being my first supporter.

A big thank you to my friends (you silly gooses know who you are) who dealt with all my late-night calls of frustration when the editing stage was *testing* my patience. Your steady, "I know you can do it," were my light in the times of the many, many rewrites.

Next, I'd like to thank the medley of online friends who first supported me when I started social media. Thank you Lilly, for your feedback and endless reposts, Lucrezia, for your help with the many translation requests and the character art, and the many others.

Thank you to my beta and ARC readers, for going out on a limb and reading and reviewing ALITA. Thank you for your excitement for ALITA, your reading reactions, and sweet DMs. And since a lot of you found me on Threads, thank you to the Threads community. I never expected to find my biggest supporters in online spaces, but it was a lovely surprise.

Thank you to my graphic designer, MG, for dealing with all my revision requests and bringing ALITA to life. I'm so glad you popped on my page that day, and your work has been amazing every time!

Thank you Kayleigh, for giving ALITA its most definitely needed refurbishing, being a joy to work with, and your lovely feedback!

And of course, a huge thank you to my readers! I've always seen ALITA as a book I needed to write for myself, but throughout every scene and every confession and heartbreak, I would hope that somewhere, sometime, my words would bring a kind of reprieve to someone in the way only books can. I hope Layla and Jaxon have burrowed into your hearts as surely as they have in mine, and to all my fellow hopeless romantics out there—don't settle for anything less than you deserve.

About the Author

An avid reader for as long as she can remember, Amal has perpetually resided in a world of literature. When not found in a research lab or in classes, she's often holed away reading or writing about swoony MMCs. Amal writes in the romantic contemporary, sci-fi romance, and romantasy genres, with her debut, *A Light in the Arcane*, being a romantic contemporary. To stalk her, she suggests her Instagram via @amalkimalbooks or on her website, authoramalkimal.com.